HE'S ALWAYS BEEN HERE

Containing the

STORIES OF TWO RECOVERING ADDICTS

Translated from Blu's mind to paper,

aiming to bless lives word by word

Blu Zaas

To everyone fighting an addiction.

To everyone that has lost a loved one to an addiction.

Be Strong.

To everyone losing their faith in God.

To everyone trying to find their way back to God.

He never left you.

He's Always Been Here

Acknowledgements

First and foremost, I have to thank the man responsible for all of this: God. Without you, I wouldn't have this beautiful gift allowing me to make an impact on others through just my words. Thank you.

To you. Yes, _you_, the one that picked up this book. I am beyond ecstatic that my book caught your eye – but even more happy that you've purchased. Trust and believe me, this is a purchase you won't regret. Enjoy!

My family and friends: I love every single one of you. Thank you for supporting my dream and standing by my side.

To my personal angel, my Daddy. I hope you know that you exceeded the role of a father/husband. Whether you knew it or not, you did an outstanding job alongside Mommy molding us into the women we are. I'm so blessed that I got the chance to say that you're mine – my earthly father. Daddy, you made a beautiful impact on plenty of lives and I promise to do the same.

Even with Heaven between us, you will always mean the world to me. I love you.

Book I.

February 27, 2016: Washington, DC

Two years of addiction. Three relapses. Two overdoses.

At 26, I'd never considered myself a heroin addict. The thing was, I wasn't in denial. As a matter of fact, I was far from it. Heroin is the devil itself, but it was also my best friend - the best friend that never turned its back on me, unlike everyone else. I love getting high. Then again, I knew if I was six feet under, I wouldn't be able to get high at all.

And that led me here: New Leaf Rehabilitation Center.

336 hours.

20,160 minutes.

1,209,600 seconds.

In simpler form, I've been a prisoner for two weeks. Yes, it was necessary to break down 14 days, so you could fully grasp the time I've spent within these walls. Two weeks felt like an eternity, especially when all I want to do was get high. The day after I admitted myself was pure torment. Before coming in, I made sure to get as high as possible.

Dumb right?

At the moment, I thought it was the greatest idea, until I was suffering from my decision 48 hours later. I couldn't stand to look at food or even smell it. I was hanging over the toilet, heaving up nothing since I had no appetite whatsoever. My hands shook to the point where I couldn't hold something as simple as tissue. My nerves were at an all-time high, leaving me isolated, feeling more alone than I already felt.

I was just thankful to be past the withdrawal stage.

Or was I?

"Shia. You decent?"

I cringed at the sound of my roommate's raspy voice on the other side of the wooden door. Honestly, I was not in the mood to be around anybody. My hands pressed into the mattress, pushing my back into the headboard of the uncomfortable twin bed assigned to me. My chocolate orbs, identical to my complexion, focused on the door as the creaky sound broke the silence.

Seeing her face, I lightly smacked my lips as she sauntered further into the room, sitting on the foot of my bed. Her hand connected with my ankle causing me to flinch. Her hands flew up, as if to surrender. I was already hoping to avoid people, and here she was, making skin contact.

My hand gravitated toward my naturally kinky hair. Growing up, I always had the habit of playing with my hair whenever I was nervous, or just on edge about something. In this case, I was on edge. Playfully, I rolled my eyes, seeing her smile, revealing her slightly yellowish teeth. As unattractive as the color of those teeth were, her smile was beautiful. It was one of those smiles that always made you smile, despite of your mood. The fact she had the deepest dimples living on her cheeks made her smile even brighter.

"Mae. I'm not in the mood," I said, sighing.

I knew what I said meant nothing to her. In fact, I'm pretty sure it went in one ear and out the other. Mae wasn't the type to mope around. I mean, she had her days like the rest of us. But for her, the good days always seemed to outweigh the bad. It made me jealous, actually. I wish I could bring myself to a good mood like she does. Just once, I would love to wake up on the right side of the bed.

It just seemed like happiness didn't exist for me.

"Now, sweetie, you need to get out of this bed and come mingle. You can't be in here alone like this."

She tried her best to persuade me to interact with others, but I wasn't really feeling it. My brows furrowed together as she began coughing uncontrollably, with her hand covering her mouth. See? That's where a bunch of cigarettes get you. And that messed up her voice, too. Which brings me to how much I can't stand her constant coughing at night or her scary, raspy voice. Nonetheless, she was a woman with a good heart that cared about my well-being, which I appreciated.

At least someone cared.

"Why are you going to admit yourself - but not take steps to get better, sweetie?"

Cringing, my eyes narrowed in on her pale face. Today, she looked more tired than usual, which instantly concerned me. Her crystal-blue hues didn't hold their usual twinkle. This was too odd. Her thin, pink lips were pursed together, and I focused on her unruly brows. She looked different today - and not in a good way.

Cocking my head to the side, I decided to ask what was on her mind. I could tell something was bothering her. There had to be something.

"What's wrong?" I softly asked.

Her striking blue orbs averted from my intense gaze to the white, bland walls surrounding us.

"Hey..." I had the urge to touch her, but since I didn't want any contact, I wouldn't make any. "What's wrong Mae?"

The silence was killing me. My simple question drastically changed the mood in the room. That alone let me know something was wrong. All I wanted was for her to speak. Unfortunately, her lips remained shut.

A sudden chill ran throughout my body once her eyes locked with mine. She shook her head.

"Nothing. I'm fine, sweetie."

I frowned at seeing the obvious pain in her features. It hurt to know that she was keeping from me something that was clearly hurting her. We'd only known each other for two weeks, but surprisingly, we had a bond. I'm not one who makes friends easily. I am what you could consider a loner. With Mae, I didn't want to be a loner. Who would've thought that I would make a 60-year-old Caucasian woman my first friend since my addiction? She gave me a motherly feeling, even though I had no clue what that truly felt like. I knew a mother was supposed to be like her. You could feel the love she held for you when she entered the room; I know I did.

"Mae. I know yo—" My words were cut short once watching her rise to her feet swiftly. She shook her head, hands doing the same.

"I'm fine, Shia. Come on. We have a guest speaker coming in a few."

I cared enough to not force her to tell me how she was feeling, at least for now. Later on, it'd be a different story.

Guest speaker? I definitely wasn't excited. Within the days spent here, this would be our third speaker. The first two was a complete drag which had me asleep midway in. I was hoping that today's speaker was nothing like the others. Knowing that it would be cold in the multipurpose room, I decided on a Nike sweatshirt and gray sweats. I slipped on my sheep slippers, sliding my feet across the tile floors closing our bedroom door behind me.

"How are you feeling, Shia?" Lisa, an attendant, questioned once seeing me enter the hallway.

"Shitty," I dryly responded, continuing to my destination.

It was required that we attend everything. I hated that rule – rules in general. I wanted to get better, right? Well, at least I think I do.

I do.
I think.

Just like I assumed, it was cold. For some reason, this room was the coldest out of the facility. Frowning, I walked towards the third row from the front and took the empty seat next to Mae. Her cold hand covered mines resting on my knee, squeezing lightly as she locked eyes with me.

"Thanks for coming."

"It's required, Mae." I said, earning a small laugh from her.

"I know. I just wanted to feel like I did something." She shrugged, focusing towards the front.

I laughed small, shaking my head. This woman always wanted to take credit for something. It could rain tomorrow. She'd say that she prayed for it, therefore, she's the reason it's here.

"Good afternoon ladies and gentleman! We have something good in store for you guys this evening."

I rolled my eyes at the sound of her voice. My therapist: Dr. Melanie Jones. I guess she was cool. I wouldn't really know seeing how we made no progress during our therapy sessions that started last week. I don't see myself willingly sharing my traumatizing past with her. It'll take some time; she needed to understand that.

"I'd like to introduce or for some people, reintroduce one of our own success stories, Dallas Raye."

A frown formed on my lips as I looked around the room, watching everyone clap with enthusiasm. A small nudge to the shoulder made my frown grow deeper, cutting my eyes at Mae.

"Clap," She said as her hands continued to slap together.

Surprisingly, I found myself joining in even though I could care less. Pulling the sleeve of my sweatshirt back some, I looked at my watch noticing my second and last dose of Buprenorphine was due soon. It was definitely needed. I was completely fine this morning after taking it but now, I was growing very agitated. I just wanted to use and since I couldn't, it was making me want to be the biggest bitch that ever existed.

"For those who know me, wassup. And for those who don't, nice to meet you. My name is Dallas. Dallas Raye, and I were once an addict, just like you guys." His husky voice vibrated against the microphone, projecting throughout the room.

My body stiffened once fixing my eyes on him. The man standing just a few feet away from me was beautiful. My tongue swept across my lip as I admired his brown, flawless skin. His lips were somewhat full but pouty, which made them even more attractive. His face would contort into this crooked smile that was a major turn-on. My lower region began to tingle forcing my legs tightly together. As much as I was trying to ignore the feeling stirring between my thighs, it wasn't working.

"You alright sweetie?"

My lips turned into a slight frown once hearing the concern in her tone.

I'm pretty sure she caught me squirming in my seat, trying to shake this sudden sexual tension. I scratched just above my right brow relieving the itch.

"I'm good."

"Mhm." She hummed while looking ahead.

I knew she didn't believe me.

All I could do was focus on how his juicy lips were moving with every word spoken. Honestly, I didn't digest a word he said - looking at him was enough to keep me satisfied.

"I was once like all of you. That was until I found God."

The room was dead silent. I looked around quickly, hoping that someone would speak up on this joke of a "God."

What God? For all I know, all I had was myself. Always have. Always will.

"What God?!"
Everyone's eyes averted from him towards me. I didn't mean for that to come out; it just did. I'm beyond tired of being forced to believe in somebody that doesn't exist.

Using my thighs to squeeze my hands together, I shied under everyone's intense gaze. My legs began shaking as I chewed on the inside of my cheek. I hated attention. I hated it even more knowing I'm the reason everyone's eyes were locked on me.

His tongue dashed across his bottom lip, clearing his throat. "I'm sorry. I didn't get your name," He spoke into the mic.

That's because I didn't give it to you nigga. The bitch in me was screaming to come out. I couldn't hold her in.

I needed a hit. **Bad**.

"That's because I didn't gi—"
"Her name is Shia!" Mae cut me off as she gave me that 'shut up' look.

I dared not argue with her. She was the *only* person in this facility that I allowed to put me in my place. It was this feeling — a feeling where I couldn't disrespect her. The respect I should've had for my mother was what I had for Mae.

That bitch wasn't worthy to be called my mother. Respect? It never existed.

"Shia, I was like you. Swearing up and down that God wasn't real… until He got a hold of me."

I released a frustrated sigh. I really could careless about anything he was saying to me especially when it came to "God."

I frowned as he chuckled in the mic, pointing his index finger at me. "And I know that face all too well. I used to look the same way when someone was trying to get through to me. I don't force anything on no one but just wait, He's going to get a hold of you too."

This odd feeling fell over my body, leaving me mulling over his last words.

He's going to get a hold of you too.

The sudden hand connecting with my shoulder caused me to jump. I held my chest, trying to calm myself looking towards the nurse standing next to me.

She had to touch me — because?

"Do you have to touch me?" I spat out, unable to hold it in.

She looked taken aback by my irritated tone while mustering up a fake smile. If the tables were turned and it was me taking care of the addict, I'd flip out.

"Sinclair, follow me so you can take your meds."

Did she have to call me by my last name?

Frowning, I pushed to my feet falling in tow behind her. Something told me to look behind me so I did. Dallas smiled crookedly as he locked eyes with me meanwhile continuing to speak.

Damn that man.

February 29, 2016: Washington, DC

My fingers tapped among the surface of the round table I was seated in front of, waiting on my visitor — my one and only visitor. The only person on the outside that loved me still. The one I was trying so hard to get clean for: my cousin Blake.

It slipped my mind that she would be coming today. Visiting days were Mondays and Fridays. During the past two weeks, she'd been alternating between the days. So with today being Monday, I wouldn't see her until I was released. Being in her presence brought me so much peace, and I hated being left behind.

With my meds keeping me at calm, I couldn't complain. I wasn't feeling that urge for a hit, so I was thankful. The corners of my lips went upward as I saw her chocolate frame emerge from the double doors. The biggest smile was plastered across her face, quickly moving to me with open arms.

Our bodies embraced tightly as my eyes shut tight, fighting back tears. I loved Blake so much. Despite my drug addiction, she never *once* gave up on me. Even when I lost all hope for myself knowing it would lead to my death, she believed otherwise. In the past, she had convinced me to go clean three times, which explain my relapses. None of the attempts went past five months. This time around I wanted to stay clean for good.

My eyes scanned her chocolate, flawless skin that resembled mine. People would always mistake us for sisters but that's because our mothers could go for twins. I smiled once realizing she dyed her hair purple; it fit her. It complimented her complexion well - it wasn't something I could pull off.

She grabbed my hand guiding me to sit down in the seat as she took the one next to me.

"I missed you Shy. You look good boo." She smiled, lightly squeezing my hand.

Blake was two years older than me. You would think I was the oldest due to her having such a baby face and height of a high school freshman.

I smiled, "I missed you more. Ugh, my hair is a mess. I'm so ready to get out of here." I pouted.

This place was a drag. Hell on earth, basically.

"Hey… you're not coming home until you're ready, okay?" Her head slightly tilted down, brows climbing her forehead. "Don't force it. God's work has already begun." She preached to me day in and day out about that guy... woman… whoever. The person or thing I'm tired of hearing about.

"Blake… please." I sighed, not really in the mood for her "preacher" ways.

Releasing my hand from hers, I ran it along my left arm suddenly getting nervous. My eyes scanned the room, feeling as if I was being watched.

No one.

"You okay?" Blake asked out of concern.

Nodding, my eyes couldn't stop searching the room and that's when I saw the one that was watching me.

Him.

He stood near the front desk, hands stuffed into the pockets of his jeans. His fitted cap was slightly tilted upward, giving any and everyone a clear view of his handsome face. The way he stood with so much confidence with that crooked smile on his face; he just knew he was something worth looking at.

"So I come visit you and you rather spend our time gawking over another patient?"

Frowning, I looked towards Blake who had a smirk spread across her face.

"Yea. I see you. What's his name?" She nodded her head his way without drawing attention.

I rolled my eyes, "He's not a patient. He used to be though, and I'm not gawking nigga."

Kissing her teeth, she waved me off. "Shy please... I know you and I know when you're gawking over a dude. So quit it."

I chuckled lightly. Leave it up to Blake to read me like an open book. She was right though; she knew me like the back of her hand.

"He's cute though… so I can see why you're sitting here staring at him."

"Shut up. If anything, he's staring at me."

"Exactly, and you wouldn't know if he was if you weren't staring right back at him."

A small laugh entered the air from me as she joined in, "whatever." I mumbled.

"You know I'm right." She teased, smiling.

My eyes locked with his again forcing my body to heat up from watching his bottom lip slip between his teeth. It was evident he liked what he was seeing but reality was, I'm a recovering heroine addict. I've complicated enough lives; no need to complicate any more.

My brown hues scanned the dining room as I sat snuggled under my black blanket. Due to Mae being at her therapy session, I was forced to eat with people that I didn't communicate with on a daily basis. But then again, they were the two people I would share a few words with here and there.

"So... Shia…"

I cringed once hearing his voice, rolling my eyes. Sighing deeply, I looked up to Mace who was seated across from me at the table. I already knew something regarding sex was about to come out his mouth. Ever since out initial meeting upon my arrival, he called himself "crushing" on me. I can admit that he was fine as hell but he didn't know what to say out his mouth 99% of the time, which was a big turn off.

I watched as he took a sip from his soda, fixating his green orbs on me. I wish he wasn't so raunchy with his approach because then he'd be a great catch; minus the fact he was a recovering addict as well.

His drugs of choice were pain killers - with his favorites being Percocet and Oxycodone.

"What Mace?" I didn't want to respond but I knew he'd keep bothering me until I did.

He chuckled, resting his elbows on the table and kissing his teeth. "Why you gotta mean mug me like that, ma?"

"Cause she already knows you about to say some dumb shit Mace, that's why." Kris said, jumping in our conversation.

Kris was around my age. 25, I think. Anyways, she was a cool chick from what I gathered during our small talks. I tried my best to steer clear from her because she had her wacky moments at times. And I'm not referring to withdrawals - I mean, the chick was loco, in a sense.

I looked her way, giving a weak smile to mutely thank her. She smiled in return. The fork rested between my fingers as I used it to pick with the peas on my plate. I really didn't have an appetite. I just wanted to get in my bed and go to sleep.

Mace smacked his lips, "Who asked you girl?"

"No one, but clearly she's not interested nigga. Leave her be."

"Says the chick who can't even get a nigga to look her way. Shut your jealous ass up!"

"Nigga, I'm cute. So quit it!"

Shaking my head, I ignored the two as they bickered back and forth. This was exactly why I didn't care for people. Wasting their breath for nothing, just to argue over something so dumb. I threw my napkin on my plate, pushing myself to my feet. The grip on my blanket tightened while grabbing ahold of my plate.

"Aye. Where you going, ma?" Mace questioned while rising to his feet, plate in hand.

I chuckled lightly, "Away from y'all. I don't need to hear that shit today." Sighing, I threw my plate in the trash turning to him. My head fell to the side, "What…do…you want Mace?" I spoke, shaking my hands with every word.

I really wasn't for his antics today.

That stupid smirk worked its way to his stunning face. His head fell back before looking down at me, "Why you always gotta be mean? You know you like being around me." He teased, biting his lip.

I laughed, turning on my heels, "Bye Mace."

"Forreal Shy?"

That was the last thing I heard before closing the door to my room.

Hugging my blanket even tighter around my small frame, I quickly moved to my bed. I loved our room. The only place I received total serenity. Pulling the covers back of my twin sized bed, I immediately got comfortable once feeling the warmth engulf my petite frame.

My hues remained fixed on the wall as I laid on my side, hearing the door softly close. I'm pretty sure Mae thought I was asleep seeing how she didn't greet me like she normally does. My face contorted with confusion, wondering why she didn't peek over my shoulder to see if I was awake.

Something was off.

Pushing myself to sit up, I looked at Mae who was sitting at the edge of her bed looking distraught. My brows met in the middle of my head as I parted my lips to speak.

"Mae. What's wrong?"

I frowned once being able to see her red eyes; it was evident that she'd been crying. Knowing that she was coming from her therapy session, I'm sure whatever was bothering her earlier was the topic of discussion. From the look of her beet red face, it had to be something terrible that was worrying her.

I've never witnessed Mae in such a weak state so I didn't quite sure know what to do. Seeing as though I've never been one to comfort the next, this was going to be new for me. I pushed my body towards the edge of my bed, sitting right across from her.

No words left my lips as I watched her sniff, using the back of her hands to wipe her tears. Leaning forward, I placed my hand over hers, squeezing lightly. I wanted her to know that I was here, just like she would be for me if the tables were turned.

"Mae. Tell me what's wrong," I soothingly said, rubbing her hand.

I frowned once she shook her head from side to side, "Nothing Shia. I'm fine." Her raspy voice entered the air for the first time.

Nothing?

"I just need some sleep, that's all."

My scowl grew deeper watching her rise to her feet to round her bed, pulling the covers back. Nothing was said between us two. Just me, watching her get situated beneath her covers, sniffing. I couldn't bare the sight of a weak Mae. It made me automatically feel like I was falling apart too and that was the last thing that needed to happen, in my case. Accepting the fact she wasn't going to speak on her troubles, I chose to get back under the covers to receive some shut eye as well.

March 1, 2016: Washington, DC

"Shia."

"Melanie." I dryly retorted while slowly averting my eyes from the window to the individual sitting not far from me.

She knew I didn't want to be in here, talking about my feelings. Matter of fact, I was never a fan of sharing my feelings with others. Whenever things got heated I was perfect at shutting down, bottling things up as well.

Softly, I chewed on the inside of my cheek as I sized up my therapist before locking on her face. Her sandy brown hair fell perfectly among her shoulders and back; the curls made it interesting to look at. Focusing on the notepad in her lap, she glanced at me over the top of her chocolate frames; I hated when she did that.

Dr. Jones was nice, pretty too, but due to me being such a reticent individual, openly speaking about my feelings was something that wasn't going to happen. I just didn't see myself sharing my past experiences with a stranger. I don't care if this was her job or not.

A deep sigh invaded my ears, causing me to kiss my teeth while watching her push a few strands of hair behind her ear. Leaning slightly forward, her palms flatly sat on the notepad, narrowing her eyes on me.

"Are we going to go through this all time Shia? This silence? You have to give me something." She pleaded, using her hands.

I began cringing at her words and it wasn't her - it was me. When I woke up this morning, Mae still wouldn't speak a word to me. I tried my best to get her out the bed but she kept put. Finally, I gave up hoping that later on she'd be in a better mood. Everything at this point was irritating me. The lady in front of me trying to get me to speak on things that weren't her concern. Then, my only friend Mae wasn't speaking to me.

I needed my Mae back.
Terribly.
She kept me upright.
Besides Blake, she motivated me to get better as well.

"What's wrong with Mae?" I blurted, staring her intensely in the eyes.

Frowning, I noticed how uncomfortable my question made her. Her body language changed immediately letting me know that Mae was going through something serious. More serious than I assumed. It probably wasn't something she would get over in 24 hours. But something that'd take a toll on her for days, maybe even weeks.

She sighed, placing her notepad on the wooden end table next to her chair. Clasping her hands together, she began speaking in a soothing tone.

"Now Shia, we're here to talk about you, not Mae. Anything concerning Mae, I will no—"

"NO!" My voice rose an octave, shaking my head frantically. "Pardon my French, but I don't want to hear that bullshit. The only friend I have in here is at her lowest right now. She won't look at me. She won't even speak to me. I can't take seeing her like this!" I said all in one breath, chest heaving up and down.

"Dr. Jones raised her hands as she parted her lips to speak, "Shia. I underst—" Getting cut off by a knock at the door, she sighed while raising her index finger in the air. "Give me a minute Shia."

My eyes remained on the hardwood floor as her black pumps clicked towards the door. My leg began shaking out of nerves; this moment was becoming too overwhelming. Mae's sudden change of behavior was affecting me, more than I expected it to. Other than

Blake, there was no one I really cared about. Somehow, Mae wiggled her way into my heart and the pain grew by the second knowing that she was in such a bad mood.

Hearing muffled voices behind me, I turned and locked eyes with Lisa, the same attendant who I had a love-hate relationship with. Once locking eyes with her I regretted even doing it. The look of pity she was giving me was something I was so used to. Being an addict, they all give you that look - that look I hated.

I didn't need anyone to feel sorry for me. I picked up that needle every day, numerous times out the day and shot myself up.
No one else. Me.
I didn't need pity.

I frowned catching on to the unexpected shift in the atmosphere from the words exchanged between Dr. Jones and Lisa.

Okay. What was going on?

"What's wrong?" I was becoming anxious, growing agitated by the pity etching her features.
She sighed, scooting to the edge of her seat making me nervous at the small space between us. I don't like people too close. People weren't allowed in my personal space unless I wanted them there.
"Shia. Mae committed suicide. I'm so—"
Before I knew it, my sock clad feet were carrying me quickly towards my living quarters as tears freely cascaded down my cheeks.

No. The only friend I had in here left me.
Why she didn't just talk to me?
We could've got through it together.
I know we could've.

The tears fell more once seeing the gurney with her lifeless body beneath a white sheet being rolled out of our... well, my room now. My breath hitched in my throat as my chest began to tighten; I felt like my world was shutting down.

This couldn't be real.

"MAE!" I screamed, rushing after them before being pulled into a pair of strong arms. At that moment, I broke down entirely. My body weakened as I allowed the person to hold me tight, making me cry even more.

"Its okay ma, I got you. Shh... I got you."

Mace tried his best to soothe me with his comforting tone, swaying us from side to side. It wasn't working. I've never hurt this bad, in a while. The last time I hurt like this while being sober was what pushed me to my drug addiction in the first place.

My body shook while balling uncontrollably as Mace's hand remained glued to the back of my head, massaging my scalp softly. As much as I didn't care for this man, I could tell that this moment between us two would be the start of something possibly good. I was just thankful to be in his embrace. I needed it.

I still needed my Mae.
I needed her to come back.
We can still get through this together.

Book II.

March 2, 2016: Washington, DC

Wrapped in my black blanket, I sat balled up in the corner of the couch staring at the sheet of paper resting on my thighs. The same sheet of paper that held Mae's last words to me. My eyes scanned over her pretty cursive handwriting adoring the lines of the notebook paper. Honestly, I couldn't even tell you how many times I've read it. Its been *that* many.

Shia,

I know you're upset with me and I would be too. Sweetie, I want you to know that you've been one of the biggest blessings to come into my life. I know you're wondering why would I take my life? Well, straight to the point, I no longer have not a soul to go home to. My son Adam was the only reason I was getting clean. This was a new start to a new life with him. & I wasn't going to get that chance since someone murdered him. I found out yesterday morning which explained my shitty mood. Shia, it's only been two weeks since I've known you and you're amazing, sweetie. Keep pushing baby. Get clean. For yourself and for your cousin Blake. You deserve to be happy instead of slowly killing yourself. Sorry that I left you so suddenly and without a goodbye. But the face you're making right now is the reason I couldn't face you. I couldn't stand to see the pain or risk you trying to stop me. This is what I wanted. I have nothing to live for anymore and that's why I'm no longer a walking vessel. Just keep pushing, and stop giving everyone a hard time. They're there to help you. Let them in how you let me in.

PS, I hope you're not mad at me forever.

Sniffing, I used my blanket to wipe the tears that fell every time I read over the letter. I focused on the last encouraging words she had to offer me.

They're there to help you. Let them in how you let me in.

Those words kept playing in my head. Mae was right. I came here for help but yet, I was being so difficult. I still couldn't grasp why she couldn't just talk to me. I knew how much Adam meant to her; she'd talk about him day in and day out. They didn't have the best relationship but one thing that was clear was that he loved his mom. I witnessed that firsthand when he'd come visit. You could see it in his eyes. Threatening to no longer deal with Mae, he gave her an ultimatum of getting clean or he was gone. Mae loved her son more than drugs. She was determined to get clean. I just really wish he didn't have to get taken away making her feel that she had to take her own life.

Folding the sheet of paper, I tucked it into the pockets of my shorts. Snuggling the blanket closer around my body, my eyes danced around the room. A few people were sitting off in the corner whispering to one another. Meanwhile not too far from me, a guy was knocked out, mouth wide open.

I just didn't want to be bothered.
I was perfectly fine sitting here by my lonesome.
I think.

The corners of my mouth was forced into a frown once feeling the empty space next to me being sunken in. Immediately, I became irritated knowing I was no longer alone. Hesitantly, I slowly looked to the left of me locking eyes with Mace. I haven't talked to him since yesterday, when he chose to comfort me. I wanted to thank him; I just didn't know how.

I'm not used to people actually caring about me. Other than Blake, Mae was the only one who I felt real love from. I can't say that Mace didn't care but honestly, I felt like it was a spur of the moment type thing. Seeing how he had a "thing" for me, witnessing me breaking down gave him more reason to be the one running to my rescue.

So, I didn't know what to think about it.
Nonetheless, I was thankful though.

"How you feeling, ma?"

I cringed hearing him call me "ma." I never really understood why he called me that and any time I brought it up, he explained that it was a "New York thing." He claimed he got attached to using it from being around one of his friends from New York. Regardless, it was irritating and I really didn't care for him calling me that. But, I wasn't up for talking shit so I'd leave it be for the moment.

Sighing deeply, my frown grew deeper as I raked my fingers through my kinky mane. Over the past few days, I haven't touched my hair nor considered it. Doing my hair was such a task and my bush was satisfying enough for me. Knowing how much I hated doing my hair, I was going to reach out to Kris since she enjoyed bringing life back to one's head.

"I'm coo. Matter of fact, I wanted to thank you by the way."

Mace's brows furrowed as his head slightly fell back, face holding a look of confusion. I'm guessing I threw him off by my sudden thank you. Around here I'm known for not communicating with people and hearing me saying this had to be a big deal. It wasn't for me. But for him, I knew it was. The nigga probably thought I wanted him, which I don't.

"For what though?"

He was *really* confused; I figured he would've known what I was referring to.

Suddenly, I felt nervous because I didn't want to elaborate further. I'd rather him just know where it came from and exactly what I was talking about. Clearly, my wishes weren't coming true right now. Another sigh escaped my lips as I felt this slight pang in my chest. Mae had been running through my mind nonstop, talking about her made everything so much more real. I mean, I knew it was real but I didn't want it to be.

I didn't want to talk about her.
I didn't want to feel.

"Yesterday. You know… With…" My voice trailed off, hoping he'd catch on.

I watched his bottom lip slip between his teeth as he nodded. His green orbs ran over my body before focusing on my brown hues.

"Naw. You needed somebody, Shy. Man. I know I irritate the shit out of you *but* I know how much Mae meant to you. Seeing you like that yesterday really hurt me. I just want you to know that even though she's gone, you're not alone."

His lips pursed together as his strong hand found my knee, giving it a light squeeze. Before I know it, he was pushing to his feet and walking away. My mouth fell slightly agape, surprised at him being so quick to remove himself from my presence. I've grown so accustomed to him doing any and everything to be around me so his quick retreat had me feeling funny.

On the other hand, I did appreciate it.

He was respecting my space.

I needed that.

Rolling my eyes, I listened to Blake get situated on the other end of the phone. I chose to call her due to me being so down in the dumps; I needed to hear her voice. The sound of faint voices in the background along with her giggling was making me jealous.

I'd rather be out there with her than in here.

"Hello. My bad boo."

Hearing her return to the phone put a big smile on my face; this would be my first time speaking to her since the incident. After my breakdown, I didn't want any communication with anyone. I didn't care who you were. My only focus was shutting my eyelids, escaping my shitty reality.

"Yea… It's coo." I dryly responded.

"What's wrong Shy? This not my Shy right now."

Like I said before, Blake knows me like the back of her hand. I couldn't keep nothing from her. She knew whenever something was bothering me; I hated it. I'm still trying to figure out if its a good thing that she knows me so well? Or not?

Clearing my throat, I found it difficult to just come out and say that my roommate and only friend I had in here was now dead. And, she was the reason behind no longer being a walking vessel. My breath hitched in my throat as I parted my lips to speak.

This. Was. Very. Difficult.

"What's wrong Shy?" I sighed, hearing the concern in her voice.

See. This is exactly why I needed to get better because I *hated* worrying her. She worried more about me than her damn self - the thought of being her burden was the worst feeling. Blake never had to help me but chose to be here for me. I truly appreciated everything she has done for me especially since she hasn't left my side.

I needed her.

I needed her energy.

"Mae… She's gone."

Tears brimmed at my lids just off the mention of her name; Mae was such a sensitive topic right now.

I don't want to talk about her.

At all.

"What?" Blake faintly said in disbelief.

Hearing the pain in her voice made the tears fighting at my lids for the past couple of seconds to fall. Blake knew how much Mae meant to me. Mae was all I would talk about when Blake would ask me about how positive my experience here was going. She knew how hard it'd been for me these past two years. I'd lost the few "friends" I had due to my addiction and the only one I'd gain was Mae.

"She off'd herself B…" I voiced, slightly getting choked up.

It felt like I was reliving everything just by letting her know what happened. Vividly, I could see the gurney rolling out of our room with Mae's lifeless body sprawled on it. Along with the others, yesterday added onto the list of bad days.

The biggest gasp left Blake's mouth, making my brows meet in the middle of my forehead. That was some big news to drop on someone but she wanted to know what was wrong, so there she had it.

"Shy… Omg."

I knew she couldn't find her words, but I expected that.

"Can I pray for you?"

Prayer? Hearing those words, I cringed. Prayer wasn't my "thing" seeing how I didn't believe in anything. Everybody has their own thing that they believe in and lived by; I didn't. Honestly, I didn't know what to think. But I did know that if it was a *God* then I would've never went through the things I did.

If He's so worth praising, why is He allowing bad things to happen?

"But... before you say no, don't. I thi— know you really need this right now."

Scooting further down into the bean bag, my eyes dashed around the secluded room I was in. Everyone was still visible due to the glass doors. The phone room was the only privacy you'd get other than being in your room; I appreciated the phone not being in the open space. My eyes shot to the ceiling, not knowing how to respond to her. It was this one side I wasn't used to telling me to agree. Then, it was me - telling me not to be bothered with this mess.

"Go head."

That was the first thing that left my lips, shocking myself. Normally, I wouldn't agree to prayer but this time was different. It was this sudden urge to say what I did. It wasn't me.

It was something else.

Blake released a sigh of relief which made me smile. I knew how hard she battled with me and this God thing. As much as I hated hearing about it, I loved her persistency; she never failed to amaze me. Showing yet another way, she wouldn't give up on me. Since she wouldn't give up on me, I could never give up on her which explains why I'm in the position I am now - in rehab.

"Father God, I come to you today asking that you keep my cousin in the good space you want her in. Lord, keep her head leveled and cease all harmful tendencies. I know right now her emotions all over the place, but I ask that you bring her to a better understanding. Let her know that none of this was her fault. Let her know that this wasn't an intentional act to target just her Lord. Let her know that you *do* in fact love her unconditionally. Also, make it clear that you've always been here and never going anywhere despite her doubts. Bring Shy peace during this hard time as well as strength..."

My heart fluttered at her words.

"Please Lord... Please... Just keep my cousin here with me. Amen."

My eyes slowly peeled open as if Blake was sitting right in front of me, reciting the prayer. I attempted to shake the weird feeling running throughout my body, but it didn't help. I huffed out of frustration earning a small laugh from Blake.

"You felt Him."

"Huh?" I asked, confused at the *Him* she was referring to.
"God. You felt God, Shy."

My hand ran over my bare arm in an attempt to warm it, removing the goose bumps. My brown hues remained focus on Kris who was sitting Indian-style in the middle of her bed. Her silence was making me regret even coming to her room to begin with; she knew I don't care for talking.

"You gonna do it, Kris?"
I watched as a smile formed on her face, continuing to doodle away in her sketch book. I've managed to see some of Kris' work and surprisingly, they all were beautiful. She was into drawing portraits of people and stunningly great at it. Oddly, the first piece of work I saw was a drawing of myself. One she'd drawn the first week I got here which was a side profile shot. I don't know if I found it weird since Mace teased her about being "gay," which automatically made me feel like she could have a thing for me.

But, who am I to assume?

Her eyes locked with mine as she rubbed her hands along her knees, "I got you. You need me to wash it too?"

I smiled, nodding my head. "Please Kris. I'd really appreciate it."

It was nothing like having someone else massaging your scalp, creating all those suds. That was one of the best feelings and if she was offering, I wasn't passing it up.

"Go get a towel. Don't worry about the shampoo, I already have some."

I watched as she closed her sketch book, scooting towards the edge of her bed and standing to her feet. All I could do was smile at this moment. My hair will no longer be untamed and I knew it was in the best of hands.

Kris worked wonders on heads.

Turning on my heels, I prepared myself to go grab an extra towel before hearing her voice enter the air.

"Never mind, boo. I have an extra one right here."

I turned around, seeing her holding a red towel in the air, waving me in her direction.

"Come on. This shouldn't take long."

The side of my face rested on the back of my hands as I watched Kris doodle in her sketch book. She had finished my hair about 10 minutes ago; I was pleased with the outcome. It wasn't the easiest task but she managed to straighten my kinky curls, throwing it into a bun. Now, if it was me attempting to straighten my hair; it would've been the ultimate failure. For some reason, I couldn't get my hair bone straight for nothing.

I hated that.

I was really thankful for her gifted hands. I loved my bush but it was becoming to be too much; I just needed some straight hair in my life and Kris delivered that.

"What you drawing?"

My curiosity reached its peak as I tried my best to figure out what she was so focused on. I still couldn't figure it out, so I knew asking would be the best option. I watched as she shrugged her shoulders lazily, lips twisting.

"I don't know. I just… Whatever comes to mind."

She locked eyes with me for a moment, feeling like like the longest second with how intense her eyes were. Don't get me wrong, Kris was drop dead gorgeous. But her eyes… Her eyes held this scary intensity.

From her eyes alone, you could tell that she'd been through more than she'd wish.

"Whatever comes to mind, I draw." She finished off, continuing to doodle away.

It's crazy how comfortable I felt in her presence right now. Mae was the only person I considered my friend in here but other than exchanging words with her, I would converse with Kris and Mace as well. Plus, I was trying to keep Mae's words in my mind so that had me more comfortable with being around Kris at the moment.

"You okay?"

My eyes were closed shut, in my own little world, as I took in the two words I could careless about hearing. I was tired of everyone feeling sorry for me; I'd rather no one care about how I felt.

I mean, I was used to it.

Clearing my throat, my eyes slowly peeled open locking onto the top of her head as she remained focused on her drawing.

"I'm fine."

My stomach tightened once her intense orbs shot up towards mine. Sighing, she ran her fingers through her straight hair, "You're lying."

"So," I shot back just as quick as her comeback.

Her brows furrowed as she rubbed on her knees; I could feel the tension settling in the air after the few words shared between us. I swear, I didn't mean any harm. After what I've been through, I'd grown accustomed to protecting myself which always had me in defense mode.

The fact she told me I was lying was the truth but honestly, who wanted to hear that shit?

Not I.

"I'm not trying to offend you, Shy. I know you're not good… And its okay. Just know, if you need anything, I'm here."

Crossing my eyes, I couldn't believe what I was hearing. Kris? Here for me? I guess I can take that. My hands shook in front of me as my head matched its pace, "I'm fine, Kris. Seriously." I grabbed her knee, trying my best to convince her of my bold face lie.

I don't want a pity party, especially from some addicts.

Well… Recovering addicts.

Kris' lip slipped between her teeth, nodding her head. With the look she was shooting my way, I could tell she knew I was lying. I wouldn't believe me either especially after everyone in the unit witnessed my breakdown. I'd be worrying about my well being too.

For now, I was fine.

Well, I hope so.

"I'll take that, Shia. Just hold your head, boo. God never puts more on us than we can bare. You're way stronger than you *think* you are."

I smiled, catching her contagious one. Sitting here with Kris made me wonder why I created distance between us from the beginning. Her presence was bringing me peace. It was something I needed, and I don't say I need anyone's presence often.

"Thank you, Kris. For my hair… The words. Just, thank you."

It was so difficult for me to express myself. One thing I *did* know was that I was thankful for her generosity as a whole. She didn't have to tame my hair and she damn sure didn't have to make it known that she's here for me.

Whether I wanted her here or not.

It was nice knowing I had someone… Well two other people here, in my corner.

My brown orbs went from one individual to the next growing uncomfortable, just like any other time we had these sessions. Along with individual sessions with our therapists, we were required to do group as well. You'd think I hated just meeting with Dr. Jones but I couldn't stand being apart of a group.

I felt like the target, just because I refused to say anything.

Fran locked eyes with me which had mine instantly rolling; I couldn't stand this bitch. She was irritating - always trying to force me to participate. If I don't want to speak, bitch I don't want to speak.

Fall back.

"You want to add anything, Shia?"

The topic at hand was how we were feeling lately. Everyone mentioned how they were having a hard time making it day by day. Some were still experiencing withdrawals while others were simply just missing their family. Meanwhile, I just wish I still had my roommate.

"I really don't, *FRANNY*... And you know that."

I hated her fuckin' name.

Who the hell names their child Francis? Forcing people to call her such an ugly nickname. So glad my carrier, also known as my mother, was in her right mind to give me a decent name.

Sighing, her hands connected with her knees, "Shia, how have you been feeling lately?"

She knew I wasn't in the best mood and her persistency wasn't applauded right now, instead, it was making me want to hit her in the face. Bringing my wrist up, I looked at the time on my watch realizing that it was nearing medication time. I sighed of relief, knowing that within the next few minutes I'd no longer be on the edge.

That was a good thing – well, for her anyways.

I knew it'd be wrong to hit her but I didn't care. It was something about her personality that just irked my nerves; I felt like everything was fake with her. Nothing seemed genuine. Don't get me wrong, Fran was one of the attractive attendants here especially being in her 40's - I just wasn't a fan of her.

"What you think?"

Me, along with everyone else in the room had to know that she proposed one of the dumbest questions. Everyone sitting in this circle with me were the same people who saw me crying a river, losing myself in the middle of the unit.

"We're not here to talk about what I think, Shia. The entire group shared *but* you. Let it out, sweetie."

I cringed hearing her utter the term of endearment which reminded me of Mae. My eyes slightly watered as Mae's words played in my head.

Let them in how you let me in.

"I don't want to talk though."

My emotions began getting the best of me as I got choked up. I couldn't take this pressure. If I didn't want to speak on it, why was I getting pressured into doing so? I just wanted to have a few hours without feeling the hot tears cascading down my cheeks.

"But it'll—"

Fran was cut off by the door opening, everyone's eyes falling on the tall individual coming through the door. My stomach tightened at the sight of Dallas' crooked smile as he moved into the room, taking the seat next to Fran.

"My bad y'all, for being late."

With every word he spoke, his eyes never left mine making me blush and shy under his fiery gaze. I watched as he leaned back in the seat, stretching his legs out while smiling.

"Alright. Y'all can ask me whatever. I'm open to all questions."

The hairs on my arms quickly stood at attention off the sight of Dallas' tongue parting his pouty lips. It slowly slid over his bottom one before disappearing in his mouth, lips contorting into a grin.

This man was gorgeous - the sad part was that I couldn't take my eyes off of him; he was breathtaking to look at.

He must've felt my wandering eyes because before I knew it his locked with mine for a second. That second felt like forever as he listened to another resident, Jimmy, talk to him.

My orbs scanned the room, suddenly becoming nervous. Chewing on the inside of my cheek, I ran my hands along my arms in an attempt to rid them of the visible goose bumps.

"What was your addiction?"

Every time it came down to me being in a room with him, words flew out my mouth before I got a chance to stop them.

Oh well, it's out there now.

Clearing his throat, his almond shaped eyes focused on me along with everyone else's. Normally, I hated being the center of attention - but this time, I was more than appreciative of having his undivided attention on me.

So, I could careless with the extra eyes in my direction. His handsome face was the only thing I kept my focus on. "Shia, right?"

Damn. He actually remembered my name.

I nodded, letting him know that his guess was, in fact, correct. "Well uh, Shia, I was an alcoholic. Today actually makes it two years without a drink." He spoke with the corners of his mouth contorting upward, revealing his deep dimples.

Everyone in the room began clapping, voicing their congratulations. Meanwhile, a small frown sat on my face, not wanting to clap at all.

Until Mae got in my head.

Clap.

This moment took me back to the first time I laid eyes on him when I refused to give him the proper welcome along with everyone else. Putting my pride to the side, I offered a quick clap just before everyone stopped.

"What drove you to drink?"

"Shia!" Fran interrupted as I whipped my head in her direction, shooting daggers with my eyes. "You should—"

"I shouldn't what? He said we can ask him whatever we want. I'm following directions for *once* Fran, fall back." I snapped, waving her off dismissively.

She really knew how to push my buttons.

I'm pretty sure everyone in the room knew to not go toe to toe with me. I knew I was intimidating; well, that's what a lot of people here have told me. The thing was, if they *really* knew me, they'd know why I'm so quick to defend myself.

I've never felt protected.

My no good mother left me to fend for myself, every time.

I had to be a tough cookie or everyone would run over me.

A light chuckle fell from his lips, looking to Fran. "Naw, it's cool Fran, she's right." His eyes moved back to me, running his hands over his mouth.

"But to answer your question, Shia, losing my best friend turned my world upside down. Liquor became my crutch… My new best friend. I completely lost my shit. I'm just thankful to still be here today, a living testimony, so I can encourage others to stay clean as well."

There was a pull at my heart once hearing what drove him to take a turn for the worst. I knew very well how it felt to lose a friend seeing as though, I just lost mine yesterday. My lip was tucked tight between my teeth as if attempting to cut the circulation.

"You ight?" He questioned, brows meeting in the middle of his head.

I'm pretty sure he saw how his few words changed my body language as a whole. My leg was now shaking, lip tucked tight, and eyes beginning to gloss over.

Got damn you Mae.

Why did you have to leave me?

I have no clue how I'm about to make it the remainder nine days in here.

Yea, my time here was coming to an end - quicker than I'd expected.

The good thing about all of this was that I haven't had an urge to use. I *think* I want to thank Mae for that. Staying clean with a leveled head was my biggest focus right now.

Nothing else.

Nodding, my eyes shot to my feet before staring back into his brown hues. "I'm okay Dallas. I'm done with my questions."

He appeared to be very uncertain on what just left my mouth; his face told it all. For some reason, I could feel that he could see right through me. He looked at me *too* intense, way too intense for my liking.

But what straight woman didn't want a fine man staring her down as if she wasn't the best thing walking?

I mean, I'm a recovering addict. But, even though I'm nothing but that, I still enjoyed some eye candy here and there.

Giggling, I took a sip from my cup of water while watching how Kris' face cringed into one of disgust.

"So, you're *not* gay?" I questioned again, really wanting to know if she is or not.

I mean, if so, oh well.

Kris was beautiful. I'm pretty sure she could pull any female or male that she wanted.

Snorting, her eyes met mine before they focused back on her sketch book that was settled on her propped legs. "Like I said before Shy, I'm not gay. I don't know why you're listening to that nigga Mace."

The disgust in her tone while speaking his name was amusing. I could tell my question was one she didn't want to hear, and could careless to answer. She answered it though, so that's all that matters.

"I didn—"

"You *were* listening to him. That's why you're even asking me this right now." She kissed her teeth, shaking her head while drawing.

I really didn't mean to offend her; it was just a simple question.

Well at least, I thought it was.

"Speaking of the devil…" She mumbled as Mace made his presence known.

He plopped down into the empty space between us on the couch. Kris rolled her eyes meanwhile I found it funny how he popped up when we were talking about him. Leaning over, he tried his best to get a look at Kris' drawing but she snatched it away before he could see anything.

"Ugh. Why you acting like that little ugly?"

Kris' hand lightly collided with the paper, irritation written all over her face. "Please Mace. Don't start with me today. It's already bad enough you have Shia over here thinking I'm gay."

"Word?" His eyes lit up with his head whipping to me, then back to her. "I just be playing though."

"Uh huh. Well, she believed you."

Mace chuckled, holding up his hands as if to surrender, "My bad Kris. I didn't even think y'all paid me any mind."

"Hm. I sure don't." Kris was quick to respond, making me laugh a little.

These two went back and forth like siblings.

Resting his head on the back of the couch, he slouched further into the cushion, locking eyes with me. My nose turned up at his intense gaze; those green eyes of his were gorgeous.

Simply amazing.

His tongue swept across his lip, "You good though?"

Pursing my lips together, I nodded averting my eyes from his for a second before catching his gaze again. My shoulder rose before lazily dropping, "I'm okay. What about you?"

His lips twisted at my question. I don't see why; I really wanted to know how he was doing, as far as staying sober and all.

"…with your soberness Mace."

His mouth formed into an 'O' as I further elaborated on my question. He nodded, running his thumb and index fingers down the corners of his mouth. He did that often - something I picked up on. I never bothered to ask why since we all had our habits of some sort.

A sigh escaped his mouth as he ran his hands down his jeans, "Yea... Yea I'm good, ma. No urges or nothing. I'm cooling. Ready to get up out of here."

I nodded in understanding. I understood how he felt; I'm ready to leave this place as well. Knowing that Mae died here was torture in itself and having to still sleep in our room made my heart ache even more.

"I second that!" Kris jumped into our conversation, looking from her sketch book to the both of us.

Mace smacked his lips, "But who asked you to second it though?!" His voice feigned annoyance but a grin played at his lips.

I smirked, trying my best to stifle my laugh once noticing the irritated expression on Kris' face. I knew she had enough of his shit. She leaned forward, giving his arm a light jab before speaking through clenched teeth.

"Stop playing with me, Mace."

He laughed, rubbing his arm. "You better be lucky you're a chick, cause I'd pop your ass right back."

Kris rolled her eyes, looking back down to her book. "Yea. Whatever nigga."

Like Mike played on the 37" flat screen mounted on the wall, as I remained wrapped up in my blanket in the corner of the couch. It was nearing 8:00 and our scheduled bedtime was 10, which I absolutely hated. At this point, they let us do as we please and I settled for watching this old movie alongside a few other residents. Kris chose to go to sleep which I honestly thought was the meds. Mace was somewhere around here, probably in some female's face, knowing him.

"And how are you?"

The deep voice entering the air startled me as I slowly looked to my left, taking in the handsome individual that occupied the empty spot next to me. My breath hitched in my throat at the sight of him. I didn't expect him to still be here; after the group session, I thought he would be gone.

Obviously not.

His eyes remained fixated on the TV as he readjusted his fitted cap on his head, looking at me.

"I'm fine." That was the only thing I could manage to utter at the moment.

His intense gaze was making me nervous, causing my leg to shake. His eyes flew to my shaking leg before running up my frame, locking on my hues.

"What's this?" He questioned, pointing towards the TV.

My jaw fell agape at the fact he had no knowledge of the movie that was playing. I mean, it wasn't a classic or anything but who hasn't seen *Like Mike*?

Clearly, Dallas hasn't.

"Like Mike…" I said in a 'duh' manner, earning a snort from him. "Why you still here though?"

I told y'all that I have word vomit. With me being around him didn't make it any better. By the look on his face, I knew my question came out in a disturbing tone. There was no recovering from that.

"I can't be here?" His brows climbed his forehead with his head slightly tilted down, looking up at me.

"I mean… You can. Do you Dallas." I fanned him off, focusing back on the movie.

He laughed while shaking his head, "Ight Shia. How you liking it in here so far?"

"Shitty. This place is somewhere I don't want to be."
He nodded, tucking that plump bottom lip of his between his teeth. "I felt the same way being in here. I'm pretty sure everyone does but you have to do what's necessary for you. You're clean right now so *stay* clean Shia. Seriously."

I nodded, taking in his every word. He spoke as if staying clean outside of these walls was one of the easiest things, when I knew otherwise. I've gone through three relapses. I'm just hoping when I walk out of these doors next week, I wouldn't commit my fourth one.

"The worst thing you can do is get out of here, just to relapse. You're in control of your addiction. Don't let the addiction take control of you."

I couldn't help but replay his words over in my head - it pretty much got stuck, in a good way.

You're in control of your addiction. Don't let the addiction take control of you.

Sighing, he rose to his feet giving me a look over his shoulder. "It was nice speaking with you Shia. Stay prayed up and keep your head up. Mae was one of a kind, she would want the best for you."

Wait. I had no clue he personally knew Mae. I thought my first day laying eyes on him was hers too. Apparently not.

I watched his retreating back while having the sudden urge to tell him what I should've earlier.

"HEY!"

He turned around, eyes narrowing in on me as he offered a head nod. "Sup?"

"Congrats on your sobriety."

I felt relieved once those words left my lips. I was stepping out of my comfort zone, and I had no one but Mae to thank for that. Her departure was devastating, and I know I'll grieve for awhile, but the letter she left behind was well needed.

This tingly sensation jolted throughout my body once seeing the corners of his lips twist upward, revealing his dimples. A man with a pretty smile along with dimples were everything.

"Definitely wasn't expecting that. Thank you Shia. You'll be where I'm at in due time. Just remember what I said."

You're in control of your addiction. Don't let the addiction take control of you.

Book III.

March 10, 2016: Washington, DC

"Shia. You have two days left, how are you feeling about leaving here?"

My eyes averted from my fiddling fingers and focused on Dr. Jones, and those blue eyes of hers. Those eyes that somewhat resembled Mae's. Ugh. I'm so tired of thinking about her. It makes me so frustrated but yet, hurts me so bad as well. I couldn't believe that in two days, I'd be outside of these walls.

I mean, I was ready. But then again, I wasn't.

Being here, sheltered me. Whereas I knew once I entered the real world again, who knows what could happen?

I'm pretty sure you all are wondering why my stay seemed so short? I admitted myself for 30 days, only. To me, it felt like months instead of just one. Nonetheless, I'm glad I decided to go through with this whole "staying clean" thing.

This was our first session since the incident. Oddly, I wasn't as tense as I normally would be in her presence. I actually wanted to talk today. My mood was very content.

Slowly looking up from my fingers, I caught her gaze. "Honestly… I'm scared."

Dr. Jones nodded as she jotted away on her notepad. I didn't expect her to still take notes especially since I wasn't going to be her patient two days from now. But, whatever floated her boat – I wasn't complaining. Despite my fears, I was beyond ready to leave here especially to be with Blake.

Surprisingly, these past couple of days for me haven't been that hard. Over the short period of time, I found myself getting closer to Kris and Mace, even participating more in group. I mean, Fran was still a bitch, like usual, but she was growing on me. Funny how she was growing on me nearing the end of my stay.

"And scared, what do you exactly mean?"

I sighed, not prepared to answer this question. I knew why I was scared but then again, why am I? I've stayed clean for 28 days thus far, what is some extra years?

Scratching my head, a slight frown graced my lips, "I just don't want to relapse..." My voice trailed off, head hanging low avoiding eye contact.

If anybody didn't have faith in me, I knew *SHE* did.

Dr. Jones rooted everyone on and even though it was something very difficult to adjust to being the person I am, it was still a great feeling. I appreciated her support, even when I didn't want it.

My eyes cut to her noticing how she slightly leaned forward, "hey." She softly spoke placing her hand on mines forcing me to look at her.

"You will *not* relapse. I speak against that now. You're strong Shia, stronger than you think you are. Just remember, whenever you have that urge to use, breathe. Don't give in. You've came too far to start all over again. Keep in mind, you're in control of your addiction. Don't let the addiction take control of you."

You're in control of your addiction. Don't let the addiction take control of you.

I cringed once hearing those words, the same words Dallas spoke to me a few days ago. I found it extremely weird how two different people managed to say the exact same thing but clearly, it was something I *needed* to hear.

I nodded, letting her know that I was taking in every word she was saying. I don't know how far breathing would get me, seeing as though I'm doing that just to stay alive. I'll consider trying it though, for my own soberness.

Clearing my throat, I moved in the seat slightly, "I hear you… I hear you. Question…"

"I'm listening." She said, throwing her right leg over her left before pushing her frames on her eyes fully.

"Out of all your patients during this year, how many actually stayed clean?"

By the look on her face, I could tell that my question wasn't one she was expecting. It had been stirring deep within me ever since our session started, and it just had to come out.

She sighed while clasping her hands together, "Honestly Shia? Not many. People come in here and do 30 days and the *first* thing they do is go back to their old ways once leaving here. Now you, I know you're different. You're one of a kind and I've known that ever since you first walked through them doors…" She said while pointing towards her office door when I knew she meant the actual doors to the building. "You've had a hard time here but Blake, she's more than enough support and love once you return home. As much as I like you and your mean ways Shia." She laughed, earning one from me as well.

Instantly, I felt bad that I treated her horribly majority of my stay here. She actually was an understanding, cool person. I should've appreciated her more but I'm just glad I realized her good intentions, before leaving this chapter of my life in the past.

"I'm not looking forward to seeing you come back here. We'll always be here for you, don't get me wrong, but I'm expecting nothing but the best when you exit our doors.

She was expecting the best. I was too.
Who knew what was ahead of me, though?
Not I, or anyone else.

March 13, 2016: Washington, DC

"Mace. Leave me alone."

I rolled my eyes, scooting away from him on the couch more to Kris who giggled while watching TV.

"Naw, ma. This our last day together." He said, reaching for my kinky hair making my nose turn up and move out of his reach.

"So!" I shot back, swatting his hand away as he laughed.

This nigga was irritating. Point blank. Period.

These two days flew. Within the next hour, Blake would be picking me up and taking me to my new home, her home. I was looking forward to seeing her townhouse. It was the same place she'd got with her boyfriend about two years ago but due to his infidelity, they were no longer an item.

I didn't blame her. She was too good of a woman to be settling for a no good ass nigga that wanted to have his cake and eat it too.

"So, means I get to bother you till we leave…" Mace laughed, "but naw, forreal though, you gon' keep in contact?"

Twisting my lips, my hand found my chin as I looked to the ceiling as if I was in deep thought. There was absolutely nothing to think about because my decision was already made up, but I was going to have Mace think otherwise. It was already decided a few days ago that when I leave here, I wanted Kris and Mace active in my life.

We were all fighting the same battle so why not fight it together?

I don't know if they needed me but right now, I **needed** them. Surprisingly.

Mace smacked his lips grabbing my arms, shaking me. "Stoppp!" I whined as he laughed.

"Speak up then, punk!" He mushed my head causing my fist to collide with his chest.

"Yes, nigga. Of course, I'm going to keep in contact with y'all."

Somehow, the corner of my lips forced into an upward position. It's been a while since I smiled this much and I had to thank the two I sat in the middle of. Spending these last few days with them made me realize that I never should've been shut off in the beginning. They were beautiful individuals, in their own way. I was glad that we built some sort of bond before departing ways.

It was comforting knowing that this, whatever we built, was going to carry on outside of these walls.

Also refreshing, I must add.

I actually felt like I can breathe again.

I nudged my shoulder into Kris' as she stared off into space, at nothing in particular. I hated when she would do that. There was no telling what or who was on her mind.

"Where are you staying once leaving here?" I questioned, looking at her side profile.

I mean, I knew where Mace would be going but Kris never mentioned where she would be laying her head every night. She began chewing on the inside of her cheek, slowly looking at me.

"With my boyfriend."

My eyes widened at her confession. At no point did she reveal that she had a boyfriend. This was a total shock, for the both of us. Once those words left her mouth, I couldn't help but look at Mace, the same guy claiming she was gay. When in actuality, she was far from it.

"You mean girlfriend right?" Mace teased, earning an eye roll from her.

Smacking her lips, she pointed at him before her hand fell carelessly upon her lap. "See. This nigga here."

I laughed, looking back and forth between them both. You know, I really was going to miss being around these two. Well, daily anyways.

Fanning him off, my nose scrunched up, "Ignore him. So when were you gonna spill the beans on your Mister? How come he never came up here?"

Her tongue swept across her lip, sighing while pushing a strand of loose hair behind her ear locking eyes with me.

"We just decided it was best if he didn't. I couldn't stand the thought of him coming then me watching him have to leave. I don't think it would've done neither one of us any good..."

I nodded my head, listening, as her legs unfolded, feet connecting with the floor.

"I love him dearly, though. I… I really want to spend the rest of my life with that man. He's such a great support system."

I smiled at how her face seemed to light up just from speaking about him. I hope one day I could feel the same way.

"Here we go with the overkill of sappy shit." Mace voiced in an exaggerated tone as Kris cut her eyes at him, making him snicker.

"Naw. You know I love messing with you, ma. I'm glad you have somebody you love that you know truly loves you, to go home to."

Kris crossed her eyes, cocking her head to the side, "What? And you don't?"

This was the first time I actually saw a hint of sadness appear on Mace's face since being here. I'm so used to him cracking jokes left and right; he always had a smile on his face. The one thing nobody could take from him – that damn beautiful smile of his.

He sighed, slouching down into the couch as his head connected with the cushion, green hues locking on Kris. "Lover-wise? Naw. I actually wish I did, though."

"Awww." I cooed, giggling once seeing him mug me.

He smacked his lips. "Naw Shy, don't start that. I'm not soft or nothing but uh, it would be nice to have something to run into when I get home." He said, chuckling with that sneaky smirk creeping on his face.

"Ugh nigga, you're the worst!" Kris spat out with disgust as I rolled my eyes.

Mace could be cool for a moment then he always manages to ruin it with his nasty antics.

I can't wait to see him outside of this environment, in the real world – the same for Kris. I really hope they stay clean throughout this transition, as well as me. Nothing would be worse than ending up back in here or worst, six feet under.

Tears welled at my lids as Blake's chocolate, flawless face came into view; it felt like forever since I've seen her. Taking one last look at the building that gained me new friends and an even better outlook on life, a heavy sigh broke my lips. Turning back around, my black high top chucks carried me quickly towards Blake who was leaned against her car, focused on her phone.

Her eyes flew to mine as I got halfway to her as we quickly closed the gap between us, hugging each other tightly. Squeezing my eyes shut to refrain from crying, the traitor tears fell anyway without my permission. I quickly wiped my face with my palm as Blake's hold tightened around me, making more tears fall against my will.

"Sucker." She teased, lightly punching me in my chest wiping away her own tears.

I laughed, sniffing, holding my bag with both hands in front of me. Here she was calling me a sucker for crying yet, she was doing the same. These were happy tears, for the both of us.

"Says the sucker." I shot back, earning a playful eye roll from her.

Quickly, she grabbed my bag throwing it into her trunk as I watched her walk to the driver side after slamming it shut. Smiling, I reached for the handle of the passenger door, pulling it open. A small sigh left my lips once feeling the cool air circulating throughout the car; it felt so good to be beyond those depressing ass walls. A strong but pleasant aroma overwhelmed my nostrils forcing my head towards the backseat as my eyes landed on a breathtaking individual.

I couldn't tear my eyes from him because he was so easy on the eyes. His unblemished caramel complexion complimented his olive green hues perfectly. His full brows were beautiful; brows that any female would die for. His beard was everything. It perfectly flowed down the sides of his face, coming down having some good length to it. It somewhat reminded me of Stalley but not as big as his.

"Girl. Don't drool now. CJ is gay. Chill." Blake laughed while starting up the car.

I rolled my eyes, face heating up as he flashed me a smile.

"Hey, boo." The hint of flamboyance could be heard in his tone but it wasn't too heavy.

His smile was contagious causing the corners of my lips to turn upward as well. "I'm Shia, nice to meet you."

His hand waved in the air dismissively, "Girl, I heard so much about you. This bih couldn't stop talking about you. I felt like I knew you already. How are you feeling boo?"

His energy was so welcoming; I was really digging it. It was the perfect energy for me to be around right now especially coming out of rehab. Finally, I faced forward nodding my head to the music softly playing, taking in the scenery. It felt like all of this was new to me. Just spending 30 days in rehab made me forget how it felt to be out here, beyond those walls.

"I'm feeling good, for now anyways."

"You'll be fine boo. Just take it one day at a time. You got this."

My heart fluttered at his words. It was crazy how I felt the support from someone I just met; it was a good feeling. Smiling, I looked over my shoulder catching his gaze. Damn, he was gorgeous. Why was he into men again?

"*WHY* are you into men?"

Blake gasped before giggling, "SHIA!"

I laughed, shrugging, "What? It sort of just came out. I mean, come on, look at him."

CJ laughed, "I know right. Look at me bitch but girl, I can't help it. I've tried women and I steer clear, not my cup of tea. Now men? Giirlll."

I giggled as a smile settled on my face. I already knew that I'm going to love him.

"Well, me personally, I wish you were into us because I'd give you a run for your money," I admitted, unable to hold it in.

I laughed once feeling Blake smack my leg, "Whore!" She teased.

My index finger pointed at her, "no, not a whore. I'm just telling the truth. He's fine."

His deep laughter rumbled throughout the car as I felt his soft touch upon my shoulder, "Thanks boo, with your cute ass."

"You hungry Shy?" Blake asked, looking at me quickly before looking back to the road.

She must've been reading my mind because my stomach growled on cue. Rubbing my stomach, I nodded, "Yes. Hungry as hell. What are we eating?"

"I'm not spending coin. I'm cooking. You eating bitch?" She questioned, looking behind us to CJ, giggling lightly.

"You think I'm NOT? Girl yes. I need to be full before I go see boo."

Blake laughed, looking into her rear view mirror at him, "Who? You know you be slinging your peen everywhere."

"Bitch. Don't play."

Simultaneously, Blake and I burst into laughter at his serious tone.

"You know I love you boo." She said, making a right turn on a street I wasn't familiar with.

My eyes widened as she pulled into the driveway of a two story townhome. Before admitting myself, I never got the chance to see the new place she called home so knowing this was now my home as well had me excited. Turning off the ignition, she looked at me with the biggest smile, "Welcome home baby."

"YAS! Turn up!" CJ loudly said from the backseat as we all laughed.

My eyes scanned the house – my new home. This all felt so surreal. A month ago, I overdosed, damn near lost my life and here I am, getting another chance at life. I couldn't let this chance pass me by. I really had to do things right this go around.

"Turn up bitch? NO! Shy can't do shit!" Blake spat back, smiling.

I never was a fan of drinking, to begin with, but I understood where she was coming from. She wanted me to come home and not do nothing at all. Basically, she wanted me to be boring Bertha.

NOT.

March 14, 2016: Fort Washington, MD

My eyes widened once my foot came in contact with the hardwood floor, stepping off the last step to the basement. Well, my new home actually – it was perfect. It was like my own apartment. Blake knew me well because the green, my favorite color, decors was making me so giddy inside. There was a small kitchen with stainless steel appliances along with a mini island, two white barstools pushed against it. Not too far from there was my living room area with a cream colored couch, three accent pillows on it, all with olive green coordinated into it. There were a few pictures scattered along the walls, adding more life to the area. I even had my own dining area not too far behind my sofa.

My smile grew even bigger once walking into my bedroom. Even when living with my mother, I didn't have such an appealing personal space. Matter of fact, I was sleeping on a twin bed every night; I wasn't complaining, though. I had somewhere to lay my head every night so I was content. Not being able to resist any longer, I plopped into MY queen-sized bed, feeling the softness of the covers take in my body.

This feeling was great.

"Someone loving their new place, huh?"

I grabbed my chest, sitting up quickly, heart racing. I didn't even hear her approach. The bitch walking like she has pillows for feet, sheesh.

"Damn. You scared me B."

She laughed, pushing herself off the doorframe walking further into my room. "My bad, I didn't mean to. You like it, though?" She questioned, looking around the room as if this was her first time seeing it.

Smiling, I looked around as well before my eyes landed on hers, shaking my head frantically. "Of course boo! I love it! You really didn't have to do this. I'd be fine with just a damn room."

She shook her head, "No Shy. I *had* to do this for you. This is a new beginning for you... For us. I'm nowhere in a rush for you to leave so I want to make you as comfortable as possible. So giving you something like an apartment will keep you with me as long as I can."

I giggled, pushing myself off the bed and bringing her into a tight embrace. I loved Blake so much. Right now, she was the only family I have. Placing a quick peck on her cheek, I stepped out of her hold, "I love you so much."

She smiled, "Like I don't love you more. Get comfy and come up when you're done."

All I could hear was music along with laughter as I moved up the stairs leading to the foyer, closing the basement door behind me. I frowned as my eyes fell on my toes; they desperately needed to be done. My bare feet shuffled against the hardwood floor heading towards the kitchen. A welcoming aroma invaded my nostrils once crossing the threshold into the kitchen, "See! Come here Shy! Your cousin tripping."

CJ fanned me over forcing me to pick up my pace, taking a seat next to him on the barstool. "Look. Look at him. Isn't he fine girl?" He questioned, shoving his phone into my hands. "Your cousin claims he's ugly."

"No. No, I didn't say he was ugly Carson. I said he was facially challenged. I don't call people ugly." Blake butted in, giving us a quick glance before tending back to the food on the stove.

CJ rolled his eyes, waving her off, "Girl bye. What you think Shy?" He asked, placing his elbows on the counter while looking at me.

I frowned, looking through the male's Instagram that he wanted my input on. Honestly, he wasn't bad to look at *BUT* his ears were extremely too big. Like, really big. He could hear everything, seriously.

"Ummm..." I trailed off, face slightly twisting. I didn't know what to say because all I could look at was them damn ears.

Blake burst into laughter, turning to face us and leaning on the counter. She pointed her finger at CJ while I handed him back his phone, "See. She thinks he's facially challenged as well."

CJ looked at me with raised brows, "Girl."

I chuckled, "No. Uh, he's okay."

I couldn't get his ears out of my head. "Them damn ears though..." I muttered, earning a loud laugh from Blake.

Slapping the marble counter, Blake slightly jumped up and down while laughing. "I TOLD YOU his damn ears was big as shit. Floppy ass hoes!" She teased, walking back to the stove.

I tried not to laugh but couldn't help it once seeing how defeated CJ looked. Reaching over, I caressed his cheek, "Sorry boo." Another laugh escaped my lips once he swatted my hand away, mouth contorted into a frown. "That's your boo?" I asked, hoping that's not the same guy Blake was referring to earlier.

"NO! Just a hoe trying to give up that neck. I told him don't even go there with Dumbo cause boo… is life." Blake butted in, turning the burner to low before opening the oven checking the food and closing it.

Everything smelled so good. Its been a minute since I've had a home cooked meal so I definitely was going to cherish this one. One thing I knew about Blake was that her cooking skills went off, but she wasn't so generous with cooking all the time.

"See girl, this why you don't have a man now... Always worrying about me and mines," CJ said, typing away on his phone. "Boo and I have an understanding but I'm pretty sure that nigga is doing him as well."

"Y'all together?" I jumped in. I was sort of confused about his situation with his "boo." Blake made it seem like they were something serious whereas CJ was acting as if it was nothing at all.

An "understanding" to me means exactly what it sounds like. Meaning, we know where we stand with each other. Nothing more. Nothing less. Yet, we're still going to fuck who we want.

CJ placed his phone on the counter, looking to me with his tongue sweeping across his bottom lip. His olive green hues fixated on me, immediately sending shivers throughout my body. Damn. I couldn't even look this man in his eyes without feeling some type of way.

Why did he have to be into peen instead of puss?

Why was I getting turned on by someone that doesn't even have women on their mind?

…Cause he's fine as hell.

"Not even together. He has just been around forever but like any other nigga, he plays endless games. Games I don't have time for." He sighed.

I could tell that he was exhausted with whatever his "boo" was putting him through. I didn't know too much about dealing with one person for years. The last relationship I had was the most toxic one I've ever been involved in because all we did was use, together.

"But you still keep him around, so shut up!" Blake yelled, bouncing to the music softly playing throughout the wireless speaker on the counter.

"You wouldn't let me get rid of him, even if I tried." CJ shot back with his phone vibrating across the counter as he quickly picked it up.

"Ya damn right! I love Loe! That's him, ain't it?" Blake asked, a smirk forming on her lips as she looked at CJ over her shoulder.

He smiled, phone glued to his ear. "Boo..." He cooed into the receiver earning a snicker from Blake.

"Yea. That's him." She said, pulling the food out of the oven and placing it on the counter.

The doorbell held a mini tune ringing throughout the house. Blake looked back at me, throwing vegetables into a boiling pot. "Can you get that for me? It's Tink."

Tink?

I nodded, not saying a word before heading to the front door. Opening the door, I was greeted with a head full of Marley twists before the individual turned to face me. She was gorgeous. Her mocha complexion shined beautifully in the sunlight, face beat to the gods. Seeing how beautiful she was, I'm pretty sure she didn't need a full face of make-up. But hey, I always loved when girls would get braids or twists in their hair, especially since I wasn't a fan of them in mine. She threw a few braids over her shoulder as the biggest smile flew to her face, "Shy, right?" She questioned, head falling to the side while pointing at me.

I returned the smile, "Yup. Tink, right?"

She giggled, "Yea. I've heard so much about you." She cooed, readjusting her messenger bag on her shoulder.

"I heard... Blake just can't stop talking about me." I pushed the door open wider, allowing her entry.

"Mmm, it smells bomb."

What was up with Blake associating with all these beautiful people? Tink was gorgeous. Stunning. She looked pretty young, though. I'm guessing she had to be at least 23, if that. I followed not too far behind her to the kitchen as CJ shrilled, jumping from his seat and yanking her into a hug.

"My boo!" He cooed, swaying them from side to side as she laughed.

I giggled, taking my previous seat while watching them embrace each other. It felt so good to feel some genuine love around me. I thought coming home after 30 days was going to be one of the hardest things for me when actually, it probably wouldn't be as bad as I thought.

Blake shook her hand in her bone straight hair, sighing. "I thought you said your car was in the shop?" She asked, looking at Tink who was finally stepping out of CJ's hold.

Tink leaned forward onto the counter as CJ tugged on one of her twists, smiling. "These cute boo."

She smiled, "Thanks, Ceej. But it is, Dallas dropped me off."

"Dallas? The nigga I have *yet* to meet!" Blake said.

Tink laughed, "yea... that nigga. You can meet him when he comes back to pick me up later."

Dallas?
What the.

Just from hearing his name, my heart fluttered. I haven't seen or heard of him since the day I found out he'd never seen *Like Mike*. Who was he to her, though? Ugh. The fact I barely knew this man and was questioning his relations with another female I just met wasn't sitting well with me.

I shouldn't care.
I don't care.
Or do I?

"What's wrong?" I looked to Blake, seeing the concerned expression settling on her face.

"Huh?"

She rolled her eyes, "What's wrong? I can see it in your face."

Dammit. I hated that my facial expressions spoke for me. I'd rather people not be able to read me just off my face alone – it was irritating. I shook my head, "Nothing. I'm good."

Blake pursed her lips before kissing her teeth, "Mhm... whatever. The food is done, though."

I knew she didn't believe me; she knew me too well. I'd be damned if I told her that I was sitting here wondering how her friend knew the handsome man she caught me staring down during our visit.

"How you know Dallas?"

She snapped her head towards me, narrowing her brown hues on me. I didn't even think before I spoke, it sort of just came out, like always. Oh well. Better out than in.

At least I'll know how she knows the man.

Book IV.

The room was silent. My eyes scanned everyone's faces as I found nothing wrong with the question I proposed. If you wanted answers, you had to ask questions. I just tend to have the "balls" to ask questions no one else was willing to. I held Tink's gaze as a small smile crept to her lips. What the hell was funny?

"Are you sure we're talking about the same Dallas?" She questioned, head slightly tilting down with her brows raising.

I mean, I'm pretty sure we were.

How many niggas out here with the name Dallas? Especially in the DMV area where everybody knew each other.

"Tall. Brown skin. Dimples with a crooked smile."

See. What I say. I nodded, letting her know that we definitely knew the same Dallas. She crossed her eyes, waving her hand in the air, "that nigga irritating."

"But you not answering my question, though..." I trailed off before taking a sip of my juice.

I really didn't mean for that to come out but then again, I did. Hopefully, she didn't take offense to it. This was me, though. Take it or leave it.

Blake nudged my arm while taking the seat next to me, "Stop Shy." My nose turned up, mugging her as CJ laughed.

"Blake, your cousin go off hunnie. I'm going to love her firecracker ass. So Ms. Tink, spill tea." He said, placing his chin in his palm while looking at Tink.

Why was she still standing there with that dumb ass smile on her face?

Tink giggled, "It's cool B. That nigga like a brother to me. Um..."

A slight frown worked its way to my lips noticing the uncomfortable expression settling on her face.

Damn, I hope I didn't overstep any boundaries.

"He was my brother's best friend. Haven't been able to get rid of him, even if I tried..." Her voice trailed off as a weak chuckle fell from her lips.

Was?

I felt that same pang in my chest when Dallas told me the reason behind his addiction. I couldn't believe I was sitting in front of his best friend's little sister, basically jumping down her throat. My frown grew deeper as I became upset with myself for even approaching the situation the way I did.

"I'm so—" My lips pursed together once she rose her hand to stop me.

The corners of her lips turned into the biggest smile before her hands went up as if to surrender, "It's good Shia. You like his ass or something?"

My eyes widened, shaking my head frantically. Naw, I didn't "like" him per say but he looked good enough to eat. I gave her a weak smile, hoping she couldn't see through the facade. The facade of the fact I was heavily attracted to Dallas and I barely even knew the guy.

"No. No. Not at all." I rushed out, knowing no one in the room believed me.

Taking a look at all their faces confirmed what I was thinking. CJ was the first to break the silence, rolling his eyes and fanning his hand around. "Girl bye. You were damn near bout to pounce on poor Tink Tink. You want the D."

A small gasp broke my lips, nose scrunching up as Blake laughed. "She does bitch. Last time I went to visit; she was undressing the man with her eyes."

I shot my head towards her, lightly smacking her arm, "No I wasn't. He's just good to look at."

Who was I kidding?

If I got the chance to climb that beanstalk of a man, I surely would AND I haven't been put to sleep in I don't know how long.

That's how long it has been.

"Ugh. I really don't want to hear this." Tink muttered, grabbing a plastic plate and heading over to the stove.

I deeply sighed, sinking further into the couch of the living room. I never thought Blake would be good at decorating but surprisingly, every part of her house was something worth looking at.

The living room was just the right size. Not too far from me was a 40" flat screen mounted on a small gray cement portion of the wall, right above the fireplace. I thought it was cute how that was the only color on the wall; it made the living room even more appealing.

Giving off such a sophisticated vibe, a bookshelf holding five shelves sat on each side of the TV. Blake had a few pictures, small plants, and books scattered along the shelves making sure there weren't any empty spots. My bare feet rested on the cream colored footrest that matches the couch and two accent seats, one sitting on each side of the couch diagonally. Allowing my head to collide with the back of the couch, my eyes sat on the ceiling fan slowly moving in a circle.

I'm tired.

The itis was kicking in, and FAST.

It's been awhile since I had a home cooked meal and to say Blake threw down would be an understatement. I forgot how much of a beast she was in the kitchen. I had no clue who she got it from cause it damn sure wasn't my aunt. I was an alright cooker. First and foremost, I didn't enjoy cooking. I'm one of those "I'd rather you cook for me" type of chicks.

A soft tap against the wall caused my eyes to avert from the fan and to my left, landing on CJ. He smiled, waving, "Alright boo. I'm out. Bae is outside."

I put on a fake pout, not wanting him to leave. Even though we've only known each other for the few hours I've been home, we have this undeniable bond between us that I'm looking forward to making stronger.

"Okay. I'll see you tomorrow?" I questioned, hoping he'd say yes.

"Mhm. I'll be back over here."

I giggled at his heavy lids due to him having a few shots of Henny. I chose not to drink even though alcohol never been a problem of mine, but it was a responsible decision to not drink because I had no clue what it'd lead to.

You're in control of your addiction. Don't let the addiction take control of you.

Dallas' words lingered in my head, making a slight frown contort my lips. I hated how he would just randomly pop in my head. I didn't see anything good coming from this.

"Okay. Be safe and have fun."

He nodded before turning on his heels, "Will do Shy. See you tomorrow."

My eyes caught Tink's frame as she entered the room plopping into the chair diagonal from my right. She released a deep sigh while rubbing her stomach allowing her eyes to slowly shut, "I'm so damn tired."

I smirked, "You too?"

That meal did a number on all of us.

She giggled, "Yea. I gotta stay up though since I'm waiting on this nigga..." She smacked her lips, "His ass need to hurry up."

My stomach began fluttering away at her reference to the beanstalk of a man I'd like to climb. Subconsciously, I bit my lip just off the thought of him. Tink laughed, "Ugh. Don't be over there thinking about his ass." She teased.

I gave her a dead glare before scoffing, waving her off, "I'm not thinking about shit..." I muttered, slightly feeling embarrassed that she called me out. "Hey! How you know Blake?"

She smiled before pushing herself up in the seat, locking her eyes on me. The sudden change in her behavior put me at ease and warmed my heart. Just from me mentioning my cousin's name, it changed Tink's energy in a positive way. From the twinkle in her eyes, I knew whatever bond she had with Blake was deep – Blake definitely meant a lot to her.

Her hand ran down one of her braids, "She's my big sister. I went into the program when I was 16 and Blake have been here for me through it all."

I nodded, smiling. I knew EXACTLY what she meant because Blake has been here for me the same way – she was truly my backbone.

"I couldn't have asked for a better big sister to get paired with, I swear. I wouldn't change shit. She told me s—"

The ringing of her phone cut her short, bringing a frown to both of our faces simultaneously. She smacked her lips with her eyes narrowing in on her phone screen before bringing it to her ear. "Nigga. Where you at? I'm tired." She slightly whined.

Sitting here watching the many facial expressions she went through was amusing to me. I could tell that she and Dallas' bond was one of a kind – something not worth letting go.

"Uh huh..." She nodded while rising to her feet, smacking her lips. "Ight nigga. I'm coming." She said before ending the call and stuffing her phone into her back pocket.

Tink looked at me, "He needs to use the bathroom. This will be quick."

I could see it all on her face that she was more than ready to get home. I was ready to hit the sheets as well. I was full. Rising to my feet, I ran my palms across my jeans while nodding, "It's cool. Let him go Tink."

She nodded, turning on her heels heading towards the front door. With every step she took, my stomach would tighten even more. Dallas was beautiful to look at but this hold he had on me this early was bothering me. I didn't like thinking about some nigga, especially after my last. No nigga was worth my time at this point. I needed to focus on me, and me only.

"Shia?"

Snapping out of my thoughts, I locked with his chocolate gaze as his tongue swept over his lip with that sexy smirk settling on his face. I felt like he was removing every piece of my clothing with his eyes, but I won't assume. His fitted cap wasn't giving me a full view of his face which automatically had me pouting.

"Dallas." I softly responded, giving a weak smirk.

He chuckled running his hand over his mouth, "Wassup? Everything good?" I giggled watching him slightly squirm while trying his best to keep his composure. "Aye. Where's the bathroom? A nigga gotta piss."

I pointed towards the direction of the only bathroom on the main floor, "First door on your left." I guided him.

My stomach fluttered against my will once he smirked my way; this man was gorgeous. "Thank you Shia." He said, never allowing that sexy smirk to fall from his face.

Damn you Dallas.

I pulled my legs into my chest, resting my chin on my knees as my brown hues averted from the TV to land on Dallas' tall frame. How could such a fine specimen exist? I couldn't tear my eyes from his astonishing physique as his arms raised above his head into a full stretch. His eyes slowly batted once completing his yawn before landing on me.

Against my will, I blushed terribly once locking in on his intense gaze. He rubbed the back of his neck, chuckling lightly, "My bad man. A nigga really had to go."

I giggled while fanning him off, "Its cool. Its cool."

He nodded, "Cool. What about you? You good? How it feels to be home?"

I smiled catching his contagious smile.

Damn those dimples. Damn that smile.
Shit.
DAMN this man.

Allowing my bare feet to collide with the floor, a soft sigh broke free as he moved further into the living room. My stomach went haywire every step he took my way; I can't take this man right now. Its been entirely too long since I've had some and having him in my presence wasn't helping my hormones in any way.

My fingers raked through my kinky curls, "I'm good."

I actually was good so I can't say that I was lying. Since being home, the urge to use hasn't surfaced and I wasn't looking forward to it happening either. I'm just dying to stay clean right now.

That is my main focus.

The way his tongue swept over his plump bottom lip had me biting into mine just off the sight. He cleared his throat before smirking and pointing behind him towards the front door, "I'm going to get going. Tink waiting."

I nodded, chewing on the inside of my cheek. The way he was looking at me had my stomach flipping crazy. It was as if there was no ending to it – to this feeling he gave me every time we were in the presence of one another.

"Aye!" His baritone voice sent a ripple of chills throughout my core.

I locked eyes with him. "Huh? Wassup?" Just like that, he snapped me out of my mini daze.

"You gonna walk a nigga to the door?" He questioned, nodding his head in that direction while narrowing his eyes in on me.

With no words coming to mind, I just simply nodded my head while pushing myself to my feet. Falling in tow not too far behind him, I watched as he opened the door turning to face me. Cocking his head to the side, he flashed me another beautiful smile revealing those dimples of his.

I wonder who he acquired them from? Mother? Father? Either way, they added more emphasis to his already amazing face. At this moment I couldn't do anything but mentally thank the two people who laid down to make him.

"You look good though Shia. I don't know how you looked before but soberness got you glowing. I can tell you're in a good place right now." He said while rubbing the back of his neck, looking down at my short frame.

I smiled. It was as if he was reading my mind because I definitely was in a good place right now. Losing Mae was one of the most difficult things I've had to endure in a long time. She had become so dear to me and having her suddenly snatched away ripped a piece of me. I'm still hurting, but I know she would want the best for me. As long as I had Blake by my side, I'm going to fight my hardest.

Accepting your addiction is the first step but overcoming it is the final one and right now, it's the hardest battle I'm in the midst of.

A soft sigh fell from my lips, "I'm feeling good, real good Dallas. I didn't forget what you said."

His hand connected with my shoulder causing a jolt once connecting with my skin. I knew he felt it too once seeing how his brows met in the middle of his forehead. He was just as confused as me. I didn't know how to digest this "connection" we had when we barely knew each other.

Regardless, I enjoyed the comforting feeling his presence brought to me. I don't remember the last time I felt completely comfortable in the presence of the opposite sex.

He cleared his throat stepping back as his hands found a home in the front pockets of his jeans. He chuckled, "You better not but uh, I'll be seeing you around Ms. Lady. Have a good night Shia."

I couldn't help but smile. "You too Dallas." I softly responded, hand resting on the door before closing it after watching him jog towards his car.

March 15, 2016: Fort Washington, MD

A frown contorted my lips once hearing voices at a distant. They weren't too loud but it was loud enough to wake me out of my sleep. Rubbing my eyes, I struggled to pry my eyes open against the sunlight overwhelming the room. Squeezing my eyes shut, I used my left hand to push my body up into a sitting position. Yawning, I finally was able to beat the battle against the sunlight as my lids fluttered trying their best to adjust. My frown grew deeper once realizing I was sitting on the living room couch.

Smacking my lips, I instantly grew irritated with the fact I didn't make it to my bed last night once catching *Hardball* from the beginning. I haven't seen it in so long so catching it from the beginning had me losing my shit. The fact I didn't stay up for the entire movie irritated me even more.

Yawning, I rose to my feet stretching while raising to my tippy toes to receive the full extent of it; I swear morning stretches are the best.

"Aw bitch. You woke Shy up!"

I laughed once hearing a light smack followed by an even harder one. Moving towards the kitchen, I took a place on the barstool locking my eyes on CJ and Blake standing on the other side of the island.

"Morning boo!" CJ smiled while pouring a glass of orange juice.

I parted my lips to speak before Blake's hand rising in the air stopped me. "Uh uh bitch, go brush your teeth before you say a word."

CJ squealed, bursting into a fit of laughter and giving the island a smack. "Bitch! STOP playing with her cause I'm here for her beating yo ass!" He said, sipping from his glass.

I wasn't worried about her; Blake loved talking shit. She didn't do it to hurt feelings or anything, it was just all fun and games. BUT when she *does* talk shit intentionally, I promise you that she could back it up. Her mouth could go off but trust, her hands spoke even louder.

I will never forget the first fight I witnessed her in. I felt bad for the poor girl because Blake wasn't playing. The bitch felt it was okay to keep coming sideways at her over a nigga that Blake didn't even want. Funny how broads act a fool over niggas that could careless about them. Blake made sure to let it be known to her and any other female that wanted to come her way, that she wasn't a force to be reckoned with. That day, it ended with the girl heading to the hospital and having a slight concussion. Surprisingly, she didn't press any charges like what any scary bitch would do. After the fight, she would offer a wave and a smile whenever she saw Blake – I found it hilarious how she had such a sudden change of heart because she got her ass whooped.

But, I guess that's a scary bitch for you. First, they want to fight then befriend you.

Shaking my head.

Blake's head slightly went back, giggling, "Shy not gonna beat me. She knows wassup. Ain't that right?" She looked at me, grinning.

A sneaky smirk slowly crept to my face. This girl knows I'm not one to be played with as well. These hands work perfectly fine. "Nigga, YOU know wassup."

Blake started laughing before popping a piece of gum in her mouth. "Girl, go get dressed so we can go buy you a phone."

My nose turned up at her reference to a phone. For what? She knew I wasn't too big on those. Throughout me using, I never had a reason to keep in contact with no one. Probably one of the main reasons I lost the few friends I had. When it came down to Blake, she knew where I laid my head every night so she would make it her duty to get in touch with me regardless. I gave up on having a phone a long time ago because I'd always lose them due to me being high.

"Why though?"

"Ooh." CJ uttered, holding his hand to his chest. I playfully rolled my eyes at his dramatics. "This your new beginning Shy. If the bih offering a brand new phone, you better take it or I will."

I laughed once seeing Blake whip her head in his direction with a screwed up face. "I'm not buying YOU anything. This is for Shy."

He fanned her off, "Bye. I already know. I have coin if I needed a new phone but that's not even necessary since I have bae." He said before sticking his tongue out his mouth while bending over to bounce his ass.

We all laughed once Blake's hand collided with his backside making him bounce it even harder to no music. Being around them had me looking at life in such a positive way again. It had me how I used to feel before I started using. I needed them – they were truly a breath of fresh air.

Blake released an exhausted sigh looking to me, "Hurry up Shy. I don't want to be out long."

I rolled my eyes allowing my hands to push me from the island and standing to my feet. I gave her a straight face, "Ight. Shut up."

I sat Indian-style in the middle of my bed, having no clue whose number to store. The only two contacts I had were Blake and CJ. I knew having a phone would be a bad idea; I had no clue what to do with this phone, honestly. When I did have one, it was a flip phone. I needed something to make quick calls here and there. Regardless of me not being up on technology, Blake insisted on buying me an iPhone 6s. Her and CJ showed me the basics, as far as contacting people, so I'd try to learn the extra things on my own.

My eyes lit up once remembering that Kris and Mace had given me their numbers before going our separate ways. Scooting towards the edge of my bed, my feet collided with the rug before swiftly moving to the corner of my room wildly searching through my bag for the piece of paper. The biggest smile spread across my face once feeling the white torn sheet between my fingers as I moved back to my bed, taking my previous seat in the middle. After storing their numbers, I sent them both a quick text letting them know it was me and to save my number. I wasn't really looking forward to hearing back from them because even though we "somewhat" built a friendship before leaving, I was sold on the fact it wouldn't go far outside those doors.

My heart slightly picked up its pace once feeling my phone vibrate as my brown hues scanned over the text from Mace. For some reason I found myself smiling. Surprisingly, I actually missed his irritating ass; something I'd never expected myself feeling.

Mace
<u>Received</u>
I've been waiting to hear from you dawg.

I giggled once seeing the red angry facial expression he sent my way. What was that? With me not being used to this "texting thing," it took me a while to type out my response. Ugh, I really got to get used to this new phone.

Mace
<u>Sent</u>
What is that? That face?
I told you I'd reach out Mace… stop

After pressing send, I noticed three dots appearing on the text conversation. What the hell?

Mace
<u>Received</u>
Uh, an emoji nigga. Duh.
Green ass. Wassup tho?
How you feeling boo?

Rolling my eyes, I scoffed knowing that he was going to be that same Mace I remembered. Calling me out of my name, not in a disrespectful way but a way I didn't want him to. Either way, it was good to be hearing from him right now.

Mace
<u>Sent</u>
Shut up Mace.
I just don't know how to work this shit.
Stop calling me boo nigga!
I'm good actually, no urges or nothing.
What about you? Everything good?

Mace
<u>Received</u>
Exactly. Green af.
Girl, you are boo. Shut up
That's good Shy. You know I'm rooting for you.
We gotta stay clean ma. I'm good tho.
A nigga just happy to be home & moms is too.

58

I cringed once knowing his mother was happy to have him home when I didn't even have a mother that loved me to even come home to. It's cool. Everything happens for a reason, right? Just as my fingers began dancing across the screen, a knock at the door stopped me midway, "Yea." I said, letting the unknown person it was okay to come in.

My eyes remained on the door as it began opening revealing Blake's head peeping through, "What you doing?"

"Nosey." I giggled, looking back down to my phone.

"So..." I heard her say while seeing her body fully move into the room out of my peripheral vision. "We're going to Tink's tonight. Her birthday is this weekend and they're having dinner for her."

Huh? I barely knew the girl for me to be going to her house to celebrate her birthday. No disrespect or shade, I just don't know how I feel about being around someone's family so early. I don't even have one to call my own; all I have is Blake.

"I'm not going," I murmured typing away on my phone.

"Yes, you are." Blake spat back.

My head whipped to her, frowning. "How are you going to tell me that I'm going?"

"Because, I won't allow you to be cooped up in the house. You're home now and trying to get better, you need to be social boo. I'm not trying to force anything but I know how much fun we used to have before your addiction and I just want my girl back. Just… Just come out with me tonight, see some new faces and if you're not feeling it, I won't pull you out for nothing else."

Looking into her eyes, she was practically begging me to accompany her to this dinner. I could eat. I just didn't want to be in the vicinity of a bunch of people I had no clue existed. Blake had made more than enough sacrifices for me so attending dinner with her could be the least I could do.

I can't be selfish.

For the past two years, I'd been selfish allowing my addiction to replace who I really am, stealing me from her, so I owed her this one. Actually, I owed her more than this.

"I'll go," I sighed, giving in completely.

Book V.

March 15, 2016: Greenbelt, MD

A small frown contorted my lips while tugging at the bottom of the black bodycon dress Blake let me borrow. It amazed me how I fit my curvy ass in this thing, but I did. It stopped a little above my knees showing off my thick chocolate legs, having my phat ass on display. There was a cutout on the shoulders giving the dress a more appeasing look instead of just being simple. It's been a minute since I wore something on the "sexy" side. When I was using, I could care less about my appearance because all that mattered was my next fix.

With us wearing the same size shoe, Blake insisted that I wore these black chunky heel shoes. I loved that they were open toed with a thick anklet, making my heels visible to everyone. Not trying to go over the top, I decided on wearing a nude lip just to keep a more natural face. My long, wavy hair flowed freely along my shoulders and back. To top it off, I put on a pair of small gold hoops and gold leaf cuff on my upper arm.

I sighed softly, stopping in my tracks. With every step we took towards the house, I was growing nervous. I wasn't ready. I'm not too worried about everyone else but Dallas… I'm so nervous to be around him in such an intimate setting. As much as I enjoy seeing his face, being in his presence was too overwhelming for me.

Frowning, I turned to face CJ and Blake who stopped once I did. "How do I look? Really, do I look okay?"

Simultaneously, they both rolled their eyes; I know they were tired of me asking the same question.

Blake smacked her lips, "You're blowing me."

"Me too," CJ added. "You look fine girl. Calm your ass down." He said, turning his nose up while waving me off.

"Agreed." Blake grabbed my hand pulling me along, "You'll be fine Shy. Just be yourself."

That was the thing.
Who am I now?

When Blake said it'd be a dinner party, I was expecting a full dinner table of people. It was the complete opposite. Matter of fact, it wasn't a dinner party at all. It was more of a kickback. Either she got the wrong memo or purposely told me birthday dinner so I could come.

I was feeling out of my element, leaned up against the wall while sipping from my juice. I haven't seen Dallas all night which was a relief but then again a disappointment. I was looking forward to seeing him but then I wasn't.

Shit, I'm confusing myself.

I giggled watching CJ bounce through the crowd towards me with his drink in hand. One thing I gathered about him since being home is that he was ALWAYS with the turn-up. The fact he didn't turn into one of those angry drunks was a plus.

He laughed once reaching me, "You over here looking all bored."

"Cause I am," I muttered, looking around the room at the bodies occupying the large basement.

This used to be my type of scene but I really wasn't in the mood for it. Maybe I needed a drink to take the edge off a bit? Eh. I never was a drinker so I don't know how that would work out for me.

Fuck it.

"Where the drinks?" I blurted out, hoping he could hear me over the music since he was in his own zone dancing.

"Huh?" His voice rose an octave, cupping his ear while leaning into me.

I gripped his shoulder pulling his body to me before speaking in his ear, "Where are the drinks?" I repeated myself.

His brows furrowed in confusion once I released my hold on his shoulder. He grabbed my hand, "You gonna be good?"

I nodded as he searched my face before leading the way, "Come on boo."

I wasn't too worried about drinking. One or two should do to get me comfortable for now. They always say you don't need to drink to have a good time but honestly, I needed to at the moment.

My eyes scanned over the various types of liquor along the bar; I had no clue what to drink. I shook my head as CJ grabbed a red plastic cup, "I got you boo."

"Please don't make it too strong. I'm not a drinker," I stressed.

I'm not trying to wake up tomorrow with a hangover, at all. He nodded while grabbing one bottle before another then lastly pouring some juice in the concoction. I became nervous once CJ pushed the cup in my direction. Before taking a sip, I brought the cup to my nose taking a sniff.

"Bitch. This smells strong." My lip turned up, pushing it his way.

"Girl. It's not. I got you."

Hesitantly, I took a sip and surprisingly it was good. I could tell he knew I liked it once he started smiling.

"Good right?"

"Actually…" I took another sip, "It is."

His smile grew wider, "I told you, girl. I bartend for part-time; I won't set you up boo."

"I would've never known."

He gave me a sneaky smirk taking a sip from his cup, "Well now you know boo. Turn up." He said raising his cup in the air as I did the same.

Rihanna's "Work" blasted through the speakers as I danced in the middle of the many bodies. It was more bodies than it was when we originally got here but it wasn't bothering me one bit. I was surprised to be having such a good time but the one drink did it for me. Bending over, my hands found my knees while twerking my butt from side to side to the beat.

I love this song especially since I LOVE me some Rihanna.

I sang along while swaying from side to side with closed eyes, winding my hips. Slowly, I peeled my eyes open as my body couldn't find it in itself to stop moving. Feeling as if I was being watched, I began searching the room through heavy lids. I knew someone was watching me; I could feel it.

Dallas.

Once locking in on his intense gaze, my body became still as my heart picked up its pace. THIS is what I was talking about when it came down to me being in his presence; it was as if we were being pulled to each other against our will. My stomach fluttered once he threw a head nod my way as that cute ass, crooked smile blessed his face.

WHY must he be so breathtaking? Seriously. I never came across such a fine specimen. Even from here, I could see his long tongue sweeping across that fluffy bottom lip. I can't. I need some air.

I broke our intense gaze, turning on my heels making my way through the crowd towards the sliding doors leading to the backyard. I sighed of relief once feeling the cool air hit my face. It was more people out here too, using this area for smoking. Pushing a few strands of hair behind my ear, I walked to my left to take a seat on the patio couch. I crossed my legs at the ankles still nodding to the music that could be heard from inside.

I turned my nose up at the marijuana smoke invading my nostrils, fanning the smoke away from me. A light skin guy not too far from me must've caught my action seeing as though he moved away slightly, "My bad love. We'll move over here." I wasn't expecting such courtesy. I flashed him a smile, "Thank you." He nodded as they moved further away.

Before I got heavily involved with heroin, I did a lot of experimenting especially with weed. I started smoking that during my freshman year of high school but of course, it got boring so I ventured out to get a different high. You'd be surprised at the many drugs I chose to do before falling in love with heroin.

The sound of the glass doors opening caused my eyes to avert from the guys smoking towards the doors. My heart jumped once seeing him look around the backyard as if he was looking for someone. I blushed once his eyes landed on me, smiling while moving my way.

Why is he coming over here?

My heart picked up its pace with every step he took my way.

Why did he have this affect on me?

Finally getting in front of me, he towered over me still smiling while stuffing his hands into the front pockets of his jeans. My eyes scanned over his choice of clothing: A black tee, black jeans, and black high-top Air Force Ones. The most simple outfit ever but yet he looked so fuckin' good; I'm pretty sure he could make anything look good.

"Why are you being a creep?" I broke the silence, looking up at him trying to see his eyes despite it being dark and his black fitted cap pulled low.

"Why are you running from me?"

What? Running from him? For what? What is he talking about?

A tiny mug settled on my face, "Running… From you?" I kissed my teeth before looking around the backyard then back to him, "I doubt it."

He chuckled before occupying the empty space next to me.

"I didn't say I wanted your company."

"You didn't have to. I can feel it." He shot back, leaning back into the couch while brushing off his jeans.

Twin
Received
Wya???

I giggled at Blake's over exaggeration of question marks.

Twin
Sent
Outside. I needed some air.
I'm good.

"Hmm."

What did he mean by he can feel it? Feel what? He probably feels the same thing I feel whenever I'm around him. I'm hoping that's what he was referring to but I won't dig any further.

"Hm what?" I looked his way, mugging him earning a laugh from him. "Why you so mean?"

"I'm not mean." I shot back, feeling somewhat offended. I mean, I know I could be kind of difficult at times but when you get to know me, I'm one of the sweetest people.

He nodded, looking around the backyard. "If you say so Ms. Lady. Wassup though? Why you was running?" His eyes landed on mine.

Why is he stuck on this running shit?

"Running Dallas? There was no running involved."

"So, you admit that you were trying to get away from me."

I huffed out of frustration, giggling lightly, "I'm admitting nothing. I know I wasn't running, though."

"Hm. I was trying to get a dance with you."

"I can't dance." I shot back, lying.

He chuckled, "Shit'n me."

I laughed, "What you want Dallas?"

He smiled, "Nothing forreal. I'm just surprised to see you here. I assumed this wasn't your type of scene."

I scoffed rubbing my hands over my bare legs as the wind hit them, "Cause it's not. Well, it used to be but I'm not really feeling it tonight."

"You've been drinking?" He questioned, sitting forward to get a better look at me.

"Just one, to take the edge off a bit. I've never been a drinker."

He nodded, "Just don't let it turn into too many."

I nodded, mutely agreeing with him; I'm pretty sure I'm done for the night.

The hairs on my arms rose as his eyes scanned my curvy frame with his tongue sweeping across his lip, "You clean up nice Shia."

I giggled, rolling my eyes, "Thank you, Dallas. You do too."

He leaned towards me nudging my shoulder, "So, can I get that dance you ran away from?"

I laughed, shaking my head. This guy wasn't going to give up. Blake brought me here to have a good time so one dance wouldn't hurt. I rose to my feet as I felt his eyes land on my ass. I giggled once seeing him quickly avert his eyes from my backside to look me in the eyes.

I tilted my head down slightly, "You coming?"

Not a word was said which was fine because seeing his lips contort into that crooked smile was enough for me.

Chills danced down my spine once his cologne swarmed my nostrils with my hand gently resting in his above my head, him giving me a spin around. His thick tongue swept across his chunky bottom lip with his chocolate gaze locking with mine, making my knees somewhat tremble. The corner of his lips turned up revealing his deep dimple upon one cheek with the other one hiding. The way my dress was hugging my curvaceous frame, I could barely move the way I wanted to. Standing before this man had me squeezing my legs tight from becoming moist between the thighs. I really want to know if he knew the effect he had on me.

He had to.

I felt like he was looking over my body forever. The lust dancing in his eyes was evident as he brought my hand to my side, stepping in closer while turning me around allowing my rotund ass to collide with his front. Once feeling myself bounce off his semi-hard front had a smirk forming on my face; he wanted me.

I wanted him too but I knew that *this*, us trying to start something, wasn't going to have a pleasant outcome. We're both recovering addicts. So, I'm going to have this dance with him and leave it at that. My body shuddered once feeling his lips graze my right ear as his masculine hands took a strong grip of my tiny hips.

"Who you wearing this dress for?" His tone had become deep with a hint of raspiness which sent my hormones into overdrive.

"Not you." I smartly responded earning a resonant chuckle, developing from the pits of his stomach and flowing from his parted lips.

A small hiss broke my lips once feeling his hands rest on the front of my bare thick thighs, giving them a light squeeze causing the butterflies in my stomach to flutter faster. His chin rested on my shoulder, lips falling right by my right ear, "I wasn't expecting you to wear shit for me anyways. I was just seeing who you were trying to impress."

Quickly, a frown took over my face as I attempted to look over my shoulder at him but failed once Juvenile's "Back That Azz Up" came booming through the speakers. THIS was one of my favorite songs of all time.

Using my hand to throw my hair over the left of my shoulder, I bent over as my hands found my knees beginning to bounce my ass to the beat. A small grunt from him graced my ears as his hands took a hold of my hips tightly. He met my bouncing ass which I didn't expect; Dallas looked like one of those "non-dancing ass niggas." I'm glad he was picking this moment to prove me wrong.

He rapped along with the song in my ear once I stood upright, continuing to give him this work. I rolled my eyes at the part he decided to rap along with when Juvenile referred to slanging wood. I found it crazy how one moment he had me nervous as if I was some little school girl but then still could manage to make me so comfortable. Just as I was about to really get into it since the chorus dropped, I was being turned around swiftly forced to lock eyes with him.

I frowned once seeing the discomfort settling on his face as my hand softly grabbed a hold of his shoulder, "Everything fine Dallas?"

I didn't understand what happened within a matter of seconds.

He nodded while looking around the room before focusing back on me. He chewed on the inside of his cheek for a quick second before parting his lips to speak, "Yea. I'm good Shy. I just wanted to look at you for a minute."

I blushed, not really understanding his reason for wanting to look at me but regardless, it sounded so good falling from his lips. His soft hand caressed the side of my face as his head fell to the side, never taking his eyes off mine.

Normally, I couldn't hold eye contact but it was something about his eyes – that something that made me want to look into them eternally. My teeth captured my bottom lip as his thumb rubbed small circles on my cheek before raking through my kinky hair. I frowned once he removed his hand from my face causing a scowl to appear upon my pretty, chocolate features; I now felt empty. Having his touch was satisfying and now, I felt nothing. I stepped back creating some space between us while pushing a few strands behind my ear.

He didn't look like the normal Dallas right now.
That confident Dallas.

Instead, he looked like a frightened little boy which was bothering me. His sudden change of behavior was making our good night turn into an awkward one. Clearing his throat, he rubbed the back of his neck while looking at the floor which instantly annoyed me. Even though I wasn't a fan of eye contact, I wanted his focus to be solely on me.

Bending my knees, I moved my face in his sight forcing his eyes off the ground and on me. "Wassup? You ight?" I questioned, hoping this time he'd give me more than before.

He sighed, digging his hands into the pockets of his jeans while nodding. "Ye-yea. I'm good."

My brows met in the middle of my head, not believing this facade he called himself putting on, "You're not."

"I am." He shot back as quickly, brows furrowing.

I rolled my eyes, not in the mood to go back and forth with him – he could have it. I wasn't one to argue especially if you're no one special to me and "special" people in my life right now was very limited. I wasn't going to stand here, looking dumb and feeling awkward. The fact he was standing here silent and just staring at me had me growing agitated but managing to turn me on as well.

I turned on my heels being spun back around just as quick; this time he enclosed the space between us. My breath hitched in my throat once feeling his fingers snake from my hip before resting in the middle of my lower back. His other hand swept through my hair as I focused on Blake and CJ across the room, not trying to make eye contact whatsoever.

He chuckled, sending a jolt through my being, "Now you can't look at a nigga?"

He mocked my actions from a few minutes ago forcing me to lock in on his chocolate gaze. That crooked smile danced among his handsome features with his brown hues moving rapidly around my face as if he was searching for something. For what? I have no clue. Whatever was on his mind must've been bothering him because it was evident through his furrowed brows and the slight mug now sitting on his pouty lips.

Those damn lips.

"You running away from me again?" He teased with his minty breath directly hitting my nose as he inched his face closer to mine.

His other hand rounded me resting on top of the other as he began swaying us from side to side to Trey Songz's "Smartphones." Just a few minutes ago, he was acting weird and now that sexy confidence is back; he is something else. What did he want from me? He knew I had to be such a tarnished individual yet here he was, showing me all the attention in the world.

I managed to tear my eyes from his even though it felt like one of the most difficult things to do. A heavy laugh rumbled throughout my chest, eyes landing on the ground.

"What you want from me?" I softly spoke to the ground.

Against my will, my hands wrapped around his waist as we continued to sway to the beat.

"You gonna direct that question towards me or expect the floor to respond to you?"

Smartass.

Rolling my eyes, I looked up to him watching his tongue wet his pouty lips. My mouth slightly fell agape before tucking my lip between my teeth. Those damn plump lips – I couldn't keep my eyes off them. Even in the dark with limited lighting, all his striking features stood out.

"Want to ask your question again? To me this time." The playfulness was radiating through his tone causing me to blush.

I shook my head, "you heard me."

Raising a brow, he looked over my head before back down at me, "Naw. The floor did, though." This time his smile spread widely across his face, bringing his deep dimples to the forefront.

How was he so beautiful? Without even trying.

I laughed, "Whatever Dallas."

I wasn't going to repeat my question because I know he heard me. His shoulders rose and dropped as he laughed, shaking his head.

"Stubborn Shia. You don't have to repeat yourself. Just know from here on out, look at me when you're talking to me. No more floor conversations."

A small frown contorted my lips once my eyes fixated on the red almond shaped nails that appeared on Dallas' shoulder. His nose turned up while releasing me from his hold, turning to face the individual. A smile blessed my face once seeing Tink wrap her petite arms around Dallas' large frame. She locked in on my gaze with her smile growing bigger causing mines to do the same.

"Shy," She cooed before releasing from Dallas' embrace and bringing me into one as well.

This moment felt hella awkward because I wasn't a "hugger," especially with people I barely knew. But, I'm trying to turn over a new leaf so I guess I'm a hugger tonight. I wrapped my arms around her, giving her a light squeeze.

"Happy Birthday Tink! You look cute!"

"Thank you, boo. Talking bout me. Look at you...All these curves and shit." She complimented, tapping the side of my butt.

She was so beautiful – probably the main reason I sort of got jealous once finding out she knew Dallas. My eyes scanned over her choice of clothing: a strapless black crop top and high waist matching black skirt. Her hair was now in thick faux locs sitting on top of her head in a massive bun. I wasn't sure of her ethnicity but she definitely had something mixed in her by the way her edges laid down so perfectly. A pair of large grandpa-like frames covered her eyes; they were adorable on her.

She smiled, "You know it's not my birthday, right? But thank you boo!"

I nodded, "Yea. I know. I didn't know your actual birthday plans so I'm saying it now just in case I don't see you. What're your plans anyways?"

My eyes fell on Dallas for a second, who was focused on his phone, before looking back to Tink. Her eyes lit up with every word she spoke, "My parents are taking me to the Dominican Republic."

Wow, that's a damn good trip. I wish I could be taking trips like that or better yet, have parents who would finance it.

"Aww. I know you're going to have fun. Take lots of pics!"

She smiled, "You know I will. But umm..." She looked to Dallas, tapping his arm to get his attention.

She looked back at me, "You mind if I borrow him for a minute? My parents acting all anal, pressing me out to find him."

I shooed them off, "Girl. He's all yours."

We laughed as I caught Dallas' gaze that sent a jolt to my lower region. He smirked before wetting those attractive lips of his. He threw Tink a head nod, "I'm right behind you Tink."

"Okay. I'll see you, Shy. Have fun." She waved as I returned it, watching her retreating back.

Dallas stepped into my view as I released the breath I didn't realize I was holding. His hands found my waist bringing my body into his. I hissed once feeling his face nuzzle into my neck, enjoying being in his hold once again along with his intoxicating cologne overwhelming my nostrils.

"You tryna get rid of a nigga?" He spoke in my neck causing the hairs on my arms to rise.

I bit my lip, fighting back a moan. My neck was definitely one of my spots and his sexy ass face being buried into it was making me hot and heavy. Frantically, I shook my head bending it in an attempt to squeeze his face, forcing him out of my neck. It worked seeing as though he started laughing while removing his face, standing upright. A mug sat on my face, "You're irritating," I hissed.

He shrugged squeezing my hips, "So. You not going to go into hiding while I'm gone, are you?"

I narrowed my eyes in on him before shrugging, "Maybe. Maybe not." I said in a playful tone.

He kissed his teeth, "Yeah igh. Don't go nowhere bae." He grinned while walking backward, keeping his eyes on me.

Leaving me with a damn pool between my thighs.

March 15, 2016: Fort Washington, MD

My eyes shot open as my head nodded once again from falling asleep. I looked out the window through heavy lids from the backseat as CJ occupied the passenger with Blake driving. I was so damn tired; I was just ready to get back in my bed. Crazy how Dallas was telling me not to go anywhere when I didn't see him again for the remainder of the night. I'd saw Tink and actually danced with her for a few but, no Dallas.

I didn't bother to ask either. I might've been pretty parched when it came to him but I wasn't going to let anyone know that, not even him.

I frowned once feeling my phone vibrate against my thigh, I squinted looking over the text from an unknown number. Who th—

(240) 698-0056
<u>Received</u>
Bae?

(240) 698-0056
<u>Sent</u>
How you get my number?
& I'm not your "bae."

(240) 698-0056
<u>**Received**</u>
Don't worry bout all that.
Lol, whatever BAE
Wya?

(240) 698-0056
<u>**Sent**</u>
Where you're not.
I shouldn't even be talking to you.
You never came back.

(240) 698-0056
<u>**Received**</u>
Don't trip.
I'll meet you at your house.

(240) 698-0056
<u>**Sent**</u>
Who said you could come over?

(240) 698-0056
<u>**Received**</u>
You.

(240) 698-0056
<u>**Sent**</u>
I did not.

(240) 698-0056
<u>**Received**</u>
My point.
You didn't have to. I can feel it.

I didn't even bother to respond. Yawning, my mind began to drift off on Kris; I haven't heard from her since I sent her the text when I stored her number. I was beginning to become kind of worried but I'll remain positive. She was okay.

"Which one of y'all gave Dallas my number?" My voice rose over the John Legend song that played softly.

CJ laughed, "Don't look at me boo."

"Why Blake?" I sighed.

She looked at me through the rearview mirror, "Girl stop playing like you don't want that man. I saw y'all hugged up in the middle of the room and shit." She hissed, coming to a stop at a red light.

Sighing, I ran my fingers through my hair, "We weren't hugged up. Just dancing."

"Bitch lies. WE saw you girl. It was more than dancing. We could feel the connection from across the room." CJ butted in causing me to roll my eyes.

How are they going to tell me what we were doing?

"No connection. Just dancing." I sang, trying my best to convince myself as well

I knew there was a connection between us but I don't want to pursue it. I want Dallas to stay on his end and me on mine. But then, being around him made me feel so giddy inside. I truly enjoyed his presence which was scaring the shit out of me. I just wanted to focus on my sobriety. The last time I was involved with a guy, I was turned onto heroin so who knows what could come out of involving myself with a recovering addict.

I don't think it'd end well.

"Expecting company?" Blake said in a teasing tone causing me to sit up in the seat, getting a better view of outside.

My eyes locked on the all black 2-door Dodge Challenger parked right out front our house with Dallas leaned up against the passenger door, attention on his phone. Shit, he actually came. I huffed out of frustration knowing it would no longer be a room full of people but just me and him, alone. I haven't even recovered from earlier; my panties were still very soaked.

"Don't be huffing and puffing big bad wolf. Just don't give up that puss tonight." CJ teased, looking back at me before stepping out the car.

I couldn't help but laugh but there was no way in hell I was giving it up. Since Dallas insist on being around me, I was going to make sure that whatever *this* was, stayed on friend terms. I couldn't risk possibly turning back to heroin just because I couldn't control my emotions. My past situations had me turning to drugs as an escape and I'd be damned if I created a new "possible" toxic situation and I'm fresh out of rehab.

Slowly, I trekked towards him as eyes ran up my frame before landing on mine once stopping in front of him. He weakly smiled, reaching to grab my hand into his pulling me closer. It was like once I got around him, I turned into putty. The way he looked at me would have my heart beating faster than normal and off his touch alone, my body always got excited.

I've never had a guy make me feel the way Dallas do.

It was something about him holding my interest but still, I wanted to push him away, far away. This feeling was overwhelming but in a good way, which is what scared me the most.

The pad of his thumbs rubbed the back of my hands before lightly tugging at my wrists. "Didn't think I was going to come, huh?"

"I really didn't. I'm going to fall asleep on you; I'm tired." I said, hoping that'd make him want to leave.

He shrugged as if it was nothing, "It's cool. I just wanna be round you..." He yawned before talking again, "I wouldn't be surprised if I nod off at some point."

I cocked my head to the side, "Then why stay if you're tired?"

Dallas smacked his lips, "This all in God's plan. I'm here for a reason..." He paused for a second, thumb strumming at his fluffy, bottom lip. "Just... Just chill. Let Him move the way He see fit. We didn't cross paths for nothing..." He pointed between us, "*This* wasn't a mistake." He finished.

Here he goes again with this God stuff but the crazy thing is, I couldn't help but to have chills running through me as he spoke about this God. I'm not too big on religion. I actually gave up on it once I was given up on but I DO enjoy Dallas' presence so whatever or whoever brought him to me, I'm thankful.

The sound of Dallas smacking his lips entered the air causing me to giggle, cutting my eyes his way.

"Slim. I'm not tryna watch this shit." He huffed out of frustration, running his hands down his face.

For the past 30 minutes, I had him watching *Catfish* which was one of the shows on his "shit list," so he says. It didn't matter to me because regardless I was going to watch it; this was one of my favorite episodes.

It was the second episode of the second season where Antwane got catfished by "Tony." With "Tony" being his cousin Carmen that was with him the entire time of the taping. It wasn't funny but then again it was hilarious once I found out the reason behind it. All because he called her a "fat Kelly Price." What the hell. I laughed at my thoughts, feeling Dallas bore a hole into the side of my face.

"You mind changing the channel?" He hissed as I looked at him, shaking my head.

My stomach fluttered focusing in on how good he looked with such a blank expression, jaw clenching and all.

"Nope." I quickly responded while leaning forward to grab my Sprite, taking a sip before returning it back to its respectable place.

He was in my home so he was going to watch what I wanted to watch.

He sighed slouching further into the couch as a small smirk worked its way to his lips. His head connected with the back of the couch, still staring at me.

I hate how he looks at me, for the simple fact, he makes my insides go insane when he does.

"You gon' get enough of playing with me Shy."

I kissed my teeth while fanning him off, "Nigga. Stop. I'm not playing with you. We're watching what I want to watch."

He continued to smile while nodding, "Yea, I hear you."

"Why are you staring at me?"

"Cause..." His voice trailed off, wetting his pouty, plump lips.

He didn't finish his sentence but cleared his throat instead, looking at the TV. I already know he didn't want to watch this so him faking like he did wasn't going to get him out of answering my question. I watched as he ran his hands over his jeans before parting his lips to speak, "Wassup though? Why are you staring at a nigga?" He questioned, eyes remaining on the TV.

"You didn't finish your sentence." I stated obviously.

A chill ran through my body once he looked at me, "So." He nonchalantly shrugged as a smirk settled among his handsome features, tucking one side of his lip between his teeth.

I could tell he was getting a kick out of this, not telling me what he was going to say and whatnot.

I huffed, waving him off dismissively, "Whatever boy."

I didn't have time for his shenanigans.

Dallas chuckled, with it coming out in a deep tone hitting me like a ton of bricks, and I say that in the best way possible. It was driving me nuts that he didn't have to utter a word but had my body reacting to the smallest things he did.

I couldn't say that I'm against the good feeling his presence brings me but however, this connection between us two had me scared shitless. I jumped slightly once feeling his cold hand come in contact with my naked thigh. Soon as we entered the front door, I rushed to my room to change into a pair of loose fitting pajama shorts and a white V-Neck shirt.

I locked in on his chocolate gaze as that notoriously crooked smile played at his lips before sweeping his broad tongue across his lip. "What you jumping for?" He questioned in a teasing manner giving my thigh a light squeeze as he enclosed the space between us.

He was too close for comfort.

My heartbeat picked up its pace with his hand resting on my thigh as I couldn't find a word to say; all I could do was stare right back at him. I watched as his eyes darted down to my heaving chest as a low laugh fell from his lips before removing his hand, running it over his mouth.

To say I felt relieved and disappointed, all in one would be an understatement. Relieved that he was no longer physically touching me because I felt at any minute, I was ready to throw all of this on him. But disappointed because without his touch, I felt weird.

Oddly, I felt deserted.

Dallas sighed before rising to his feet forcing my brows to meet in the middle of my forehead in confusion.

Where is he going?

Leaning over, he grabbed his black fitted cap off the coffee table running his hand over his slight waves before shielding his head. He nodded behind him towards the door, clearing his throat, "Walk me out, girl."

My brows rose at his choice of words, "Girl? Rephrase that. And how about please as well?"

He smirked reaching out to grab me, pulling me to my feet. His face was a few inches away from mine to the point I could feel his breath with every word spoken, "Please bae?" He grinned while tugging on my wrist.

I couldn't help but smile at the childish begging face he put on – it was adorable on him. Removing my hand from his hold, I extended my pointer finger his way, "I'm not your bae."

"Whatever. Come on." He pulled me along as I stayed close behind him towards the door.

He stopped suddenly without warning causing me to collide into his back earning a laugh from him. He kept his hold on my wrist while swiftly turning to face me, bringing me into a tight embrace. His mind blowing cologne overwhelmed my nostrils causing them to expand out of enjoyment. Releasing from our hug, his strong but soft hands took a firm grip on the side of my upper arms.

"I'll let you know when I get in."

I turned my nose up, "Who said I wanted to know?"

The grin his face held quickly fell causing me to burst out in laughter and throwing my hands up in surrender. "I'm just playing Dallas. Please let me know you made it in safely." I batted my lashes in an innocent manner earning a kiss of the teeth from him.

My stomach tossed for a bit watching how his juicy lips held a slight mug to them. Maybe I should make him mad often? I definitely could sit here and admire how even better he looked when upset.

"FUCK!" I hissed, jumping back from him, rubbing my fleshy thigh where he just delivered a hard pinch.

That sneaky smirk appeared on his handsome face as he reached behind him to grab a hold of the doorknob, pulling it open. "I told you to stop playing with me Shy."

Fucker.

I couldn't think due to how bad my thigh was stinging. More than ready to get him out of my presence now, my palm collided with the door applying pressure to rush him across the threshold.

"GoodBYE nigga." The annoyance was evident through my voice.

Dallas laughed, "Don't forget to say your prayers little girl."
I scoffed, rolling my eyes.

Prayers. For what?

They did nothing for me. All those nights I "prayed" for a better life, it never happened. All those nights I "prayed" that I didn't get taken advantage of by the man who was supposed to protect me as one of his own. All those nights I "prayed" that the one person that carried me would love me first.

Prayers weren't for me and clearly didn't work either because here I am, just a torn soul trying my best not to relapse.

Book VI.

March 16, 2016: Fort Washington, MD

Groaning, I turned on my side grabbing my phone. It's been vibrating for the past 10 minutes which I tried to ignore but to no avail, I couldn't manage to fall into a deep sleep with it vibrating continuously. Not even bothering to glance at who was calling, I slid my thumb across the screen bringing it to my ear.

"H-hello," I groggily answered, clearing my throat.

Slowly sitting up in Indian-style, I began rubbing my eyes as the other end of the phone remained silent. Frowning, I pulled the phone away from my ear allowing my hues to fixate on the screen, eyes widening at the caller.

"Kris. KRIS!" My voice rose an octave, confused as to why she was still silent.

Small sniffles erupted into my ear before her pain-filled voice cracked through the receiver, "S... Shy. I need you."

Instantly, I hopped to my feet more than ready to be there for her because she was doing the same for me in rehab. I had no clue where she was or how I was going to get to her but I knew at this moment, I just needed to make my way to her side. Frantically, I looked around my room for something quick to throw on.

"I'm coming. What's wrong? Where are you?" I questioned, jumping up and down into a pair of jeans.

I blame my mother for my phat ass. My blessing and curse especially whenever I went shopping and had trouble finding something to fit my bottom just right.

"KRIS!" I somewhat yelled trying my best to hold her attention.

With me not being in front of her, she could possibly do anything to herself and I just wanted to keep her in a positive mind state.

"Where you at?" I begged, slipping on my Adidas slips and rushing to my bedroom door.

"At the hospital."

My eyes widened knowing that this was more serious than what I assumed. I thought she was having one of her moments like I would, randomly out of the three times I tried to get clean.

"What the fuck. What's going on Kris?!"

"Th-they killed him." She struggled to finish the sentence before breaking down uncontrollably.

My heart dropped knowing that it was only one guy that we mutually knew that actually meant something to the both of us.

<u>Twinnie</u>
<u>Received</u>
I'm pulling up now.

Once receiving the text from Blake, I stuffed my phone into the back pocket of my jeans as I stood to my 5'5" frame. A deep sigh escaped my lips still trying to find out what was going to be the ending result of where Kris would lay her head every night. For at least ten minutes, she struggled to tell me how she came home and found her boyfriend of five years murdered. He was shot three times with his body dangling through the window of their kitchen as if he was in the midst of escaping. I couldn't even imagine seeing someone I love laid out as if their existence didn't mean anything to someone, anyone.

It pulled at my heart, driving my mind crazy if I ever lost Blake. Honestly, she was my heart. I've never cared so much about someone like I did Blake, not even my own mother.

"Kris..." I softly said, listening to her soft sniffles. She'd been crying ever since I got here which was about 20 minutes ago.

Wiping at her eyes, her bloodshot hues locked on me. Her lip was tucked tight between her teeth as if she wanted blood to surface. Noticing the tension in her body language and face, I gave her shoulder a light push. Her expression became uncomfortable.

I knew that look too well – she was going off the deep end.

Losing her boyfriend was enough but to turn around and have police officers in her face questioning her didn't make the situation any better. I just wanted to get her away from the chaos tonight. I wasn't sure on what tomorrow would bring but I *do* know that my plan wasn't to leave Kris tonight.

I watched her use the back of her hands to dry the tears that were practically begging to stain her gorgeous features. She quickly rose to her feet matching my exact height as I extended my hand, her taking it.

Using my hand, I fanned myself trying my best to circulate a little bit of air. Blake was complaining about the fact the air conditioning was too cold so the "outside wind" would do. My brows furrowed while my plump bottom remained irritated by sitting on this barstool. Upon arrival, I got Kris comfortable in my room resulting in her falling asleep. Whereas now I was sitting across from Blake who was standing on the other side of the island, looking at me with concern.

I rolled my eyes. "Why you looking at me like that B?"

"So what is this?" She folded her arms, placing them on the island.

I rolled my eyes, sighing out of frustration. I already knew what she was referring to and honestly, I had no clue. Blake didn't sign up to take in two recovering addicts. I was going to talk to Kris but everything was so fresh; I just wanted to give her some space to breathe. I ran my hands down my face, shaking my head.

"I don't know. She just lost her dude B. This is too much." Instantly, I started feeling overwhelmed and nothing good ever came out of me not being able to control my emotions.

I'm assuming Blake felt the sudden tension radiating from my body because she offered a comforting hand upon mine. Slowly I looked to her, "Hey. I can't have you losing yourself trying to help someone else. Your main focus right now is yourself, Shy." She spoke in a soft, soothing tone.

My lip was tucked between my teeth as I fell in deep thought but still managed to nod, letting her know I heard her as well – I understood what she was saying.

She was scared which I fully understood but I also understood that Kris needed somebody right now.

She needed me.

I cleared my throat, "I hear you B but she needs me right now."

Her brows furrowed, kissing her teeth. "So what's your plan, Shia? Cause you know she can't stay here, right?" Her voice rose an octave causing me to roll my eyes.

Doing. Too. Much.

"And I know that... just let her stay for the night. I'll talk things over with her when she wakes up. Don't trip." I shut the conversation down, placing my hands on the island to push to my feet.

Blake's expression remained emotionless before she gave me a slow nod, "Ight."

"Thank you."

Dallas
<u>Received</u>
No good morning text for your bae?

I giggled once scanning over the text from Dallas. This nigga had the audacity to throw the sad face behind his message too. This was my first time hearing from him since parting ways last night and honestly, I didn't plan on reaching out. I wanted to stay far away from him as possible. This connection between us was terrifying me and it was something I didn't want to grow. Deciding to ignore him, I opened up the conversation with Mace. He was the first person I reached out to once Kris called me; I couldn't handle this alone.

Mace
<u>Received</u>
How is she? Y'all good?

Upon arriving at the hospital and the entire time I was there, Mace made sure to keep communicating with me. Having him as that extra support just so I could be strong enough for Kris was very helpful, and I was truly thankful for him.

My slim digits began moving quickly across the screen just as my phone began vibrating, another text coming in from Dallas.

Dallas
<u>Received</u>
Lol, ignoring me now slim?
Your read recipients on punk!
Bet you don't know how to turn them off either.

Read recipients? Staring at the previous messages, I realized that every message I sent to him had "Read" beneath them along with the time. What the hell. He was right too because I had no idea how to turn it off, but I damn sure was going to find out.

Mace
<u>Sent</u>
We're fine. She's sleep… for now.
Idk where she can go after 2nite.
Mace… how do you turn off read recipients?

The corners of my lips went upward once seeing the dots pop up on the screen, signifying that Mace was responding.

Mace
<u>Received</u>
Coo. What you mean?
She don't have nowhere to go Shy?
Lmao, dawg... You so green.
Who you trying to ignore? Lol

Why does he have to be so difficult? I rolled my eyes, fingers moving swiftly to respond.

Mace
<u>Sent</u>
We haven't talked bout it.
I plan on it once she gets up.

Mace
<u>Sent</u>
I wish you'll tell me how instead
of being difficult nigga!!

Mace
<u>Received</u>
Just tell me how that goes.
Lls, pressed you know how to use emojis huh? Go to your settings
then Messages, you'll see it.

83

I let out a small sigh of relief now knowing that Dallas won't be aware of me seeing his messages. Quickly, I followed the directions Mace had given me. Any other time I'd be damn near ready to get rid of him but he has been very helpful with getting me hip to this "iPhone thing." Not too long ago he taught me how to screenshot which I thought was one of the best things invented.

Mace
<u>Sent</u>
Ight nigga, thank you!

March 17, 2016: Fort Washington, MD

Yawning, my slender arms flew above my head as my body stretched itself out simultaneously. A soft moan escaped my lips, covering my mouth as another yawn slipped through. My hands collided with the mattress pushing myself to sit upright as my brown hues fluttered open, scanning my room. My heartbeat went into overdrive once noticing the empty space on the other side of my bed, covers pulled back signifying that Kris once occupied that space. Instantly, I went into a frantic state not knowing the whereabouts of my recovering friend. I quickly pushed my body towards the edge of the bed allowing my chocolate bare feet to collide with the soft carpet. Wanting badly to find Kris, I chose to ignore the pressure that built between my thighs over the night.

Pulling my door open, I jogged up the stairs leading to the foyer.

"KRIS!"

Nothing.

I began moving around the two-story townhome but there were no signs of her or even Blake for that matter. My feet quickly carried me back down to my room, snatching my phone off my nightstand. The main screen came to view after holding my thumb on the home button, immediately going to Blake's name. Bringing the phone to my ear, the back to back rings invaded my ear before Blake's soft voice flowed through the receiver.

"Hello."

My chest heaved up and down as I tried to find it in me to calm down. "Wh-where's Kris?! You've seen her?!" It sounded as if my words were coming out as gibberish because of how worked up I was about her not being here.

"Calm down Shy. I just dropped her off to her cousin." I sighed out of relief knowing she was safe.

What? What cousin?

Shaking my head, I brought a finger to my temple trying to register everything. "Cousin? What cousin?"

She sighed, "Girl!" Her voice rose an octave with a hint of annoyance. "I don't know. She just asked me to drop her off."

I sucked my teeth, not believing that she actually just dropped her off somewhere. "So you're telling me that you just dropped her off somewhere?" I questioned.

"Yea Shia. I just dropped her ass off somewhere." She retorted with the most sarcasm before the smacking of her lips sounded off in my ear. I just knew for a fact that she was rolling her eyes, hard as hell too. "Naw nigga. I met her cousin and all, said she's going to live with her for a bit."

My head began shaking as I found some comfort in her words; I just wish Kris would've told me her plan before just dipping out. I did just come to her rescue off one phone call.

"Ight B. Thank you. I'll see you when you get here."

"Kay boo. I love you."

"I love you more."

My phone fell from my hold, falling next to me as I hopped to my feet ready to release the pressure between my thighs. After finishing up in the bathroom, my body slightly jumped once the doorbell went off. Stopping in my tracks, I headed towards the front door swinging it open as my eyes collided with his brown orbs.

Dallas.

My breath hitched in my throat at the sight of him. I wasn't expecting a pop-up from him especially since I've been ignoring his texts since yesterday – I thought he would've got the point. A teasing grin settled upon his lips as his eyes began ogling my curvaceous frame. It'd totally slipped my mind that I was dressed in nothing but a white crop top that my D-cup breasts freely sat under. A pair of black mini shorts adorning my lower region with my waist beads wrapped around my flat stomach.

His tongue swept across his lip as he welcomed himself into the house, closing the door behind him. Now I took my time to take in how good he looked. Black must be one of his favorite colors because I noticed that was one thing I always saw him in. I looked over his choice of clothing for the day: a black hoodie with a white V-Neck peeping through due to his zipper being midway zipped. I bit my lip focusing on his gray sweats; I love a man wearing gray sweats.

Dick prints.

After noticing the pair of Infrared 6's cladding his large feet, my eyes flew to his face blushing at the crooked smirk dancing on his face. He looked really good today. The fact he had a fresh haircut that could be seen under his black fitted cap sitting backward on his head had me blushing even harder. He looked so clean and put together.

Dallas cleared his throat enclosing the gap between us with two steps, hovering over me with his 6'2" structure. His muscular hands grazed the side of my thighs with his breath bouncing off my face once parting his lips to speak, "You always chill in the house like this? Little ass shit on?" A small mug worked its way to his lips as I enjoyed the sight of the tension taking over his handsome features.

I rolled my eyes, turning quickly to head towards my room to cover myself better. I could feel his presence not too far behind me as he fell in tow; I could feel his eyes on my ass as well.

"STOP looking at my ass Dallas!" I hissed, catching his eyes fly from my ass to my face once I looked over my shoulder.

He laughed, "I can't help it, baby. You got on that I want you to fuck me wear."

Rolling my eyes, I smacked my lips as I pulled out a pair of pajama pants from my dresser before quickly throwing them on. I watched as he stood in the middle of my room looking around; my room wasn't much to look at. I planned on going shopping at some point once I had a steady income, add my own spice to my living quarters. I sat on the edge of my bed, keeping my gaze on him.

This undeniable feeling I experienced every time in his presence was the main reason I wanted to stay away from him.

"Wassup with you, though? Ignoring me n' shit…" His voice trailed off as his eyes finally fixated on me. "Thank you for putting on some pants bae." Once that last statement left his lips my body shivered.

I assume he knew what his words were doing to me because that sexy, teasing grin painted his features once again. Before I knew it, he was standing over me forcing my head to tilt back in order to look me directly in my eyes. How was it even this possible to look this fuckin' good? I don't understand. I was being pulled to my feet once our hands connected before being brought into a tight embrace. My nostrils took in his intoxicating scent as my knees slightly buckled from being in his hold.

"You can't run from me, Shy. I told you this God's plan..." The hairs on the back of my neck began to rise once feeling him take a tight hold on the back of my thick thighs, squeezing lightly. "Got me hitting your phone like a stalker or sum'n. Stop playing with me girl." His voice dropped an octave giving off a raspy, deep tone.

My lips parted as I finally found my words, "I'm not playing with you."

"Oh. She talks!" He joked, releasing me from his hold as his hands snaked to my hips. I can already tell his hands on my hips were one of his favorite things to do.

"You owe me though."

My mouth contorted into a slight frown, not agreeing with me "owing" him anything.

"I don't owe you shit." I spat back.

He smiled revealing those straight pearly whites, chuckling. "THIS the Shy I was waiting on but yea, you do though."

His eyes fell into thin slits as his index finger found my chin, tilting my head back. My stomach churned watching him admire me. His brown eyes moved around my face before locking on my succulent lips – mine locked on his as well. It felt as if everything in the room closed in on us once feeling his lips against mine. The feeling of our lips connected was one to always remember. I never experienced such an igniting kiss. He smirked once pulling away as my hues lazily peeled open, stuck in a daze.

"You owed me them lips." I couldn't help but blush as he stole another kiss. "Soft ass lips girl." He muttered, strumming his thumb against my bottom lip.

Damn you Dallas.

Dallas released an annoyed sigh causing me to giggle as I remained sprawled out on my stomach, chin resting on my hands.

"Naw. Do we really have to watch this shit?" He hissed earning an eye roll from me.

Honestly, I was starting to believe that Dallas was a control freak. This was his second time being over and he was trying to control what we watch as if he wasn't in my home. I gave him a quick look over my shoulder, smirking at the little mug dancing among his pouty lips.

My eyes trailed down his long frame, starting from his fresh haircut that was now fully revealed due to his fitted cap resting on my nightstand. After complaining about how hot it was in here, he'd removed his hoodie that was sitting on the doorknob of my closet. His 6's were the first thing he had kicked off before getting situated in my bed, back against the headboard and legs crossed at the ankles.

A slight frown blessed my face once my eyes fixated on his white socks especially since I wanted to see how his feet looked. Many would say that I had a "foot fetish" but I looked at it as I just appreciated a man with well-kept feet. I was fighting the urge to ask to see his for the simple fact I didn't want him to look at me weird.

"I'm not changing the channel, Dallas." I simply said, turning to face the TV again.

He smacked his lips, "Don't nobody want to see this *Love & Hip Hop* shit."

I shrugged, waving him off as I continued to remain intrigued in my ratchet TV. I could careless if he wanted to watch it or not.

My room.
My rules.

I smiled, feeling his intense stare which was causing back to back tingling sensations throughout my body. I hissed once feeling his warm hand trail up the back up my thigh causing me to whip my head towards him, mug strongly painted amongst my beautiful features. That crooked smile of his was tearing me down, quickly at that. His thick tongue swept across his bottom lip leaving a wet sheen causing me to lightly bite into mine.

He was the epitome of sexy, and I hate using that word. This man was perfectly made, in every way.

His hand gave my thigh a light squeeze as he chuckled, back colliding with the headboard, "I'm hungry bae."

I sighed turning onto my side, "Well I'm not."

His brows rose, "You not gonna feed me?"

I rolled my eyes swinging my legs over the side of the bed, looking back at him. "Come on. Blake cooked the other night, it's some leftovers upstairs."

The biggest smile spread across his handsome features as he stood to his feet with a quickness. Walking towards my door, I felt his presence closer than normal which had my stomach fluttering away.

"Bout damn time you feed me."

My elbows rested on the counter as I watched Dallas devour the leftovers as if it was his last meal. My nose turned up as I took in the animalistic sight, giggling softly. He didn't give a care in the world that I was staring at him while he ate. Matter of fact, he wasn't paying me any mind.

"You always eat like this?" I queried causing him to stop eating, brown hues locking on mine.

He licked his lips before grabbing the napkin nearby and wiping his mouth of the food residue. My hands found my arms giving them a rub once feeling the sudden goose bumps appearing on my skin. The sound of the turkey bone hitting against the glass plate was the only thing that could be heard as he kissed his teeth.

He cleared his throat clasping his hands together, "Cause a nigga haven't eaten all day. That's why."

My head fell to the side, "So you was more worried about seeing me than eating?"

He nodded, "That's right."

I watched as his soiled napkin collided with the plate before rising to his feet. His long limbs stretched towards the ceiling before grabbing the plate and rounding the island, towering over me.

His jaw clenched while looking around before focusing back on me, "Trash can?"

I giggled, completely forgetting that the trash can was basically hidden. It was placed in this sort of cabinet door closet. It was pretty creative, especially whenever the fumes from the trash would start moving around; they would be sealed to one spot. I nodded my head towards the spot causing his brows to rise in question.

"Over there?"

I nodded, "Yea."

His tall structure moved around me heading towards that spot to dump his remnants into the trashcan before heading towards the sink.

"You don't have to wash that, I will," I called out once noticing him turning on the water and grabbing the rag.

He gave me a quick look over his shoulder before turning back around, "It's cool. I got it."

I blushed, shaking my head as my back collided with the island admiring his muscular back. The way his well-defined arms looked from the back as he washed his dishes was turning me on. Every little thing about him was a turn-on. The sound of the water being turned off had me meeting his brown gaze. He grinned while wiping his hands on the dry dish towel, eyes never leaving mine.

"Shia."

"Dallas." His smirk grew deeper.

"Bae." My stomach tossed at his term of endearment. "Come 'ere real quick." He motioned me over with his head causing me to blush.

I shook my head, not wanting to get any closer to him because he already had me feeling some type of way, "I'm good right here."

Dallas chuckled before pushing himself off the counter, "Cool. I'll come to you then."

My heartbeat quickened with every step he took my way, making me weak by the seconds. His hands took a firm grip of my petite waist bringing me closer, breath hitting against my face. His lips pressed against my forehead before pulling away, looking at me.

"Why you don't like to listen?" That sneaky grin played at his lips causing a shiver to run down my spine.

"Cause I don't have to listen to you. That's why."

A deep chuckle rumbled throughout his chest before exiting those beautiful lips of his, hands tightening on my waist.

"Can I have another kiss though?" His voice dropped an octave making me want him even more.

Smiling, my head began shaking frantically from side to side. "Nope!" I quickly shot back turning my head to avoid his intense stare.

Dallas leaned in to place a soft but yet sensual kiss on the corner of my lips. I slowly looked at him, eyes fluttering at his gesture. His pouty lips connected with mines before slowly disconnecting, brown gaze fixating with mine.

"It's something about you girl." He mumbled, keeping his forehead against mine.

Little did he know, I felt the same way about him. It was something about him as well.

"SHIA!" Blake's voice rang out in the foyer causing us to quickly step out of each other's embrace just before she came into view.

A sneaky smirk fell upon her chocolate features looking back and forth between us both, "Well. Hello, Dallas." She said in a teasing manner.

Silence.

"So. Are you going to properly introduce us, Shia?" She questioned with a smirk tugging at her lips, looking at me.

Blake knew what she was doing and I could tell, just from that stupid smirk alone. Dallas released a deep chuckle once I smacked my lips followed by an eye roll. What was I introducing them for? First of all, she already knew his name and secondly, she was talking as if he wasn't right in front of her.

She can introduce her damn self.

"For what?" I shot back, giving her a taste of her own medicine. My heart warmed once seeing the discomfort settling on her face.

Little bitch.

My heart jumped once feeling Dallas' hand come in contact with my thigh, locking my eyes with his. Just from his touch alone, my body relaxed as well as those ill feelings developing towards my cousin at the moment. Dallas' tongue slowly snaked across his bottom lip before disappearing into his mouth. The corners of his lips turned upward as that sexy grin made itself known, making my insides go crazy.

"Chill bae." He soothingly said, never tearing his eyes from mine.

Just like that, I was back to myself. Not annoyed or feeling on the edge. Honestly, I've been feeling pretty annoyed with Blake once finding out that she dropped Kris off. I don't care if I was sleep; I should've been woken up to know my friend's next destination. The only thing I believe Blake was worried about was getting her out of her home, instead of her well-being also.

That was irritating me the most.

That same feeling of emptiness revisited me once Dallas removed his hand from my body, bringing it to the marble island top. A frown found my lips admiring his side profile, smiling once the dimple appeared upon his brown cheek before disappearing just as quickly as it appeared.

"Bae?" Blake teasingly questioned, looking between us both with raised brows.

I rolled my eyes, getting irritated with her all over again. Her finger rose to motion back and forth between us, shock plastered over her face. She was overthinking this "bae" term; she was about to make a big deal of it.

"Wh-? Y-?..." I couldn't fight the laugh that was pleading to surface from Blake not being able to find her words. She took a deep sigh while putting her hands in surrender, "Okay. Y'all two fuckin' or something?" She bluntly asked causing me to smack my thighs, head falling to the side.

Normally Blake wasn't this blunt; she left that to me. Dallas' laugh invaded my ears as my face heated from embarrassment. Why was Blake choosing a moment like this to act an ass?

"BLAKE!" I shrilled as she laughed, looking at me as if she did nothing at all.

"What? I'm just asking a question." I rolled my eyes hard as she looked to Dallas. "So. Are y'all?" She asked in a softer tone, barely audible but reached both of our ears.

"Don't answer that." I quickly interjected as Dallas couldn't find it in himself to stop laughing.

Meanwhile, I didn't understand what was so funny. At this point, I've accepted the fact that Blake was being nothing but a nuisance. All she had to do was come in and mind her business, leaving me to my company. But of course, like old times, she just had to pry in my shit.

Dallas shook his head, licking those beautiful lips yet another time. So badly I wanted them pressed against mines; they were terribly addicting. Blushing, I focused on how one corner of his mouth formed into a crooked smile before parting his lips to speak.

"Naw… Naw…" His voice trailed off, fixing his gaze on me causing an overwhelming wave to hit me suddenly. "Not at all. She bae though." He finished off while keeping his eyes on me with every word, ending with that damn smirk.

My brows quickly rose with my head tilting down some, keeping his intense gaze, "Bae huh?"

Dallas kissed his teeth as I giggled once seeing him quickly cross his eyes towards my question.

"What I tell your ass earlier?" The way his voice dropped an octave taking on a demanding tone had my thighs squeezing together.

His hand fell from the countertop falling on his leg as his head cocked to the side, narrowing his gaze on me. I hissed watching how his lip flew between his teeth, scanning my frame. There wasn't much to see especially since I've thrown on pajama pants but from the look on Dallas' face, he was mentally undressing me, I'm pretty sure.

The sound of Blake snorting forced me to look her way, laughing at the disgusted expression plastered on her face.

"I'll be in my room. I can't stand here and watch y'all eye fuck each other."

Dallas and I laughed watching Blake's retreating back, "Your cousin wild man."

I nodded before sighing, "Tell me about it. Don't pay her any mind."

He cleared his throat, "It's cool." His voice was now husky which was like music to my ears.

I watched how his brows met in the middle of his forehead while pulling his phone from his back pocket. A deep sigh parted his lips, index finger raising in the air while standing to his feet.

"Hol' up Shy." I nodded.

Giving me his back to focus on, I watched as he moved towards the living room with his phone attached to his ear. His hand rose to scratch his head while a frustrated sigh entered the air. Clearly, this phone call was one he wasn't expecting; his body language was showing how agitated he was with the caller on the other end. The way his brows met in the middle of his head, lips contorted into a mug, and fist squeezed tightly by his side showed me how irritated the call left him. The sudden change of his demeanor was putting me in an uncomfortable space.

I didn't know to ask if everything was okay or not?

I didn't want his anger directed towards me but then again, I wanted to be here for him.

"Everything okay?" The words left my lips before I could consider stopping them.

Dallas fixed his brown hues on me, face softening a bit but the tension was still there. From a distance, I scrutinized his handsome countenance, noticing a different look in his eyes.

One I was too familiar with: Pain.

Honestly after dealing with Kris, I couldn't stand the thought of possibly being thrown in another situation of being there for someone. I needed to put myself first. Despite my hesitance, I found myself sauntering in his direction allowing his tall frame to hover over mines.

Something in me badly wanted to be here for Dallas right now.

He would be here for me.

Well, I'd hope so.

Looking up, I bit my lip watching how his jaw continuously clenched as he continued to bore his hues into mine. I really didn't know what to say; I just wanted to make sure that he was okay. Dallas' face remained stoic, eyes sweeping across my physiognomy before landing on my lips. It was killing me not knowing what had him so upset but oddly, I was grateful for this silence. I loved how comfortable Dallas kept me, even in silence.

My hand rose to connect with his upper arm giving it a light shake, "You okay?" I asked again in a much softer tone.

Silence.

My lips developed into a small pout earning a light chuckle from him with his hand taking a hold of my chin, tilting my head back. Silence engulfed us as we studied each other's gorgeous features. My stomach tossed as he slowly leaned in towards me, placing a soft kiss against the corner of my lips. A frown quickly took over my face in response to me not feeling his lips against mine.

That's it?

"I gotta roll," His husky tone entered the air, clearing his throat.

Mace
<u>Received</u>
Wyd tomorrow?

Mace
<u>Sent</u>
Nothing. Wassup?

Mace
<u>Received</u>
Let's go on a date!

Mace
<u>Sent</u>
Mace.
I don't want to go on a date with you.

Mace
<u>Received</u>
Girl. It's a friendly date.
I miss you slim.
Wanna get lunch or sum'n? On me.

Actually, I missed Mace and I could always go for a free meal. My thick ass loved food. I need to be enclosed with positive vibes and one thing Mace was good at was making me laugh.

Mace
<u>Sent</u>
Lol, kay. FRIENDLY date.
I miss you too. Yea, we can def do that.

Book VII.

March 17, 2016: NW, Washington, DC

The beeping of the hospital machines and intercom calls seemed to fade into the background as I quickly maneuvered my way through the main floor. My pace quickened once seeing the elevator doors meeting in the middle. My main and only focus was getting to her.

"HEY!" I yelled, hoping that the person on the elevator would bring the doors to a halt.

I sighed out of relief once noticing the doors slowly open, revealing a gorgeous woman.

Sighing, I took my place against the wall making sure not to invade her personal space. There's been plenty of times that females would act out of pocket because they claimed you were "too close."

"What floor?" Her soft tone invaded my ears, bringing a smirk to my face once locking in on her green gaze.

Those eyes.

Clearing my throat, my hands found their usual spot in my pockets, "Five please. Thank you."

She smiled, "No problem." Her focus turned towards the numbers, making my destination floor light up.

Running my large hands over my face another exhausted sigh broke free. I was tired of this shit. Within the past month, a lot of time was spent by my mother's side due to her being in and out of the hospital. I'm just tired, Lord. It's bad enough I already lost my best friend and brother-in-law.

Can my mother *not* be next?
I got clean.
I got myself together.
What else you need me to do?
All I ask is that you keep your loving hands upon my mother.
Please.
She needs it.
I **need** her.

Two years ago when I stepped out of the doors of New Leaf Rehabilitation Center, I was a changed man. I'm not quite sure how seeing as though I had to have a drink every day of the week, just to keep a leveled head. Knowing how strong-willed I was about remaining clean along with God's help was the key to surviving soberness. Throughout my soberness, I've been able to establish a well-grounded relationship with Him and I was truly thankful for it.

The green-eyed beauty looked over her shoulder, piercing hues fixed on me as the corners of her lips turned upward. Her mouth developed into a full smile as I focused on the shape of her eyes; they had a bug-like shape to them - it was cute. Well, for her anyways.

"Have a good day," She bid me farewell.

"You too," My voice had dropped becoming croaky causing me to clear my throat.

My brown hues flew upward, looking at my reflection in the mirror stretched along the roof of the elevator. I bit my lip as Shia's curvy frame quickly rushed my thoughts; I could just imagine having her pinned against the wall and doing what I do best. I shook my head in an attempt to rid the nasty thoughts of me deep in Shia.

That damn girl.

Whatever this connection was bringing us closer together was beyond immense at this point. It was undeniable, to say the least. Our chemistry was so raw. So real.

Baby, God makes no mistakes. He places people in your life for a reason. Take heed. It can be just to solely teach you something or contribute to your life greatly. Listen to Him, baby. Don't ignore it.

My mother's words lingered in my head; those same words I've been living by since growing closer to God. Stepping off the elevator, I approached the nurse station leaning against the desk as a smirk crept across my face.

"Hey you," I voiced causing the beautiful 45-year-old woman to turn around while holding her chest.

I laughed once hearing her sigh of relief before quickly approaching me from the opposite side, "You scared me, Dallas." She said through clenched teeth with a smile teasing at her lips.

"I didn't mean to Mrs. Taylor. I just wanted to say wassup."

My mother had been here so often that I felt like the entire hospital knew us by now. They were all genuinely sweet but I could live better without seeing my mother stuck to a bed all day. Nodding in approval, I noticed the big chop she did to her hair. It was somewhat of a close cut starting from her sides and moving towards the back. The top of her head held more hair that was flared in the air, giving an edgy look.

"I see you cut your hair..." My voice trailed off, pointing at her head earning a blush from her.

She nodded while running her palm down the side of her hair. "I sure did. Listening to damn Oprah talking about women over 40 should go for a short cut to look younger."

I crossed my eyes at how much she sounded like my mother when it came to Oprah. My mother was always taking Oprah's advice when the show used to air. Why? I have no clue. I didn't bother to watch it unless my mother just so happened to really want my company that day. That's crazy. Five years later after her show stopped airing and Oprah still had hell of an influence.

All power to her.

"I already told you that you looked young. I 'ont know why you're listening to that lady." I spat in return earning a laugh from her.

The thing was, I wasn't lying. I still found it mind boggling that she was 45. She definitely didn't look an age over 30. If she wasn't married or my mother's nurse, I'd try my hand in a heartbeat.

Giving the desk a light tap with my fingers, I used my shoulders to push my frame into an upright position. Her 5'2" figure shuffled from around the desk in a happy manner, crashing into my towering one. I leaned over allowing a gentle peck to be placed against my cheek before she stepped out of our usual embrace.

"See you around baby." She cooed, smiling while grabbing a manila folder off the desk before placing it on the flexline cart, ambling in the opposite direction.

A deep sigh escaped my pouty lips once my hand connected with the doorknob of my mother's assigned room. Every time I came to visit her, I couldn't shake this unwanted feeling that overtook my body whenever it was time to enter her presence. Raising my hand, my

knuckles softly knocked on the thick wooden door before slowly pushing it open. A smile spread on my face once locking eyes with the woman of my life, along with my older sister by three years.
"My baby." My mother cooed as I moved further into the room, leaning over the bed rail placing a gentle kiss on her forehead.

My fingers softly maneuvered their way through her short black hair that wildly sat in the air. She smiled weakly through heavy lids while looking me over. I chewed the inside of my cheek, finding it hard to see her in this state. Of course, she was going to always wear a smile to put on this facade that she wasn't in pain, living with something she can't get rid of. Her beautiful visage that would normally be shining was now showing exhaustion; it was clear that she was tired of fighting.

I just couldn't take the thought of her giving up on us.
Giving up on me.

The soft touch to my back averted my attention to my sister, whose face was screaming nothing but pain. Her face was full of exhaustion as well with her eyes being the dead giveaway. Bags were sitting comfortably under her almond-shaped eyes as they held a red tint to them, signifying that she'd been crying. I pulled her into a tight embrace placing a soft kiss upon her temple.
"So what they say?" I mumbled in her ear as I slowly released from our hold.
Devyn's lip flew between her teeth parting her lips to speak before our mother's voice cut her off before the words could exit her lips.
"You act like I'm not right here Dallas." She coughed, touching my hand gently. "You can ask me."
My brown gaze fell on her frail face; it looks like the life had been sucked out of her. My eyes flew to the ceiling trying my best to keep it together while seeing her in such a fragile state. Slowly, I focused my attention back on her.
I threw her a head nod, "Wassup Ma? What the doctor talking about?"
She squeezed my hand causing my heart to swell, becoming uneasy at whatever words she was bout to speak. I don't think I'm as ready as I thought I'd be. She smiled weakly before looking to Devyn,

"Give us a minute baby?" Out of my peripheral, I caught Devyn nodding before turning on her heels to exit the room.

Silence fell over us two leaving me beyond anxious, in a bad way.

Growing impatient with the silence doing nothing but making me more nervous, my lips parted to communicate, "So wassup Ma? Talk to me." Quickly looking behind me, I grabbed the nearby chair pulling it to take a seat making sure not to let her hand go.

My constricted gaze fell on my mother's tired but still beautiful face, squeezing her hand as she offered me a smile. She deeply sighed, "I've developed lupus nephritis Dallas."

Once hearing those words fall from her lips, I released her hand quickly standing to my feet. I couldn't believe this shit. Six years ago, she was diagnosed with SLE (Systematic Lupus Erythematosis) which happens to be the most common but serious form of lupus compared to the other three. Along with other complications brought to our attention, lupus nephritis rested around the top of the list. This was one of my biggest fears as if her fighting lupus wasn't enough.

"How bad is it Ma?" Tears welled at my lids, as I did everything in my power to fight them back.

"Baby don't cry." She soothed, rubbing the back of my hand softly.

My brown hues flew to the ceiling as tears cascaded down my cheeks. I wasn't about to cry but once hearing her comforting words, the tears played against me choosing to fall anyways. Frantically, my head moved from side to side, "How bad is it Ma?"

"Nothing that God doesn't have control over sweetie."

I rolled my eyes, giving her a dry expression, "Ma." This beating around the bush thing she was doing had me growing impatient with a hint of agitation.

"I don't want you stressing Dallas because I know how you are baby. The doctors said it's a mild case right now. They will keep me for a few days and I can come back home. I just have to take care of myself and keep taking my meds. If..."

"If what Ma?" My brows rose in question.

She sighed, looking away for a second before focusing back on me. "If my kidneys fail, I'll be on dialysis."

My heart cringed at the possible outcome of everything and the thing is, I knew it didn't stop there. I knew failing kidneys possibly meant that we could be burying our mother. Knowing I could be burying my mother sooner than later wasn't an option.

I know you'd keep her here with us God.
I just know you would.

Pursing my lips together, I nodded while using the side of my index fingers to wipe my tears away before leaning over to kiss her forehead. I weakly smiled, knowing how much she hated to see her son hurting.

"You gon' be ight Ma. I already know it." I voiced, trying to convince myself more than her.

My mother is and always been a God-fearing woman. She was the reason I grew closer to God after becoming sober and I knew for sure she knew that she was going to kick lupus' ass. Then when I looked into her eyes, she appeared as if she didn't want to fight any longer. I've never witnessed the look before but I had that feeling - it didn't feel right. Regardless of this feeling, I was going to continue praying and never let my faith waver.

"I will baby. God has the last say so. I'll be needing your and Devyn's help more around the house since I'm so weak right now."

I nodded knowing completely what she meant. This wasn't the first time she'd been in such a weak state. I or Devyn never minded helping her, EVER.

I sniffed, "You already know I got you Ma. It's nothing. I love you, Fat Girl." I teased earning a soft laugh from her.

That was her biggest smile since I've stepped foot in this room.

She found it so amusing that I'd use that nickname on her. At some point, she gained a lot of weight due to one of the medications she was on but it was a healthy weight, though. I loved it on her. Technically, she wasn't fat but since I grew up only seeing my mother slim, it was the only thing I could come up with.

"I love you more my Dally baby." Her smile grew wide making me catch her contagious one.

I kissed my teeth, hating that she called me that but her along with my babies were the only ones I'd let get away with it.

March 18, 2016: Greenbelt, MD – Olive Garden

"You look good Shy," Mace complimented with a grin playing at his pink, full lips.

Mace had blown up my phone about four times this morning. It slipped my mind that I agreed to us going to lunch today. After having enough of him irritating me during the last time he called me, I pushed myself out the bed and got dressed.

My brown hues searched his face as his lips remained wrapped around his straw, keeping my gaze. Mace was handsome - VERY handsome I might add. Anyone could tell that he wasn't of just one ethnicity and me being nosey, like always, I'd asked him awhile ago. He told me that he was of Paraguayan, Argentine, and Saudi descent. Originally he's from Canada to be exact, but moved to the US with his mother when he was six.

His soft texture hair peeked from beneath his blue NY Yankees baseball cap as he pushed it off his head some, giving me a better view of those gorgeous eyes of his. Since the last time I've seen him, he had less facial hair. Now, there were brown hairs neatly starting from the sides of his face moving downwards to cover under his jaw and chin. A small neat mustache rested above his lips.

"So do you Mace." I returned the compliment, smiling. "Thank you." My gaze connected with our waitress as she placed my plate in front of me before placing Mace's in front of him.

"Thank you," Mace thanked her as well.

Ever since arriving at Olive Garden, she was making sure to give us the best service. I giggled once catching a glimpse of Mace rubbing his hands together, eyeing the hell out of his meal.

"Hungry ass." I muttered, still giggling while picking up my fork.

"Man. I haven't eaten all day boo." His words came out in a rushed manner before taking the first bite of his Tilapia Piccata.

Crossing my eyes at the term of endearment he just won't seem to let go, I took a stab into my Stuffed Chicken Marsala. I wasn't in the mood to go back and forth with him especially when I knew he was going to keep calling me boo regardless of what I say.

That was Mace for you.

"I see..." I responded after swallowing the delicious chicken breast, eyes closing in satisfaction. "Mmm, this is so good." I complimented the chef as my eyes peeled open landing on Mace staring me right in the face.

"Stop looking at me like that," I rolled my eyes, digging into my plate again.

His lips turned to the side, "Lemme get some."

Before I could get the chance to tell him no, he was leaning over his side of the table with his fork heading for my plate. "UH UH nigga!" With one swift motion, I moved my plate out of his reach earning a smack of the lips from him.

He sat back in his seat, "Come on Shy. That shit looks good."

I grinned, "And so does yours, now eat your own food." I conveyed, using my fork to point at him in an attempt to get my point across.

"Ight. How bout this? I'll give you some of mine and you give me some of yours." He began cheesing as if he came up with the brightest idea.

I scoffed, waving him off dismissively, "I'll pass my nigga."

His hands went in the air before lazily hitting his legs, "Shit. I tried." He exaggerated with a grin settling among his countenance, digging into his food.

A laugh flew from my lips while shaking my head, "You get on my nerves."

His green hues flew to me, "Like you don't get on mines and you better shush."

A smirk slowly contorted my lips, "Or what Mace?"

"Or this fine nigga here won't pay for the food you have the audacity of not sharing with me."

My face deadpanned with my orbs scanning his expressionless visage; I couldn't tell if he was serious or not. I huffed out of frustration, shoving my plate in his direction.

"Try it… Irritating ass." I hissed.

I was getting full anyway.

That gorgeous but irritating smile of his took over his face while grabbing my plate, pulling it quickly towards him. I watched as he stabbed his fork into the chicken before moving it into the mashed potatoes, looking at me with the fork not far from his mouth.

"I was going to pay for your shit regardless boo." He teased, stuffing the food in his mouth while closing his eyes mocking me from earlier. "I truly do thank you though." He said, eyes peeling open to lock in on my brown gaze.

He irritated me to my soul.

Reaching across the table, I yanked my plate back towards me, "Give me my shit." My voice was filled with annoyance as he laughe

A nudge to my shoulder had my lips contorting into a frown, cutting my eyes at the irritating individual that was my lunch date just a few minutes ago. We walked side by side through the parking lot heading towards his car.

"You talk to Kris?" This was the first time he'd brought up Kris since the day I was texting him about her.

Honestly, I wasn't trying to worry about her because her situation tends to put me in a bad mood - a mood I didn't like to revisit. I do wonder how she's doing, though.

I shook my head, "Naw. I actually haven't. I haven't spoken to her since the day I went to the hospital to meet her." I responded while opening the passenger door and sliding into the leather seat.

"Fuck you mean you haven't spoken to her since then?" Mace queried while giving me a confused look causing me to roll my eyes, grabbing my phone out of my pocket.

"Exactly what I said, nigga. I'm not trying to relapse and the way I felt that day was something I'm not trying to feel again. Dealing with all that shit had me on the edge." I spat back while unlocking my phone.

Mace started up the car forcing air out the vents to fan against our faces, "Yea, I hear you. I still think we should reach out to her boo." I nodded, hearing every word he said but keeping my focus on the text I'd just received.

Dallas
<u>Received</u>
Shia

My brows furrowed in confusion scanning over the text from Dallas. We haven't spoken to each other since his awkward departure last night; I believed it was best to give him his space.

Dallas
<u>Sent</u>
Dallas

"So we going to reach out to her or..." Mace's voice trailed off as we came to a red light, me finally averting my attention from my phone to him.

His head rested against the window with his gaze on me. I nodded, "Yea. Yea. I'll call her later on."

He chortled, "What about right now? At least while we're both together."

That didn't even cross my mind especially since I wasn't ready to face Kris. Honestly, I was scared to see what was going on with my friend. I was scared to feel her pain once again. I wasn't ready but having Mace here as some sort of support, I probably could manage.

"You right. Hold on."

I navigated through my phone going directly to my contacts as an incoming text ceased my movement.

Dallas
<u>Received</u>
Busy? I need you right now.

Need me?

Butterflies rushed my stomach at Dallas' choice of words. The only person that made it known that they needed me was Blake. To know someone of the opposite sex needed to be in my presence was such a warming feeling. My cheeks heated, still stuck on his words. I've never blushed so hard in my life and here I am, doing it over five words.

"Must be a nigga, huh?"

Mace's question pulled me out my little moment, clearing my throat before studying his sharp side profile. I found it amusing how Mace could read me like an open book and we haven't known each other that long. He was so observant and I appreciated that. He's the type of nigga that'd notice if I did the slightest cut to my hair. He paid attention to all the little things, and that mattered.

"Yea," I softly responded receiving a quick look from him before focusing back on the road.

"Forreal Shy?" His voice rose an octave as if he was surprised.

I laughed, "Don't sound so surprised but yea."

"Aww, look at you. Fresh out of rehab and getting some dick." He teased in a playful manner, giving my arm a light jab making my nose turn up.

"NO nigga. I'm not on no one's dick. We're just cool." I shot back, looking back to my phone.

There was no way in hell I was going to reveal the man that had me blushing. Mace would never let me hear the end of it.

Dallas
<u>Sent</u>
Need? Strong word.
Everything okay?

Dallas
<u>Received</u>
I mean exactly what I said.
Can I pull up?
Yea. I'm good.

Dallas
<u>Sent</u>
Yea.
I should be there in 10.

Dallas
<u>Received</u>
Ight bae.

My stomach did that thing it normally does whenever he called me that; it sounded even better falling from those pouty lips of his, though. Those lips I missed against mine. Just thinking about him had me squeezing my thighs together as that familiar feeling found its way back to my lower region.

Damn you, Dallas.

"Shy! Stop thinking bout fucking your text buddy and call Kris!" He hissed earning an eye roll from me.

He was so dramatic and irritating.

I gave him a dead glare as a smirk settled amongst his features. A chuckle escaped his lips as he looked at me out the corner of his eye, "Your fingers can start moving now nigga."

Kissing my teeth, I pressed on Kris' name that already was plastered across my screen before placing it on speaker allowing the rings to radiate through the car once Mace turned the music down.

"We're sorry. You have reached a number that is no longer in service. If you feel you have reached this recording in error, please check the number and try your call again."

The automated voice caused our faces to contort into confusion simultaneously.

What the fuck.
Where's Kris?

March 18, 2016: Fort Washington, MD
My brows furrowed at the sight of Dallas sitting on the hood of his car, staring off as if he was stuck in a daze. I could tell something was heavily on his mind by the way his lips were pursed together with his brows meeting in the center of his head. The tension was written all over his handsome face and it was making me hesitant on getting out of Mace's car.

"Oh shit. That's bruh from rehab." He chuckled as I tore my eyes from Dallas, looking to him. "That's who you fucking Shy?"

I rolled my eyes at his assumption. This nigga just wants me to be fucking someone.

Smacking my lips, I mugged him, "I told you we not fucking nigga."

He waved me off twisting his lips, "You know I don't care, ma. Your uptight ass needs some anyways."

I rolled my eyes again, "BYE Mace. Me and my kitty are fine." I countered, pushing the door open.

He laughed, "She'll be fine once she gets some attention." He shot back earning a giggle from me.

Mace was the definition of a fool.

My feet collided with the pavement before closing the door, bending over to focus on his striking visage holding that stupid smirk he always does. Cocking my head to the side, I clasped my hands together, "I'll see you nigga. Be safe. Stay sober."

I began laughing at the twisted expression settling on his face as he waved me off dismissively. "I'm good boo. I'm not going back to that shit. You do the same though and let me know if you hear from Kris."

I nodded, making a mental note to relay any messages concerning Kris. "I will. Let me know when you make it in."

He gave me a quick nod as his hand rested on the gearshift, "Got you Shy." I backed away watching his car disappear down the street before turning around, locking in on Dallas' brown gaze. His face softened once settling his eyes on me while pushing his body off his car. Chewing on the inside of my cheek, I slowly sauntered his way stopping not too far from him.

"You know you could've gone in to wait for me, right?" I spoke, taking notice of Blake's car in the driveway.

His lips twisted revealing one of his dimples while shaking his head, still moving towards me. "Naw, I'd rather wait on you."

His voice held that deep tone but had a hint of softness to it as if he was trying to whisper. His towering frame enclosed the space between us as his tongue swept over his lip. Narrowing my eyes, I studied his countenance trying to read him but he remained stoic. I already knew something had to be bothering him. From him leaving upset last night to a whole day of not communicating with me then suddenly needing to see me.

I was just hoping this was something he'd want to speak on.

My brows rose in question, "You good?"

He nodded, looking around before back down at me, "Yea bae. I'll be ight."

Realizing this was something he didn't want to speak on by his response, I chose to leave it alone. He'd tell me if or whenever he was willing to.

Nodding, I motioned for him to follow me as I began trekking up the driveway only to be stopped by him grabbing ahold of my wrist.

"Where my hug?" His voice held some huskiness this time which shot a jolt to my lower region.

He smirked, tugging my wrist again before wrapping it around his waist as he wrapped his arms around my small frame. A soft sigh fell from my lips once being in his warm embrace. I could literally stay in his arms forever and not complain once. Being in his arms was *that* comforting for me.

My nose wiggled from his intoxicating natural scent that I enjoyed whenever in his presence. So many thoughts ran through my mind as he held me longer than usual. Whatever on his mind was definitely heavy, and eating away at him quickly. The sudden release had a frown forming on my face as we stepped back from each other. His bent index finger flew under my chin giving my head a slight tilt to look into his brown orbs even better.

"Bae."

Chills ran down my spine at his term of endearment. If it was any other nigga, I'd throw a conniption if he acted like he couldn't use my name. Coming from Dallas though? One of the best things I could hear falling from someone's lips.

"I really needed to see you. Thanks for letting me fall through." His brown hues danced along my chocolate features before landing on my lips.

Once noticing what his eyes were focused on, I became anxious. His lips were truly my kryptonite so I couldn't imagine what a night in the bed would be like with him. Just thinking about us going further than hugs and kisses had my knees weak. He began leaning down towards my lips as I rose on my tippy toes to meet him halfway, heart picking up its pace while enclosing the space between us. He stopped just inches from my lips as that sexy grin settled on his face. A small hiss fell from my lips once feeling the tip of his tongue graze my bottom lip before disappearing into his mouth. Shivers went throughout my body once our foreheads connected with his breath fanning against my lips once he parted his lips to speak.

His hands moved to my hips, gripping tightly. "Fuck you getting nervous for?" He spoke lowly with that smirk still teasing at his lips.

I released the breath I didn't realize I was holding once feeling his hand run through my hair, massaging his fingers through my mane. His lips gently pressed against mine before pulling back, looking deeply in my eyes. I could see the pain in his brown hues even though he was trying his best to conceal it; I know that look anywhere. I looked at myself daily with that same look in my eyes.

Pain.

"You're welcome." It was the only thing I could manage to say right now.

This man had me going crazy on the inside and as much as I was scared of this feeling, I loved it all at the same time.

He chuckled before placing his sweet lips against mine again, "That's all you can say bae?" The cockiness was spilling from his tone along with his facial expressions causing me to lightly punch his chest, making him stumble a bit.

He laughed while rubbing his chest, looking my curvaceous frame over while grabbing ahold of my hand. "We going in or what?" He questioned, nodding in the direction of the house.

My brown hues remained on Dallas' side profile as his attention remained on the TV. For a change, I decided not to be selfish and allow him to watch what he wanted which resulted in me not being able to tear my eyes from him. I could care less about the basketball game playing especially since I was in the presence of a fine ass specimen. We'd only been in the living room for a good 10 minutes and I can honestly say that my eyes stayed on him for half that time.

He gave my feet a light squeeze bringing a small frown to my lips as I focused on how his jaw clenched before smacking his lips. He'd been so intrigued by the game while massaging my feet, which was one of the best massages I've ever received to mention.

He comfortably sat on one end of the couch while my back rested against the armrest on the opposite side, with my feet resting in his lap. Dallas took me by surprise when grabbing my feet once I slipped off my sandals; I wasn't expecting it but it was greatly appreciated.

"W'sup?" His deep voice entered the air, never tearing his attention from the game. He smacked his lips again while creating small circles on the top of my foot. "Come on ref!"

"Why you ask that?" I wetted my lips, bringing my fingers to twirl in my kinky hair.

He looked at me causing my stomach to flutter like usual. "Cause you staring n' shit. Why else would I ask?" He smartly shot back.

I playfully rolled my eyes in return, "Your favorite color black or something?" I questioned referring to his choice of clothing today.

His entire outfit was black, like always. A black tee with D&G plastered in big white letters along with Dealers&Gangstas right under it covered his torso. His well-built arms painted with a few tattoos were on full display as I tried to get a good view of his artwork at the short distance. A pair of black jeans with zippers at the knees fit his bottom half perfectly. Leaning over slightly, I caught a glimpse of the Tim Hardaway Nike Bakin's clothing his feet before looking back to him. My heart slightly jumped once seeing him grinning my way making me giggle.

His brows rose, "You checking me out?" He questioned with his opened palm outstretching to take a tight hold of my thick thigh, shaking it forcing a laugh from me.

"Stopp." I whined while swatting his hand away earning a chortle from him as his back collided with the couch, kissing his teeth.

His hands went back to massaging my feet, "You didn't answer my question, Dallas."

He cleared his throat before cutting his eyes at me, shrugging, "Sum'n like that." He smoothly spoke while sinking further down into the couch.

My face contorted into a twisted expression from his response, "Something like that Dallas?" I countered earning a chuckle from him as he looked to me.

He nodded, "Yea. It's my favorite color. Good to see how observant you are."

I rolled my eyes at how sarcastic his words came out even though I'm pretty sure he didn't mean it in that manner. Nodding, I pursed my lips together, "Well it looks good on you."

Dallas' head slowly turned to face me while wetting his pouty lips before the corners of his lips turned upward revealing his deep dimples. His hand smacked my thigh before squeezing it forcing my plump lips into a small frown, "This looks good on you as well but thank you Shy." He spoke.

I'm pretty sure he was referring to the fact my ample ass was on full display from my gray leggings for his eyes to ogle. I couldn't be mad though because I've been basically eye fucking him ever since getting in the house.

"No problem Dallas."

He smiled, shaking his head turning his attention from me then back to the game.

"What?" I questioned in a whiny tone.

Dallas looked at me tucking his lip between his teeth before allowing it to slowly fall from his mouth. "Nothing. You just—" He stopped mid-sentence as loud laughter radiated off the walls forcing our attention to focus on the two bodies emerging from the foyer.

I smiled once my brown orbs fell on CJ; I so missed his loud ass.

"Oooo, look what we have here," CJ said, stopping not too far from us with a teasing smirk on his face.

I could already imagine what was going through the both of their heads. Dallas chuckled, shaking his head at CJ's silly antics.

"Wassup," Dallas voiced, throwing a head nod their way.

"I didn't know the both of you were here." I said as Blake's hand found her hip while she made one of those 'mhm' faces.

"You would've known if y'all weren't down here boo loving. I know you saw my car."

"Yes, bitch. I know you saw her car." CJ added, laughing earning one from me as well.

"I did but y'all see I have company, right?" I shot back in a smart tone earning a taken back look from them.

"Oh. Don't show off for Mr. Dallas here." CJ teased making me giggle.

I rolled my eyes, "Whatever. Y'all leaving?"

Blake grabbed her chest as CJ did the same with them looking at each other in shock. "Did she j—?" CJ said pointing at me before looking back to Blake.

"Yes, she did," Blake answered his half question.

These two together were a handful, and then some.

I laughed, "Stop playing y'all. Y'all know I don't mean it like that."

"Mhm. So you say. We're going for dinner so since you have company, we'll see you two later. Practice safe sex kids." Blake threw over her shoulder as they turned to head for the door. "Love you Shy! Bye Dallas!"

I shook my head at her forcing this sex thing on us, "I love you too. BYE CJ!"

His striking green hues landed on me, tilting his head to the side with pursed lips. "BYE heffa!" He laughed once seeing my jaw drop as Dallas chuckled, "Ight y'all."

A sigh parted my lips looking to Dallas' stunning countenance with him staring right back at me. His head tilted back keeping his eyes on me, smiling.

Damn creep.

Just as quick as his beautiful smile appeared, it disappeared just as fast. Why the sudden change? His unruly brows furrowed while sucking his lips into his mouth, sitting fully up and sighing.

"What's wrong Dallas?"

I had no clue what was on his mind but I'm pretty sure it was the same thing which had him wanting to just to be in my presence suddenly. His jaw clenched showcasing his amazing bone structure that I grew to love whenever I'd admire his good looks.

His hands rubbed along his jeans while clearing his throat, "I'm good bae." He sounded as if he was trying to convince himself more than me.

"Bullshit," I spat, really wanting to know his reason behind suddenly needing me.

I regretted calling him out once receiving the dead glare he was shooting in my direction, causing the hairs on the back of my neck to rise. His face held so much tension, "You right but I don't wanna talk about that shit. So chill." He spat back at me as if venom was on his tongue.

It's been a short period of us knowing each other and I never expected to see this side of him so soon, but I somewhat did bring it on myself by being persistent. Still, his choice of words along with tone put me in a salty mood. Throwing my legs off his lap, I quickly rose to my feet - I needed to get out of his presence for a minute. The fact Dallas had this affect on me was beyond me. He could make my body react with simple touches and clearly, he could get me upset just as quick. A hold of my wrist had me stopping in my tracks towards my room before I was swiftly pulled onto his lap.

"Get off of me Dallas," I spoke through clenched teeth.

He chuckled while tightening his hold on me, "So now you mad cause I don't wanna talk?"

I remained silent looking at anything but him.

"Huh?" He questioned, breath bouncing against the exposed skin of my arm.

My eyes shot towards the ceiling once feeling his lips come in contact with my arm. He released a deep sigh, "Don't even act like this girl. I came over here to get my mind off shit. Not talk about it." He explained.

"I'm sorry for snapping on you bae..." Another sigh fell from his lips, "It's just some shit I really don't want to speak on right now. I just want to enjoy being with you slim. That's all."

I turned to him, nodding scrutinizing his face that softened once locking in on my brown gaze.

My brows rose in question as a grin settled on my face, "Slim?" He laughed allowing his head to fall on the back of the couch, keeping his hues on me. My body jumped from him using his legs to bounce me causing me to giggle, punching his chest lightly.

"Yea. *Slim.*" He responded, putting an emphasis on 'slim' while beginning to rub my hip.

Where did he come from?

He was sent my way right on time.

Book VIII.

March 18, 2016: Fort Washington, MD

A frown quickly took over my face once hearing the loud burp exit Dallas' mouth as I watched his silhouette move in my darkened room, with the TV light making some of his features visible.

"You can say excuse me," I shot out with an attitude once feeling his weight shift the opposite side of my bed.

The sound of him smacking his lips had my head whipping in his direction within seconds, him staring right back at me. The corner of his lips twisted, "Can you give me time to say it? Damn." He said, shaking his head.

Instantly, my expression became apologetic not knowing that his plans were to excuse himself.

My bad.

His palm rose in the air seeing the look settling on my face. I know I looked dumb as shit, mouth somewhat stuck in the position of an 'O.'

"You good Shy but chill," I nodded, totally agreeing with him.

I had the habit of speaking without thinking first and it was something I needed to work on.

Pulling my black blanket up to my nose, I snuggled under it more turning onto my side facing Dallas. We chose to have a movie night and he had me in here watching this sick shit, *Saw*. Honestly, I wasn't in the mood to see a bunch of gory stuff tonight knowing I have to go to sleep but, it wasn't so bad.

"Oh shit!" His voice rose an octave, lightly biting into his fist as the screaming voice of a man sounded throughout my room.

"Turn that shit down," I hissed, watching him lean forward to grab the remote.

A smile graced my lips once hearing the volume lowered, "Thank you." I politely said earning a snort from him.

"You welcome mean ass." He shot back causing my jaw to slightly drop. A chuckle fell from his lips once catching a glimpse of my shocked expression.

I offered a light jab to his arm, "I am not mean." He nodded, face still painted with that beautiful smile.

"So you say," I smiled at the sight of him cringing. My attention averted from his handsome side profile towards the movie. My face contorted into one of disgust once seeing the man using a saw to cut through his ankle.

Snuggling beneath my blanket more, a light chuckle entered the air causing me to focus on Dallas. My body warmed up from him looking at me through thin slits. He was so damn attractive that it was hard to fathom at times - I appreciated having someone so handsome to look at.

"What?" I nervously asked, growing more turned on under his intense gaze.

He didn't have to lay one finger on me and still managed to make my body react. Dallas remained silent, never breaking our gaze. His pink flesh darted across his fluffy bottom lip, leaving a wet sheen. Staring at his lips was giving me the urge to connect mines with his. His kisses ignited this fire in me that I wasn't aware of existing. A taunting smirk began to appear among his stunning features, heating my body more than before.

"Nothing..." His voice trailed off causing my eyes to narrow at his response. I knew that wasn't all he had to say. "I just like looking at your beautiful ass." His bent pointer finger brushed against my chin, making me blush.

I crossed my eyes, "Whatever." I muttered. He began yawning with his long limbs stretching in the air. "I know you're tired Dallas. Go home," I urged. This was probably the fifth time he'd yawned since starting the movie. My brown hues shifted to my phone, pressing the home button to reveal it was a little past one in the morning.

"You don't have to work in the morning?" Dallas chuckled while shaking his head.

"You call yourself trying to get rid of me bae?" He teasingly questioned, resting his head against the headboard while keeping his attention on me. I parted my lips to speak before getting cut off by his husky voice. "I'm not ready to leave you yet."

Before I knew it I was being wrapped up in his masculine arms, face nuzzled deep in my neck. A giggle passed my lips while squeezing his face with the side of mine, "Stopp," I whined as his muffled laugh sent vibrations throughout my being.

His face remained in my neck as my chin found a home on the top of his freshly cut hair. My dainty fingers trailed their way up the nape of his neck causing his body to flinch slightly under my gentle touch. I massaged the exposed skin, releasing a deep breath as well.

This was such a fortifying feeling being wrapped up in his arms. It felt good to feel needed.
Wanted.

He couldn't begin to understand how therapeutic this was for me. Being in his arms was a new feeling - one that I actually enjoyed. For once, I felt safe.

A comfortable silence fell over us. The movie ended not too long ago, leaving the ending credits moving across the screen. A frown contorted my lips once feeling Dallas remove his face from my neck, tugging on my blanket.

"Lemme get some." The grogginess in his voice gave him away; he definitely was way more tired than he'd lead on.

Letting up my grip, his tall frame easily slipped under the blanket permeating a new heat to my frame. Within one motion, I was being pulled into his body causing a slight gasp to fall from my lips. My hues surveyed my room before traveling back to the handsome man I laid entangled with. My heart jumped once locking in on his intense gaze. His deadpan face sent shivers down my spine. The only thing I could find myself focusing on was his dancing fingers moving across my lower back and those lips.

Those fuckin' lips.

A smirk lifted the left corner of his lips while his warm hand began creating circles on the side of my thigh. His brown eyes never tore from mine. Smoothly his hand moved towards the back of my thigh before pulling it to rest on top of his. The more his hand warmed my thigh, the faster my heart picked up its pace.

"What's on your mind?" Somehow, from deep down, I was able to find my words.

His brows met in the middle of his head with confusion, sweeping his pink flesh across his plump bottom lip. Dallas began moving slightly as if trying to get more comfortable, clearing his throat before parting his lips to speak.

"A lot..." His voice trailed off, brown eyes still holding that hint of pain in them.

He was hurting, and I could see that just by looking in his eyes.

The movement on my thigh abruptly stopped forcing my hand to move and caress his cheek softly.

"Talk to me, Dallas." I softly cooed, hoping he'd give in to my request.

I understood that he came here to be in my presence but it was killing me not knowing what had him so bothered. I'm pretty sure it was something that I couldn't fix. But just maybe, maybe I could offer some encouraging words despite the fact I'm fucked up myself. My brown hues searched his handsome countenance while my thumbs began rubbing against his soft flesh gently. A frown painted my full lips once focusing on the shaking of his head forcing my hand from his face.

"I already told you… Not tonight." I nodded, completely understanding if he didn't want to elaborate on his sudden appearance tonight.

I'd leave it be.

"Okay."

There was nothing else to be said. He didn't want to talk. Who was I to force it out of him?

A weak smile blessed his lips while leaning in, placing a gentle kiss on mine bringing a swarm of butterflies to my tummy. He offered a faint smile, rubbing the pad of his thumb along my bottom lip. Narrowing my hues, I nodded.

"Just... When you ready to talk. I'm here," I watched as he chewed on the inside of his cheek before leaning in, blessing me with another kiss.

I'm assuming that was his way of saying 'thank you.'

A deep scowl settled among my gorgeous, chocolate features watching Dallas remove himself from the bed. Using my elbow, I pushed myself to sit upright as I confusingly watched Dallas putting on his shoes.

"What did I say?" He chuckled, looking over his shoulder.

"Nothing bae. I'm just gon' get going."

My scowl grew deeper at his words. I mean I was trying to convince him to go home at first but now that the moment presented itself, I didn't want him leaving. He smirked while grabbing his fitted off my dresser, placing it on his head with the brim pointed in the air.

Wetting my lips, my eyes danced up and down his tall frame. This man was impeccably beautiful, even when he wasn't trying. My breath hitched in my throat as he leaned forward, closed fists coming in contact with the mattress. A smirk tugged at his lips with his breath fanning against my nose, sending a tingly sensation down my spine.

"I'll let you know when I get in." His husky tone caused my body to tense for a second before relaxing once feeling his lips upon mine. My lips fell into a pout as his forehead rested against mine, pecking my lips again.

"Ight bae." His weird way of bidding me farewell, returning to his 6'2" frame while peering at me through heavy lids.

I'm pretty sure he wasn't aware of the tantalizing look in his eyes, but it was damn near driving me insane on the inside. He nodded towards the door while beginning to walk backward, "Come lock up."

I rapped along with one of my favorite rappers, J. Cole, "Too Deep For The Intro," while nodding. With me being a fan of Erykah's music as well, I thought it was clever how he rapped over "Didn't Cha Know" beat while incorporating her soulful voice in it as well. That man never failed me when it came to his music - he was definitely underrated. The light of my iPhone illuminated my car as I came to a red light, retrieving it from the cup holder.

Gi
<u>Received</u>
You up Daddy?
We miss you.

The vibration shook my hand causing my eyes to widen at the picture coming in quickly after the text. A chuckle parted my lips, shaking my head at the wide open legs giving me a full display of her pink pussy. It belonged to Gizelle. A blonde-haired, mixed chick I happened to stumble upon at a club. Out of all the chicks I've dealt with throughout my 28 years spent on this Earth, I'd never came across a female that intrigued me enough to actually spend time with her as well. Gizelle was definitely a dope chick but honestly, I never saw us going beyond the fuck buddies title.

Ever since meeting Shia, I found myself wanting to spend more time with her and throwing Gizelle on the back burner. It's been a good week now since the last time I've been balls deep in Gizelle so I know she was itching for her fix.

I pulled into the parking lot of my apartment complex, relieved that I was home after being away for a week. Due to my mother being in the hospital, if not at work, the majority of my time was spent at my mother's helping my sister out with my twin nieces. With my mother being back and forth in the hospital, it was taking a toll on all of us especially my babies. With them being four, Devyn tried her best to explain to them what was going on with their grandma but knowing she was in the hospital always ended in tears from them.

Father God, please keep my baby here with us all.

Grabbing my phone, I pushed the door open allowing my Bakin's to collide with the cement before closing the door behind me. Trekking the short distance to my building, I pressed the key on my car remote to lock the doors, chirping ringing in the air signifying the alarm being turned on. Jogging up the stairs to the second floor, I singled out my apartment key before unlocking the door. Sighing out of exhaustion, I locked the door before throwing my keys on the coffee table and heading towards my bedroom.

I always felt at ease in the confines of my own personal space. Being in my room felt like I was in my own Heaven - one of the greatest feelings.

Scratching the nape of my neck, I moved towards my closet slipping my shoes off, too lazy to return them to its respectable box. Exhaling, I rounded the corner going into my bathroom turning the shower on full blast, making sure it was hot enough. After ridding my body of today's outing, my bare feet moved across the white tile before crossing the threshold into my bedroom. I sat on the edge of my bed, palms resting on my knees. Looking to my right, I grabbed my phone seeing that I received another text from Gizelle. A smirk pulled at the corner of my lips as I began responding.

Gi
<u>Received</u>
Wake up Daddy.
I know you miss us too

Gi
<u>Sent</u>
Daddy got you later today.
A nigga had a long day. Take your ass to sleep.

Gi
<u>Received</u>
We can't wait

I laughed, shaking my head. I mean, I'm fully aware that I can throw dick and very well at that. Main reason why I had to slow down with how much I ran into bitches; they began getting too crazy for my liking.

After throwing my phone beside me, I pushed myself to my feet heading to my dresser to retrieve a pair of black Calvin Klein boxers along with a pair of basketball shorts. After slipping them on, I moved towards my bed, throwing the covers back before allowing my body to soak into the memory foam mattress. This mattress was definitely one of the best investments I've made to lay my head on every night. Devyn had kept bragging about hers and after sprawling out on hers one day, I had to get one of my own.

Outstretching my arm, I took my phone in my hand scrolling to Shia's name. Bringing the phone to my ear, my eyes closed at the two rings before her sweet voice overwhelmed my being. Hearing her voice put me in a state of tranquility; something I haven't felt in a long time. Dealing with my mother's sickness has been weighing heavily on me so having someone like Shia to suddenly cross my path was definitely God's doing.

"Hello." I could tell I'd woken her.

"My bad Shy. You fell asleep that fast?" It didn't take me but a good 15 minutes to get home. She was trying to tell me how tired I was when she was as well. "I just wanted to let you know that I made it in. I'm not gon' hold you."

I also wanted to hear her voice till I fell into a deep slumber. I didn't plan on expressing that to her though.

"Hmm..."

I chortled at the grogginess seeping through her tone. She probably didn't hear a word I'd said.

"Nothing. Don't worry bout it. Go to sleep bae."

A sudden whiff of air attacked my bare chest forcing me to pull the covers up, covering myself completely while turning on my side. I smiled at her smacking her lips before whining, "I want to stay on the phone with you."

A small grimace took over my lips at the thought of her whining my name while filling her to the hilt. Shaking my head of the nasty thoughts, I licked my lips before clearing my throat. "But you sleepy. Go to sleep." I responded, voice dropping an octave at my last words. I already could tell being on the phone with her off the late night would be a problem for me. The fact I was laying in complete darkness with her soft breathing and sultry tone tickling my ear was enough to probably make me bust a nut. As much as I wanted to stay on the phone with her, I knew I couldn't.

A nigga needed some pussy, and now.

Shia huffed out of annoyance which I'm pretty sure was directed towards me, seeing as though she wanted to stay on the phone. There was movement on her end along with a few choice obscenities under her breath before she returned to the phone.

"Okay. Since you're trying to get rid of me, Dallas." I laughed at her mocking me from earlier. She giggled which sent an unexplainable heat through my body, "I'll talk to you later?" She queried, knowing damn well there was no way she wasn't going to hear from me.

"You already know you will bae. Stop that shit, but sleep good. Ig—?" My nose turned up once hearing a stream of liquid connecting with water letting me know that she was on the toilet. "Oh naw Shy. You on the toilet?" She laughed at my question where I believe I should've received a warning or something.

"Yup!" I smacked my lips, "Man, goodnight slim." Her laughter got louder bringing a smile to my visage before her laughter was covered, still audible to my ear.

"Sorry." The innocence in her voice made my smile grow even bigger.

"It's cool but get some sleep, ight?" At that moment I envisioned her nodding.

"Kay Dallas. Night night."

Sitting up while running a hand down my face, another smile took over my lips, "Night baby."

Gi
<u>Sent</u>
You still up Gi?
I'm bout to come thru.

Fuck sleep right now. A nigga needed his nut.

March 19, 2016: Laurel, MD

My lip remained tucked tight between my teeth as I focused on the ample flesh within my hands while my condom coated dick plunged in and out of her wetness.

"Shit," I hissed, head falling back as my eyes fell on the ceiling. This shit was long overdue.

"Daddy," She whined as my strokes sped up, knowing she was almost to her peak as well as me.

My brows met in the middle of my head as my palm came across her ample ass, smirking once seeing the jiggling wave. Not only did Gizelle have an amazing physique but also had a plump ass to go along with it.

"Move your hand girl!" I barked, swatting the hand that was trying to push me away.

She was begging for the dick about an hour ago and now acting like she can't take it.

Fuck outta here.

Spreading her cheeks apart, my attention fell on my dick that I fully removed from her before filling her to the hilt again, making her pussy fart.

"Oooh," She cooed, fisting the covers.

A teasing grin contorted my lips once hearing the smacking sound of my front connecting with her rear, balls slapping against her bare skin and all. Rotating my hips in a circle, I knew I was hitting her spot once receiving a loud yelp from her. Her hands were placed firmly on the mattress as she lifted her body, giving me a sexy look over her shoulder. Those piercing blue eyes was fixed on me as she began throwing her ass back, sending a hard grunt from my lips. I thrust my hips upwards meeting hers.

124

"Fuuckk." She moaned, encouraging me to go faster and even deeper.

Another squeal fell from her pretty lips as I continued stabbing at her sensitive spot, taking a hold of her shoulders. One hand softly took a hold of her neck, knowing how much she was into that choking shit. Her loud cries filled the room as I tortured her from behind, enjoying the sound of her pleasure filled moans.

"I-I'm..." I already knew what she was about to say and I was right there with her.

"I know Gi. I'm right there with you." My husky voice completed what I knew she was trying her best to get out.

I sent one hard stroke into her spot causing her body to immediately go into convulsions. Her body went limp, falling into the bed as I grabbed a hold of her ass, digging in her so I could get mines as well.

"Damn Gi," I muttered as she continued moaning.

I knew she was gone off my dick, but little did she know, what she had between her legs had me considering actually dating her at times. Then it becomes just another figment of my imagination once I'm out of her.

"Fuuckk," I groaned, swiftly removing myself and pulling off the condom before busting all over her ass.

I wasn't into nutting on a female until I met Gizelle; she would practically beg me to coat her beautiful skin with my kids. I wasn't one to protest either so I did what was requested of me. I shook my head, satisfied with finally getting my nut off. Smiling, I watched as her palm came across her ass before her long tongue made my seed disappear.

This bitch was nasty and she knew it.

Her heavy lids honed on me once rolling on her back, legs sprawled open giving me an excellent view of that pretty pussy of hers. I grunted, grabbing myself trying to calm him down as he was trying to work his way back up. Her white manicured index finger disappeared in her wet pussy as her tongue swept across her fluffy bottom lip.

"Come on Daddy, one more round."

I chuckled, shaking my head while bringing my boxers and sweats around my waist in one motion. "Naw Gi..." I trailed off, heading to her bathroom to flush the condom down the toilet.

Grabbing my white tee off her dresser, I threw it over my head before focusing on the pout marring her gorgeous features. I slipped my sock clad feet into my Nike slides before nodding towards her bedroom door, "Come lock up."

She smacked her lips, not moving. I shrugged before giving my back for her to focus on; I could care less if she had an attitude. A nigga was tired, got a nut, and now ready to be back in the confines of my own space.

"You really not going to fuck me again?"

I chuckled at the annoyance in her voice, looking over my shoulder, "You see I'm dressed right? Come lock the fuck up, Gizelle." I hissed. Not another word was said as she scooted her naked body off the bed, stomping in my direction.

"Move nigga," She murmured while brushing against me as hard as possible. I chuckled, eyes fixated on her phat ass following her to the front door.

Like I said before, I could care less if she has an attitude.
My dick. My rules.

March 22, 2016: Hyattsville, MD - *Chipotle*

Blake sighed, "How are you feeling? Any urges lately?" She asked me before wrapping her lips around her straw.

Since I missed out on dinner with Blake and CJ a few nights ago, she made it her duty to treat me to Chipotle for lunch. I bit into my burrito, shaking my head. After swallowing the food, I parted my lips to speak.

"Nope. I'm surprised I haven't been thinking about it. I'm just in a good place, surrounded by positivity. Now... If some bad sh—"

My words were cut short once her hand went into the air, "Don't start talking like that. You control who and what surrounds you. Just keep the right people in your presence and you're good." She preached.

I always considered Blake to be somewhat of an optimist especially when she began ranting about "God" and whatnot. Sometimes it was encouraging how positive she was and then at times, it could be pretty annoying. At the moment, I appreciated what she said.

I took another large bite into my burrito, savoring the igniting flavors taking over my mouth. Chipotle was one of my favorite food spots, hands down. Blake thought it was so irritating how I would eat it every day when it first hit this area.

"Bitch, you blow me." My eyes popped open, already knowing what she was referring to.

Wiping my mouth with a napkin, a smile contorted my lips as well. I fanned her off, "Girl. You know this my fave."

She kissed her teeth, "Yea. I know. Gon' turn into a damn burrito." She teased earning an eye roll from me.

Grabbing my cup, I took a sip of my Dr. Pepper, relishing in the burning sensation it sent down my throat. My eyes remained on Blake whose attention was now on her phone, typing away. My face twisted at how quick her fingers moved. I was getting better at texting but I definitely wasn't able to text like Blake, speed-wise.

After wrapping my burrito in the given foil, I returned it to the bag before locking eyes with my cousin. Her brows rose while throwing her purse on her shoulder, grabbing her bag.

"You ready?" I nodded, grabbing my bag and standing as well. My lips warped into a frown as I looked at the incoming call which was an unknown number. Moving not too far behind Blake towards her car, I brought my phone to my ear.

"Hello," I placed my bag on the floor between my legs.

"Hey. Is this Shia?"

My brows furrowed even more at the unfamiliar voice that knew my name.

"Yea. Who's this?"

My brown hues moved towards my cousin, shrugging as she mouthed 'who's that.'

"Ron. I'm Kris' cousin… The one that she's been staying with."

Oh shit.

A weak smile worked its way to my lips, "Really? Hey, Ron. How is she? Is she good?"

Ron laughed lightly at my rambling. I was excited. I've been worried about Kris these past few days and with her phone cut off, it brought my worry level to the highest.

A short silence fell upon us as she sighed, "I was calling because Kris wanted me to. Sad to say, she's back in rehab. Relapsed the same day she came home with me."

My heart dropped, not prepared for what was just relayed to me. See, if she'd stayed with me for a few days, I'm pretty sure she wouldn't have. I can't believe this shit.

"Shia. You still there?"

I chewed on the inside of my cheek, trying my best to keep my anger at bay. It was stirring rather quickly and I was beyond ready to lash out on the individual occupying the driver seat.

"I'm here. I just really don't know what to say. Shit hurts..." I trailed off, sulking in my feelings.

"I know. I really had high hopes for her staying clean this ti—"

I squeezed my eyes shut, feeling the pain as she began getting choked up. I looked out the window fighting back my tears, hoping Blake didn't say a word to me. If so, it wasn't going to end pretty. Hearing her sniffles was damn near tearing me apart; I couldn't take this.

"She just lost it when she lost Cole. We all did. I've never seen Kris so in love with someone before. So for him to be snatched away so suddenly during one of her weakest states was too much. The praying won't stop because I know God has wonderful things planned for her."

I rolled my eyes once hearing her reference to God. If there was a God, *why* was my friend back in rehab? *Why* was her one and only love taken away from her? *Why* did she put in all that work to stay clean only to start over, and possibly be worst?

"But she definitely wants to see you and Mace so whenever y'all can, please go see her."

I nodded, already ten steps of her. Of course, I was going to make it my duty to go see Kris - she needed to know that she still had us behind her 100%.

"We definitely will Ron. Sorry for your loss and hold your head. Stay in touch please."

"Thanks, Shia. I surely will. Have a blessed day boo."

"You too."

Dropping my phone into my lap, I shook my head trying to allow everything to sink in. I squeezed my fist, feeling the anger more than ready to spill out of me.

"So who was that?"

Blake had no clue of the anger directed towards her right now, and she was better off not saying shit. I shot an evil glare her way, "Shut the fuck up." I spoke through clenched teeth as her eyes widened, tension settling among her chocolate features.

"The fuck wrong with you?" Her voice was laced with exasperation.

"You Blake. Don't fuckin' talk to me right now."

I rolled my eyes once hearing her sarcastic chuckle, "Naw. We gon' talk bout this shit right now."

She continued mumbling obscenities to herself while pulling into a parking lot, coming to an abrupt stop. My jaw clenched in vexation as I felt the piercing stare on my side profile.

"So. Speak." She spat out, making me even more furious.

Narrowing my eyes, I shot my head towards her and by the shocked expression on her face, I knew she knew how mad I was. I was livid. All I wanted to do was help my friend and Blake completely interfered with that.

"You're the fuckin' reason Kris is back in rehab!!"

Her jaw dropped, pointing to herself with a tipped brow. "Me? I'm the reason?" She kissed her teeth, waving me off. "Don't throw your friend's drug habit on me. *She's* the reason her ass is back in rehab, not me."

My jaw fell agape slightly, "Are you fuckin' serious?! If it wasn't for you being so fuckin' pressed to get her out of the house then maybe she'd still be clean!" At this point my chest was heaving up and down, eyes stinging due to the tears blurring my vision.

Blake's face softened, shaking her head before speaking in a softer tone. "Look Shy, you just said it yourself. *Maybe* she'd still be clean. So you knew as well that it'd be a possibility she might relapse after what happened. She wasn't strong enough to fight the urge right now..."

I looked away, wiping my tears quickly.

"I admit. The way I handled the situation at the moment was fucked up..."

I looked back to her, searching for the genuineness in her eyes, and I found it.

"But I didn't want you to relapse. We're not God Shy. We can't be Omnipresent nor save everyone. That's just life. I mean, we can try but that doesn't mean we'll succeed. Now you? I don't want you too focused on everyone else's problems when you have the biggest problem in your face right now. I can't lose you again Shy. I've never seen you fight so hard to stay clean and I know for a fact that you're going to win this time. That night with Kris just threw me off. I didn't want her breakdown to affect you, putting us back at square one. So yes, I do apologize for how I handled things that night *but* my intentions were good. You know how I am when it comes to you."

At that moment, I felt my anger slowly leaving my body coming back to a calm state. That's all I needed to hear. The apology was long overdue but hearing it along with everything else was worth the wait. I nodded, tucking my lip between my teeth. My palms flew across my cheeks, ridding them of my tears.
"I understand. It's just... I wish I could've saved her. She's my friend. I felt like I've abandoned her." I softly spoke, fiddling with my fingers.

"Shy..." She called, forcing my eyes to fixate on her matching brown ones. "She knows you're her friend. She knew that the day you hopped a few buses just to make it to the hospital. Don't beat yourself up over this. Like I always tell you, a minor setback for a major comeback. That's all this is. Kris will be fine. Just pray for her like you'll pray for yourself."

Praying being the last thing I want to hear right now.

March 22, 2016: Uptown, Washington, D.C.

Throwing my keys on the entryway table, I slipped off my black Adidas shell toes kicking them under the table. A smile took over my face once hearing the giggling of my favorite little women.

"Hey! Stop running girls!" Just off my sister's voice alone, I could tell she was exhausted. This was Ma's first day back home so after getting off, I ran home to take and shower and came right over. Work had me ready to eat dinner and lay up with my nieces, watching whatever they pleased. I was beat for the day.

The pattering of little feet coming towards me as I moved through the corridor brought a frown to my lips. "Didn't your mother say stop running?" I hissed, looking back and forth between my nieces who abruptly stopped with wide eyes set on me.

They were so beautiful it didn't make any sense. They had the cutest button noses, just like my sister. Their dark brown, curly hair wildly went whichever way it chose. Their brown, doe eyes complimented their golden skin perfectly. Once finding out that Devyn was pregnant with identical twin girls, I knew they were going to steal my heart.

I stooped to their eye level, smirking at the pouting faces they were throwing my way. They both stood with clasped hands in front of them, shoulders touching. These two were inseparable especially when it came down to them getting in trouble. One would never let the other take all the heat which I loved. They understood the true meaning behind having an unbreakable bond with your sibling.

"Grandma is home now so you two need to be on your best behavior. Kay?"

They nodded, not saying a word. My crooked smile returned as I opened my arms to embrace them. "Give Uncle D some love." They looked at each other before giggling and bum-rushing me.

Their laughter grew as I placed sloppy kisses all over their faces, bouncing back and forth between the two. I kept a tight hold around their tiny bodies as I moved towards the kitchen. My dimples revealed themselves once laying my eyes on my sister that was making plates and taking them to the table.

"It smells good in here big head." My nostrils flared, taking in all the delicious fumes.

She looked over her shoulder as that bright smile of hers blessed her face, "Hey ugly." I chuckled while placing the girls on their feet. "Yani. Yuri. Go wash your hands." She demanded, nodding her head towards the foyer where the only bathroom on the main floor was.

Rounding the island, I leaned up against the counter watching my older sister prepare our plates. Devyn cut her eyes at me while continuing to prepare my plate, I'm assuming, from how much food was piled on it.

"You need to go wash your dirty ass hands too," She teased earning a snort from me.

I nodded, "Yea. I'm headed that way. Ma in the living room?"

She nodded, "Yea. Can you get her please?" Her brown orbs locked with mine, pushing a few stray hairs behind her ear.

"Of course."

Slowly sauntering towards the living room, Yuri brushed against my leg with Yani doing the exact same thing seconds later.

"Stop running!" I barked as their running turned into skipping.

"Sorry Uncle Dally!" They said in unison, making my heart flutter as I shook my head.

Those damn girls. They have my whole heart.

Against my will, my face began heating up once fixating my gaze on the love of my life. She must've felt my presence because I didn't get far into the living room before I got a full view of her frail but beautiful face. Despite her sickness, she was still beautiful in my eyes - always will be. I smiled, moving quickly to her placing a gentle kiss on her forehead.

"Sup Ma," I voiced while sitting on the footstool that went along with the rocking chair she was sitting in. The one seat you'd always find her sitting in if she was in the living room.

My elbows rested on my legs as I cocked my head to the side. She offered me a weak smile, "Hey baby." She softly spoke.

"How are you feeling Ma?"

She giggled, "I'm still here so I am blessed baby." My heart jumped at her positive attitude; I love how positive she can be during the worst situations.

I always fed off her positive energy.

"How was work?"

I twisted my lips at her question, "Work is work Ma." I chuckled, "Nothing great but I'm thankful for God providing me with a steady income."

She smiled while nodding, "Ya damn right."

I laughed, "You're not supposed to be cursing when I just mentioned God."

Her face twisted while fanning me off, "God knows my heart."

I burst out in laughter once hearing her use my own words against me. It was my favorite thing to say whenever she threw God in the mix and me just so happened to slip up with some foul language.

"You too much Ma..." I managed to say as my laughing subsided, "You ready to eat?"

Her smile grew at me mentioning food, "I sure am!" She replied in an excited tone.

**Shy
<u>Received</u>
Dallas.
I need you.**

After helping my mother to the dining room, I excused myself to step outside for a minute. Closing the sliding glass deck door behind me, I retrieved my phone from my back pocket. Once unlocking the screen, I immediately scrolled through my contacts landing on Shia's name. I didn't know how to feel once receiving that same text I sent her four days ago. I couldn't leave my family's side at this very moment but the least I could do was call her; I had to be here for her just like she was for me.

My nose turned up once hearing the rings cease before movement flew through the receiver, "Shia." I called out her name before her background became silent allowing her sultry voice to attack my ear, sending a tingly sensation through my frame.

"Dallas... Hey." Her greeting was very soft, pain-filled actually.

"You crying?" My face contorted once hearing her sniffles before a short pause fell between us.

"I'm alright."

I smacked my lips, "What's wrong bae? What was that text about?"

She sighed, "I. I really don't want to talk about it right now. I just need to be around you for a bit... take me out this funk."

Sweeping my tongue across my lip, my brown hues flew towards the sky as I leaned against the deck railing. For us to have known each other for such a short amount of time, I found myself wanting to be near her even after just leaving her presence. Making this even more difficult to tell her that I couldn't make it; well at least, not right now.

I sighed deeply, running my free hand over my face, "Shy..." I was actually nervous to tell her that I couldn't drop everything and come running. "I can't come right now."

"Cool. I'll talk to you later." She quickly shot back causing my face to contort, thrown off by her sudden attitude.

"Hol' up slim. You didn't even let me finish." I rushed my words, making sure to catch her just in case she was about to hang up.

"What Dallas?!" Her tone was too snappy for my liking especially when she was being selfish, thinking only of herself.

She didn't know a damn thing about what was going on on my end and didn't bother to ask either.

"Chill with that attitude shit Shia. Seriously." She had me snapping right along her, which I was trying to avoid.

But my emotions were at an all-time high just from dealing with my mother's sickness and then the one female I couldn't help *but* be drawn to was acting an ass.

"That's your problem slim. You catch these little attitudes left and right. I'm not gon' tolerate that shit." I said, speaking with my hand as if she was in front of me.

"Sorry." She mumbled, almost inaudible but I caught her apology.

I nodded, "Yea, you good but just chill out. That's all I'm saying. You didn't even let me finish. I'm with my fam right now but I got you later. I'll definitely make sure to come lay up with you for the night. So be up."

"Okay. I'm really sorry though Dallas."

Now she was making me feel bad for snapping at her the way I did. But that was nothing compared to how I've done to other females.

The sound of the glass door sliding open had me turning my head around, focusing on the oldest out of the twins: Yuri. I pulled the phone down from my ear, nodding to acknowledge her presence.

"Sup baby?"

"Uncle Dally, Mommy said come eat before your food gets cold."

Her sweet, angelic voice could have the hardest nigga's heart melting at every word.

I smiled, "Tell your mother I'm coming."

She nodded, smiling before closing the door. Bringing the phone back to my ear, my smile never left. My nieces just had that special affect on me, which I loved. They could put me in the best mood even after a bad day.

Thank you, God, for my babies.

"Bae," I called to her.

"I'm still here."

"I'll be there..." I pulled the phone away to look at the time, "No later than 10, ight?"

"Okay. I'll be waiting for you."

March 22, 2016: Fort Washington, MD

Mace
<u>Sent</u>
Kris is back in rehab.

Before I had the chance to put my phone down, it was ringing with an incoming call from Mace.

"What you mean she's back in rehab?!"

"Just like I said... she's back in rehab."

I didn't want to believe it either, but it was bound to happen - I knew there was no way she was going to be sober after that tragedy. Somewhere deep down, I was just hoping that she'd be strong enough to fight through it.

I guess not.

He released a heavy sigh, "Damn man," He mumbled.

In this moment, we were sharing the same sentiments towards this situation. We all came out of rehab with high hopes that we'd stay clean. It was just unfortunate that Kris had to undergo finding the love of her life dead, in the one place they called home. The police have yet to find the person behind Cole's death which made the situation even worst; he deserved justice.

"FUCK DAWG!"

His sudden yelling got a jump out of me, holding my chest.

"Mace." I softly said.

He smacked his lips, "Yea man."

I could hear the pain in his voice.
I felt the exact thing.
I was hurting as well.

Kris and Mace bickered like siblings but the one thing I did know was how much we cared for one another. I never would've imagined me losing Mae bringing me closer to two beautiful individuals - two people, I wanted nothing but the best for.
"She wants us to come visit."
"Shit, we were showing face even if she didn't want us to. When you wanna go up there?"
I shrugged as if he could see me.
"I dunno."
I really didn't. I was actually scared to return to that place. Bad memories. And now for me to be the one visiting was one of the weirdest feelings ever, but I'd do it for Kris.
"Ight. I already see I'm going to have to make the decision for the both of us. What you doing Friday? I can come get you round uhh..."
Friday? That was two days away.
"Is 3 cool?"
I couldn't back out now.
"Yea. That's fine. I'll be ready."
"Ight boo. Cool. Be ready ma. I gotta go, though. Hitting the streets with ma dukes."
A smile graced my lips knowing how much love he held for his mother. I admired their bond. The way he talked about her. They were best friends, and I was jealous. Jealous because I never got the chance to experience that with my own mother. I can't even say I love the woman, honestly. But I know the love is there because she is my mother, half of the reason for my existence.

Bitch.

"Have fun. Tell her I said hey!"
He laughed, "I will. She keeps begging to meet you. Wants you to come over for dinner one night."
When we were in rehab, I would talk to her through Mace whenever he'd call home. She grew a liking to me I guess from hearing

him talk so highly of me. That's because he was called himself crushing on me. In my eyes, we were nothing but friends. Nothing more, nothing less.

I smiled, "I'd love that. Just lemme know when and I'll get Blake to bring me.

The clinking of our forks hitting the plates was the only thing being heard before my mother broke the silence.

"So baby... Girlfriend?"

My brow tipped, giving her a ridiculous look. Those meds must be getting to her. She knows damn well I don't do girlfriends. Titles bring way too many complications; I'm good on that.

"What you talking bout Ma?" I questioned, shoving a forkful of mashed potatoes in my mouth.

Devyn did the damn thing with dinner tonight: fried chicken, mashed potatoes, and collards.

She gave me a teasing smile, "You know what I'm talking about. Whoever has been giving you this glow lately." She responded, using air quotes to emphasize 'glow' earning a snort from me.

"Mommy, tell Yani to leave my food alone." Yuri whined, tilting her head back in exaggeration.

I fixed my hues on my nieces sitting across from me as Devyn reached over to pop Yani's hand that was reaching into Yuri's plate.

She threw a scolding finger her way, "Stop messing with your sister's food. Eat your own."

I shook my head at my nieces bickering antics before slowly bringing my eyes back to my mother who had the biggest smile.

I chuckled, "What you smiling for woman?"

"You baby. I know you're involved with someone. So..." She placed her folded arms on the table, "Tell me about her."

I rolled my eyes, suddenly feeling funny at the thought of Shia. That damn girl had the ability to have control of me, even at a distance. Using my fork to stab at some greens before eating it, I kept my eyes on my food.

"She's nobody Ma," I shifted my gaze to her.

"Aww, so it is somebody?" Her tone was pretty excited offering me a tipped brow.

My mother always had this habit of asking me when I would be giving her the next grand baby. She stressed how much she loved witnessing me interact with Yani and Yuri. That's different; they're my nieces. I don't know how I'd be with a child of my own. 30 was right around the corner and the thought of creating a little me wasn't first on my list.

Unfortunately, it was first on my mother's.

I caught Devyn's gaze who was wearing a teasing smirk as well. "Yea baby brother. Who is she?"

I smacked my lips, hand going in the air, "And here you go."

She giggled, putting her hands up in surrender causing me to smile.

I looked between the both of them.

"Ight. Y'all got me. I've been chilling with this one lady. She's cool... Nothing serious."

I attempted to downplay whatever it was developing between me and Shia. Whatever brewing between us was serious, very at that, but I wasn't going to relay that to the two nosey women questioning me. It was difficult for me to explain how she made me feel but, I couldn't shake her. I'd never had a female on my mind constantly especially after just two weeks.

Shit was crazy.

It was even crazier that I relished in the feeling of wanting her... Wanting her near me.

March 22, 2016: Fort Washington, MD

Tucking my bottom lip tight between my teeth, my eyes ogled the stunning, chocolate physique belonging to Shia. Got damn. This girl was beautiful. My hand came in contact with the door frame, cocking my head to the side as I continued admiring her beautiful face and body.

"Hey baby." My voice came out low and husky which I knew was exciting her by how quick she bit into her lip.

My nose turned up once really focusing on the little bit of material covering her private parts. She was covered in a pair of black Calvin Klein boxer briefs with a gray waistband along with an Adidas gray crop top and toes out. My attention stayed on her feet a little longer than expected, appreciating how cute they were. I didn't have a foot fetish or anything but women with cute feet was a plus in my book.

She sighed, opening the door wider, "Dallas..." She voiced as if she was trying to catch her breath causing me to smirk.

My smile grew as she stepped to the side with me still admiring her amazing frame, biting even harder into my lip. I adjusted myself while watching Shia close the door before her brown hues fixed on me.

"Stop eye fucking me," She dryly said, pushing past me as I fell in tow.

I focused on the movement of her phat ass with every stride, imagining I was deep between her cheeks. This girl was driving me fuckin' crazy. Closing the door behind me, I slipped out of my shoes kicking them to the side near her dresser. My lustful gaze remained on her as she crawled into the bed, paying me no mind while getting comfortable under the covers.

"You feeling ight?" I questioned, throwing my shirt on the chair leaving me in my white wife beater.

Normally, I wasn't the type to spend the night but a nigga was exhausted and the last thing on my mind was going home. Shia wanted me here so I'm pretty sure she didn't care if I'd crash as well.

"I'm cool," She softly responded even though I knew otherwise.

Slowly, I trekked my way towards her as her brown gaze followed my every move. There was nothing but lust twirling in her hues. The sexual tension that settles whenever we're in each other's presence grows every time. The corner of my lips twisted into my infamous crooked smile, earning a blush from her. She giggled as I flipped the covers back to join her. I sighed, softly caressing the side of her face holding her intense gaze.

Something was on her mind but I didn't want to push her to speak on it by any means.

"Thanks for coming Dallas." She softly spoke causing me to turn my nose up slightly, using my thumb to rub her cheek.

"I told you I was coming through bae. Thanks for waiting on a nigga."

She nodded before quickly moving her body towards me, wrapping her arms around me tightly and nuzzling her face into my chest. My nostrils welcomed her intoxicating scent; whatever she had on was making me hard. Being this close to her was becoming too overwhelming. I can't lie as if I didn't want to be balls deep into her because I would love to be. The thing is, I have way more respect for Shia and rather wait for when the time is right; I don't think our moment presented itself yet. I wasn't into rushing anything with Shia because whatever this was, I wanted it to be a good outcome.

Along with titles, sex complicated things too.

We already had enough on our hands so me sliding in her sounded like a good idea, but I knew it wasn't right for us right now.

"I missed you." Her words came out muffled as her warm breath soaked into the thin material of my wife beater.

Every little thing she was doing was making me *that* much harder.

My eyes fell on the ceiling, hands roaming her ample ass forcing a small moan from her, "Shy. Don't be doing that shit man." I smacked my lips, head slightly falling back as she giggled.

"What I dooo?" She whined earning a grunt from me.

I swear. Everything she was doing was sexy as shit.

I frowned once feeling a light punch to my chest as her intense gaze locked on me, "I told you that I missed you nigga." She hissed, making my smirk grow into a big smile.

My voice dropped an octave as I cleared my throat, "I missed you too bae." I continued rubbing on her ass as her fingers trailed up and down my arm, sending chills throughout my being.

I placed a gentle kiss on her forehead as her eyes locked with mine, me placing a soft kiss upon her plump lips. Her hand gripped my chin coming in for another kiss. This one being more passion-filled, hungry. Her tongue snaked into my mouth as I savored the sweet taste of her. I gripped the back of her neck, deepening the kiss before slowly pulling away. My lips hovered over hers for a second making sure to keep our foreheads connected even though our lips weren't.

Her brown orbs bored into mine, "Dallas..."

"Yea bae?" I rubbed her waist.

"Kris is back in rehab." Her gaze left mines, looking down.

Using my index finger, I tilted her head up to look at me, "And my mother has lupus."

Book IX.

March 22, 2016: Fort Washington, MD

Lupus. The one word I dreaded hearing. The one thing that took the only parent that mattered to me. My Daddy. Unwillingly, tears began forming at the brim of my lids as I quickly sat up. Using the side of my hands, I wiped at my eyes.

I spent my days throwing my father in the back of my mind. Off one word alone, he was brought to the forefront. That one word being the sickness that sent him to an early grave.

He was only 42 when he was snatched from me, leaving me absolutely devastated. Leaving me weak and willing to do any and everything to ease the pain. Making me even more vulnerable to the sins of the world. Making it that much easier for me to start experimenting with drugs, leading to me falling in love with heroin.

The gentle touch of Dallas' hand to my back forced my attention on him, concern etched across his handsome face particularly those eyebrows. Those eyebrows I found amazingly beautiful especially since he strongly expressed himself through them. Any look he gave me had to follow with some sort of movement of his brows, which was a complete turn-on by the way. He'd probably grown so accustomed to it that he had no clue how much he does it, and how attractive it was.

He licked his pouty lips leaving a wet sheen, "What's wrong Shy?" His brows fell deeper as his concern grew stronger at my sudden breakdown.

I wasn't expecting it either. Hearing that one word just reminded me of the pain I felt when my entire life changed. I was never the same after I witnessed my father take his last breath.

Tearing my brown hues from his, I focused on my fiddling fingers searching for my words. I knew I had to elaborate on my unanticipated tears but when I parted my lips to speak, I got choked up. My body slowly relaxed from Dallas rubbing circles into my back.

"Talk to me, baby. Please." His voice was gentle and laced with concern.

"My father had it," I muttered, not being able to look him in the eyes.

That was the only thing I could gather myself to say.

My father had it.

A brief silence fell over us before a sigh exited his body, forcing my head towards him. A gloomy expression marred his beautiful face, shaking his head. I know he caught on to me using past tense in reference to my father which explained the same face everyone was giving me during the funeral. I hated people feeling sorry for me.

"Damn Shy. So sorry to hear that."

I nodded, looking away from him focusing on nothing in particular. I just couldn't take keeping any type of eye contact with him, in fear that I'd offer up my body because I'm in such an emotional state. The sexual tension was obvious between us but if I came on to him right now, it'd be for all the wrong reasons. Something like a quick fix just to get me out of my head. And I'm trying to get better as an individual so I couldn't fall back into my "addict" ways - always looking for a quick fix. I need to learn how to cope on my own, without the drug.

Unfortunately, Dallas was slowly but surely becoming my new drug. Which honestly is scaring the hell out of me because I'm gaining a new addiction.

"I just don't understand why my father had to die," I spat out, anger taking over.

The anger from that day was beginning to hit me. Out of all the fathers in the world, mine had to be taken? When there were kids out here who didn't appreciate their parents for shit and here I was, fatherless.

"You know what baby. I used to wonder the same thing when I lost Aaron..."

Never had he once mentioned the name of his best friend to me. That alone got my undivided attention as I turned to face him, him taking a hold of my hand. He looked me deeply in my eyes as if he was searching for something. His brows furrowed together meeting in the middle of his head, giving off a tensed expression.

"It's crazy cause I was mad..." He shook his head, "Real live mad with God, for awhile."

I rolled my eyes at his reference to God. I lost every piece of faith I had after losing my father. I haven't been able to believe in im ever since.

"That was until I realized that he wasn't mine to keep. None of us are. We're all simply put here to bless one another. From the beginning to the end, we belong to God. We all have to return to Him so this..." His index finger moved in a circular motion. "Is all just temporary. Our bodies... are temporary. But our spirits will live forever so I know it hurts baby, but he's with you. Always. God gives His toughest battles to His strongest soldiers."

I found that hard to believe because clearly, I wasn't strong enough, turning to drugs and all.

"I don't think He's real."

Dallas' eyes widened, head moving back with a smirk settling on his face, "That's because He hasn't got a hold of you yet Shy. I've lost my faith before but trust me when I say, God has a funny way of bringing you back to Him."

I chewed on the inside of my cheek, eyes scanning my room before fixing back on him.

"I hear you," I muttered, not really interested in the conversation any longer, growing uncomfortable by the seconds.

God just wasn't something I believed in anymore.

He must've felt my energy shift because he simply nodded, "You still need the light?"

Shaking my head, I leaned forward to bring the covers up to my chin sinking further down into the bed while keeping my undivided attention on the beautiful specimen across the room. I blinked a few times allowing my eyes to adjust to the darkness, with the little bit of street light peeking through the windows. A jolt shot to my center once catching his fiery gaze as he stepped into the light, showing off his sharp features.

Even in the dark, he was beautiful. A smirk tugged at his pouty lips before curving into that sexy crooked smile of his. Every little thing he was doing was beginning to create a pool between my thighs, causing my heartbeat to pick up.

"Move over," I frowned once feeling him tap my arm before scooting over to give him enough space. "Thank you." My heart fluttered at his manners as he got comfortable next to me.

Getting comfortable on my side resting my cheek on my hands, I admired his stunning side profile. Dallas cleared his throat before licking his lips, "Wassup bae?" His voice held a hint of raspiness, sending chills through my body. Slowly he looked my way making the existing butterflies flutter even more. I giggled, loving how his dimples were making themselves known as he smiled.

"You all staring n' shit…" He muttered, making me blush at the devious smirk tugging at his lips.

A jolt flew to my wet center as he looked to me, back resting against the headboard. His eyes scanned over my frame before tipping his brow, "You like something you see?"

The sexy voice he was putting on along with his lustful brown eyes was sending my hormones into overdrive.

I nodded, "Yea." I softly responded, not even sure where that came from.

There was no point in me lying to him - he already knew. He was definitely worth looking at and not one second would I get tired of it. Dallas chuckled while shaking his head, smacking his lips. He grunted before descending his body into the bed, turning on his side to face me.

"Go to sleep Shy."

March 25, 2016: Washington, DC

"Come on Shy. It's just Kris, ma."

He made it seem like this was easy, coming back to the place that haunted me. I never thought I'd be back here so soon especially visiting a friend that I hoped would stay clean. This shit was slowly but surely killing me on the inside; I was even scared to see how she looked. Frowning, I watched Mace who stood by the front door waiting for me. We'd got here not too long ago but honestly, it took Mace about five minutes just to get me out of the car and now my feet felt stuck to the ground.

I don't want to go in there.

Mace smacked his lips before trekking my way, face softening in the process. I knew he was growing irritated with me but I also knew that he'd make sure I was comfortable before anything. My body somewhat relaxed once he took a hold of my hands with his piercing green hues boring into my brown ones.

"Boo, you good. I got you. We got a friend in there that needs us more than anything. It might not seem like it but I'm fucked up just like you coming back here, but I know Kris would do it for us. We all got each other. She can't forget that she has us two in her corner."

Somehow, his words managed to relieve just enough tension from my frame which had my feet moving along with his. His grip on my hand tightened as we approached the glass double doors. I took a deep breath as his hand connected with the handle. A wave of chills rushed through me once he looked my way.

His head tilted down slightly with his brows rising to the top of his head, "You ready Shy?"

I bit my lip before shrugging, "I have no other choice."

The shaking of my leg ceased once Mace's cold hand brought it to a stop. He chuckled, "Chill Shy, it's just Kr—" My brows furrowed from him stopping mid-sentence. I noticed how the corners of his lips began forming into a smile with his piercing orbs focused behind me.

At that moment I knew exactly who he was looking at. Her soft voice entered the air sending chills down my spine as Mace rose to his feet, rounding me. I took myself by surprise once I began rising to my feet, turning slowly around. My heart jumped at the sight of Mace squeezing Kris as if he was holding on for dear life, her reciprocating the tight embrace.

"Why you standing over there?"

Being deeply in thought, I had no clue she was looking at me with Mace by her side - she looked gorgeous. I was expecting her to look as if she was crying all day but there were no tear stains in sight. Matter of fact, her skin looked flawless. Kris' smile grew as my feet swiftly moved across the tile before colliding my body with hers. From her hug alone, I could tell that she missed me and I missed her just as much. We released at the same time, looking each other over before stepping back in for another hug.

Mace smacked his lips, "So y'all really gon' hug the entire time?"

I rolled my eyes while Kris smacked her lips, "Can you shut up Mace?" She hissed, throwing a playful mean mug his way.

That stupid smirk when he was about to say something smart worked its way to his pink, full lips. He ran his hand down his mouth with his thumb and index fingers specifically paying attention to the corners.

"Yeaaa..." Kris dragged, "Get that shit off your lip." She teased.

I giggled at how playful she was today; I guess seeing us was something she really needed. Shaking my head, I began moving towards the table as they started bickering back and forth. I remember how annoyed I used to get by their back and forth but now find it pretty amusing.

Mace would say how he was crushing on me when I truly felt otherwise; I believe Kris was the one he wanted.

"With them little ass tennis balls for titties. Fuck outta here." He scoffed while waving her off, smirk still playing at his lips.

Kris gasped before reaching across the table to hit his chest, laughing. She looked down grabbing her boobs before looking back up at us. "I like my titties just fine. Thank you," She spoke confidently, smiling.

I was beyond amazed at the good spirit she was in. Was it really just off our visit alone? If so, we definitely needed to bless her with our presence more often.

I leaned forward resting my elbows on the table, taking her in fully. She blushed while smiling at me, "What?" She questioned, cheeks growing red by the seconds.

"Your hair. It looks bomb," I complimented as I caught Mace crossing his eyes in my peripheral, mumbling some bullshit.

Her smile grew wider as her fingers raked through her black, bone straight hair. I loved her long hair. It freely fell upon her shoulders and back, stopping just below her breasts. It was rare seeing females wear their natural hair and I loved that Kris never wore weave.

"I did it last night. Thanks Shy. So..." She looked back and forth between us, "How are y'all?"

My face twisted up at her question seeing as though she was the one back in rehab. That question was one we should be asking her.

"How are we? Girl, how are you? How you holding up, ma?" Mace asked leaning forward before placing his elbows on the table.

My eyes scanned over Kris' visage as her nose slightly scrunched up before a deep sigh passed through her thin, pursed lips. Silently we watched how she used her right hand to rake through her tresses, looking away. Narrowing my hues on her side profile, I noticed that her eyes were beginning to water as her bottom lip flew between her teeth. Out of my peripheral, I saw Mace take a hold of her hand forcing her attention back towards us. Tears slowly cascaded down her rosy cheeks as she began nodding her head.

"I-I'm managing."

My brows frowned at the pain in her voice as I reached to grab her other hand. The corners of her lips turned upward offering us a weak smile which warmed my heart.

"I know this shit not easy Kris but we got you. Just get better cause we can't lose you slim. We in this shit together." Mace soothed as I found comfort in his words as well.

I wasn't expecting him to be the glue to hold us together. But he was and I loved it.

Kris nodded, looking my way through teary eyes before looking to Mace. Simultaneously she squeezed our hands sending a jolt to my heart.

"I love y'all. Thank you so much for being here for me cause..." Her voice trailed off as she looked down at our connected hands. She sniffed before looking back up, "He was my everything. I never felt this bad in my life." Tears began descending quicker down her blood filled cheeks causing me to frown, pain rapidly filling my chest.

This was so fuckin' hard to witness.

It was as if Mace and I were thinking the same thing because we both rose together, rounding the table to embrace Kris. With Mace in front of her and me behind her, we squeezed her just enough so she could feel our love for her. I *needed* Kris to know that we were here; she *needed* to know that we loved her.

I lacked love in areas of my life and I'm grateful that I know how to give it and allow it in as well.

March 25, 2016: Uptown, Washington, DC

My pouty lips connected with the foreheads of my nieces as Yani remained tucked under my left arm on the inside of the couch with Yuri laid out on my chest. They had me watching *Frozen* which was their favorite movie at the moment, meaning we watched it every single time I was with them. Due to this being my day off, I decided to spend some time with my babies. After being laid up with Ma talking about everything, she eventually fell asleep on me. Even though I tried to maneuver my way around Shia, she always found her way back to her name. While talking about how we met, I accidentally slipped up and said her name which had the biggest smile spreading across Ma's face. She finally had a name to the "mystery girl" and wouldn't let up; she even suggested that I bring her over for dinner.

I didn't know how to feel about that.

There was nothing I wanted more than for Shia to meet my family but then again I've never done anything like this before. Feeling strongly about a female who wasn't my babies, mother, or sister was something that didn't happen. I didn't even have female friends because the majority of the time, they didn't know how to be just a friend. Plus, I wasn't trying to rush things between us. Who knows if Shia would be around months from now? And then I'd introduced her to the only people that mattered to me. It was something I definitely had to put thought into; I wasn't too sold on the idea as of right now.

The sound of keys hitting the table had my eyes averting from my phone to my sister, looking over my shoulder. I greeted her with a head nod as her slim, tall frame came into view blocking the TV as the *Frozen* credits rolled up the screen.

"Aww," She cooed while bringing her phone into view.

I smacked my lips once noticing what she was doing, "Man, gon' with that camera Dev."

Any chance she got to snap a quick photo of me and the girls, she took advantage of it. They always came out nice but Devyn was obsessed with us; the shit was scary. Crossing my eyes, I twisted my lips as she continued to snap away.

"You done nigga?"

She rolled her eyes before putting her phone on the coffee table, sighing and plopping in Ma's favorite seat.

"Tired?"

She yawned, "Tired not even the word. I had so many clients today." I nodded, catching her contagious yawn.

Devyn was one of the top hair stylists in our area right now, working at the most known salon too. Growing up, she always shared her dreams of becoming a hair stylist and I'm happy she was doing everything she talked about. For a couple of months now, she'd been networking and trying to get involved with the right people and I was beyond proud of my sister. Devyn was really out here making a name for herself and I know that all her hard work was going to pay off sooner than later.

With patience comes all good things.

My arms tightened on Yuri and Yani as I readjusted myself before looking to their mother.

"Were they good?" Devyn asked while leaning forward to grab her phone.

I caught her gaze as she looked at me before focusing back on her phone. I ran my hand over my face, "Come on slim. They were with Uncle D. Their asses better been good."

She giggled while rising to her feet, "Whatever nigga. I'm about to put them down. I'm pretty sure you wanna get out of here."

Once passing Yuri off, I made sure not to wake Yani as I moved her tiny frame towards the center of my body rising to my feet. After placing Yani in her bed, I trekked towards Devyn bringing her body into mines before placing a kiss on her forehead.

"Aight ugly, I love you." She voiced as I stood in the threshold of the doorway, looking back to her.

"I love you more ugly son."

She burst out in laughter making me chuckle as well, "Bye nigga!"

March 25, 2016: Camp Springs, MD

Rubbing my palm over my bare chest, I moved out of my steam filled bathroom walking around in all my glory. This was one of the things I enjoyed most about having my own place - being butt ass naked. Shit felt great. My stomach grumbled even louder forcing my lips into a frown as I sat on the side of my bed grabbing my phone. Scratching my head, I scrolled through my contacts landing on her name.

Shia
<u>Sent</u>
Bae. Get dressed.

A nigga couldn't take another second not eating anything and I'd be more than happy for Shia to accompany me to lunch plus, I missed her pretty ass face. It's been an entire week since I seen that face of hers.

Shia
<u>Received</u>
Trying to adultnap me?

I chuckled, shaking my head while typing my response.

Shia
<u>Sent</u>
Lol. Tf. Just get dressed girl.
I'll see you in 20

Shia
<u>Received</u>
Demanding ass
I'll be ready handsome face.

March 25, 2016: Falls Church, VA – *Red Lobster*
Tension settled within my brows as my fiery gaze remained on his retreating back. Wetting my lips, I rubbed my thumb across my bottom one as my scowl grew deeper before parting my lips to speak.
"I want another waiter," I dryly stated, watching him disappear into the kitchen before looking to her.

Tucking my lip between my teeth, I admired her flawless chocolate skin in her colorful outfit. Every time I'd see her, she was wearing something simple so witnessing her in bright clothes made her even more appealing to look at. She was so damn beautiful; it didn't make any sense. The pink, sheer top draped loosely over her torso exposing her chocolate cleavage just enough but not too much. It was tucked into an olive green Aztec patterned skirt that stopped mid-thigh showcasing her thick thighs. Her hair held a bunch of life today; it was something I wasn't used to but I loved it. A side part sat on the left side of her head as her natural, kinky hair was thrown to the right side of her face leaving some falling down her back as well.

I loved a woman in her natural state - and Shia didn't wear make-up which made her even more attractive.

Her nude glossed lips formed into a wide smile as she continued laughing at my expense - I didn't find shit funny. Placing my elbows on the table, I leaned forward slightly twisting my lips while admiring her beauty. The way her eyes squinted together while laughing. The way her hand gravitated towards her mouth to stifle her giggles because we were in public. She was gorgeous and for the past 20 minutes we been here, I couldn't tear my eyes from that face of hers.

"Why you want another waiter Dallas?" She questioned while sipping her raspberry lemonade, already knowing exactly why someone else should be serving us.

I smacked my lips tilting my head to the side, "You already know why I want another one."

I reached out to grab my glass while holding her intense gaze, sipping from my straw. "That nigga was damn near eye fucking you."

I couldn't help the smile that developed on my lips once hearing her cute laugh again. A smirk pulled at my pouty lips as her brown hues bored right back into mine, sending chills down my spine.

She's fuckin' beautiful.

"He wasn't eye fucking me, Dallas. You're over-exaggerating sweets." She fanned me off, rolling her eyes before sipping from her drink again.

I shook my head while leaning back into the booth seat, "Naw baby. He was. He definitely was."

There those damn eyes go rolling again. It was doing nothing but turning me on, thinking of all the ways *we* could be the reason behind them eyes rolling. My eyes scanned the room just out of habit; I always had to be fully aware of my surroundings.

I observed as she raked her fingers through her hair as her eyes danced around the room, head softly bobbing to the music that was playing lowly. Clasping my hands together, I leaned forward narrowing my gaze on her side profile.

"Why are you staring?" She softly questioned, still looking off before locking her fiery gaze on me.

I never could explain the looks she gave me but every time her eyes landed on me, it brought this weird feeling to my body. It was something no female could ever make me feel, even Gizelle. Wetting my lips, my hues scanned over her gorgeous features as her lips began contorting into a full blown smile earning a laugh from me.

"What you smiling for?"

"You," She shot back just as quick.

My head went back with my face twisting up at her vague response.

"Me? I didn't say anything to make you smile."

Her smile grew wider as if it wasn't already wide enough. "You didn't have to. Just looking at you alone is enough."

To say I felt like a bitch right now would be an understatement. Shia happened to have this strong hold on me and I barely knew anything about her. All I know is that she's once where I used to be and just trying to stay strong enough to remain clean.

Smirking, I raised my hand to my chin rubbing it softly while holding her gaze. "Is that right baby?"

My dick jumped once seeing her bite into her plump bottom lip, lust swirling through those almond shaped eyes. A small grunt invaded my throat as I moved in the seat, attempting to get me and him comfortable. The more I had Shia in my personal space made my sexual attraction for her grow even more. My eyes gravitated towards her cleavage but were quickly forced back on her face once her hand covered that area as she laughed. My hands flew up in surrender mode once seeing the shocked expression plastered on her face, still laughing off her expression alone.

"Stop looking at my titties Dallas." A playful smirk still played at her lips keeping the smile on mine.

"I can't help it..." My index finger pointed towards her cleavage before shrugging. "I mean. They're all out on display n' shit. You knew what you were doing…" My voice trailed off as I twisted my lips earning a giggle from her.

She playfully rolled her eyes, "Whatever…" She mumbled even though I caught the simple response. "But honestly Dallas, I could look at you all day. You're handsome."

This girl had me feeling like putty - I felt like a smooth bitch right now. It should be me having her blushing but the reality was, she had my face hot as shit.

"Thank you, baby. You're just as beautiful. As if you already don't know."

Clearing my throat, I focused on that nigga coming our way with I'm assuming our food. I kissed my teeth, locking my eyes back on her.

"He's coming back, isn't he?"

My scowl grew deeper at how teasingly she questioned me as if this all was a joke to her. Shia thought I was playing but I was serious when I said that I didn't appreciate how that nigga was looking at her. How are you here to service the both of us but yet keep your attention on just the female? The female that I'm here with. Niggas disrespectful as shit.

I didn't respond. I just kept my intense gaze on him until he made it to our table.

I sized him up as he placed my plate in front of me. As much as I didn't want to thank him due to his disrespectfulness, I still exercised my manners. My mother taught me better than that. Twisting my lips, I grew more annoyed watching Shia flash these flirtatious smiles as if I wasn't sitting right across from her. I gave him a once-over as he continued laughing and exchanging small words with her.

The fuck.

"Ight bruh. You good. We good." At this point, I had to shoo his ass off because clearly, he didn't know boundaries. Knowing my quick temper, I chose to play it cool not wanting Shia to witness that side of me.

I matched his mug as he sized me up as well, not intimidating me one bit. I watched as he slowly looked to Shia before parting his lips to speak as I cut him off just as quick.

"I said we good bruh. You being all disrespectful n' shit," I hissed as his face twisted up at my comment.

Catching Shia's gaze, I noticed how she looked taken aback by my statement but I was serious. Both she and I knew how disrespectful the nigga was being but I already knew I was going to be the one to voice how I felt, not her. Honestly, the nigga needed to get the fuck from our table. He sized me up once again before looking back to Shia.

"Let me know if you need anything," He voiced before giving me one last look earning a chuckle from me.

This nigga had balls.

"Nigga not getting a tip for shit and you better not give him one either." I said, cutting into my steak before stabbing a piece and eating it.

Shia giggled while twirling her fork into the Cajun Chicken Linguini Alfredo she decided on. Chewing my food, my gaze didn't pull from her beautiful visage as she shook her head while wrapping her lips around the fork.

"You didn't have to do all of that Dallas. He was being nice."

I kissed my teeth at her attempt to convince me otherwise. The nigga was flirting with her, simple as that, and she was feeding into it. She's disrespectful as well. Cute ass.

"Naw. You already know that wasn't him being nice..." I said using air quotes to emphasize this nice word she chose to use. "Nigga was being disrespectful. Here I am on a date with you and he's acting as if I'm not sitting right here. Like I said before, the nigga disrespectful ass not getting a tip." I finished off, stuffing a forkful of mashed potatoes in my mouth.

I watched as she ran her tongue over her teeth before a sexy grin settled upon her face, turning me on. Every little thing she did with her face had my shit going haywire. Grabbing her napkin, Shia wiped her mouth of the alfredo sauce before folding her arms across her chest perking those pretty titties up more. Still devouring my food, I licked my lips before looking up to her as chills shot down my spine. Her brown orbs narrowed on me, leaving me confused on why she wasn't eating but instead ogling me.

My lips contorted into my infamous crooked smirk. "Wassup baby? Them eyes of yours never can stay off a nigga, huh?" I chuckled at the amused expression appearing on her face.

Shia continued to stare, not saying a word. It was like she was looking at my soul. She was searching for something. I just didn't know exactly what it was. Leaning back, I wiped my mouth as a small sigh escaped my lips. My brown hues danced up and down her upper half before locking into her gaze.

"What are we doing Dallas?"

My brows furrowed, thrown completely off by her random question.

What are we doing Dallas?

The thing is I've never put any thought into what we had going on. All I know is that I appreciated the time spent with her and didn't want to rush anything. Feeling even an ounce of care for a female that wasn't my family was foreign to me. Having her around was throwing me off but at the same token, it made me the happiest guy just to be in her presence. I rubbed my hands against my distressed black jeans tilting my head to the side trying to come up with a response.

I didn't want to say anything stupid.

I sighed, "I don't even know, honestly. I'm just going with the flow. You dealing with shit as well as me but all I know is that I enjoy every moment spent with you."

A smile slowly crept to her full lips as she picked up her fork, twirling it back into her pasta.

"So wassup? How you feeling? What you want us to be doing?"

My eyes caught the gaze of a female waitress as I signaled for her to come over. Her bright smile had one forming on my lips as well. My index finger bounced back and forth between the both of us, "Can we get two boxes please?"

"Sure!" Her high pitched voice replied as she turned on her heels to disappear towards the kitchen.

"How you know I wasn't going to eat all my food?"

My nose scrunched up as I looked to her, "Because I know you're full. Shit. I am, but are you going to answer my question?" I questioned while taking a sip of my drink.

She giggled as her eyes scanned the room before looking at me. I could tell my question made her nervous by the way she was acting all giddy like a little girl. It was really cute to witness her like this though.

Outstretching my hand, I grabbed hers with my thumbs soothingly rubbing the back of her palms.

My eyes focused in on how her chest rose and fell letting out a deep sigh. "I don't want us to be doing anything. I just want whatever *this* is that is developing... to be genuine. I really like being around you Dallas and I don't want anything dumb to mess things up."

My brow tipped, "Dumb as innn..." I dragged, hoping she'd elaborate more on what she meant.

"Meaning I don't have the time nor stable feelings for you to be toying with me. I'm fresh out of rehab and I truly enjoy your presence as well, but I won't tolerate bullshit. I'm trying to be a better person and if you're just another nigga that's going to hold me back, I'll leave this where it's at now."

My mouth fell slightly agape with my brows still meeting in the middle of my forehead as I scanned her face. We both were fully aware of the strong connection between us and the shit was scary. I sighed letting go of her hands before running them over my face.

"The thing about all this is that I don't like my feelings being fucked with so that's the last thing on my mind baby. I can't sit here and tell you how this is going to end but just know, you don't have to worry about being played with..." My lip twitched as I looked around, growing more nervous with the fact I was sitting here expressing myself to a female. "This shit rare for me. I've never had a female that actually had me considering building something but with you, I don't know what it is. All I know is that I've never felt this shit before and it's scaring me. But I'm scared enough to know that I don't want to miss out on whatever this is."

March 25, 2016: Fort Washington, MD

Sighing, my brown hues scanned the scenery through the wet passenger window as the cold air flowing through the vent fanned against my face. A small hiss broke through my plump lips to the touch of Dallas' cold palm coming in contact with my flesh, forcing my eyes on him. Narrowing my hues, I admired how his bone structure was perfectly sharp as he comfortably looked relaxed driving with one hand. This man was handsome beyond words, seriously. My eyes averted to his rubbing hand on my thigh causing my nose to scrunch up from the gesture. It wasn't that I didn't like it because I didn't mind but it was surfacing a new set of hormones that I wanted to get rid of. I despised the way Dallas made me feel but all at the same time, I was angry because I adored how I felt about him as well.

My nose twitched at the sound of him clearing his throat. "Shy." His voice was soft, making the slowing rain louder than him.

I swiftly looked his way, scanning over his side profile as his attention never tore from the road.

"Yea?" I responded, wondering what was on his mind.

Resting my elbow on the armrest of the door, I kept my eyes on him as he cut his brown orbs at me giving off that sexy smirk like always. Dallas began nodding his head to the radio music softly playing as he kept a suitable speed on the wet road.

"How did the visit with Kris go?"

My heart jumped at the mention of her name - I wasn't expecting him to care about how our visit went. I know I made a big deal out of it this morning but since it ended well, I wasn't really tripping. But now with him bringing it up, it made a bunch of unwanted emotions hit me at once.

I'd rather not speak on it.

Looking away at nothing, in particular, I felt a short calm fall over me once feeling Dallas' hand brush against mine as he reached for the gear shift, putting the car in park. As I looked out the window, I noticed that we were now in front of my house. Time seemed to fly seeing as though I didn't keep up with the route he took; I was just enjoying the ride. Locking into his chocolate gaze, my chest somewhat tightened as he looked at me through heavy lids.

"I can spend the rest of my rainy day with you, baby?" My stomach flipped as his words came out low and husky, giving off the sexiest tone ever.

Without him knowing, he was making me want to throw all my morals out the window and just jump on him and have my way. The only response he got from me was a head nod since I was unable to find my words. I bit hard into my lip enjoying him watch me. I know he feels this between us. The air was thick.

He chuckled, "You always want to act like a fake mute." He teased while resting the side of his face on the headrest keeping his hues fixated on me.

Suddenly I became nervous under his lazy, intense gaze. He wasn't trying to look good but in every aspect, he was damn gorgeous without attempting. I appreciated being able to be in this man's presence. His brows rose as if he was growing impatient with my silence forcing a giggle from me.

"You can stay Dallas."

He smiled showcasing those beautiful dimples. "Aww, you found your words, Shy?"

I playfully rolled my eyes while grabbing the door handle but was stopped once feeling his hand on top of mines, face closer than ever. His breathing was slow and steady as his lips remained in kissing reach with him staring deeply into my eyes.

Why was every moment spent with him so intense?

Damn you, Dallas.

My breath hitched in my throat as he inched forward, lips almost grazing mine. I'd be damned if I broke eye contact first; I felt like that's what he wanted. From being around Dallas lately, I've noticed that he loved to be in control but tonight, I wasn't going to give him that satisfaction.

"Fuck you tryna run for?" With every word, his breath bounced against my lips causing chills to flow throughout my body.

Not giving into his intoxicating ways, I shot back. "Run? What I'm running from? You not gon' do shit." I hissed, twisting my lips as I gazed out the window at the falling rain before opening the door preparing myself to rush to the front door.

The only thing I could hear was his deep chortles as I felt his presence getting closer from behind me. I was trying my best to hurry and get to the porch before my hair was wetter than I'd like. The chirping of his car alarm was the last thing I heard as his masculine arms wrapped around my waist, face nuzzling in the right side of my neck. Against my will, a moan escaped my lips once feeling the wetness of his perfect lips come in contact with my spot.

Softly I pushed him away before sticking my key in the door and rushing in as he followed suit. I frowned watching him laugh while shaking his head.

What was so funny?

"Take off your shoes," I demanded while following my own demand.

I didn't have the time nor patience to hear Blake's mouth. Today was one of those days. Ever since being home, some days were better than others seeing as though I wasn't trying to be dependent on my meds. Therefore, here I was winging it and doing well even though I felt on the edge at times.

That's where my snappy ways were stemming from.

Biting my lip, I appreciated the quick glance of Dallas' v-cut as he pulled his black hoodie over his head. Shifting my weight to one side of my body, I intensely watched him throw his hoodie on one of the coat rack hooks. My full lips curled once hearing a deep chuckle resonate in the air.

"You watching me n' shit..." He mumbled while brushing his hands against his shirt, slowly turning to face me.

A smirk contorted my lips as I continued looking him up and down, not giving a care in the world that I was boldly checking him out. This man is everything to look at. This was my first time seeing him with a low fade and I actually liked it.

I began ogling his bulging biceps popping from beneath his white shirt. The word "Pop" was printed four times going down the shirt in bubble letters, different colors. A pair of black Levi's covered his lower half with white, high-top Air Force ones clothing his feet. My hues took their time moving back up his frame, locking in on his chocolate gaze.

His deep dimples took over his cheeks as he ogled me the same way. His head tilted back slightly but never moved his hues from mine. Another intense moment. We had far too many of these and I was strongly starting to believe that it would lead us to clothes dropping. I shook my head of my nasty thoughts, biting my lip before turning on my heels.

"Come on," I whispered as my bare feet moved across the hardwood floors.

Even though I had my own living room area downstairs, I always found myself upstairs but tonight was different. I wasn't looking forward to seeing Blake whenever she came home. She didn't do anything to me but I know me not being on my meds was playing a part in my ill feelings. Until they subsided, I'd rather keep my distance. It's best. For the both of us.

Bending over, I grabbed the remote off the coffee table turning the TV on. Dallas' tall structure collided with the couch as I proceeded to my room to grab a blanket. Plopping into the cushion, my eyes slowly shut as my head rested on the back of the couch.

"You can watch whatever you want," I voiced.

"You falling asleep on me over there?"

His voice was raspy and low, sending a jolt to my box forcing me to squeeze my legs together. I peeled my eyes open looking out the side of them to him, catching his grin. Pulling the blanket up to my shoulders, I giggled before folding my legs next to me.

"I'm not going to sleep, Dallas." My words came out muffled from speaking into the blanket.

He nodded, looking back to the TV.

"So. How did the visit go?"

There goes that thump to my heart again once being asked that question. Sniffing, I turned my head only to be looking at his side profile.

I cleared my throat, "It went well."

Dallas' head snapped my way, brows meeting in the middle of his forehead. I knew he wanted a better elaboration on exactly how it went but honestly, I didn't want to speak on it. Everything was still fresh. I was still angry that she'd relapse; I was also hurt. I just wish my friend was out here with me but the reality was, she wasn't.

"Cool," He smoothly responded which threw me way off.

I was expecting him to press the issue but he didn't. Honestly, his nonchalant but smooth response put me at ease but disappointed me as well. It was like I wanted him to care enough to bother me until I spoke on it but appreciated him respecting boundaries. This man had me beyond confused. He had me feeling ways I've never experienced before.

The sound of his iPhone rang over the music video that was currently playing on the TV. I watched as the biggest smile took over his face once bringing the phone up accepting the FaceTime call.

His dimples seemed as if they grew even deeper as I could feel his happiness pouring from his body. A smile graced my face just off witnessing his happiness alone. Whoever was about to come on the screen definitely had a special place in his heart.

"Hey, baby." He cooed, showing off his pearly whites.

I was trying my best not to be nosey but I couldn't look away from him for shit. The high pitched voice sounded on the phone making my heart flutter - I adored kids.

"Uncle Dally!" She screamed before sighing deeply, "Move Yani!" She shrieked as another voice shot back.
Dallas chuckled while shaking his head. "Aye!" His voice rose an octave. "Y'all can share the camera. Uncle Dally has more than enough love for the both of y'all."

I giggled once hearing her smack her lips; I could only imagine the face she was making.

"Wassup though Yuri?" He questioned, sliding down into the couch.

"Where are you?"

My hands flew to my mouth trying my best to stifle my laugh. The fact she questioned him as if she was his mother or girlfriend was hysterical. His lips twisted cutting his eyes my way before focusing back on the camera.

"At a friend house baby. What you need?"

My brows furrowed at him referring to me as a friend. I mean, we were just friends but what friends kiss? What friends felt such an undeniable force to each other that we both had no control over? What fri—

Whatever.
We're just friends.
Fuck it.

After hearing that, I pretty much zoned out from annoyance along with not trying to listen in on his convo. Suddenly, a wave of anger overwhelmed my body which I couldn't fight. I had to get away from him. Throwing my feet to the floor, I wrapped the blanket around me as I caught Dallas' confused expression. I swiftly moved to my room plopping into my bed, hoping that somehow I could get my anger under control.

Shia. You're too beautiful of a person to allow your anger to control your life. Step back, take a few deep breaths and reevaluate if it's really worth getting angry over.

Taking a few deep breaths, I remembered Dr. Jones' words as my lips parted allowing the air to break through. My eyes tore from my bed cover focusing on Dallas who was leaned against the doorframe.

"Everything good bae?" His voice was laced with concern and it was visible on his face as well.

It wasn't him.

It was me.

My nostrils flared, suddenly irritated with his presence. He stood quietly awaiting my answer. I was beyond irritated and the thing was, I couldn't help it. I wasn't trying to run to my meds either. Scratching the side of my face, I continued to do my breathing exercises but they weren't helping.

"The fuck you mean we're just friends?" I could tell my random, snappy words threw him off by the taken aback expression taking over his handsome features.

I mentally cursed myself for my angry ways. I was in no place to question Dallas as if he was mine. I never knew how to express myself the right way which always resulted in me snapping on whomever, wherever.

"The fuck..." He hissed which turned me on. He rose his hand while shaking his head, "Don't start that shit with me Shia."

Out of the few times, Dallas did snap at me I loved seeing how he looked angry.

"Answer the question Dallas!" I shot back, not feeling intimidated by him one bit.

His tongue dashed across his bottom lip as he rubbed his chin. A chuckle fell from him with his eyes going to the ceiling before intensely landing on me. In that moment, I somewhat felt nervous. His gaze was too fierce forcing my eyes to look away at nothing in particular.

"Naw slim. Don't look away now. What I tell you bout that shit Shia?"

My eyes whipped back to his, not saying a word.

"Huh?!" His voice rose an octave bringing a jolt to my being.

How can you look so good when angry?

"Bout what Dallas?" I mumbled.

"You and that damn attitude of yours. You do far too much. If you want to ask a question, ask me like a damn adult. You can kill all that snappy shit slim." His intense gaze never faltered nor did he break eye contact.

As much as I wanted to look away, it was that force keeping my eyes locked with his. I couldn't look away, even if I tried.

"But to answer your question, we are friends Shia. Friends that just so happen to be drawn to each other. What the hell you were expecting me to say to my niece? Huh? I was stating facts slim whether you want to accept it or not. That doesn't mean I feel any less about you because we're *friends*." He said within one breath meanwhile putting an emphasis on friends.

After seeing how upset I'd gotten him, I cowered under his fiery gaze while chewing on the inside of my cheek. Literally, I was at a lost for words. Parting my lips, I tried to gather something to say to him. But I couldn't.

Dallas threw me a head nod as his brows lifted to the top of his head, running his tongue over his lip. I silently watched his thumb glide over his plump bottom lip before narrowing his hues on me as that sexy grin settled on his face. My face scrunched up once seeing him shake his head as he pushed himself off the doorframe.

"You don't know no better slim but uh, walk me out. I'll holla at you."

I did it again.

Huffing out of frustration, I followed not too far behind him knowing that I was the only reason we were departing ways so early.

Me and my smart ass mouth.

Book X.

March 28, 2016: Fort Washington, MD

Sighing, I looked at my phone for probably the 100th time today, just to see if I had a text or call that I missed. Nothing at all, like I expected. It's been two days since I've talked to Dallas and to say I felt like shit would be an understatement. I didn't mean to snap the way I did. Ever since knowing him, he's been trying to be here for me and like typical me, I was doing nothing but pushing him away. Pushing him away like I do everyone that tries to help me. I sighed out of frustration, having an internal battle with myself. I wanted to text him but then the fear of getting ignored constantly crossed my mind.

I hated being ignored.

"Girl, if you don't call or text him already. I'm tired of you moping around." He said out of annoyance.

I was too but I missed Dallas, terribly.

Rolling my eyes, I locked in on CJ's piercing gaze as his full lips wrapped around the Corona bottle.

"I can't," I whined while running my fingers through my wavy hair.

CJ waved me off while sitting his bottle on the marble top counter. "Well then sulk in your misery hoe." He replied before focusing on his phone.

Shaking my head, I chuckled not finding it in me to be mad at his response. He was right. I could either reach out so I can get out of my feelings or not and just suck it up.

"Anyways, where is your cousin?" He questioned as if I was her keeper.

"You should know. That's *your* best friend." I snapped back in a playful manner causing his mouth to form an O shape.

His index finger rose as his green eyes landed on me, "Uh uh bitch, don't do me. You and your salty ass can stay on that island by yourself. Don't try to bring my cute ass down with you. Tah!" He fanned me off again before rolling his neck.

I burst out in laughter at his antics. Despite my funky mood, CJ's personality alone was bringing me to a good place. I glanced at my phone again, hoping that it'd light up.

Nothing.

The sound of his phone coming in contact with the counter forced my attention on him. He folded his arms on the counter with his head falling to the side.

"Seriously though Shy. Go ahead and reach out. I mean, it was your fault bitch. Tripping off being called his friend and whatnot..." His finger rose to his temple as if he was thinking before pointing it my way. "Weren't you the one swearing up and down y'all weren't shit anyways? Girl bye." He waved me off again.

I rolled my eyes allowing everything to settle in, knowing that there was truth behind his words - that's what was irritating me the most. I appreciated what was said but then again I was so on the edge that I didn't want to hear shit. Picking up my phone, I took a glance at CJ to see a sneaky smirk sitting on his face.

"Go head girl." He pushed causing me to smile weakly.

My thumb scrolled through the few contacts before pressing on his name. My heartbeat picked up its pace as my thumb hesitantly hovered over his name, scared to press the message icon.

I can't believe Dallas had me this shook right now.

Unbelievable.

I sighed deeply once gathering the guts to open up our text convo looking over the last words exchanged between us. Turning my nose up, I took another deep breath before typing.

Dallas
<u>Sent</u>
I don't like you not talking to me

After returning my phone back to the counter, I felt as if a weight had been lifted off my shoulders.

Now, I was just hoping that Dallas responded.

March 28, 2016: Uptown, Washington, DC

"Sup Ma," I placed a kiss on my mother's forehead earning a lazy smile from her before sitting on the edge of her bed.

"Hey, my baby." She cooed before pushing a few strands of hair behind her ear.

She looked much better than she did the other night I was here. Her face didn't look as dull. Instead, you could see the life slowly returning back to her features. She was also gaining her strength back, using her walker less which had me glad.

I was getting my baby back.

"How you?" She questioned with a tipped brow, looking back and forth between me and the TV.

This woman loved her day talk shows - she lived for them.

I kissed my teeth, "I should be asking you that."

She chuckled before fanning me off. "Boy. Answer my question."

The thing was, I didn't want to answer her question. Honestly, these past two days had been some shit seeing as though I haven't spoken to nor seen Shia. I could easily reach out but I wanted her to see that this was all on her, not me. I wasn't the one pushing her away, instead, it was vice versa. That attitude of hers was really beginning to irritate the hell out of me. I've dealt with females and their ways but with her, she brought another feeling that I couldn't shake. Anytime she snapped, I felt that shit, *hard*.

I sighed, "I'm good Ma."

"You're not." She shot back just as quick causing me to frown.

My mother knew me like the back of her hand.

"Did something happen with you and your lady friend?" She questioned causing my eyes to look towards her, chuckling at her raised brows as she slightly leaned my way.

This woman was a mess.

Knowing I couldn't keep anything from her, I shrugged my shoulders as the corner of my lips twisted upwards.

"Something like that," I dryly responded in hopes that she'd leave it at that.

"So..." Her voice trailed off forcing my hues on her identical brown ones. "What happened Dallas?"

I shook my head, sighing deeply. I could tell my mother anything but for some reason, it was difficult for me to let her know how this chick I barely knew had me wide open. Out of all the bitches I've dipped in, I found myself getting attached to one who's just as damaged as me.

I ran my hands down my face. "Trippen'... like any other bi—"

My words were cut short once catching her piercing gaze and pursed lips - the look I was terrified of as a kid. That look meant you're about to get your ass whooped in .5 seconds. I cleared my throat while rubbing the back of my neck, feeling uneasy.

"My bad Ma. She's just trippen'. It's coo..."

My brown orbs locked on my phone lighting up on my lap forcing my brows to furrow. I wasn't in the mood to talk to anyone; I was spending time with my favorite lady.

She nodded her head my way before sipping from her glass. "I bet that's her. She came to her senses baby." She raised her glass in the air offering me another head nod.

I shook off my mother's words as I unlocked my phone going to my messages. A jolt hit my body once realizing that it was, in fact, Shia being the one behind the text. I looked at my mother in disbelief wondering how she knew. A big smile spread across her lips as she slightly bounced in glee.

"I told you, baby. Mama knows." She leaned forward rubbing my back softly.

I chortled at the fact she thought she knew everything, but then again, the outcome was always her being the right one.

The sound of her back hitting the headboard averted my gaze from my phone to her.

"Talk it out. You know I've told you about holding on to good things. Clearly, this young lady is something good for you right now because I've never seen you in such a good space baby. You're always so worried and stressing over me. You deserve your place of peace and she just might be it. Don't fuck it up." She expressed.

My eyes widened at her one choice of vulgar language before laughing.

"Come on Ma..." I said between laughs, "Chill out man." I waved her off.

She joined in on my laughter, "I'm serious baby. You don't come across many good women. I've seen the little girls you've fooled around with."

"What?!" My voice rose an octave surprised at what she was saying especially since I've never brought anyone around.

Her lips tightened as she slowly nodded her head, putting on her ghetto face.

"Trust me, Dallas. I know more than you think." She voiced as her head tilted down while looking up at me.

I put my hands up in surrender while laughing, "You got it Ma."

"But go ahead baby, go fix that happy thing you got going on." She waved me off dismissively while handing her empty glass to me.

A tingly sensation shot through my body knowing how much my favorite lady supported my happiness as a whole. All she knew about Shia was her name. It felt great knowing that I had Ma's support in regards to Shia, whether I truly decide to pursue her or not.

Leaning my back against the island counter, I read over the text bringing a small grin to my lips while shaking my head. We haven't spoken in two days and all she could say was how she doesn't like me not talking to her as if I was supposed to reach out first. Clearly, she still didn't get it. I wasn't the type to drag things out so I'll let it go for now cause I missed her little ass.

Mean Ass
<u>Sent</u>
A nigga wasn't even mad at you baby. Just waiting on you.

A minute didn't even pass before my phone was buzzing in my hand.

Mean Ass
<u>Received</u>
I know
I should've said something sooner, but I was scared.

My nose scrunched up.
Scared?

Mean Ass
<u>Sent</u>
What you scared fo?

Mean Ass
<u>Received</u>
Thought you'd ignore me.

I smacked my lips at her response. She had no clue how I operated because I was far from petty. The one thing my mother made sure I lived by was to not hold grudges - it did nothing but hinder your blessings. I already know God has major blessings coming my way and I wouldn't dare be the one standing in the way of that.

Mean Ass
<u>Sent</u>
Naw Shy. Not even.
Miss me, huh?

A teasing grin pulled at my lips as I suddenly became anxious, wondering what she'd say back. It was mind boggling how this girl could make me feel. Even that night she popped off at the mouth, I was pretty much over it halfway home. I couldn't be mad at her for shit because having her near put me in the best space.

Mean Ass
<u>Received</u>
I did & I still miss you.
I'm sorry Dallas.

Mean Ass
<u>Sent</u>
I missed your mean ass too.
You good. We'll talk bout it face to face. Fyd?

Pushing myself off the island, I put my phone in my pocket before moving towards the living room. I let out an exasperated sigh once the sound of Elsa from *Frozen* reverberated against the walls, making me cringe. These girls wore this movie out. I don't see how

169

they could watch it over and over again. As many times as I tried to wean them off this movie, they always found their way back to it. I smiled at the sight of them sitting cross-legged on the floor, entirely too close to the TV for my liking.

"Aye!" My voice rose over the loud music making sure that they were aware of my presence.

I chuckled at them jumping simultaneously before looking back at me, identical smiles spreading across their beautiful faces. As I continued sauntering further into the room, they refocused their attention back on the movie as if it was their first time seeing it. I plopped into the couch made for three as my phone vibrated against my thigh.

"Y'all two need to back up. Too close." I demanded while retrieving my phone from my pocket.

They both gave me a weird look before scooting back, just a little bit. I was requesting them to move further back than that but these little girls do what they want.

Mean Ass
<u>Received</u>
Fyd?
Um. That means?

I burst out in laughter receiving furrowed brows from my nieces as they raised their index fingers to their lips, shushing me simultaneously. My heart warmed at their cuteness. The smallest things they did meant the most to me, even with them telling me what to do. The one thing they got from my sister was their bossy ways. At times I couldn't believe how fast they grew before my eyes. I'm a proud uncle and grateful to have them blessing my life.

Mean Ass
<u>Sent</u>
Lol, you need to keep up baby.
It means "fuck you doing."

After sending my response, I could only imagine the sour face settling on her pretty ass face.

Mean Ass
<u>Received</u>
No.
Just ask the entire question instead of shortening it.
But nothing at all... in here with CJ & Blake.

My fingers hovered over the screen as I watched the dots pop up on the screen, signaling she was still typing.

Mean Ass
<u>Received</u>
& don't curse at me Dallas
Wyd?

Mean Ass
<u>Sent</u>
Naw, I'd rather be difficult.
Talking bout me but yet you're being lazy about asking me what I'm doing.
In here hoping my damn nieces don't go blind from sitting too close to the TV.
Wanna show me that face of yours?

My nose turned up once noticing that Yani and Yuri had scooted back to their recent spot. I leaned forward giving the coffee table a light tap to grab their attention. Their heads whipped towards me as their lips fell into a pout once seeing my index finger summoning them my way.

"Come 'ere... y'all don't listen."

Their pouting faces grew deeper as I patted the empty space on my right that could fit them two.

"Why we have to sit here Uncle Dally?" Yani, the youngest by two minutes, whined.

I locked with her doe, brown eyes, as they created a warm blanket over my heart like it did every time I looked my babies in their faces. They were absolutely my world and then some if that was possible.

My pouty lips tightened before parting, "Cause I said so. Y'all good right here next to Uncle D."

"We don't want to sit next to you." Yuri spat out earning a deep chortle from me.

Mean Ass
<u>Received</u>
Guessing that means you're bout to come over?

My eyes averted from my nieces to my phone, reading the text before replying back.

Mean Ass
<u>Sent</u>
Naw, I'm coming to get you so we can kick it at my crib.

A wave of nerves rushed my body at the thought of Shia entering into my place of peace - my personal space. Out of the three years I'd been living there, I never brought a female to where I laid my head every night. But like I keep stressing, Shia was one of a kind. So with me taking the initiative to invite her into my world was a big deal for me. It was nearing a month since we crossed paths and she already had me changing my ways that I've been accustomed to for years.

Shia Sinclair was about to be the **first** woman other than my mother and sister crossing the threshold into my sanctuary.

March 28, 2016: Fort Washington, MD
"Don't do anything I won't do!" CJ yelled after me as I pulled the front door open.

Looking back, I met the smiling faces of the dynamic duo as one crept to my face as well.

"Bitch. There's nothing you won't do so spare me!" I shot back, laughing once seeing his jaw drop at my comeback.

"BI—" The only thing I heard once closing the door behind me, locking up.

My brown hues fixated on the familiar black, 2-door Dodge Challenger, creating a flutter of butterflies in my stomach. Just a few minutes ago I was eager to see Dallas but now that the moment presented itself, I was nervous. Glancing around, my dainty fingers raked through my wavy tresses before releasing a deep sigh. Ambling my way down the driveway, I rubbed my hand against my thin, gray crop sweater as I felt a sudden chill.

Dallas always brought me chills.

I glimpsed at my crisp white chucks before fixing my gaze on the handsome individual occupying the driver seat. It was as if my heart skipped a beat once seeing the corners of his lips curve upward. Offering him a weak smile, my feet continued moving me towards his car. In the inside, I was going insane but trying to keep my composure on the outside. In spite of my nerves, that familiar force between us pulled me quicker to him by the seconds.

He threw me a head nod before that beautiful tongue of his swept across his fluffy bottom lip.

I missed his kisses. Who am I kidding? I missed him.

"Sup baby." His husky voice vibrated against my eardrums as I got comfortable in the passenger seat.

"Hi," I softly responded, suddenly feeling like this was my first crush.

He smacked his lips before twisting his lips. "Naw Shy. Get on with that shy shit." He fanned me off, chuckling while putting the car in drive.

I giggled, looking out the window before focusing on his side profile.

"They don't call me Shy for nothing," I joked earning another smack of the lips.

"Baby."

I sat there waiting for him to finish his sentence but realized that he was waiting for a response.

"Huh?"

He looked at me while coming to a red light, straight face and all.

"Shut up."

His loud laugh invaded my ears once he saw my face deadpan. I tried to fight my smile but failed before reaching over to give his arm a light jab.

His laughter died as he cut his eyes at me.

"What?" I softly asked with a toothy grin.

He kissed his teeth before using his right hand to rub his chin. His face contorted into that cute crooked smirk, giving me a quick look over. The lust was swirling in his brown hues making me melt under his gaze.

"You look cute..."

I parted my lips to thank him but was stopped once he spoke.

"Or whatever."

That sexy grin was set on his face as I giggled at his silly antics. He was in a really good mood which was making me even happier for reaching out; I missed his positive vibes.

His deep chuckle met my ears. "Who you trying to look cute for?"

Crossing my eyes, I kissed my teeth while fighting back a smile, looking his way. That question alone had me thinking about the night at Tink's house when he asked who I was wearing my dress for. Butterflies began engulfing my tummy at the thought of being in his embrace that night.

"Not you nigga!" I spat back as a smile tugged at my lips, bringing one to his as well.

He chortled, "You can't even keep a straight face, my nigga."

March 28, 2016: Camp Springs, MD

Just as I was about to respond, I realized that we came to a complete stop. Immediately I began observing my surroundings, taking in the nice apartment complexes. My hand gravitated towards my chest trying to calm my racing heart from Dallas unexpectedly appearing on my side. My brows met in the middle of my head as I locked in on his chocolate gaze, his hands raising in surrender.

"My bad baby. I didn't mean to scare you." He softly chuckled while pulling the door open.

A jolt shot through my heart once his hand connected with mines helping me out the car.

Who knew he was such a gentleman?

The corners of my lips curved upward once he brought me into a tight embrace. The butterflies in my stomach swarmed faster as he rested his chin softly on the top of my head.

"I didn't get my hug..." His voice trailed off sending shivers down my spine, his breath brushing against my ear with every word.

Inhaling deeply, my eyes rolled at his intoxicating scent invading my nostrils. This man was going to be the death of me. His warm hands slowly moved to my lower back before releasing me. I instantly felt bare once he let me go - I adored being in his arms.

I always felt **safe**.
Something I haven't felt since losing my father.

"Come on." He mumbled while motioning for me to follow him.

Smirking, I ogled his tall frame from behind as he jogged up the stairs leading to the second floor. Dallas could absolutely make any and everything look good. He didn't have to try for shit. His hair was freshly cut making his face even better to look at as if it wasn't already handsome enough. A navy blue collared shirt with scattered white dots adorned his muscular upper body. His broad shoulders sat perfectly under the thin material showing his hard work in the gym was paying off. My brown hues fell on his dark denim jeans that loosely clothed his bottom half with a pair of low, white Stan Smiths sheltering his feet.

Dallas locked eyes with me once glancing over his shoulder, brows rising to the top of his head.

"You eye fucking me?" He mocked me from the same question I've asked him before.

I bit my lip as I stepped onto the top step, standing not too far from him as he looked me over with a teasing grin.

"I'm not eye fucking you at all, Dallas." I innocently responded.

In return, I received a deep chuckle and shake of the head as he opened the door allowing me entry first. My open palms flew to my arms in an attempt to warm myself seeing how cold it was in here. My eyes fell on his back as he lightly jogged towards the thermostat as I continued to admire his home.

To my surprise, his personal space was well put together than I anticipated. I wasn't expecting this.

"You decorated yourself?" I questioned.

His head whipped in my direction as a smirk contorted his pouty lips, nodding.

"Actually I did…" He voiced. "It's aight, huh?" He asked while looking around, clearly proud of his work.

A black sectional couch rested against the single brick wall complementing the tan walls perfectly. The dinner table resembled a black desk with four tan stools, two seated on each side. His kitchen was gorgeous. Stainless steel appliances everywhere.

"Surprised, huh?" He asked while moving towards me.

My awkward ass was still standing by the front door, waiting to get the "okay" to move further into his home. He grabbed my hands pulling lightly as I continued to scan the gorgeous space. His flat palm connected with my lower back causing a small scowl to take over my pretty features.

"Make yourself at home baby." He voiced while pushing me towards the couch as I fell into the leather cushion. "You like alfredo?" He asked while washing his hands.

His brows rose while tilting his head slightly down, not tearing his orbs from me as he turned off the water before drying his hands.

"You can cook?" I asked in a surprised manner.

I've never met a guy that could cook and if Dallas could, that just made him even better.

I bit my lip once fixing my gaze on his back muscles flexing through his white wife beater once removing his shirt. I admired how he moved around the kitchen, grabbing what he needed to prepare dinner. He stood on the opposite side of the island, chuckling while grabbing his phone before Travis Scott and Young Thug's "Pick Up The Phone" came through the speaker.

"You used to fuck niggas, huh?" He questioned with a tipped brow, bringing the cutting board into view.

My nose turned up as my hands collided with the couch pushing myself to my feet. His chocolate gaze remained on me as my feet moved across the hardwood floor. Smiling, I placed my elbows on the island as I watched his every move. Witnessing a man know his way around the kitchen was something new for me - it was a sight to see.

Dallas seemed to surprise me every day; I loved it.

Tilting my head to the side, I ignored his question not wanting to revisit my past niggas.

"Who taught you how to cook?"

He grinned before looking over his shoulder while standing in front of the stove, throwing dry noodles in the boiling pot of water.

"My Ma. What? You don't know how to cook?" He teasingly asked forcing a scowl to my face.

I fanned him off while rolling my eyes, "I know how to cook nigga."

I lied through my teeth knowing I *barely* knew how to make anything. I could do simple things but I left the extravagant dinners to Blake. She was the beast in the kitchen, not I. Leaning forward, I attempted to get a better view of what he was cooking on the stove.

"Whipping up some chicken and shrimp baby."

I smiled once seeing his bright smile he flashed once making eye contact.

"Mmm," I hummed enjoying the enticing fumes invading my nostrils. "You like cooking?"

I watched as his shoulders rose before lazily dropping as he moved to grab the alfredo sauce, dumping it into the pan.

"I mean... it's cool. I'm not trying to be a chef or anything but I live alone, so a nigga gotta cook for himself."

I nodded, fully understanding what he meant. From him mentioning a chef career, it put a vivid image in my head of him in chef attire which I know would be such an attractive sight.

"I hear you." I finally voiced as I focused on how the beautiful pasta fell from the pan with ease into the glass container, wetting my lips at the sight.

My stomach growled forcing my hand to it, rubbing softly hoping that he didn't hear. I know I failed once hearing him chuckle while shaking his head.

He smirked, "I'm making your plate now Shy."

His contagious laugh met my ears causing me to laugh as well.

"Shut up Dallas." I retorted, swatting at him as he dodged my hit before placing my bowl in front of me. "Thank you." I cooed as he took the seat across from me.

"You're more than welcome beautiful." He responded while twirling his fork in the pasta.

I blushed while smiling at my food, looking like a complete creep.

"What?" I whined noticing him smiling, showing off his deep dimples.

I stuffed my mouth while watching him rid his face of the alfredo sauce with his napkin before parting his lips to speak, placing his elbows on the island.

"Nothing man. I just..."

My brows furrowed once he cleared his throat glancing away before fixing back into my confused gaze. I narrowed my eyes at him, searching his eyes for something - anything at all. His pouty, juicy lips were slightly agape as he looked at me, tension apparent in his brows.

He sighed deeply as if he was having an internal battle, running his hands over his face.

"I don't know man. I just missed your ass slim, more than I thought. With you being right here in front of me made me realize how two days without talking to you was some shit."

Chewing on my food, my cheeks heated up as I broke our gaze finding it difficult to look him in the eyes after his confession. I felt like it was more to it but that alone had my stomach flipping more than I would like. Fiddling with my food, his deep chortle brought me back to reality forcing my hues on him.

"You always wanna play fake shy baby. I know you missed me just as much..." He shrugged. "I can't even front. You got a nigga feeling some type of way already."

From his tone of voice alone, I could tell that these emotions that were stirring within were something he didn't want to deal with head on. It was clearly frustrating him and honestly, it was annoying me especially since I've never felt this way before for the opposite sex. Here I was getting rid of one bad habit and gaining a new one, knowing that he was going to be one hell of a drug.

Dallas Raye.

Book XI.

March 28, 2016: Camp Springs, MD

Leaning forward, I dodged the accent pillow that Shia threw my way as I continued laughing. Standing to my full 6'2" structure, I sauntered towards her before leaning over placing my hands on the back of the couch, on either side of her face. My dick jumped once she placed a quick peck on my lips, leaving me wanting another one. I leaned down placing a slow, sensual kiss on her full lips earning a small moan from her. Quickly, I pulled away not wanting this to go any further knowing that things could get out of control quickly.

A smirk played at my lips once Shia grabbed a fistful of my wife beater pulling me back towards her lips. My dick hardened as she moaned in my mouth with our tongues wildly playing with each other. I quickly placed two pecks on her lips before prying mines from hers, not wanting to at all.

Sighing deeply, I stood upright as she looked at me through lidded eyes. There was nothing but lust dancing within her brown hues which was making me want her more than I already did.

I scratched the side of my head, finding it sort of difficult to keep my composure.

"Naw baby. We can't." I voiced before clearing my throat as I tried to convince myself in the process.

Shia turned her nose up while abruptly standing to her feet, throwing me off guard once her small frame collided with mines. She wrapped her slender arms around my waist with the side of her face resting on my chest.

"Why can't we Dallas?" She whined in this sultry, soft tone while tightening her hold on me.

My eyes flew to the ceiling as I tried my best to keep my hormones and dick under control. I'm pretty sure she could feel me but I'm going to remain my cool as if I didn't feel how stiff I was. Chills flew down my spine once her fingertips danced at my lower back making me begin to tap my foot against the hardwood. My hands caressed her hips, rubbing them softly as I wet my lips.

"Cause. I'm not trying to fuck up whatever we have going on and sex... sex just complicates things." I spoke truthfully.

I've had too many bad experiences with females from having sex with them, and I'd be damned if that messed up what we had going.

Her face pulled from my chest forcing me to look into her eyes. "But—"

"But nothing Shy. Trust me, there wouldn't be nothing more that I'd love than to put your ass to sleep." My voice dropped an octave as my hands continued to warm her hips. "BUT I know that I'm not about to allow sex to jeopardize whatever we call ourselves working towards."

A grin contorted her lips as her head tilted back some. "I thought you said we were just *friends*?" She retorted, making sure to put an emphasis on that "friends" term.

I kissed my teeth. "Cause we are. Two friends that have some strong shit sitting between us. You and I both know that. We feel it too."

I looked into her eyes and off her expression alone I could see that she was allowing my words to sink in. Raising my left hand, I raked it through her wavy tresses. Biting my lip, I vividly imagined being deep in her while pulling on her hair.

I needed a breather.

A scowl marred her pretty visage as I stepped out of our small embrace, turning my back towards her.

"Where you going?" She questioned as I began heading to the back, trying to shift my mind to one thing and one thing only.

My blunt.

I disregarded her question grabbing the perfectly rolled blunt off my dresser, placing it between my lips. Shia's face scrunched up as she watched me move towards the balcony doors, giving her one last look.

I raised the blunt in the air, "I'll be out here bae." I said, nodding my head towards outside. "You'll be aight?" I grabbed my shirt, throwing it over my head.

The thing was I wasn't a smoker but I knew in order to keep my dick in my pants, I needed to hit this jay. Hitting a blunt always put me at ease, brought me to this indescribable state of solitude. Knowing that Shia was fresh out of rehab, I refrained from asking her to keep me company. I wasn't sure if weed could possibly have a negative effect on her or not but I wasn't going to take any chances.

"Can I keep you company?" She put her hands up in surrender as those full lips of hers curled in disgust. "I don't wanna hit that shit."

I chuckled at the disgusting but cute expression settling on her face, nodding while pushing the door open.

"Yea, you can join me."

The cool air brushed against our faces once stepping out on the spacious balcony with me leaning against the banister and her taking the only seat. Reaching into my back pocket, I lit the fat cylinder resting between my lips as her eyes remained glued to me causing a wave of nerves to rush my body.

Clearing my throat, I crossed my right leg over the other at the ankles keeping her intense gaze.

"Why are you smoking?"

She broke the comfortable silence between us.

I took a slow, long drag before allowing some smoke to seep through my parted lips, sucking the remainder back in.

"To keep from fucking you," I responded truthfully, bringing the blunt to my lips again.

Her eyes widened in shock before a giggle entered the air forcing a grin to my face. I loved hearing her laugh. She had one of those squeaky, irritating laughs but then again it was cute.

"Seriously Dallas?" She asked with a tipped brow.
Raising the blunt, my heavy eyes honed in on it before darting back in her direction. This was some good shit. Plus, I haven't smoked in some months so a nigga was high as shit.

My tongue swept across my bottom lip while nodding.

"Deadass baby." My voice fell into a husky tone which I can tell turned her on witnessing how she squirmed in the seat.

Softly kissing my teeth, the side of my lips curled in annoyance once feeling the vibration of my phone. It's always interruptions when it comes down to me spending time with Shy. Digging into my pocket to retrieve my phone, my brown hues ran over the text.

Gi
<u>**Received**</u>
Wya Daddy?

I chortled at my convenient pussy, not in the mood to entertain her seeing as though I had all I needed at the moment. Ignoring Gi's text, I returned my phone back to my jeans. The thick smoke fell from my lips before slowly moving upward to dance in front of my face. A lazy smirk worked its way to my lips as my entire body relaxed.

Reaching forward, I ashed the blunt in the ashtray causing Shia's eyes to avert from her phone to me.

"What?" She softly asked with a glint of happiness dancing in her orbs.

I shook my head, "I didn't say shit."

Her lips pursed together as her eyes restricted on me, right leg crossed over the other. Why was she so beautiful? Even when she wasn't trying. Everything about her was natural. No make-up. Her real hair. That curvy body. That phat as—

Shit.

Biting my lip, I shook my head to rid my mind of the nasty thoughts that were trying to sneak their way to the forefront. After finishing off the blunt, I threw it in the ashtray as a sigh parted my lips. Crossing my arms, I fell into her fiery gaze with a stale expression contorting my countenance.

This weird chill flew up my spine once she rose to her feet, quickly closing the gap between us. That familiar pang to my chest returned once feeling her hands fist my shirt on both sides. That blunt didn't help because that undeniable force was making the air thick between us. Huffing out of frustration, my arms curled around her waist.

"You feel that?" She spoke just above a whisper which sent chills through my body.

This girl had me feeling like a cold bitch.

One of her hands moved to rest on my chest, deeply looking into my eyes.

"Huh?" She questioned as I tried to find it in me to answer, her hand toying with my shirt.

I nodded slowly. "I told you God had us cross paths for a reason."

Shia rolled her eyes hard while stepping out of our embrace. She gave me her back to look at before turning to face me again, arms flailing before falling to her sides.

"Why do you always gotta bring up that shit?!" Her tone feigned annoyance forcing my brows to furrow.

The fu—

"I don't wanna hear about that. That *thing*. Ight?" Her voice escalated as my brows fell deeper glancing around making sure we didn't gain any onlookers.

I raised my open palms motioning in a "calm down" manner. "You need to chill," I spoke calmly, trying my best to not allow her random attitude change to affect me. "What are you even talking about?"

Her crazy ass flipping out all randomly.

"Matter of fact, let's go in," I suggested while pushing her towards the door as she shrugged away from me, moving further into the living room.

"I'm talking about you mentioning God, Dallas. Stop it."

I chuckled while shaking my head, closing the door.

"And what I'm going to stop doing that for? He's been great to me but to be real with you..." My voice trailed off as I sauntered towards her direction. "I don't talk about Him enough. Maybe you should try it slim." I shot back, plopping into the couch while keeping my eyes on her.

I'm tired of her being wishy-washy. It's been occurring more often which is really beginning to get under my skin.

"No. Maybe I shouldn't, SLIM." She retorted causing me to laugh at her childish antics.

"Shia. You really need to figure out what you want to portray consistently. Cause this up and down shit you doing is really blowing a nigga." I huffed, tipping a brow at her.

She rolled her eyes while crossing her eyes. "All I ask is that you stop bringing up God."

I twisted my lips, growing more annoyed at how she had no respect for the one man that's behind all of our existence.

"And all I ask is that you respect me and my beliefs. I understand you're not feeling the idea of God but I can't help but to speak about Him. And like I said before Shy... once He gets a hold of you, you won't be able to stop speaking on Him either."

Keeping my fiery gaze on her, I could see her eyes softening as she moved towards me with pouty lips. She threw her head back in an exaggerated manner, mouth wide open.

"I'm sorry Dallas." She whined, slowly looking down at me.

I raised my brows in hopes that there was more she was going to say. This girl was crazy. Seriously. Her body brushed against mine as she sat next to me.

"I just…" She began while fiddling with her fingers. "I just don't believe anymore. From all the shit I've been through, He wasn't there."

Shaking my head, I knew exactly how she felt. I was once there. I was once her. I grabbed her hands into mine looking deeply into her orbs.

"Look bae, I get it. Trust me, I do. I believe at some point everyone has lost their faith because they felt God wasn't there. But the thing is, He's *always* there. To this day, He STILL is here for you whether you believe it or not. It's up to you to place your faith within Him again. Regardless baby, His love for us is unconditional. I used to ask myself the same thing…" I scratched the side of my head, clearing my throat. "Y'know, why was all the bad things happening to me? I see it now, though. Somebody had to go through it and obviously, God knew I could handle it. I'm a living testimony, as you are too. You'll find your way back. Just don't wait till it's too late."

Caressing the side of her face, I leaned in to place a gentle kiss upon her lips. Her eyes fluttered as if she was in a daze, them pretty lips sitting slightly agape. I used my thumb to rub across her soft skin just by the corner of her eye.

"He's always been here, baby. Don't forget that." I spoke softly but stern enough so she'd know I meant every word said.

"Your ass crazy slim."

My face scrunched up at his random outburst, hues narrowing on his well-defined side profile. He was trying so hard to not smile but was failing, terribly at that. Quickly, I leaned forward poking the one dimple on his right cheek making itself known.

Dallas was so damn cute.

My smile grew wider once seeing the annoyed expression marring his handsome visage. Focusing in on his pouty lips curled into a deep frown created a vivid image of me sitting on his face. Squeezing my thighs together, I folded my arms across my chest, trying my best to rid my mind of the freaky thoughts.

"What?" I hissed once hearing his deep chuckle vibrate against my ears, sending a jolt to my center.

Nervously, I pushed a few strands of hair behind my ear before my arms fell lazily in my lap. His eyes quickly ran over me while licking his lips, returning his gaze to the TV without another word said.

"You." He softly spoke but still, I managed to hear him.

I crossed my eyes at his vague responses knowing I was only going to get as much out of him as he wanted to give me. I was a piece of work but Dallas was as well. He had no problem with giving me short answers, leaving my mind to wonder for however long it may.

Silence consumed us as the screeching from the basketball player's shoes was the only thing sounding into the air. I glanced at the TV, somewhat getting into the game before Dallas' question threw me off.

"Huh?" I heard him clearly but I wanted him to repeat himself, just to hear his husky voice. It was heavier now and I believe it was due to him being high and tired.

That familiar pang overwhelmed my chest once hearing him smack his lips before twisting sideways.

"You heard me. You bipolar or something?"

"What make you ask that?"

Dallas cleared his throat while shifting further down into the couch, never tearing those adorable brown eyes from me.

"Why wouldn't I? You give me every reason to think you are."

My eyes widened slightly at his words before shaking my head.

"No. Just… just a little on the edge." I confessed while running my left hand over my clothed right arm.

His eyes scanned over me again before a lazy smirk snuck its way to his face. He slowly nodded averting his gaze to the TV for a hot second before honing back on me.

"I understand that completely Shy but I'm not your enemy. So you need to chill out with that flipping out shit. You taking your meds?" His brows rose in question.

Pursing my lips, I broke our gaze looking at nothing in particular.

"So that's a no. Why not? You know it helps, right?"

He wasn't saying anything I already didn't know. I knew it would help me but the thing was, I wasn't trying to be dependent on it. I was just hoping to come home, not relapse, and not use the meds my doctor prescribed me.

Finally, I locked in on his chocolate gaze, nodding slowly. My full lips parted allowing words to break free, "I know. I just don't want to become dependent on it."

Dallas was two years sober meanwhile here I am only a good six weeks and two days in. It was easy for him to say but for me, I was terrified that even an ounce of me could become addicted to it.

I watched as his brows shifted into confusion, "Dependent? Dependency should be the last thing on your mind baby. What they gave you is what you need right now. It'll definitely help out with that little attitude of yours. You swear you're scaring somebody…" His voice trailed off as I giggled at the expression settling on his face.

I rolled my eyes. "I'm not trying to scare anybo—"

He cut me off with a smack of his lips, shaking his head.

"Naw Shy. Naw." His index finger rose towards me. "You do be trying to scare people with those nasty lash outs. Remember, I've witnessed it firsthand during groups." He spoke while moving his finger along with every word.

I sighed, fiddling with my fingers. I used to lash out terribly on everyone which I was now regretting, especially since they were there to help me.

"Yea, I know. I just hated being in there. The atmosphere always had me on the edge."

"Just like how you're feeling now, right?" He questioned, tipping his brow.

I bit my bottom lip, nodding.

"Yeah," I softly responded.

"Ight then. I know them meds put you at ease. Just think about it, baby. I know how you're feeling though because I went through the same thing when I first came home. I tell you, it really helped my days go by easier. It got rid of the slight urges I'd have as well as keeping my mood intact." He confessed as I took in every word he said. "Had any urges lately?"

I thought it was adorable how he was so concerned about my well-being. Like where did this man come from? I offered him a lazy smile before shaking my head.

"Nope. The last time I had a slight one was when I was dealing with Kris. I understand now why Blake wasn't too sold on the idea of Kris staying around."

He nodded, sweeping his tongue over his lip. "You gotta understand Shy that your cousin loves you. She wants to see you stay sober just as much as you do. At times it might seem as if she's being heartless but that's not the case. Just always keep in mind that she's on your team, always been on your team."

I smiled small, loving the positive words he was sending my way. He was right, about everything too. Blake wanted nothing but the best for me. Kris was my friend, not hers. She didn't owe her anything. I know everything came from a good place but I just wish Blake would've approached the situation differently, that's all.

"Why you care so much? You barely know me."

I didn't understand how someone I've known for a little over a month caring more than the one person who carried me - it just didn't make sense. Why was he sent to me? Why was he brought to me just at the right time? The time I needed someone else in my corner.

Dallas' handsome countenance contorted into a confused look as he softly began rubbing my right ankle that rested near his thigh. A smirk crept across my lips as I scanned over his frame, taking him in as a whole.

This man was gorgeous.

A hiss fell from my lips once his grip slightly tightened on my ankle sending a rush of chills to my being.

"I ask myself the same thing…" His voice trailed off with his gaze tearing from mine. It was as if he was searching for his words. His brows furrowed as he looked down at his lap before looking at me. I watched as his chest rose and fell while sighing deeply. "I don't even know why I care this much Shy; I'm not even gon' lie. This shit crazy… but I feel like I've known you forever. I care cause that's all I find myself doing when it comes to you. I can't help it." He shrugged lazily, "It's like that shit natural or something." He confessed laying his head on the back of the couch.

I smiled wide, cheeks burning and all. Never would I have once thought that I'd be sitting before a wonderful man that couldn't get enough of me. A man that really cared about me. This felt good. So damn good. My eyes flew to his hand that was moving up my lower leg, rubbing gently.

"You know I've been eye fucking you ever since I met you?" I honestly spoke, covering my mouth once I realized what just left my lips.

He chuckled before reaching over to pull my hands from my face. My cheeks heated up as I admired that beautiful smile of his.

What did his father look like? I could look at Dallas forever.

His mouth fell slightly agape as amusement swirled through his eyes looking me over. His head tilted down as his infamous crooked grin took over his lips, "Oh yeah? And don't be hiding that pretty ass smile of yours."

I giggled, "I didn't mean to say that."

He chuckled, "But you did, though. Don't trip. I saw you, little baby. I was watching you watching me."

My head fell to the side, "Did you ever think we would be kicking it like this?"

It always crossed my mind if getting to know me was in Dallas' plan.

He shook his head, "Yeah cause I've been drawn to you. We were bound to kick it at some point."

He continued rubbing my leg before a deep chortle rumbled throughout his chest.

"You done playing 21 questions?" He asked with a tipped brow.

I laughed, "I'm done nigga."

"You mind keeping the other side of my bed warm for the night?"

The sleeping butterflies in my stomach instantly woke up at his cute way of asking me to spend the night. My mouth spread into a big smile as he silently waited for my answer.

"Is this your way of asking can we have a sleepover?"

He scoffed, "Sleepover? I wouldn't say that per say. Little kids have those. You see us… we're two adults."

I slowly slid my tongue across my top lip. "So what would you call this then?"

His face twisted, "You staying over my house, the fuck." He spat causing a big laugh to break free from me.

My laughter died down, "I'll keep the other side of your bed warm tonight, Dallas."

The vibration of my phone against my thigh forced my eyes on the lit up screen, scanning over the text from Mace.

Mace
<u>Received</u>
Free Saturday night?
Say round 7:30. Moms wants you over for dinner.

Book XII.

March 28, 2016: Camp Springs, MD

Crossing my feet at the ankles, I gradually rubbed my sock-clad feet together bringing more warmth to them. Despite me wearing socks, my feet were always the coldest part of my body. I hated that shit. I chuckled at *Crooklyn* as I cleared my throat, moving further down into the bed while waiting on Shia to get out the bathroom.

"You taking a shit in there?!" I yelled, making sure she heard me over the TV.

Next thing I know the bathroom door was swinging open as she stood with a screwed up expression sitting on her face.

She rolled her eyes, "Nooo, I wasn't taking a shit."

My brown orbs steadily ran up and down her curvy frame in *my* clothes. She stood leaning against the doorframe, grinning.

Her wavy, black hair fell freely down her shoulders and back as I caught onto the lust dancing in her eyes. My hues fixed on her every move as she sauntered her way into my room. My long sleeve Stussy World Tour tee clothed her upper half, giving off an oversized appearance due to my larger frame. My red Polo boxers gave off the same look as it stopped just above her knees.

I tapped the little bit of exposed skin of her thigh, "My clothes look good on you baby." I licked my lips, still looking her over.

She blushed while giggling, "Thank you, Dallas." She voiced while using the scrunchie from her wrist to throw her hair into a messy bun on the top of her head.

Using her index and thumb, she wiped at the corners of her mouth as her eyes lit up once focusing on the TV. She quickly folded her short legs into Indian-style.

"What you looking at?" She asked, eyes still forward.

A lazy grin worked its way to my lips as my right hand gravitated towards the inside of my basketball shorts, resting just over my shit.

"You." I dryly responded, bringing my other hand to rest behind my head, scooting further down into the bed.

Shia cut her eyes at me, looking away then quickly looking back at me with widened eyes. The hairs on the back of my neck rose once seeing her hues shift towards my crotch before looking at me with a perplexed expression.

"You being a creep?"

I laughed once seeing her look at my crotch again with her brows furrowing once looking back up at me.

I shook my head while allowing my laughter to subside. "Naw. No creep shit. I'm just comfortable."

Her deep-set eyes narrowed as if she was trying to figure out if I was lying or not. She slowly began shaking her head realizing that I was telling the truth. A cute little smirk settled on her lips as her attention went back to the movie.

"I love this movie." She whispered to herself causing me to chuckle.

"I fuck with this joint too."

Crooklyn had been one of my favorite movies since I was 12 when Devyn first put me on to it. I haven't been able to let it go ever since.

Fixing my gaze back on Shia, I couldn't seem to keep my eyes off her. That flawless, chocolate skin that seemed to glimmer without the need of anything. The euphoria dancing in her eyes as she watched what I assumed one of her favorite movies as well. Her few baby hairs laid perfectly along her edges. Those well-rounded lips that forced me into some sort of spell whenever ours connected.

She was beyond prepossessing.

I was strongly beginning to feel that this girl was going to be my new healthy addiction. After a two-year sobriety, I never would've imagined myself gaining a new dependency. But here she was, sitting right next to me in my personal space.

Shia Sinclair.

Snapping out of my daze, I caught her puzzled mien. Her thick brow tipped as her tongue broke free snaking across her top lip before disappearing back into her mouth. A low grunt resonated within my chest as she tucked her lip into her mouth. Trying my best not to think about being balls deep in her, I broke from her fiery stare.

She knew what she was doing. At least, I believe she did.

"Dallas." She softly spoke causing that well-known twinge to radiate throughout my chest.

I cleared my throat before hesitantly looking back to her, "Yeah." I answered, finally finding my voice.

"You okay?"

I could see the concern in her eyes but she had nothing to worry about. I was simply having an internal battle with keeping my hands to myself and my hormones under control. Scrunching my face up, I scratched at the side of my face before a lazy grin spread across my lips.

"I'm chilling."

She snickered before playfully rolling her eyes.

"Whatever you say..." Her voice trailed off as the sound of her back connecting with the headboard sounded off while throwing her legs under the comforter.

March 29, 2016: Camp Springs, MD

Yawning, a soothing sensation built within my small frame as I continued stretching my limbs whichever way. Slowly peeling my eyes open, I turned on my left side fixating on a still sleeping Dallas. Just from seeing how peaceful he looked in a deep slumber brought the biggest blush to my face. He absolutely brought me to a space of tranquility which I was grateful for.

I raised my hand using my index finger to trace the outline of his pouty lips earning a twitch before a breath of air freed his lips. I smiled weakly once hearing him clear his throat while raising his bent arm to cover his eyes. He was a sight to see while sleeping but I no longer wanted to be up alone.

A loud whoosh of air exited his mouth leaving his lips partly agape, making his lips look even fluffier. My smile grew wider at the sight; he was so damn handsome. I couldn't believe I was laying here ogling a sleeping man.

"Dallas," I whispered, hoping that he'd hear me.

He didn't budge, instead, I received a few light snores in return. My nose scrunched up as my open palm rested against his wife beater clothed torso, shaking lightly. My hand throbbed from the groan stirring within his chest. I began using my fingers to tap against his chest, bringing him out of his slumber quicker.

"Come on, baby." His voice made my body quiver with the low, husky tone it was giving off.

His arm covering his eyes lowered to cover my hand. "You had me up all night n' shit. Let a nigga sleep." He complained.

He was right. Every time he fell asleep on me, I'd wake him up. We stayed up till about three in the morning, doing nothing much. We spent hours digging into each other's personal interests, getting a better understanding of one another. I learned a lot of things about Dallas last night that I wouldn't have expected.

It was a very cute bonding moment for us.

"But I want you u—" My words were cut short once his intense brown hues shot open, locking on me.

He licked his lips, "But you had me up all night, though." He sternly retorted.

"So," I shot back, grinning.

A creepy smirk found its way to his face as his muscular arm wrapped around my back, pulling me into him with one motion. I giggled once he began digging his face into my chest.

"Stop, nigga!" I squealed while mushing the side of his head.

His hold on me tightened as he got comfortable with his head on my chest, sighing deeply. My hand drifted towards the back of his head beginning to create small circles.

"You going back to sleep?" I asked.

He nodded his head, "Fuck yea."

I scoffed before pushing his body from mine as the smacking of his lips bounced off the walls. His face became tense, brows meeting in the middle as he shook his head giving me his back to watch. I giggled at his attitude, reaching for his arm before quickly being shrugged off.

Pushing my body up, I cocked my head to the side. "You mad?"

Silence.

This nigga was giving me the silent treatment. Petty ass.

A sneaky smirk contorted my full lips as I crawled towards him, throwing my leg over his waist while holding the bottom of his oversized shirt I was wearing. I lowered my weight on his crotch as he kept the pillow covering his face, not paying me any mind at all.

I knew how to get a rise out of him.

My flat palms rested on his chest as I began slowly grinding while leaning over speaking into his ear.

"Come on. Wake up… for me." I softly spoke in the sexiest tone I could muster up.

I knew I was getting to him once he grunted before taking a tight hold of my waist. The smirk never wavered from my face as I removed the pillow revealing his deep scowl.

Fuck.

He was gorgeous with this mad façade he was putting on. His brows were damn near touching with his lips pursed together. A comfortable silence blanketed over us as he moved his head sideways, staring into my soul. The more we sat here silent, the more I felt my chest feel as if it was going to burst.

"What you doing Shy?"

I innocently smiled, "Nothing. I just wanted you to wake up."

"Shit. You didn't just want to wake *me* up." He said, thrusting his hips upward forcing a moan from me, feeling him grow harder beneath me.

He tapped my thigh. "I gotta piss," He quickly said as I removed myself allowing my bottom to collide with the mattress.

I watched his every move as he smoothly ambled towards the bathroom, holding himself. My head whipped towards the vibration sound of his phone against the comforter. It instantly made me think about the many times it was ringing last night when he kept falling asleep.

A bitch, perhaps?

"Dally, your phone ringing!" I yelled over the flushing toilet as his tall structure emerged from the bathroom while yawning, covering his mouth.

"Don't call me that shit. I only let my nieces call me that." He muttered while moving towards the bed.

I waved him off dismissively knowing I'd call him what I pleased. By the look settling on his countenance, I could tell whoever it was obviously was someone he didn't want to talk to. I glanced at his phone connecting with the bed as I leaned back into the headboard, crossing my ankles. A loud yawn hit my ears once Dallas sat on the side of the bed with his back facing me. I could feel him boring a hole into the side of my face, chuckling.

"The TV not even on, nigga. Stop acting like you watching sumthin'." He spat causing me to roll my eyes, facing him.

He threw me a head nod before slightly turning his body, getting more comfortable to hold my glance at an angle.

"Sleep good?" He asked, taken me by surprise seeing as though every time I've slept next to him I slept the best.

Tucking my lips into my mouth, I nodded my head in response.

"Good... go—" His words were cut off by a big yawn, hand covering his mouth. "Cool. You hungry?"

My eyes lit up at his question due to me being a fat girl at heart. I dramatically began rubbing my stomach, licking my lips like a little kid earning a chuckle from him.

"Starvinggg." I dragged out, tossing my head back with pouty lips.

His pointer finger brushed beneath my chin as his lips held that infamous crooked smirk before pushing himself to his feet.

"Sicing ass."

March 29, 2016: Fort Washington, MD

My phone vibrated in the cup holder as I took a glance at the name, smacking my lips. The fuck. It's only been a few days without me dicking down Gizelle and the bitch was going crazy. All this begging she was doing was starting to blow a nigga. My lip twitched once hearing the giggle from Shia as I looked her way.

"What you laughing at?"

"You."

I gave her that expression to continue speaking before focusing back on the road, readjusting myself in the leather seat. Shia pushed a few strands of hair behind her ear before smiling, pointing her finger my way.

"Go ahead and answer it. I'm not paying you any mind." She smoothly said, grabbing her phone from her lap.

I chuckled, shaking my head. There was no way I was going to pick up any of Gi's calls while I was with Shia. All she wanted was some dick and that was something she could get later.

"Naw. I'm good."

A secure silence fell over us as I pressed the "volume up" button on the steering wheel making The Manhattan's "Kiss and Say Goodbye" sound louder through the speakers.

There was nothing like old school music - it put me in the best mood. I had nothing against today's music but I had my chosen few such as Kendrick, Cole, and KRIT who I really connected with compared to other artists. But when it came down to old school music, any and everything goes. It had **substance**. The one thing a lot of music nowadays is missing.

Her soulful voice flowed into my ears as she sang the chorus, forcing me to quickly look her way.

"You can sing slim?"

She laughed before twisting her hand side to side, "Sum'n like that." She mocked me of one of my favorite things to say.

I chuckled, "Blow some real quick baby, go all in." I pushed her, hoping she wouldn't get shy on me.

Seeing her out my peripheral, she took a deep breath before her full lips parted as a tone so sweet surfaced from her little body. Chills started from the top of my head to my toes once hearing the hint of raspiness making itself known in her voice. Her shit was powerful. I couldn't believe such a big voice was coming out of her little body.

Finishing off the chorus, she connected eyes with me as I put the car in park, us now sitting in front of her house.

I leaned back keeping my eyes on her, still in awe over her voice. A lazy smirk sat on my face as I readjusted my hat before licking my lips.

"Damn. You really can sing Shy," I voiced.

My smile grew once seeing how much she was blushing, covering her mouth. "Thank you." She muttered in her cupped hands as I reached over pulling them down.

"You gon' have to sing for a nigga more often. I'd really appreciate all of that."

Shia playfully rolled her eyes, "We'll see." She teasingly said while releasing her seatbelt.

"No lips?" I asked, face showcasing a bewildering expression as I focused on her hand preparing to open the door.

There was a pang in my chest once she faced me, quickly enclosing the space resting between us leaving her lips in kissing reach. I smiled crookedly before puckering my lips, making a light kissing noise making her laugh.

"Play too much." She mumbled while gripping my face within her hand, bringing my face to hers.

This electrifying sensation shot throughout my being once our lips connected. There was this ongoing fire burning in the depths of my chest spreading quickly. The tip of her tongue flickered against my lips asking for entrance before our tongues quickly danced with each other. I gently bit her bottom lip just as she tried to pull away, bringing her full lips to cover mine once again. She began pulling away softly as I could feel her smile against my lips, bringing one to my face as well. I leaned forward placing one last peck to her succulent lips as our heads rested against each other.

I watched her chest rise and drop, clearly worked up by just our kiss alone. I pecked her lips again before completely pulling away, resting the side of my face on the headrest fixing on her dazed gaze.

"Hit me later on or sum'n."

Clearly, she was at a loss for words since all she could do was nod while hopping out the car.

"I will. Thanks for breakfast and a good time boo."

She closed the door, flashing me a seductive look before turning on her heels heading up the driveway.

I released the breath I didn't realize I was holding shooting my eyes towards the car ceiling, running my hands down my face. This girl had a hold on me and didn't even know it. I couldn't stand this shit. I didn't even want to leave her ass. Retrieving my phone from the cup holder, I navigated to the one chick that I knew would get my mind off

Shia for the moment. I could definitely go for some neck right now seeing how Shy left me rock solid.

April 1, 2016: Alexandria, VA

"You sure I look fine?" I asked, suddenly feeling as if what I chose to wear wasn't good enough for meeting his mother.

This was probably the 20th time he'd smacked his lips since he picked me up. We'd just arrived at his house and once laying eyes on it, a wave of nerves hit me out of nowhere. I don't know why I was making a big deal out of this - it was just Mace's mother. We've talked plenty of times on the phone before but this time was different, we were actually meeting and I've never met a guy's mother before.

His piercing hues scanned over my voluptuous frame before a lazy grin appeared upon his full, pink lips. His tongue made an appearance before returning to his mouth, nodding slowly. He rose his thumb to his lip, rubbing it softly while continuing to nod.

"You always beautiful, boo. I don't know why you trippin'." He said so smoothly, waving me off.

At this moment, I took the time to admire his ensemble he threw together. Before picking me up, he told me that his mother wanted us to "dress up" - not anything extravagant but decent.

My eyes shifted downwards taking in the spaghetti strap black dress that hugged my curvy body perfectly. Not in the mood to be walking in heels, I decided on a pair of ankle cut black, suede booties. To top my simple fit off, I added two gold necklaces and a three-ring arm cuff to match it. My thick hair freely fell down the middle of my back, full of wand curls that Blake had created about 20 minutes ago.

"You look nice," I complimented earning a small chuckle from him.

"Thanks, boo." He smiled showing off his pearly whites and deep dimples.

My smile widened at the sight of Mace looking so spiffy. Who would've ever thought his annoying, cute ass could clean up so well? A white button-down shirt which was halfway buttoned revealing some of his white wife beater complemented his dark denim jeans well. A pair of white shell toes covered his large feet. Fixating on his hair, I noticed that instead of getting a complete cut he settled for just a shape-up which looked really nice by the way. Also since the last time I've seen him, he'd trimmed his facial hair down making him look younger.

Mace looked good, *damn* good.

He nodded towards the front door, "Come on, though. Ma waiting."

I nodded, slowly falling in tow behind him before he smacked his lips and took my hand into his. The various fumes filled my nostrils once we crossed the threshold into his home. Intertwining my fingers, I stood awkwardly in the foyer while taking in my surroundings. I jumped slightly at his palm coming in contact with the middle of my back, pushing me forward.

He chuckled, "Chill out with your scary ass."

I rolled my eyes while allowing him to guide me, growing more nervous by the steps we took. The soft voice of his mother sounded through the living room, heels clicking against the hardwood floors.

"Yea Ma. It's us!" He yelled, stepping next to me while nudging my shoulder with his.

I caught her contagious smile once honing in on her brown gaze as she rounded the corner, coming into view. She was beautiful. Her wild, brown curls were pushed off her face from a black headband causing her hair to fall loosely down her shoulders and back. Her olive skin was free of blemishes, making her face something you could look at forever. Her lips were covered with red lipstick as a pair of large, peach colored frames sat over her eyes. Looking her over, I took note of her cute sense of style. A dark denim dress stopping just above her knees covered her slim frame topped off with a pair of red pumps.

Her smile grew as she began softly tiptoeing our way with opened arms. Not a word left her lips and I already could feel the love - it was spilling from her body. All I could do was smile back as she got closer, stopping just in front of us.

"You didn't tell me Shia was *this* beautiful." She complimented earning a blush from me as her hand gravitated towards my shoulder, looking me over.

Mace kissed his teeth as I giggled at his uneasy expression sitting on his face.

"Ma. I told you endless times that boo was legit."

She laughed looking back to me, "He did sweetie. He talks about you and Kris all the time."

I looked to Mace with wide eyes as he chuckled, waving his hand in the air.

"Ight Ma. You're doing the most now. I don't talk about them like that. They ight." He downplayed earning a playful eye roll from me.

"Give me a hug Shia! I've been waiting so long to meet you. All I used to hear was your voice."

I giggled as she brought me into a tight embrace, swaying us from side to side. I couldn't believe I was feeling so much love from someone else's mother. I longed for my mother to hold me like this, just be happy that I was in her presence. Off this one hug alone, it stirred a bunch of unwanted emotions that I'd dare not bring to the forefront.

I offered a weak smile once she released me.

"Mace told me that you love tacos so, that's what we're having for dinner. Cool?" One brow climbed her head in question as I frantically nodded. "Good. Dinner's ready!" She happily said, clasping her hands together.

My brows met in the middle of my head as she began to turn around before I stopped her by grabbing her arm. Her curls got some air as she looked back to me with curiosity swirling in her brown hues.

"Yes, baby?"

"What do you want me to call you?"

She laughed as her hand collided with her chest. "I'm sorry Shia. Ma, Angie, or Mrs. Wolfe is fine. Whatever you like." She replied with ease.

I nodded, letting her know that I was listening but already knew the one name I thought was suitable to call her.

My nose turned up as the biggest belch broke free from Mace's lips before he burst into laughter, dodging the dish rag that Mrs. Wolfe threw his way. Over dinner, we talked about a lot of things and surprisingly I was very comfortable. His mother is a sweetheart and she knew her boundaries in regards to questions, which I loved.

Hearing the churning of Mace's stomach forced my scowl to grow deeper, looking at him with disgust. He stood leaning against the island rubbing his upset stomach with a discomforting expression marring his features.

"Go to the bathroom." I spat earning a scoff from him as he flipped me off.

I looked towards his mother, hoping she caught it. "Mrs. Wolfe!" My voice rose an octave as she turned her attention away from washing the dishes. "Mace—"

"Snitch!" He cut me off, laughing and rushing towards the bathroom. "The bathroom calls!" He yelled as I watched his retreating back moving down the hall until it disappeared before looking back to his mother.

"You need any help?" I asked, raising from the bar stool rounding the island moving towards her side.

I leaned against the counter admiring her beauty. A smile graced my face watching her wash the dishes as she began smiling.

"You staring again." She teasingly said earning a giggle from me.

It has been a couple of times during dinner that either she or Mace would call me out on my temporary staring problem. She was gorgeous and I couldn't keep my eyes off her. Plus, the mother vibes she gave off was hard to ignore which was drawing me to her even more.

"I know. I'm sorry. You're just so pretty Mrs.Wolfe." I complimented.

She wiped her wet hands with the dry towel while turning to face me. Her hand cupped the side of my face bringing heat to that same cheek.

"So are you sweetie." She returned, smiling wide.

I felt as if I lost something once she removed her hand causing me to frown. She began moving towards the living room motioning for me to follow her.

"So, how have you been doing baby?"

I knew this question was coming.

Two months ago, I would've had a conniption about someone I barely knew asking me about my well-being but I was far from feeling that way. In fact, I felt a sense of serenity at her concern. Being in her presence reminded me of the exact way I felt around Mae.

I nodded, pushing a few strands of hair behind my ear.

"I-I'm fine." I choked over my words, clearing my throat.

I kept it short seeing as though I didn't want to go in depth about how some days were better than the others. The fact some days I think about using, just because it's something to do. The fact I can't get out my head at times. The fact I wish I never turned to heroin in the first place and then I wouldn't be like this: a shitty individual.

Mrs. Wolfe offered me a bright smile as her head fell to the side, looking deeply in my brown hues.

"Don't worry Shia. Just take everything one day at a time. He never puts more on us than we can bare. You'll be fine baby. I know you will." She paused for a moment. "I can see it in you... your strength. You are a living testimony and your struggle will help others get through theirs. Never forget that." She finished, gripping my shoulder firmly.

April 1, 2016: Fort Washington, MD

"Thanks, Mace." I softly said, looking from my house to his green piercing orbs.

He licked his lips while keeping his gaze completely on me as we sat with the radio softly playing.

"Ma loves you already." He voiced breaking the short silence between us.

A genuine smile graced my full lips as I began nodding, "I can tell."

Mace chuckled while shaking his head, "Y'all two a mess." His mouth stretched open as a loud yawn escaped making me catch it as well. He ran his hands down his face before giving me a view of his exhausted eyes.

"I'm tired as shit." He mumbled, talking more to himself than me.

"I know you are. Let me let you go..." I grabbed a hold of the door handle, pushing it open. "Thanks for the invitation Mace and tell your mother I said thank you again."

"No problem boo. Sleep good ma."

"You too ugly."

His deep chortle was the last thing I heard before progressing up the stairs towards the front door.

⚜

April 7, 2016: Fort Washington, MD
Dallas
<u>Received</u>
Wats good bae?

Closing the refrigerator door, I grabbed my phone off the island as a Sprite can rest in the other before moving towards the couch. It was just hitting noon and I'd spent the majority of my morning downstairs in my own space especially since Blake didn't get off until six. Today was the first day of my follow-up therapy sessions with Dr. Jones and when I'd let Dallas know a few days ago, he offered to take me.

Dallas
<u>Sent</u>
You didn't forget about me, did you?

Sighing, I raked my fingers through my hair before leaning forward to grab the remote off the coffee table and flipping through channels.

Dallas
<u>Received</u>
Forget about you?
What you talking bout baby?

The butterflies in my stomach went erratic just from texting him; I missed him so much.

Dallas
<u>Sent</u>
My therapy session

Dallas
<u>**Received**</u>
Aw shit… the follow-up.
I forgot that was today.
My bad. What time?

Something told me to remind him.

Dallas
<u>**Sent**</u>
If you can't Dallas, it's fine.

Dallas
<u>**Received**</u>
You blowing me.
Slim, what time you gotta be there?

I chuckled, imagining the irritated expression taking over his handsome face.

Dallas
<u>**Sent**</u>
Lol, 2:30 nigga.

Dallas
<u>**Received**</u>
Lls.
I'll see you in a few. Just getting off.
Boutta take a shower then I'll be omw.

Dallas
<u>**Sent**</u>
Okay.
Thank you Dally pooh.

I knew how much he hated when I called him Dally. He barely liked when his nieces and mother would do it but could tolerate it since it was coming from them.

Dallas
<u>Received</u>
Lol, you blowing me dawg.
I'll see you when I get there slim.

Book XIII.

Schoolboy Q's "Studio" blared through the speakers as I nodded my head to the beat, waiting for Shia to come out. A smirk blessed my face once seeing her plump backside making itself known through her white shorts stopping mid-thigh. After locking the door, she descended the stairs with the biggest smile on her face earning a chuckle from me. That was that same smile she wore every time she saw me.

Cute ass.

My nostrils caught a whiff of her perfume sending a pang to my chest. I frowned small at the effect she had on me without trying.

"Why your hair in that damn bun?" My frown grew deeper, loving her long hair out rather than confined into one knot.

She rolled her eyes in return while waving me off, "Do you *not* feel the heat out here today, Dallas?" She smartly responded earning a chuckle from me.

Licking my lips, I gave her a once-over as she began blushing causing me to laugh.

"Stop eye fucking me." She softly said as a cute grin contorted her succulent lips.

I shrugged my shoulders putting my car in drive. "Naw. I'd rather keep eye fucking..." I paused shortly, looking to her as I came to a stop sign. "You." I finished off before proceeding onto the main road.

Her cute giggle sent a jolt through my body.

"Whatever nigga." She mumbled, looking out the window.

"How are you feeling, though?"

I caught her confused expression out of my peripheral, locking eyes quickly before focusing back on the road.

"About the session, bae." I finished, making a right turn.

"Oh." She sighed deeply and I instantly knew she wasn't digging the idea of meeting with Dr. Jones. She shrugged lazily while scrunching her button nose up. "I guess I'm okay. I'm not too excited but I know it'll help." She said all in one breath.

I nodded, glad she was seeing the positive outcome ahead despite her fears.

"Just keep that positive mindset. You'll be aight. Don't think too much on it. Just go in there and be open to talking, meanie."

I laughed once hearing her snort.

"I am not mean." She mumbled as if I didn't hear her.

Her ass knew she was mean.

"Yes, you are."

I pushed my back into the seat once coming to a red light, looking to her. Smiling lazily, I took pleasure in witnessing the upset expression marring her beautiful features. Using my bent index finger I brushed under her chin, wetting my lips.

"Come 'ere," I muttered in a husky tone as I saw the excitement swirling in her brown hues.

A teasing grin crept to her full lips as she leaned towards me slowly, lips resting not far from mine. I placed a peck on her lips but was quickly pulled back in for a deeper kiss once her hand found the back of my neck. The car horn sounding off had us breaking apart against our will earning a laugh from us both.

"You always take it too far." I laughed as she rolled her eyes, waving me off.

"No, I don't. You liked it." She teasingly said earning a grunt from me because whether she knew it or not, she pretty much knew me like the back of her hand already.

April 7, 2016: NW, Washington, DC

Shaking my head frantically, I looked over the building for about the 5th time since we'd been sitting in the emergency lane with the hazards on. I couldn't gather myself to allow my feet to clash with the concrete, knowing I had to face my fears beyond those automatic revolving doors. My hands began to become sweaty as I wiped them against my exposed thighs, watching the perspiration bring shine to my skin. The heavy chuckle forced my nose upward as I snapped my head towards Dallas who was staring right back at me.

"You're making this bigger than it is Shy. Go in there slim. I can't sit right here forever." He smoothly voiced, looking around for I'm assuming any sign of cops.

"I know," I whined, looking back to the building before honing in on his chocolate gaze again. "You coming up?" I innocently questioned with raised brows.

Dallas kissed his teeth while shifting down in his seat, nodding. "You already know I'll be up there. Right in the waiting room for you. Second floor. 216, right?"

A weak smile managed to warp my plump lips at not only his physical support but moral support as well. My stomach fluttered once his warm, soft hand took a hold of mine intertwining our fingers immediately. A wave of heat took over my being with him looking deeply in my eyes.

"You got this, baby. I'm right behind you. Lemme go park right quick. Go ahead." He pushed which surprisingly lit a fire under my ass because my free hand was opening the passenger door.

He smiled, letting go of my hand as I stepped out the car releasing a breath I didn't realize I was holding. I sized up the building one last time simultaneously coaching myself in my head.

You got this Shia.

216.

My brown orbs swept over the three numbers engraved into the light brown wooden door. Here I was, stuck again. I felt as if I'd been standing here forever, probably about a good five minutes now. My heart felt like it was going to break free from my chest and fall at my feet.

"Shit!" I hissed once feeling a hand come in contact with my back forcing my body to turn around, coming chest to chest with Dallas.

His strong cologne swarmed my nostrils as he took a firm grip of my waist with his pouty lips resting just above the top of my nose. The warmth from his breath breaking through the small gap of his lips had my knees becoming weak. He chuckled as his other arm wrapped around my small frame, keeping me upright as if he knew I'd fall to the floor any second.

He huffed before swiftly turning my body to face the door, giving my back a light shove forcing me forward.

"It'll be over before you know it." His husky tone sounded off behind me as I opened the door as we crossed the threshold together, him right behind me.

If I was *this* nervous, I couldn't imagine how I would've felt going back to New Leaf for a session. When Dr. Jones proposed the idea of us meeting at her outside office, I agreed quickly. Dallas took a seat in one of the chairs against the wall, one leg sprawled out with the other in its normal bent state. There were about three other people in the waiting area - a couple and a young female.

The contagious smile of the receptionist had the corners of my lips curving up as I approached the desk.

"Good afternoon. How are you? I will need your name and who will you be seeing today?" She sweetly asked.

"Afternoon. I'm good. I'm Shia Sinclair and I'm here for Dr. Jones."

She smiled, pushing her black tresses behind her ear before clicking away on the computer. "Okay. You can sign in on the clipboard and may I please have your ID and insurance card?"

I nodded after signing in, grabbing my ID and insurance card out of my back pocket and handing it over.

"You can have a seat and I'll let her know that you're here."

"Thank you," I smiled, turning on my heels to head towards the empty seat next to Dallas.

He looked my way with a screwed up expression after my body bumped into his as I plopped into the seat. I giggled before picking up an Essence magazine and beginning to flip through it. I frowned once feeling my phone vibrate in my back pocket as I leaned to one side retrieving it.

Mace
<u>Received</u>
Let me know how your session goes boo.
Good luck!

Mace
<u>Sent</u>
Lol, Thanks Mace.
You know I will.
You gotta chill with the kissey emoji, lol.

I giggled to myself, feeling Dallas' eyes boring a hole in the side of my face causing me to suddenly grow nervous. Slowly I turned towards him, smiling wide earning a laugh from him as he shook his head.

"You irritating slim." He laughed, still shaking his head.

I shrugged as the receptionist called my name while holding up my cards as I went to grab them. My heart skipped a beat once I heard that familiar voice, "Ms. Sinclair."

Her dark brown tresses were now mixed with honey brown highlights, bone straight. I'd grown so accustomed to seeing her hair one color and in loose curls that I never imagined it straight. Instead of her usual suit, she was sporting a gray high waist pencil skirt with a white blouse tucked in it along with black pumps. Her brown frames sat on the edge of her nose giving me a full view of her brown eyes as she looked over the top of them.

I couldn't help but smile once seeing hers. Surprisingly, I actually missed her.

"Dr. Jones." I responded as she pushed the door open wider, motioning me in her direction.

"Dallas. How are you?" Her voice rose an octave bringing his attention from his phone to her, smiling while showing off those deep dimples at the same time.

He gave her a head nod, "Sup Dr. Jones. I'm good and yourself?"

"I'm just fine." She focused back on me as I stood uneasily next to her. "Come on Shia. Let's get started."

The ticking of the clock on the wall was the only noise cutting the thick silence in her office. My attention remained focused on my dainty fingers, twisting them around each other out of pure nervousness.

"So Shia, you're telling me that you've come all the way out here to be quiet?"

My brows furrowed, fingers ceasing movement as my eyes traveled up her crossed legs before locking on her face. For her to be 38, she looked *really* good.

I shrugged, twisting my lips, "What you want me to say?"

"What's on your mind?"

I sighed, looking around her office searching for anything to keep my eyes away from her intense gaze. My shoulders rose and dropped lazily again, "I don't know."

She nodded, gripping her iPad within her hands. "Okay. Well let's start here, I see Dallas is here with you. What do you two call yourselves building?"

Out of nowhere, I became annoyed at her questioning about Dallas and I. I wasn't quite sure on what we were myself so attempting to explain it to someone else on the outside was annoying and I definitely was unprepared.

"That's the thing. I don't know…" My voice trailed off as I began fiddling with my fingers.

"Shia. Make eye contact when you speak." She demanded.

I huffed while looking up, "Dr. Jones. I don't know. All I know is that I feel my best when I'm with him."

She smiled that bright smile of hers while pushing her frames up the bridge of her nose. "So we're getting somewhere. When did things begin developing between you two?"

I smiled at the thought of being alone with Dallas for the first time - at New Leaf when I discovered he'd never seen *Like Mike*. I made a mental note to show him that movie sooner than later.

"Honestly…" I raised my brows, "At New Leaf. He was on his way out and was checking on me. But ever since first seeing him, something was drawing us together. I don't know what but the more we hang out, the stronger the feeling hits me."

She nodded, looking back and forth between me and her iPad. For some reason, after that small confession, I was comfortable. I felt at peace with sharing things with her because I knew she wasn't here to judge me whether I sounded crazy or not.

"I just really enjoy his company, Dr. Jones. Also, I find my sobriety flowing easier with him being in the picture. I know it's too early to be gaining new addictions or any for the matter, but I truly feel

Dallas is a healthy one for me. He's opening my eyes to the positive side of things instead of my overbearing negativity." I expressed with my hands while speaking.

Since I started talking about him, her smile never wavered.

"Sounds like you both are becoming a great asset to each other's lives."

I nodded while smiling wide, "You can say that."

"Well from what you're telling me, things are going well. I know with things like this it can be downs as well, but it's up to you Shia to not allow it to get too overwhelming where you could consider using. Have you had any urges lately?"

I broke her gaze looking towards the cracked window, "Actually I have. When Kris was going through her shit, it took a toll on me as well. Lately, the urges would pop up whenever I'm bored or something."

"And have you used?"

My eyes widened, "Hell no!" My voice escalated, shaking my head. "No. No. I'm not going to use." I stressed to her as well as myself.

"Good. That's good. Have you been using the meds I've put you on?"

I knew that question was coming.

"I haven't but that's the one thing Dallas suggested I should start doing. I sort of, kind of spazz out on him from time to time."

I giggled at her wide-eyed expression plastered across her face.

"And he's still tolerating?" She asked with a surprised tone causing me to burst into laughter.

"Am I *that* mean?"

Dr. Jones' face deadpanned which made me laugh even harder. Honestly, I didn't think I was that much of a bitch but I guess I was.

"I can't say that you're mean Shia but your lash-outs are always unnecessary and over the top. It all stems from pain. Your past. In regards to the tarnished relationship with your mother, losing your father, and having your body taken advantage of. I don't blame you for always playing defense, making sure that you'd protect yourself. That's fine. But, you just need to know those who are genuinely here and who's not so you won't have to be defensive 24/7."

My leg began shaking at her words as I reminisced on my fucked up past. The best part about growing up was spending it with my father. Everything after that was hell on earth.

"I hear you. I just wish I didn't have to go through what I did... but somebody had to, right?"

My brows furrowed as the door closed behind me with my curvy body moving further into the waiting room, narrowing my intense gaze on Dallas. His body language was extremely different than what I left him in - I could tell something was bothering him.

"Dallas," I voiced, watching his brows deepen before looking up to me.

"You down to ride with me real quick?"

His voice was low and shaky, jaws clenching and all. Before I knew it, his tall structure was towering over mine while holding my gaze. The slight glistening filling his eyes had me worried, scared that he was going to have a breakdown any moment.

"What's wrong?" I asked, concern heavily lacing my tone.

I don't know about everyone else in the room but the tension was in existence, and it was thick. I frowned once reaching to grab his arm only to be shrugged off. He stepped back creating more space between us looking towards the ceiling before looking down at me.

"I'm ight. We just need to head to the hospital."

April 7, 2016: NW, Washington, DC

Silence consumed us.

The only thing that could be heard was the wheels darting across the gravel as Dallas hit about 80 down the freeway. Not a word was spoken between us since we left Dr. Jones' office which was killing me, but I'd rather leave him be until he was ready to talk. I had no clue who we were rushing to the hospital for but if my assumptions were right, I'm pretty sure it was for his mother.

I wasn't ready for this. None of this.

Looking to my left, a frown worked to my lips once seeing how tensed he looked. That tight expression never left his face since the waiting room and many things crossed my mind to say, but my lips wouldn't allow them to enter the air. Accepting the fact he wasn't going to look my way, I remained silent and looked back out the window more than ready for this intense ride to come to an end. My brows furrowed once we pulled into the parking lot of one of the places I wasn't expecting to ever return to.

Instantly, my body tensed as Dallas pulled into a parking space. I didn't want to move for shit. My mind was telling me to get out the car just as quickly as Dallas did but my body wasn't having it. I remained seated, staring at nothing in particular. Out of nowhere, my heartbeat picked up its pace as slight anxiety started to kick in. There were too many horrendous experiences in that hospital; I didn't want to go through those doors again.

"Come on." His husky, stern voice vibrated against my ears with his large frame towering over me as he opened my door.

"I can't," I whispered, not able to find the courage to fight my fears more than once within a two-hour span.

Dallas smacked his lips releasing an exasperated sigh. "Look. Shy, I'm not doing this shit with you. You're either coming or your ass can sit right here in this car."

I whipped my head towards him as his words managed to break me out of my daze. Annoyance etched his handsome features as he stood with his weight shifted to one side of his body. I could tell that he was losing his patience with me which I completely understood. I'd lose patience with myself. He'd just finished supporting me but here I was allowing my fears to get in the way of me returning the favor. Before I knew it, Dallas was turning on his heels walking towards the hospital entrance.

As much as I didn't want to go in there, I know I had to. Not just for myself to face my fears but also to be right there, for Dallas.

At this point, Shia was getting on my last nerve.

I found it crazy how I willingly dropped everything to be by her side today yet, she was being difficult in returning the favor. It was evident on her face that this hospital was what she wasn't expecting but none of that shit mattered. The only person I was trying to get to was my mother and nobody, Shia included, was getting in the way of that.

Standing with my back against the elevator wall, I glanced her way shortly admiring her beauty. A chuckle wanted to make itself known at her irritated look but due to the serious matter at hand, my face was stuck in a stoic state. I wanted to apologize for how rude I'd been acting but also I figured she understood that I was acting off emotions right now.

"You aight?" I asked as her eyes landed on mine, constricting and all.

"I should be asking you that." She shot back. "I want to be here for you, Dallas. You're already shutting down on me before I get the chance to." She finished with her tone softening.

She was right.

I wasn't use to this shit. I wasn't used to having a female other than my family in my corner. Despite me being uncomfortable, I understood that we both were placed in this position. Neither one of us could fight how we felt about each other. So while I had the chance to express my gratitude, I was going to take advantage of it despite my own fears.

Shia sized me up as I moved towards her, taking her hands into mine while looking profoundly into her hues.

"Thank you, baby. Thank you for being here right now cause I really need you right now." I spoke, shaking our connected hands for emphasis.

She bit her lip, nodding her head. "Of course, Dallas. I will always be here for you like you're here for me."

"Stage 4?" My voice rose an octave as I shrugged Devyn's hand off my shoulder in her attempt to calm me down. "Fuck you mean stage 4?"

"Calm down, Dallas," Devyn spoke in a relaxed tone while trying to grab my arm as I shook her off like before.

I don't know how she remained unbothered during difficult circumstances. Honestly, I desired to have her patience when it came to things like this but I couldn't. Ma was just doing fine. She was moving around more, using her walker less only for me to be seeing her looking worse than my last visit. I took a big breath, digging deep to bring myself to a relaxed state before asking the doctor more questions.

I caught Devyn's gaze before looking to my Queen, silently sleeping with the life sucked from her beautiful features. When I left her yesterday, she was doing perfectly fine or at least I thought so. Looking at her now, it was like witnessing her last hours - she didn't look like herself. Devyn's hand touched my back once again and this time I allowed the contact. Water began to build within my eyes as I looked from my mother to the brunette doctor who held nothing but sympathy in her orbs.

The one look I hated. That same look I received when I was told my best friend was dead.

"So what we do next?"

Her eyes darted towards my sleeping beauty before focusing back on me. "Well, her blood pressure was highly elevated when coming in but we've managed to get that under control which is great. As you can see, there are great amounts of swelling in her legs which have become quite painful making it difficult for her to walk. She'll be bed-ridden for a few days until the swelling goes down. Due to the nephritis going from stage 3 to 4, she is on a high dose of corticosteroids to reduce the swelling and pain as well as immunosuppressant medications. We want to monitor her for about two days to keep an eye on the swelling and blood pressure. I highly suggest she begin immunotherapy immediately."

My brows climbed my forehead, "Immunotherapy?"

"With your mother now being at stage 4, it can develop into End Stage Renal Failure which will result in dialysis or a kidney transplant. But with immunotherapy, she would have a better chance at preventing further damage to her kidney. This is a new therapy that we'd been practicing for some years now which many of patients have benefitted from. It improves immunity and reconstructs kidney function. Due to the fact we've caught her at the beginning of the stage, she could benefit greatly from the therapy so I recommend her starting as soon as possible."

God, I don't understand. What's going on here? Why are we going through this? Why our mother?

Hearing Devyn's sniffles, I grabbed her hand giving it a squeeze to let her know that I was right here. We were going through this shit together. Always have been.

I nodded, not able to find my words as I saw Devyn wiping her eyes out of my peripheral.

"A nurse will be in later to check in. As of now, she's stabled. I was told she wasn't getting much sleep because of the painful swelling so now that we've got that under control, she's been resting. If you have any further questions, don't hesitate to contact me."

Once the door closed giving us our privacy, I wrapped my virile arms around Devyn's minuscule figure as she began bawling in my chest. My eyes found the ceiling as I allowed my older sister to let out every ounce of pain. Tears welled at the brim of my lids but I refused to let them drop; I had to be the strength of the family. I'm nowhere near prepared to carry them all but this had to happen.

It was something I **had** to do.

"I'm scared," She muttered into my chest.

I was too. I wouldn't admit that, though.

Placing a kiss on her temple, I grabbed her shoulders removing her body from mine looking into her bloodshot orbs, still filling with tears. The pain emerging from her body was becoming contagious, making my chest heavier. With Devyn being the oldest plus a mother of two, she carried the majority of the load since she was with Ma 24/7. Looking at her pretty face similar to mine, I noticed the exhaustion. She was tired and I didn't blame her.

"Dev, you already know the way God is set up and the strength of our mother. Miracles exist and doctors love to downplay that whenever things are out of their control. But you know what, Ma is in

God's hands and that is the best place for her. I got you, sis. You're not carrying this load alone. I swear you're not."

As I spoke, more tears cascaded down her cheeks as she forced a weak smile to her face before wrapping her arms around my abdomen. I rested my chin on the top of her head, squeezing her tight.

"I love you, Dallas."

"And I love you more."

Rubbing my soft hands against my exposed arms, I attempted to radiate some heat from the friction. During the hour I've been sitting here, I was getting colder with every passing minute. My attention locked on the tan blanket being brought into my view forcing me to lock eyes with the kind stranger. I smiled once locking eyes with a beautiful woman who looked as if she was in her mid-30s. Pink scrubs adorned her small body as her short hair was parted on the side, cute swoop in the front.

"Thank you," I said while grabbing the blanket.

She smiled wide revealing her two dimples, "No problem, honey. I see you came in with Dallas and wanted to make sure you were well taken care of. I know how chilly it can get in here."

I returned the smile, "Thank you so much." I softly giggled while spreading the blanket out allowing it to fall freely over my body.

"You're welcome, sweetie. No problem at all."

She turned on her heels heading down the hallway Dallas disappeared into an hour ago. Within seconds, a slim brown-skinned beauty emerged from that same hallway. For some reason, I couldn't tear my eyes from her - she reminded me of someone. The frustration was visible as she roughly raked her hands through her hair. I frowned, feeling her frustration from where I was sitting.

This was exactly why I hated hospitals. Pain was everywhere.

I looked away quickly once we made eye contact. Hesitantly I looked back her way only to find her focus solely on me. The way her eyes were constricting as if she was trying to figure out who I was had me doing the same exact thing because I swear her face looks familiar.

My brows furrowed once seeing her feet amble towards my way before stopping in front of me.

I didn't say a word and neither did she.

I studied her beautiful visage as I assumed she was doing the same - that was the only explanation I could come up with for the silence. That's when it hit me. My jaw fell agape at how beautiful she was, lips beginning to move before my mind had the chance to register anything.

"You're Dallas' sister?"

She giggled, "And you're Shia." She stated more than questioning, tone laced with curiosity.

Huh? He actually told his sister about me?

The swoosh of air from her body colliding with the empty seat next to me fanned against my face. I never would've thought our initial meeting would be in a hospital. Nor did I expect his sister to come off so sweet; I assumed meeting a guy's sister for the first time would've been filled with tension.

"You look even cuter with your eyes open," She broke the short quietude blanketed over us.

"Huh?" My voice rose an octave as I looked her way, confused.

She laughed, "My creep brother took a pic of you while you was sleep. He was telling me about you and that happened to be the only one he had of you." Her elaboration earned a giggle from me. "I'm Devyn by the way."

I smiled, "Nice to meet you, Devyn."

"Likewise love. Sorry you're stuck he—"

I cut her off with a wave of the hand, "Don't worry about that. I'm fine. I'll wait all night. Dallas has been a great solace to me lately and I've been waiting for the chance to do the same for him."

Devyn offered a genuine smile, holding my gaze. "You're not mean at all."

I laughed bringing my hand into the air, "Hold up. Wait. He said I was mean?"

She nodded, "Girl. I'm pretty sure he told you his damn self already. That man never bites his tongue."

I giggled, finding it cute how well she knew her brother and at the fact she was accurate about him informing me on my "mean" ways.

"But, I've never seen him invest time and energy into no one else but us. So to know that somehow you're bringing my brother peace, it makes me happy. I haven't seen him this happy since we've lost my husband and Aaron..." Her voice trailed off as her attention averted towards her fiddling fingers.

The same thing I had the habit of doing when I found it grueling in search for my words.

Once seeing the single tear bounce off her hand, I placed mines over hers silently letting her know that I wasn't just here for Dallas, but all of them as well. Devyn sniffed while using her free hand to wipe at her eyes before looking to me.

"He's been through so much, Shia. We all have. If it's not one thing, it's another. I just... I can't lose my mother. I can't take losing someone else I love." Her words came out shaky, lips trembling.

My scowl grew deeper at her negative thoughts. Crazy how I did nothing but thrive off negativity, allowing my past to create such a battered individual. But being showered with Dallas' positive energy was molding me into a different person - someone I never imagined seeing myself evolve into. An unexplainable feeling rushed my body before parting my lips to speak.

"Devyn, if there's one thing your brother has taught me was to have faith. Despite how things are looking at the moment, remember you have the best person in your corner… God."

I surprised myself once those words of encouragement flew from my mouth so easily. Where did that come from? A tingly sensation started from the top of my head shooting to the soles of my feet at the thought of God. He was here. I felt His presence. Allowing Him to make Himself known to me was such an overwhelming feeling, in a good way. The warm tears blessed my cheeks as I suddenly felt as if I'd been released from a hold of pain - I felt free. This moment was bringing things into perspective for me. I didn't realize how much pain Dallas was enduring until now. Despite his losses, he still managed to lean on his faith. On God.

I truly admired that about him. And I admired him even more for bringing me back to God.

"You sound just like Dallas. Where did you guys meet anyway?" Her eyes narrowed on me.

"New Leaf."

My heart skipped a beat once hearing his husky tone forcing my eyes from Devyn to him. He stood with his hands stuffed in his pockets, eyes holding a slight red hue to them.

"Are you serious?!" Devyn's voice rose an octave out of surprise, eyes wide in shock.

Was this reaction good or bad?

Book XIV.

April 7, 2016: NW, Washington, DC

"You ready Shy?" I asked before Devyn got the chance to begin drilling us with questions.

Back when I was a patient at New Leaf, Devyn would always tease me about being with someone fighting an addiction just like me. I never would've expected her words to become my reality. I was just as shocked as she was but I definitely wasn't trying to hear a million questions she was conjuring up to shoot our way. Another day would have to do.

"Only if you are." She sweetly responded which brought the first smile to my face since we arrived here.

Shia stood to her feet turning to Devyn, outstretching her arms for a hug. My brows met in the middle of my head surprised to see Shia being the first to initiate physical contact. She wasn't much of a hugger and if someone wanted to hug her, she didn't deny it but her face screamed "I'm uncomfortable." That was one of many things I observed about her when we began hanging out. So to witness this was mind blowing. I watched as they embraced one another before releasing, Shia's hands holding Devyn's.

"Remember what I told you."

Devyn chewed on the inside of her cheek, nodding. "I will Shia. Thank you." My brows deepened once seeing Devyn lean in to whisper something before a giggle came from Shia, turning to smile at me.

"You know I will." She spoke before turning to give Devyn one last hug.

Wanting to have any type of physical contact with Shia, I outstretched my hand as she took a hold. Her thumb softly rubbed against the back of my hand bringing a blanket of comfort over me.

"I'll be back Dev."

April 7, 2016: Fort Washington, MD

"Thanks for coming, baby. I appreciate you." I thanked her while keeping my focus on the road.

My eyes began growing heavy as a loud yawn parted my lips. I was tired as shit. From working early this morning, Shy's session, and ending my day at the hospital was enough for me. As much as I'd love to be sprawled out in my bed sleeping, I knew I had to make my way back to the hospital for the night. I wanted to be there when Ma woke up.

"Anytime boo." My heart jumped once her hand grabbed mines. "You tired?"

I shook my head, "Nawww." I dragged out while beginning to play with her fingers.

Her cute giggle filled the car as a smirk contorted my lips.

"What you laughing at?" I asked, cutting my eyes at her.

"You." She quickly shot back, boring a hole into the side of my face.

"Oh yeah?"

"Yeah. You're tired as shit. You need to come in and sleep for a bit."

Smacking my lips, I twisted them as I turned on her street. "Naw. I need to get back to the hospital, bae."

Shia sighed as I felt her fiery gaze on me forcing me to look her way once I parked in front of her house.

"Dallas, come in and take a nap. I'll wake you up within an hour or two."

The more she talked about sleeping, the more I was leaning towards the idea of cuddling her to take a nap. Turning my car off, I stuffed my keys into my pocket.

"Aight. An hour and 30 max."

Crazy how it didn't take much to convince me.

She laughed while pushing her door open, "Whatever nigga."

My footsteps were slow and ponderous as I trekked into Shia's personal space of the basement. After slipping off my shoes by the steps, I sauntered towards the couch allowing my heavy frame to fall into it. I snorted once Shia's hand smacked against my back.

I could fall asleep right here - I was *that* worn out.

"Uh uh. Come get in the bed."

Her sultry tone had my body reacting against its will, shivering and shit. I don't think she was aware of the way her words came out. Pushing my flat palms into the cushion, I raised from the couch standing to my feet. I caught a glimpse of her round backside as she disappeared into the bedroom. Following not too far behind, I made sure to flick off the living room light before crossing the threshold into her personal domain, closing the door behind me. Alicia Key's "Butterflyz" filled the air as I frowned at the mood the slow jam was setting.

My brown orbs fixated on Shia as she quickly stripped her body of her clothing, leaving her in nothing but black lace panties riding up her ass with a bra to match. Wetting my lips, I grabbed myself trying my best to keep my shit under control, but this was long overdue.

I don't think self-control was going to be considered tonight.

Biting my lip, my sock-clad feet slid across the floor as I swiftly moved across the room grabbing her from behind. A soft moan escaped her pretty lips as the back of her head fell into my shoulder. Using my warm hand, I began rubbing her flat stomach earning a hiss from her.

"What are you doing Dallas?" Her question entered the air in a breathy tone; I know the contact was driving her insane.

The contact alone was enough but with Alicia playing softly in the background was making it worst. This was some baby making music.

"What you want me to do," I raspily spoke into her ear as my hand trailed down her thick thighs.

My dick stiffened against her ass which explained her quickly removing her backside from my front, turning to face me. A lazy grin sat on my face as I looked over her perfect body. Locking into her fiery gaze, I could see the strong passion sitting in her brown hues. I swept my thumb across my lip, kissing my teeth as my eyes continued to scan every crevice of her structure.

"On mute?" I teasingly questioned as I noticed her squeezing her thighs as she backed into the wall.

Quickly I enclosed the space between us gripping her face in my hands. My brown hues scanned over her beautiful features like any other time, placing a gentle kiss on her lips.

"Fuck this," I spoke through clenched teeth as my hands slapped against her ass, bringing her body into mid-air only to have her legs wrap around my waist.

I rested my forehead against Dallas' before placing my lips onto his, reciprocating the strong kiss he was giving me. His kiss was filled with passion; he was kissing me like his life depended on it. As if I was fulfilling his appetite.

Bringing my hands to cup his cheeks, I pulled away from him looking intensely into his eyes. That strong pang to my chest that I grew accustomed to surfaced like any other time I looked into his eyes, but this time it was different. It was stronger, stirring numerous emotions within me. I sighed deeply, grabbing his shoulders firmly.

"Let me down, Dallas."

His face was filled with confusion but he obliged, allowing my bare feet to connect with the floor. Moving towards my dresser to cover myself, I raked my hands through my long tresses.

"Baby." His husky voice sent chills throughout my body causing the hairs to rise on my arms.

A gasp broke my lips as Dallas' hand covered mine stopping me from pulling up my shorts. I licked my full lips once his hot breath bounced against the side of my neck. His grip on my shorts tightened as he pushed them to the floor in one motion.

"Dallas," I whispered in a shaky voice.

"Baby." He said low and sexy in my ear.

"We can't do this," I whined as my knees shook lightly.

"But we can, though."

Swiftly I turned to face him as my eyes honed in on his pouty lips before locking into his gaze. I touched his cheek softly.

"Dallas, we just left the hos—" My words were cut short as his index finger rose to my lips, shushing me.

"I already know what you're about to say, Shy. How I'm just hurting and want to use sex to feel better. Right?"

I nodded slowly as my expression contorted. "Pretty much," I agreed.

He chuckled, "I know. But..." He looked away shortly before looking back to me. "That's not the case. This is just our moment. That moment I've been waiting on. Being at the hospital today made me realize a lot. Today, I came to terms with my feelings for you. I'm not ignoring or fighting it anymore."

He licked his lips wrapping his arms around my waist. "I heard everything."

"Huh?" I asked, completely thrown off about what he could've possibly heard.

"You and Dev. Just to hear you speak of God when you were about to bite my head off the other night from mentioning Him was beautiful, baby." He smiled while shaking his head, eyes shooting to the ceiling before looking back down to me. "I can see the change in your eyes. They don't look dark anymore… less pain. This whole day made me appreciate you even more. In the beginning, I was iffy about you but this shit real. I can't even back out nor shake how I feel about you."

With every word he spoke, my body felt as if it was on fire. He made me feel like no one else ever had. Was this possible? To fall for someone so deeply within just a month? If not, we just made the impossible, possible.

He bit his lip, "And you don't have to say anything. I already know how you feel because I can feel it. It's always like this fire between us. It's strong as hell too. Y'know my Ma always tells me that God will bring certain people in my life just to teach me something for the moment or be a great contribution. She always said don't ignore it because He makes no mistakes..." His voice trailed off as I nodded, butterflies fluttering wildly throughout my stomach. "Like I told you before, this between us wasn't a mistake. We have imperfections and still have things to work on but honestly, I can't see myself working on me without you. I need you just as much as you need me."

By now, warm tears were flowing down my cheeks at his heart-filled confession. I would've never expected Dallas to feel like this towards me especially since he used to be quick to shut down. To start off as complete strangers, we established a bond that scared me but was so grateful for. He chuckled, using the pads of his thumbs to wipe my tears.

"Baby, stop crying." He continued chuckling earning one from me as I swatted his hand away.

"I can't." I sniffed, "You shouldn't have said all that sweet shit to my mean ass."

He burst out laughing with his head cocking to the side, "Oh yeah? You gon' hold that mean shit over my head, huh?" He teasingly asked, sweeping his thick tongue over his lips leaving a wet sheen.

His warm hands began creating heat to my exposed hips as he rubbed them gently, hands creeping to my plump ass. I smirked, locking into his lustful gaze.

"Mhmm," I hummed.

Alicia Keys and Maxwell's "Fire We Make" began falling from the speakers, making the air thicken around us creating more sexual tension. My hands flew to my mouth trying to stifle my laugh at Dallas' annoyed expression. He smacked his lips, looking towards the stereo before back to me. He pecked my forehead as I wrapped my arms around his neck, swaying us from side to side.

"Fuck you tryna do? Make a baby?" He joked earning a laugh from me. "You knew what you were doing when you turned that music on before stripping n' shit."

I burst out in laughter, head falling back. Actually, I'd been listening to my R&B playlist earlier today and wanted to cuddle Dallas to it. I just happened to throw it on the moment Dallas wanted to get it popping.

I pushed his chest, "Shut up." I mumbled before rising on my toes, kissing his lips.

"You tryna make a baby?"

My brows furrowed at his serious tone before a teasing grin worked to his lips. "I'm just playing baby but, you gonna have my first. I already know that shit."

My face heated up as I waved him off, loving the idea of having a family with him but wasn't going to feed into it. Whatever happens, happen. He pecked my lips resting his forehead against mine.

"So... you gonna let me put this thang on you?" He asked, rotating his hips against my body making me giggle.

I tipped a brow at him, stepping out of his hold before reaching behind me to unfasten my bra allowing my perky, chocolate breasts to fall free. His eyes held excitement as they remained on my bare boobs.

I grunted once her full titties bounced in the air, hovering over her flat stomach. Alicia's voice was really making a nigga want to put a baby in Shia. I shook my head of the family thoughts, enclosing the space between us before taking her face in my hands and falling in a deep kiss. Her hands roamed freely over my body causing me to mumble obscenities once she began fiddling with my pants. My left hand slowly moved up her spine before taking a hold of her hair, pulling her head back.

A moan escaped her pretty lips as I placed a gentle kiss on her chin before diving into her neck. I was enjoying the way she was squirming in my hold - her knees were going to give out at any moment. Flicking my tongue across her sweet skin, my lips latched onto that taut area as her fingers wildly massaged through my rough curls. I chuckled at the cute frown settling upon her lips as I abruptly pulled away from her, looking her over intensely.

I'm. Going. To. Tear. Her. Ass. Up.

"Get that ass on the bed," I demanded, smacking the side of her ass.

She smirked with glee dancing within her eyes before obeying my request. There was no time to be wasted as I removed my shirt before suddenly stopping, focusing on Shia bent over removing her panties putting that phat ass of hers on full display.

DAWG.

I mirrored her smirk while holding her fiery gaze as she leaned back on her elbows in her striking birthday suit. Dropping my pants and boxers to the floor, my dick sprung in the air as Shia's eyes fixated on it. I looked down to the one thing that never failed me since I've put it to work.

"Shit." I hissed, remembering I didn't have protection.

Her face held concern as she sat up, "What?"

"Fuck," I muttered. "I don't have protection, baby."

The biggest smile etched across her lips as she got off the bed, ass jiggling with every movement. I bit my lip watching her bring a gold wrapper in front of my face. One side of my lip turned up, "Fuck you doing with this?" I questioned, looking back and forth between the condom and her.

Shia giggled while returning to her previous position as I held her gaze moving towards the bed. Alicia and Maxwell began singing the chorus of the song, sending chills throughout my body as I placed my body over hers.

"Boo." Her hands rested against my chest as my frame hovered over hers, dick sitting at her entrance.

"Hm?" I hummed while placing soft kisses across her collarbone moving down to her titties.

Flicking my tongue across one nipple, I grabbed the free titty with my hand massaging it as I devoured the one I was on. I chuckled, looking up to see her biting her lip with closed eyes. Snaking my tongue over to the other titty, I gave the same attention loving her moans hitting my ears.

"Didn't you have something to say?" I asked between kissing and sucking.

"Mm." I moaned as my hand found the back of Dallas' head.

It's been so long since I've had someone pay my body attention and I was more than ready to get to the best part.

"Ba..baby," I said in a breathy tone, unable to form my words.

"Hm?" He hummed moving down my stomach to my thighs.

A yelp fell from my lips as a loud smack to my thighs turned me on even more. I could feel my box getting wetter by the seconds. My body softly shook as he placed kisses on the inside of my thighs getting closer to my love below. My mouth dropped once feeling his hot mouth wrap around my pussy, tongue breaking my wet folds.

"Mmm," I moaned loudly as my hands quickly went to my hair, fisting it.

The feeling he was creating between my legs was indescribable. It hadn't been 5 minutes and I could already feel that good feeling stirring within the depths of my stomach. I gripped the few curls he had, moving my hips recklessly against his face.

"Thought you had something to say, bae?" He mumbled in my pussy sending vibrations through my body.

Moans continued to exit my mouth as I continued to hump his face, still unable to gather my words.

"Fuuckkkk," I said between heavy pants as he brought my clit between his teeth softly before his tongue dug deep.

I could feel him smiling against my hot center before his strong arms pulled me towards his face as I tried to back away.

He chuckled, "Naw nigga. No running." He spoke into my pussy before two fingers dug into me causing my back to arch.

This man was driving me crazy.

"Dallas," I whined but moaned at the same time.

The strong sensation built at my toes traveling up my body, hitting me HARD. My body jerked wildly against his face as he continued feasting away with my juices coating his face. He licked up every drop before kissing his way back up my body, placing a soft kiss on my lips. I licked my lips, tasting myself enjoying the sweet flavor.

He smiled showing those cute dimples of his. "Baby, what you wanted to say?"

I blushed, finding it cute that despite the heated moment he remembered I attempted to say something.

"Take it easy on me." I broke his gaze, giggling once he kissed my jaw.

I moaned with a pout marring my features once a loud smack was created against the side of my ass. The feeling of his hard dick against my folds had me squirming. Once I witnessed him release himself, I was in shock. I always felt it through clothes but to see it bare was a different story. This nigga was PACKING. He held length and girth. Looked like one of them long ass flashlights, thicker version. I don't even know if I could take it but shit, I was gonna try.

It looked beautiful especially since my weird ass had a thing for dicks. I don't know why but I always found them sort of attractive.

He laughed before the gold wrapper came into sight as he ripped it with his teeth.

"Baby, I got you. Daddy gon' take it easy on you."

Beyoncé's "Rocket" made love to our ears as Dallas comfortably positioned himself between my thighs, me growing terrified by the seconds once coming to terms that the monster swinging between his legs was going to be in me. His grunt met my moan as he slapped his member against me forcing a moan from me. My hips thrusted upwards once feeling two fingers sweep at my opening, making me drip even more. A slow hiss exited my lips as his teeth nibbled on my ear before speaking raspily into my ear.

"The fact you're wet as shit, though..." His voice trailed off before placing a kiss on my lips.

My head dug into the mattress, mouth falling ajar in pleasure as his fingers continued to go to work between my thighs. A sly grin pulled at my full lips once seeing his wet fingers enter his mouth.

He smirked, "You want to taste, baby?"

The sight of him enjoying my juices made my shit even wetter. I nodded as his lips pressed against mine while his hand took a firm grip of my right thigh, placing it around his waist. I moaned against his lips feeling his plump head resting at my opening.

Our tongues intertwined with one another causing it to feel as if a blanket of heat covered us.

He slightly jumped at my nails digging into his sides, frown contorting his lips. "Baby, ease up. Just relax." He coached while using a hand to run through my hair. The soft kisses he was placing all over my face was bringing some sort of comfort to my being. Oddly, it was helping and had my legs spreading wider preparing us for the spiritual connection we were about to embark on.

Releasing a deep breath, I mentally coached myself to relax. Knowing the large mammoth waiting to invade me had my heartbeat picking up its pace and the hairs on my body to rise. It's been so long since I laid down with someone and seeing what Dallas held between his legs was terrifying. His hands grabbing ahold of my face brought me out of my head, staring deeply into his brown orbs.

Hissing, my body went tense once feeling him slowly enter me. This felt like my first time all over again.

"Baby, get out your head. I got you. Just relax..." His voice trailed off with me nodding as he pushed further into me, shushing me with a kiss.

Squeezing my eyes shut, I took a hold of his shoulders as his tongue ran from the bottom of my neck up to my chin. I wrapped my legs around his waist trying to ignore the hint of pain. Dallas leaned back taking a hold of my thick thighs, pushing them towards my chest allowing him to get deeper. Biting my lip, I honed in on his fiery gaze as his hips rhythmically moved with Beyoncé's voice.

The pain slowly but surely disappeared as I began to wind my hips against his, admiring how he was looking at me in this moment. This look was different than any other time he'd look at me - this was more emotional. He was making everything known at this moment how he felt about me with just one look. It was driving me crazy because I felt the same way, if not more.

I grabbed the back of his neck forcing his face into my neck with him picking up his pace. My moans grew as his hand took a hold of my right thigh keeping it in place, him digging into me relentlessly forcing my cries to challenge the music.

"Oh... mmm." I hummed, barely able to vocalize due to his powerful strokes.

The hold on my thigh tightened as he thrust upwards sending an unfamiliar jolt to my body making a loud moan to escape. I bit my lip hard as his hand grabbed a handful of my ass.

"Fuckkk." My voice came out shaky with every stroke.

A smirk came to my face once seeing the pleasure plaster across Shia's beautiful features. Her expression was everything I dreamed about. I'd been waiting to see the faces she would make while I was in her and this moment made that wait worth it. Biting my lip, I picked up my pace enjoying the sight of her struggling to keep her composure. Her hands flailed wildly, clearly not knowing what to do with them. Her leg shook violently in my hand as I continued to punish her shit without remorse.

Beyoncé was making this moment more intense as her sweet voice blessed the air. A grunt left my lips as I delivered a sharp stroke earning a loud yelp from Shia. The gushy sound entered the air every time I pulled away before slamming back into her, smirking at how wet she was.

Her shit was amazing.

My arm curved around her body, hand holding the back of her neck as I stabbed at her opening forcing her mouth to fall open, eyes rolling to the back of her head. Leaning down I placed a tender kiss to the corner of her full lips pushing a loud hiss from her mouth. Rotating my hips, I aimed for that one spot I found when I received that loud squeal from her. She was going to cum, and HARD.

My hand trailed up her left leg cupping her heel as I pushed it further back with my hips slowing down to the beat, poking at that sensitive spot. I smirked once locking into her hazy gaze, fixing my eyes on her bouncing titties before taking one into my mouth. Grunting, my hand slowly began moving back down her leg before taking ahold of her left ass cheek, squeezing tightly.

"Ooh… Dallas... Slow down baby," She said between pants which encouraged me to go faster.

I wasn't slowing down for shit.

My husky voice sounded off in her ear, "Naw. You taking all this dick tonight, girl." I demanded before sending a striking stroke.

This was way past overdue between us; I was going to make sure I fucked her right to sleep.

Shia grabbed my shoulders while biting her lip - possibly being the sexiest expression she's made since I've known her. My hues shot to the ceiling as I relished in how good it felt to be in her, not slowing down one bit. I looked down between us noticing the wetness coating my condom clad dick.

"Fuck." I murmured, feeling that usual feeling stirring from deep within.

There was no way I was about to nut... not right now.

A cute scowl marred her beautiful features once I pulled out, tapping the side of her ass with my index finger.

"Turn that ass around," I hissed while circling my index finger in the air.

She shot a mischievous expression my way before turning onto her stomach, tooting her voluptuous ass into the air. Shaking my head at how good she looked from the back, my feet collided with the floor. Within a swift motion, I pulled her towards me by her thighs earning a giggle from her. A lazy grin sat on my lips as she threw a sexy look over her shoulder. Grabbing myself, I slapped at her wetness enjoying the sight of her ass jiggling as she squirmed from the contact.

Smacking her ass, I positioned myself at her opening, shoving myself into her as we simultaneously allowed our sounds of pleasure to fill the air.

Chills trickled throughout my frame as Dallas leaned towards my ear, hand wrapped around my neck forcing my head backward. I was enjoying every second of what Dallas and his best friend were sending my way.

"You hear Bey. You want daddy to punish you, baby?" He teasingly spoke into my ear.

Licking my lips, my hand took a hold of the hand he had resting on my tiny waist.

"Please," I whined.

"Please what?" He delivered another strong stroke causing my mouth to drop at how amazing it felt.

"Daddy, please," I whined once again.

I could only imagine the smug look taking over his face as I begged for him to fuck me. His blows against my pussy became deeper and faster while smacking my ass. Turning my head to the right, my hair fell to the side allowing the little bit of air to come in contact with my neck. Fisting the covers, I began throwing my ass back as I looked over my shoulder to find Dallas with low eyes, lip tucked tight between his teeth. Possibly being the sexiest look he's made since I've known him.

His hands parted my cheeks, stabbing at my spot earning loud moans from me.

"Mmm," I cooed while tightening my walls before earning a sexy groan from him.

"Fuck." He mumbled in a low, raspy tone.

His warm hand slowly moved up the middle of my back as my body shuddered from him taking the skin of my shoulder between his teeth. His strokes slowed as my pussy walls began contracting around him which I knew was driving him crazy. I bounced one cheek at a time as I felt his dick pulsate within me. Him and I both were nearing our peak and honestly, I was ready.

I **needed** this release.

Throwing my hair back while meeting his thrusts, the obscenities he was murmuring seemed to hit my ears over Beyoncé's soothing voice. Dallas grabbed a hold of my shoulders drilling himself into me forcing me to cry out in pleasure. The shit this man held between his legs was golden and perfectly fit me. Dropping my face into the same covers I fisted, I screamed out as the tingly sensation stirred from deep within before bringing my body into convulsions. I could only imagine the cocky grin sitting on his fuckin' handsome face as he continued ramming into me, intensifying my orgasm. His strokes slowed down with his body beginning to jerk behind me as his hands gripped my plump ass hard.

"Fuuuckkk," He dragged out.

A cute moan broke his lips as he delivered one long, last stroke sending my curvy frame face forward into the bed. Slowly turning on my side, I honed in on his intense gaze as he removed the condom before heading towards the trash can. My brown hues followed his every movement, even in the dark, admiring how the street light hit various parts of his naked body. Dallas chortled while standing at the edge of the bed, stroking himself slowly while holding my gaze. By the look on his face, I could tell he wasn't done with me but shit, I already felt sleep taking over.

Before I know it his long frame was hovering over me, pecking my full lips. Fluttering my eyes, I twisted up my lips as his fingers begin playing between my thighs causing me to moan against my will.

"Dallas," I whined.

His deep laugh in my ear sent a jolt to my pussy.

"Fuck sleep, baby." He voiced, extending his arm towards the dresser grabbing a brand new condom.

Book XV.

May 5, 2016: NW, Washington, DC - *Carmine's*

For the past month, Dallas and I had become inseparable. You would think we were attached at the hip as much as we were together. Also, we couldn't keep our hands off one another either. We'd definitely been going at it like rabbits since our first night together. And it seemed as though every moment shared was better than the last, deepening our connection even further.

Taking a sip from my Pepsi, I locked eyes with Blake.

"Why are you looking at me like that?"

She crossed her eyes, "Cause, this the first time I'm seeing you in like... forever."

I rolled my eyes at her over exaggeration. If I wasn't spending the night at Dallas', she would see me at home *if* she wasn't already at work.

I waved her off, "Stop it. You know you see me."

"Like hell we do!" CJ butted in earning a giggle from me. "You get a piece of dick and don't know how to act." He teased, rolling his neck.

The smile never moved from my lips as I picked up my fork, twisting it in my pasta before stuffing it into my mouth. Noticing the silence across the table from me, I looked up only to have those two staring at me with blank expressions. After swallowing my food, a laugh erupted from my lips.

"Can y'all stop staring, please? Thanks."

Blake giggled as CJ pointed a finger my way. "Dallas got you glowing n' shit. He really makes you happy, huh?"

My stomach began fluttering at the mention of his name. We'd already had that weird connection between us but now that we indulged in sex, I was slowly beginning to grow deeper feelings for him. This was something I haven't shared with anyone and wasn't too sure on when I would.

All I know is that I'm thankful for that man.

"Aww, look at her blushing!" Blake teased while nudging shoulders with CJ.

I laughed, "He really does y'all. I'm so grateful to have him."

"So. Are y'all together?" Blake questioned before digging into her chicken marsala.

Out of nowhere, this weird feeling hit me as if someone was staring, hard as fuck at that. My eyes searched the restaurant before locking eyes with a blonde bombshell. She was gorgeous. I just wanted to know the reason behind her mugging me, when I had no clue who she was.

"What you looking at?" CJ's question had me bringing my eyes back to them.

"That chick," I responded with a hint of annoyance in my tone.

"Who?!" Blake asked, placing her hands on the table while slightly standing up to look around.

"Sit your ass down girl." CJ spat earning a giggle from me as he yanked her down.

I shrugged, not trying to make a big deal out of it.

"I don't know her so whatever."

A smile blessed my face once locking eyes with Tink, her smile mirroring mines. Due to her being a model, she was always on the go or either out of town. She was pretty difficult to keep up with at times. I was glad she agreed to meet us for lunch straight from the airport; I missed her dearly.

"Tink," I cooed while standing to bring her into a tight embrace.

I found it mind blowing how showing love through something as simple as a hug was becoming a part of me - I had Dallas to thank for that.

Her hand ran over my ample ass, bringing a grin to my lips. This girl couldn't get enough of it. Whenever we were together, she would take it upon herself to feel it up which never bothered me. Actually, I found it amusing plus flattering.

"I see Dallas been putting in work." She voiced while rounding the table to give hugs to CJ and Blake as well.

"Shut up," I giggled, feeling my cheeks heat up.

I plopped into my seat as she took the empty one next to me.

"You look cute!" I complimented.

"You do too!" She returned before picking up the happy hour menu, sighing. "I need a drink."

Personally, I didn't think I looked up to par today. I wasn't in a dress up mood resulting in me wearing a white wife beater, my waist beads, and a pair of distressed jeans. Since the weather was really nice,

I threw on a pair of black sandals that went well with my simple fit. Not really in the mood to bother with my hair, I threw it into a messy bun before tying a folded scarf midway on my head.

"Drinking already missy?" CJ questioned.

Tink released an exasperated sigh, "Hell yeah! I *need* this. That trip just took everything out of me."

"Bad or good thing?" Blake asked.

"Eh…" Her eyes began darting around the room before looking back at us, "Who's our waiter?"

CJ laughed, sipping from his own drink. "Girl, your ass must *really* need one."

She tipped a brow at him, giving a look. "I told you that I do. So who—"

Her words were cut short once the blonde bombshell with the staring problem was heading our way. Seeing her seated at a distance, I wasn't able to make out her shape. But now that she was sashaying our way, I couldn't help *but* admire her curvaceous frame similar to mines.

"Y'all know this chick?" Tink looked between all of us with furrowed brows.

Out of the time I've spent with Tink, I gathered that she was trained to go, always. If a chick had a problem? She had no problem with resolving it with her hands.

Blake kissed her teeth looking at me, "This her? Ain't it?"

I nodded, holding blondie's intense gaze.

"This bitch bold," CJ added with irritation lacing his tone.

Everybody including me was on the edge, especially since we had no idea what her problem was.

All of our eyes remained on her while hers remained on me, approaching our table rather quickly. A fake smile crept to her lips while shifting her weight to one side of her body, placing a hand on her hip.

"I thought I should come over and introduce myself. The n—"

"Who asked?" Blake cut her off.

"Exactly," Tink added, sizing blondie up.

Immediately, I fed off their angry energy which had me shooting daggers at the brave individual standing before us.

Who was this bitch?

I bit my lip in vexation as my leg began to shake, prepared to smack that stupid grin off her face.

"Like, what do you want girl?" CJ questioned, annoyed as well.

Never did she once acknowledge any of them, paying their words no mind at all. Instead, her crystal blue orbs remained stationed on me. Her tongue swept across her lip as her finger rose to point at me causing Tink to shift, forcing my hand to come in contact with her arm. Tink looked at me as I gave her a "chill out" look, not wanting to make a scene in public.

"You know Dallas, right?" She questioned, moving her finger with her words.

May 5, 2016: Camp Springs, MD

The sound of my 992's screeching across my apartment complex steps as I descended them bounced off the walls of the empty hallway. Brushing my thumb across my nose, I got situated in my car after unlocking the doors. The first thing I did was roll down my window - it felt too good out today. Things were starting to look up lately. Shia and I were on the best of terms. Ma returned home three days ago and was making progress, and my babies would be five on Saturday.

Mean Ass
<u>Received</u>
Who the fuck is Gizelle?

Retrieving my phone from my joggers, I glanced over the text from Shia which immediately shifted my mood, forcing an irritated sigh past my lips. Ever since the night with Shia, I'd been giving Gizelle the cold shoulder, really hard. She'd been practically begging for the dick but I was trying to do right by Shy, despite the fact we weren't together. I knew if I continued to lead Gizelle on then that would make matters worst.

But, I wasn't making it any better since I was ignoring her. Who knows what that broad said to Shia? Even though Gizelle was cool, she still had those conniving ways about her.

"Fuck dawg," I muttered, seeing my phone vibrating in the cup holder.

Kissing my teeth, I slid my index finger across the screen allowing the call to connect to my car through Bluetooth. Even though I didn't want to deal with this right now, I knew I had to.

"Wassup," I dryly greeted focusing in on the noise in her background before it got silent.

"Dalls, you didn't get my text?"

Coming to a red light, I ran my hands over my face knowing that this conversation was about to turn bad within seconds.

"I did," I shortly replied.

"So, was you going to respond?"

I could hear the aggravation in her tone and I knew I was making it worse by how calm I was being. With her, she loved for me to get worked up as well but I wasn't for none of that today. All I wanted was to go kick it with my family, having a drama-free day.

"Did you give me a chance to?" I snapped, not really trying to.

A sarcastic chuckle entered my ears before the beeping sound resonated through the speakers signaling the end of the call. Chuckling, I shook my head.

"Childish ass."

Like I said before, I have enough on my plate and dealing with Shia's attitude at the moment wasn't one of them. I know I've been doing right by her and whatever bullshit she allowed Gizelle to feed her was her fault. I'll fix it later. My sole focus was going to chill with my favorite women.

May 5, 2016: Fort Washington, MD

Shaking my hand through my wet and wavy hair, I kept a tight hold on my towel. It's been since around 3 when I last heard from Dallas and not once did he make an initiative to reach out to me after I hung up. My emotions were all over the place especially after Gizelle basically flaunted them fucking each other in my face. She informed me that it's been going on way before me but still, he was dipping in her recently. Recent as in since we've started being sexually involved.

"Yea, I'm here." I plopped into my bed while picking up my phone that was on speaker.

"You gon' have to get rid of that sad shit ma. I'm not even trying to hear all that." My full lips contorted into a frown at Mace's words.

As soon as we got back to the house, the first person I called was Mace - I missed him so much, I swear. It's funny because, in rehab, I couldn't stand him but out here we were damn near inseparable. I loved how our friendship developed over time.

I sighed, laying on my back, placing the phone on my chest. "I know. I know. How was your day?" I asked, changing the subject completely.

"Now we're talking..." His voice trailed off as I could imagine the huge smile spreading across his handsome visage, "I got some cheeks so a nigga good."

My nose turned up once finding out that the highlight of his day was getting between some female's legs.

"Uh, did you know her?"

He chuckled, "That's the best part, Shy. She was a shawdy that used to go on me cause y'know I was off the shits. And now she's the one chasing me down! Feel great. Real live living the Mike Jones life."

I burst out in laughter at his reference to Mike Jones - this boy was a fool. Well, at least somebody was in a good mood for the both of us.

"Shia." That familiar pang returned to my chest once hearing his husky voice.

"Oh shit. Hit me back ma," Mace voiced quickly before hanging up as I stood to my feet.

My hues ran over Dallas' tall structure as his face remained stoic, leaning against the door frame. As bad as I was trying to remain mad, every ounce of anger was quickly leaving my body once locking eyes with him. I shied under his intense gaze as he rubbed his chin, looking me over. Looking down, I had completely forgotten that I was just wearing a towel.

"Dallas," I dryly retorted, turning to head towards my dresser.

My body tingled once feeling his presence on my back, plump lips right by my ear. My breath hitched in my throat as he began speaking.

"Hurry and put some clothes on fo' I lay your ass out." He spoke sexily into my ear before removing himself from my back.

I bit my lip, wanting nothing more for him to, but I had to remain my composure. We had to get to the bottom of this Gizelle situation.

I could feel his eyes on me as I searched for something to sleep in. Finding a pair of boy shorts, I slipped them on under my towel before completely dropping it giving him a full view of my backside. I grabbed one of his t-shirts I didn't plan on returning, throwing it over my head. Leaning forward, I grabbed a scrunchie off my dresser before throwing my hair into a messy bun.

Letting out a sigh, I turned to face him as his orbs continued to scan my frame. He looked tired but knowing Dallas, he'd never admit it. I know these past couple of weeks were hard for him - the main reason I was doing all I can to keep my anger tucked away.

He summoned me his way with his head, "Come 'ere."

"You ready to talk now?" I snapped, folding my arms across my chest. "How did you get in anyways?"

Stubborn Shia.

On the way here, I contemplated on many ways to tell her about Gizelle but couldn't come up with a solid speech. That's when I knew that everything had to come from the heart. Seeing the fire resting within her hues was making me nervous; I'd never have to explain myself to any female before.

But I knew I couldn't lose this… lose Us.

"Yea, I'm ready to talk. You going to talk from all the way over there, though?"

She nodded, "I sure will. Talk."

A smirk graced my lips as a deep chortle rumbled throughout my chest, pushing myself to my feet. When is this girl going to let up on this stubbornness? Moving slowly towards her, she didn't budge one bit but that scowl remained on her beautiful face.

I stopped right in front of her, looking down on her tiny frame.

"What you wanna know?"

"Who is she?"

"Who she tell you that she was?"

She smacked her lips in annoyance, "So you're going to answer my question with one?"

I licked my lips, "Naw baby, I'm going to answer your question but I'm curious on to what she said she was to me. Cause whatever was said got you really worked up, and I know she can be on some other shit at times."

Shia's brows furrowed, eyes narrowing on me. "You're talking like you've known her for a while."

My eyes broke from hers for a second then returning, "Cause I have."

She slowly nodded, scowl growing deeper the more I spoke. I just wish she'd get straight to the point so we can put everything behind us.

Her index finger collided with my chest applying pressure causing me to frown. See. I'd appreciate if she kept her hands to herself. I grabbed her wrist softly placing her hand by her side.

"Keep your hands to yourself, Shy. That's all I ask."

Next thing I know I was being shoved backward by her small hands pushing my chest. I looked at her in disbelief, "The fu—"

"No! You've been fucking that bitch while fucking me Dallas?!" Her voice rose an octave as she quickly moved towards me with closed fists, me catching her fists before they could connect.

I lightly pushed her away, putting my hands up in surrender. "Fuck wrong with you Shy?! Keep your hands to yourself slim. Talk like an adult. Keep your shit at your side man."

A sarcastic laugh fell from her lips slowly moving my way with her head cocked to the side. From the look in her eyes, this wasn't even her - this side she was showing was *definitely* the hidden, crazy side.

"Or what? You gon' hit me?" She turned her cheek to the side, pointing at her face before speaking in a taunting manner. "Come on, hit me!"

The hell?

My face twisted in disbelief that she was begging me to put my hands on her.

"Fuck you used to men putting their hands on you or something?" I spat, ceasing her movement as she gave me a dead glare, tears welling at the brim of her lids.

Tears began flowing down her chocolate cheeks instantly making my heart hurt. Damn. I knew Shia was hurting but I had no idea she used to be abused.

My brows furrowed once I reached for her arm, her snatching away.

"Don't touch me, Dallas." She seethed, wiping at her cheeks. "I don't want this shit anymore." She softly spoke, looking towards the ground, sniffing.

I know damn well I didn't just hear that leave her lips. There was no way we were ending anything. Leaning down to get in her view, she brought her eyes to me.

"Go ahead, say that shit again… and actually, *mean* it."

My heart felt as if it was going to burst out my chest while I held her gaze. Her lips fell agape but nothing came out.

"You really mean that?"

She nodded slowly.

"Then say it while looking in my eyes."

She took a deep breath, looking away before looking back at me. "I don't want this anymore, Dallas. Fuck everything!" She hissed, bringing a strong pang to my heart.

I shook my head frantically, "Naw bruh. You not about to cut me off cause of what some broad said to you. Not even ME Shia but a fucking broad, slim. Yea, we fucked from time to time but nothing has happened since I've laid down with you. Matter of fact, I haven't even spoken to her since then. Been giving her ass the cold shoulder cause I want *this* with you. Not anyone else Shia, but you. And here you go throwing me away over some broad's words? Naw. I'm not letting you go, baby. You gon' have to fight me off or something. Give me one good reason why you want to let this go?"

By this time my chest was heaving up and down. I was experiencing too many emotions at once - something I've never felt before. This woman was bringing up feelings I didn't know existed. Never would've thought I'd be begging a female to stay in my life.

Not only did I want this woman standing in front of me but, I **needed** her.

God, please don't take her away from me.

"Cause I love you." She whispered, watery eyes locked on mine.

Well, Dallas, are you going to say something?

The silence covering us was killing me. Did he feel the same? Was I in this alone? My eyes fluttered once feeling his warm hands cup my cheeks, staring lovingly into my hues. The light squeeze to my cheeks puckered my lips as he leaned down to place a gentle kiss on them.

"With that being the one and only reason you *shouldn't* want to let go." His husky tone rose the hairs on the back of my neck, butterflies going crazy in my stomach.

His lips connected with mine again before releasing, his breath bouncing against my lips.

"I love you too... mean ass." He mumbled against my lips, wiping the tears from my cheeks before they could stain.

My heart swelled at him uttering those three words that meant so much meaning. Those three words that I found it hard to say to anyone other than Blake. Those three words that set me free in this very moment.

Frowning, I felt empty due to his sudden departure from my body as he clapped his hands together.

"Ight. Date night! Grab you something nice and you can change at my crib."

My brows contorted in confusion, "How we go from arguing to date night within a matter of seconds?"

Inquiring minds wanted to know.

"Cause that's the way love goes, baby." He simply said, lazily shrugging his shoulders while retrieving his keys from his pocket.

Blushing, I giggled at the thought of Janet Jackson's song popping into my head at the right moment. Dallas kissed his teeth while rubbing his stomach and the back of his neck simultaneously.

"Plus, this was already my plan. Come over here to argue it out, have make-up sex, then take you out to eat."

I laughed at this "plan" he'd come up with in advance. My brows climbed my head, "So why are we skipping the make-up part?" I teasingly questioned, slowly moving his way.

That sexy, crooked smile of his marred his features. "Aw baby, no skipping... we just putting it off for later. We need this food for energy." My heart jumped once feeling his lips quickly connect with mines before giving the side of my ass a thump.

May 5, 2016: Camp Springs, MD

Exhaling deeply, my large palms ran down my face growing impatient with Shia. It didn't take much for me to get dressed but with her, it was a different story. It's been about 30 minutes since I've been sitting on the edge of my bed waiting for her to get ready.

"Baby…" My voice trailed off while taking a glance at my watch. "Hurry up!" My voice rose making sure she heard me over the running water.

"I'm coming!" Her sweet voice hollered from the bathroom, water coming to a stop as her heels clicked against the tile floor before emerging from the open door.

"How I look?" She asked, giving a full spin around as I bit my lip, admiring her curvaceous frame.

Her hair was in loose waves flowing down the front of her shoulders and back. Pink gloss covered her full lips that made me miss her lips against mine more than I already did. A simple, thick gold chain sat around her neck, being the only accessory upon her body. Her voluptuous figure was hugged by a velvet, flamingo pink two-piece set. The off shoulder crop top exposed her rich, chocolate skin with the high-waist skirt leaving a bit of her stomach in view. My eyes traveled down her legs noticing the nude, ankle strap, open toe heels clothing her feet.

Locking in on her face, I realized that she was checking me out as well. A small chuckle broke my lips while enclosing the space between us. She giggled as I brought her in a tight embrace, nuzzling my face in her neck.

"I'm guessing I look good." She softly cooed in my ear.

I bit the taut skin of her neck earning a small moan from her.

"You look better than good, baby. Beautiful like always."

May 5, 2016: NW, Washington, DC – *Ruth's Chris*

The numerous fumes filled my nostrils as Dallas and me, hand in hand, followed the hostess further into the extravagant restaurant. My eyes continued dancing around our surroundings, taking in every little detail. The lights were dim, giving off a romantic vibe with mini lamps placed in the middle of the white table-clothed tables. We came to an abrupt stop, finding ourselves tucked off in a corner by the window at a table for two.

"Enjoy your dinner." She offered a smile, placing our menus on the table before making her exit.

"I got that baby." Dallas voiced, grabbing the back of the chair before I had a chance to.

"Aww," I cooed, looking to him with a big smile. "Look at you."

He chuckled, "Stop that shit." He muttered, helping me scoot into the table before taking his place on the other side.

"This is nice." I complimented, receiving this hint of glee within from being in the midst of such an upscale environment.

"It's Ruth's Chris, baby. Nothing big. We definitely can do better; I was just fienin' their stuffed chicken breast." He smoothly spoke, folding his arms on top of each other on the table.

"Well…" I started, picking up my menu to look it over. "I've never been here before so I'm excited." I finished, smiling while bouncing in my seat earning a laugh from him.

My eyes widened once noticing the prices, looking up to Dallas whose attention was on nothing in particular.

"These prices, boo. They're crazy."

His brown hues locked on me, kissing his teeth while waving me off. "Get whatever you want, Shy. I got you."

I shook my head, still finding it ridiculous to be paying this type of money for food. For all I care, we could've grabbed Applebee's and I would've been satisfied.

"If you say soooo," I sang while focusing back on the menu, licking my lips at all the delicious choices.

"We better not have a damn nigga tonight."

Bursting out in laughter, I immediately covered my mouth as we gathered a few wandering eyes. Instantly, I thought about our first date and how he acted an ass with our waiter. My eyes fixated on Dallas' handsome face, a sexy grin forming upon his juicy lips.

He chortled, making me squirm in my seat. Earlier, I was so upset with him but after getting our feelings into the air, I wanted to have my way with him. We could skip dinner and head straight to dessert - I don't care, I just wanted a piece of him. I'm guessing he could see the lust swirling in my eyes as he leaned forward, elbows on the table while his pink muscle swept across his bottom lip.

"Thinking bout this dick, baby?" He questioned in a teasing tone, forcing my eyes from his and back to the menu.

His deep laughter brought a small frown to my lips as I looked over the menu, finding it difficult to focus due to the puddle building between my thighs.

"Shit," I mumbled to myself. I jumped once feeling his warm hand touch my knee forcing my hues back on him. "Stop," I spoke through clenched teeth as he sat with that sneaky grin on his face.

"You don't want me—"

"Hello! My name is Mya and I will be your waitress for the night. Can I start you guys off with some drinks?" She paused for a moment looking at us both, "Unless you know what you want?"

I shook my head, "I don't have a clue what I want yet. But I'll settle for a raspberry lemonade for now."

She nodded before looking to Dallas, who kept his eyes solely fixed on me. "I'll take a water," He smoothly voiced before slowly looking her way.

Funny how in that moment, I experienced a hint of jealousy once his attention was directed towards another female other than me.

"Kay! I'll be back with your drinks in a few."

We thanked her in unison as she departed.

"You still don't know what you want?" Dallas sniffed, clearing his throat.

"Well, I could decide faster if your hand wasn't on my knee," I quipped.

"Wanna go get a quickie in?"

A jolt flew to my center averting my eyes from the menu to him - he was dead ass serious. I tipped a brow actually sitting here considering it. Allowing sense to settle back in, I found myself shaking my head.

"No. That's what later on is for."

My brows furrowed once watching him rise to his feet, pushing his chair in.

"What are you doing?"

"Meet me in the bathroom in 5."

Tugging at the bottom of my skirt, a wave of chills danced throughout my body as I progressed into the hallway. I couldn't believe I was about to do this. Stopping right in front of the men bathroom door, I gave a quick look around before leaning towards the door.

"Dallas," I whispered, hoping he was close enough to hear me.

Before I know it, the door was being swung open and my handsome beau was wrapping me in his strong arms. A moan slipped past my lips once feeling his fingertips hike up my skirt, leaving it right beneath my ass. Within a swift motion, I was brought in the air, legs wrapping around his waist as he moved us into a stall.

"O-oh..." I couldn't find my words as my back slammed against the stall wall, Dallas' face deep in my neck.

I really, *really* hope no one comes in here.

My arms lazily were draped over his shoulders as I felt his fingers began to play with my panties. I hissed loudly, head dropping back as his fingers dug into me forcing my hips to match his rhythm.

"Damn, baby." His husky tone spoke in my ear making me grip the back of his head, playing in his rough curls.

Tearing his lips from my neck, I'm pretty sure it would be a reminder there in the morning. His pouty lips crashed into mines, our tongues trying to beat each other. My adrenaline was rushing so much that I couldn't hold myself together.

"Mm, fuck me, baby, please," I whined in his ear.

I could feel his cheeks moving upward, knowing that beautiful smile of his was making itself known.

"No problem, baby."

My mouth dropped once he filled me to the hilt. I didn't even know he managed to drop his pants and throw a condom on. Biting my lip hard, I fought back the moans as his raspy voice vibrated against my ear, pumping me relentlessly.

"Go head… let that shit out," He pushed forcing a squeal from me as he hit my spot.

"W-we can't b-be loud," I managed to say between breaths.

With every stroke, my back separated and collided with the wall in a pleasing way. Dallas' face was deep within my neck which was annoying me due to the fact I love seeing his face while we're connected.

"The whole damn restaurant can hear us." He said between grunts in my ear.

He squeezed my ass, slowly pulling out before slamming back into me forcing a loud moan into the air. Our movements stopped once hearing the bathroom door open, both of our eyes widening.

He smiled crookedly, placing a soft kiss to my lips, "Shhh, don't be so loud baby." He spoke against my lips, slowing down his strokes making me feel *him* even more.

Tucking my lip tight between my teeth, I rolled my hips against his hoping that whoever entered didn't hear us. But if so, who cares. The sound of the sink water sent relief throughout the both of us; I could tell from his expression alone that we shared mutual feelings.

A low chuckle bounced off the walls, "Y'all two have a good night."

Once the bathroom door closed, we burst out in laughter, still connected as one.

Book XVI.

May 7, 2016: Fort Washington, MD

"Shy, it can't be that hard to come up with an outfit for a kids party."

Kris' voice rang over the speakerphone as I rumbled through my closet.

The twins party started in two hours and I still haven't decided on what to wear. Dallas had called me this morning, stressing me to be ready when he pulled up. Yet, here I was, hours later and still at a standstill.

Huffing out of frustration, I slapped my hands against my bare thighs before running my fingers through my kinky tresses.

"Just do something simple." Kris paused shortly, "Its Chuck E. Cheese's my nigga."

I rolled my eyes, heading towards my bed to grab my phone.

"Yes it is but I'm meeting his mother."

Kris laughed, "I'm pretty sure she's not that bad. You already met his sister; that was the hardest part."

I sighed, "You're making it sound so easy."

"Cause it is," She shot back.

There was a short pause before her voice came through the receiver in a rushed manner.

"But I'll see you in two weeks boo. I can't wait to come home. I love you and have fun."

I smiled, "I love you more and kay."

Mace
<u>Received</u>
It's Chuck E. Cheese's my nigga, not a fashion show.

A loud laugh broke my lips at Mace's text and the fact Kris had just said the exact same thing. Sighing, I moved back towards my closet to continue my search of today's fit.

May 7, 2016: Waldorf, MD – *Chuck E. Cheese's*

A deep chuckle vibrated against my chest as Shia remained tucked to my side, us hand in hand. Ever since picking her up, I could sense the nervousness radiating from her body along with it being evident on her face.

I don't know what she was scared of. Ma had been begging for me to bring her over so their initial meeting was going to go smoothly. I refused because I'd rather Shia come around my favorite women on a special day instead of just *any* day.

I gave her hand a light squeeze as my hand, holding the girls' gift bags reached for the door handle. "Baby, relax. It's not that deep," I assured her.

I laughed at the intense glare she gave me over the shoulder before walking through the door ahead of me. Grabbing a hold of her hand, I began walking but was stopped by her not moving.

"Dallas, I can't do this."

See. This girl is too much, for no reason at all. I never told her how excited Ma was to meet her because I'd rather her witness it on her own. She was making a big deal out of nothing.

My brows met in the middle of my head, turning to face her after giving a quick glance around noticing Devyn not too far from us.

"You already here now, so shut up." I dryly responded earning a snort from her.

"Dallas!" Her voice rose an octave as I turned to start walking in the direction of my sister.

A smack of the lips following a nudge to my arm brought my attention to the firecracker I had the pleasure of calling my lady. My heart jumped once focusing on the small pout forming amongst her pretty, plump lips.

Damn. I really love this girl.

Raking my fingers through my kinky tresses, I came to a stop not too far behind Dallas. My brown hues fell over the many bodies surrounding us specifically locking on Devyn, eyes lighting up with glee once seeing me. Averting my gaze, I looked over my outfit which was simple but comfortable. Not really in the mood to have my hair blowing around, I threw on my black, Nike cap. A camo tee hugged my upper half, black skinnies with a few rips squeezed my thick thighs, and red Air Maxes clothed my feet. Like any other time, I kept a scrunchie on my wrist in case of emergencies.

"Shia." Devyn cooed with the biggest smile on her face, pulling me into a tight hug.

Ever since our initial meeting at the hospital, we've taken a great liking to each other. It even came down to us exchanging numbers and going on lunch dates whenever she was able to squeeze me into her busy schedule. Honestly, I didn't expect us to kick it off the way we did especially since females and me never really got along.

"Thanks for coming, boo." She expressed her gratitude, giving me some sort of solace.

I smiled, "No problem Dev. I wouldn't have missed your girls' day for nothing."

I looked over her outfit before looking back to Dallas who was occupied with his nieces, placing endless kisses all over their cute faces. A blanket of warmth fell over my heart like any other time I witnessed them interact - I love it. Devyn smiled looking over her shoulder at them as well, shaking her head before looking back to me.

"I'm so thankful for him. He loves my babies like they're his own."

I shifted my gaze to her, "I know, and they love him just as much. It's so cute." I confessed, scanning her frame from head to toe. Raising my index finger, I moved it back and forth between her and him, noticing the matching outfits. I covered my mouth, smiling wide.

How come I didn't notice this at first?

"Aww, y'all are wearing matching outfits."

Devyn laughed, looking down to her shirt while tugging the bottom of it. "I can't believe you're now just noticing."

"Turn around," I requested while twirling my finger in a circular motion as she did a 360.

They were all wearing white baseball tees with the sleeves being black. All of them had the number five on the back representing

Yani and Yuri's age. Above the numbers were their titles in their lives: Uncle, Mommy, and Nana. I truly admired how close-knit of a family they were despite their losses. Being around them made me miss what I used to have at some point. Feeling their amount of love bouncing off each other stirred up a bunch of tucked away emotions.

"Who came up with the idea?"

"You wouldn't believe it... your boy." She said while nodding her head back in his direction.

Butterflies swarmed in my belly once hearing the cute idea Dallas came up with. This man just became more amazing by the days; I couldn't believe it. Biting my lip, I caught his gaze from where he stood, knees slightly buckling once seeing his pink muscle sweep across his bottom lip.

Forcing my hues from his and back to Devyn, I smiled, "I believe it."

"Sup babies?" My husky voice entered the air, clearing my throat.

"Are you going to come play with us?" They asked simultaneously.

My heart jumped at how in sync they were. It was rare when it happened with them saying the exact same thing but when they did, it always had the same effect on me. Even though they had identical faces, their personalities differed tremendously but were alike in few ways.

I stooped down to their eye level, "I'll be over there in a few. I got to talk to Nana for a minute."

They smiled big, nodding, before turning to run off with their shared cup of tokens.

"So, is Devyn going to hog your lady friend or she's going to let her breathe and come meet me?"

My gaze altered from my beautiful lady to my mother, who held a weak smile and exhausted eyes. Once being released from the hospital, she'd started immunotherapy immediately, spending her time at an outpatient clinic three times weekly for at least two hours. Some days were better than others and thankfully, today was one of her better ones. The doctors said there wasn't much progress but her ongoing sessions were the only option for her at the moment.

But with the way I was set up, that wasn't her only option, because whether they knew so or not - we had God working in our favor.

"That's what I'm saying Ma. Hold up, I'll be back," I said, giving her one last look before pushing to my feet to head their way.

"Ma, this my baby, Shia. Baby, this my first lady, Ma." Dallas introduced us, my heart beating against my chest rapidly.

I watched as her brows climbed her head, lips twisting before looking to Dallas. Within those seconds of silence, I felt as if my heart stopped.

Did she like me?

"Now do you think your new girlfriend wants to hear I'm your first lady when she should be?" She said in a sweet tone, grabbing a hold of the table and top of the booth to rise to her feet.

Quickly, Dallas leaned forward to lend a helping hand as she chose to swat his hand away.

"I'm fine baby. I got it."

He nodded, backing up as she outstretched her arms while moving towards me. Once in her embrace, I felt a sense of comfort fall over me. Despite this being our first time meeting, I could feel the genuine love flowing from her to me. She squeezed me tight before letting go, looking me over with a hand rested on my shoulder.

"It's so nice to finally meet you, Shia. I've been waiting for this boy to bring you my way. Trying to hide you from me and whatnot."

I blushed while giggling, "It's nice to finally meet you as well Ms. Raye. I know, I don't know why he waited so long for."

I laughed once catching Dallas' expression of disbelief as I somewhat tag teamed him with his own mother.

He smacked his lips, waving his hand. "Naw, none of that. We just needed right timing. Besides, Shia was scared to meet you anyways."

My eyes widened before quickly mugging him as that cute, crooked smirk contorted his lips. Slowly, I looked to Ms. Raye with bashful eyes, somewhat embarrassed that Dallas would even tell her that.

She laughed, "Aw. I'm not one of those mothers that run girls away every chance they get. Besides..." She looked to Dallas, smiling before honing back on me. "It's clear you're a keeper. He kept you away from me for a reason, just to know for sure if you were worth bringing around. And here you are, bringing light into my baby's world."

My smile never faltered as I relished in the sight of watching Devyn and Dallas hold the twins up so they could play each other in basketball. I haven't got the chance to properly meet them seeing as though they'd been running around ever since we arrived. Reaching for my cup, I took a sip of my fruit punch which I truly wish was raspberry lemonade. The clearing of a throat brought my attention back to the pretty individual across from me.

We'd been sitting here for the past 30 minutes getting to know each other better. Dallas was right. I had nothing to worry about because she was beyond sweet.

"So, how did you two meet?" She questioned, folding her arms on the table.

That question caught me off guard due to me assuming he'd already let her know. Looking past her, I caught his gaze as he blew me a small kiss causing the butterflies to resurface.

"He really didn't tell you?" I asked, locking on her gaze.

"Well I'm sitting here asking you, now aren't I?" She shot back, a smile slowly spreading across her lips.

My tongue dashed across my bottom lip, "Well..." I paused shortly, feeling my nerves beginning to overtake me. "We met at New Leaf," I confessed, honing on my twiddling fingers before slowly meeting her brown orbs.

She looked taken aback by my words before her expression quickly softened, smiling. "You're ashamed of that?" She questioned in a surprised tone, one brow rising.

My stomach flipped at her sudden question - a question I wasn't expecting to come from his mother. I wasn't ashamed at all. Or was I? Did I care *that* much what people thought of where I met my new found love? Clearly, I was, because Ms. Raye's question put me in an uncomfortable state.

I shifted in the booth uneasily, falling into her brown gaze. Shaking my head, I took a sip of my juice before clearing my throat and crossing my arms on the table.

"I'm not ashamed."

"Well you damn sure act like it," She shot back.

My brows furrowed along with my full lips falling into a pout - I wasn't expecting that. I shook my head, "No. No, Ms. Raye, I'm not. I just..." I trailed off, searching for my words. My leg shook under the table, "I just didn't expect to find someone at a place where I was trying to find myself."

My heart picked up its pace speaking on my handsome beau, slowly looking his way to see that crooked smile contorting his striking visage while admiring his nieces and sister.

God, what did I do to have someone so beautiful in my corner? Thank you.

"You love my baby, don't you?"

Her question had my head whipping in her direction, heartbeat picking up its pace even more. I looked over her jaded but beautiful countenance, relishing in her identical features of her son. Her genes were extremely strong especially since Devyn looked like them as well.

I bit my lip, nodding, "I do. I really do."

She smiled, "I can tell. The way you look at him is the way I used to look at their father."

My interest peaked at the mention of Dallas' father since he'd never brought him up, ever. Sniffing, I played with the end of a strand of my hair as my brown hues narrowed on hers.

"What happened to him? Dallas never brought him up."

I watched as she shook her head, chuckling, focusing on her fingers before looking to me. "That sounds like my Dallas..." She looked over her shoulder towards her children, "He just... left. I guess he didn't love me enough to stay."

My brows furrowed in confusion, "What you mean?"

She sighed deeply, "After finding out I was pregnant with Dallas, he just left. Come to find out, he had a woman on the side that he was deeply in love with..." Her voice trailed off, biting her lip. "He had a family on the side. He just didn't want this one."

"Blow out the candles babies!" Devyn coached while standing behind Yani and Yuri, camera in hand.

Simultaneously, they looked at each other before leaning towards the cake and blowing out their five candles together. My eyes shifted towards Shia who was now seated by my mother with the biggest smile on her face, clapping. Devyn grabbed the knife from the table before cutting two small pieces of cake, placing them on two individual paper plates and setting them in front of the girls. My heart jumped once seeing them smile wide before digging into their cake.

"Y'all want some?" Devyn questioned, eyes darting from me, to our mother then Shia.

Shia shook her head, "I'm good."

Ma pushed her plate towards Devyn, "Put a small piece on here for me, baby."

"Uncle Dally!" Yuri's high pitched voice caught my attention, tongue running over her plastic fork.

She pointed towards Shia with the fork before a pout fell upon her lips once her hand was swatted down by Devyn.

"What I tell you about pointing at people?" She fussed, earning an eye roll from Yuri.

I chuckled, shaking my head at my niece's attitude. I swear they were just like their mother when it came down to that. A small gasp left my mouth once seeing her head slightly go forward from Devyn pushing it.

"And stop with that damn eye rolling little girl. You act like I didn't see it."

Yani began giggling while still eating her cake. Whenever one of them got scolded, the other always had a habit of teasing. We'd tried our best to break the habit but like I've said before, they were a handful. They weren't particularly the easiest to tame.

An exaggerated sigh came from Yuri's little body, looking back to me, cute pout still contorting her adorable face.

"Soooo..." Her tiny voice dragged out, picking with her cake.

I shifted my weight to one side of my body, throwing a head nod her way. "So what baby?"

"Is this your girlfriend Uncle Dally?" She sweetly asked, nodding her head in Shia's direction, batting her long lashes.

Shia slightly choked on her juice as I started laughing at how smoothly she asked, along with the head nod since she couldn't point. All Devyn could do was shake her head at this point, grinning as our mother did the same. I nodded, moving towards Shia's side while keeping Yuri's brown gaze.

"Yes Yuri, this is my girlfriend," I admitted, suddenly feeling nervous once both of their eyes focused on me, mouths falling agape.

Yani smacked her lips, "That mean we're not your favorite girls anymore?" She pouted causing a pang to my chest.

I would never want them to feel as though they've taken the backseat to any female I'm involved with, because that will **never** be the case.

My brows furrowed as I moved to them, placing a kiss on their foreheads before looking deeply in their eyes.

"That will never be the case. Y'all my favorite girls forever. Y'all have Uncle Dally's heart." I reassured them as they both smiled before standing in the booth seat.

I leaned down allowing their tiny lips to come in contact with both sides of my cheeks. A wave of warmth filled my heart from the contact. If I felt this way about my nieces, I didn't even want to imagine how in love I'll be with my first child. The unconditional love they give me was what kept me afloat, despite the hectic shit going on around me.

I **needed** them just as much as they **needed** me.

July 15, 2016: Camp Springs, MD

"Shit," I grunted while tightening my hold on Shia's hips as she rode me like her life depended on it.

I watched as the beads of sweat starting from her neck slowly rolled down the middle of her chocolate breasts. I thrust my hips upward forcing a yelp out of her, head falling back while biting hard on her lip. That had to be one of my favorite faces she made whenever I was in her.

"Mmm." She moaned while throwing her hips in a circular motion bringing that familiar tingly sensation to my body.

"Damn baby," I grunted as her palms found my pecs while getting situated into a comfortable squat before bouncing rapidly.

It was like every time we had sex, it got better. I've had my share of women but when I tell you that Shia was a freak and did shit I've never had done to me - that would be an understatement. And to top everything off, despite my constant mood swings lately, she's been patient and haven't budged one bit.

Our bond was growing even deeper.

"Big head!"

"SHIT!" My eyes widened at the sound of my sister's voice with little feet pattering against the hardwood floor.

Shia jumped off me going into a straight panic mode, rushing to throw on her clothes that were in a pile on the floor. Shaking my head, I chuckled at her reaction already knowing that Devyn wasn't going to welcome herself in my room nor let my nieces barge in.

"If you two don't sit down!" Devyn fussed as the pattering of their feet ceased simultaneously.

"Chill baby. They're not gonna come in here," I chuckled while pulling my sweats and boxers up before throwing a white tee on, rounding the foot of my bed.

"Shut up Dallas," She spat back while mugging me as I moved closer to her.

Her beautiful, mean ass.

Leaning forward, I placed a soft kiss on her full lips before grabbing a handful of her ass causing her to burst into laughter, punching my chest.

"Stopp!" She managed to get out in between her laughs.

My lips warped into a crooked smile as my eyes wandered her half nude body. Grabbing myself, I shook my head upset that neither one of us got to get our nut off.

Thank you, Devyn, Yani, and Yuri.

"I got your ass later on," I promised her, loving how her body visibly shook at my words. "Hurry up and get dressed before I don't give a fuck that my sister and nieces in the other room."

She giggled, "I got you, Daddy."

I chuckled at her taunting response, making a mental note to have her calling me that numerous times tonight.

"Yea. Ight," I dryly responded while turning to leave the room.

Standing in front of Dallas' full-length mirror, I scanned over the clothes that were adorning my body before I was quickly stripped of them no more than 30 minutes ago. A pair of Dallas' red basketball shorts covered my bottom half with a white wife beater attached to my torso as if it was a second skin.

Twisting my lips, I focused on my sweaty, wild mane that has a mind of its own. I was not in the mood to do my hair, but there was no way I could go into work tomorrow with it looking the way it did. Huffing, I pulled the scrunchie from my wrist before throwing it into a messy bun on the top of my head.

A smile spread across my lips once hearing the high pitched voices of the two girls that happened to ease their way into my heart. Over these past two months, I've spent countless time with them especially when Dallas was on uncle duties.

"My Ying and Yang!" I rose my voice over their laughter from Dallas bouncing them on his outstretched legs as he sat on the couch.

My heart jumped once their brown, doe eyes locked on me before hopping off their uncle racing towards me. I laughed, stumbling back slightly as their miniature frames striked my legs.

"Hey babies," I cooed before stooping down to their level placing a kiss on their cheeks. "Y'all spending the day with Uncle Dally and me?"

Dallas kissed his teeth, "I told you bout that Shy."

I rolled my eyes, waving him off, not one bit intimidated by his so-called threat in regards to me calling him Dally. I hugged them tight as they giggled trying their best to wiggle free.

"Guess what I have for y'all?" I looked between them as I held their shoulders, smiling at the excited expression rushing to their faces.

They began bouncing in anticipation causing me to laugh. It still bothered me that Dallas hasn't seen *Like Mike* so yesterday during my break at work, I ran to the Target that was in walking distance from my job. His nieces' sudden appearance gave me, even more, reason to play the movie today; I know they'll enjoy it especially since it's kid friendly.

"What you have for us?" Yani asked, rocking back and forth in anxiousness.

"A movie. I know you two will like."

"What movie you got for them?" Devyn asked, forcing my eyes to her as I rose to my full stature.

"*Like Mike*. Your annoying brother never saw it so I bought it yesterday. Now that the girls are here, we can watch it together."

"You never saw that movie nigga?!" Devyn looked to her younger brother, questioning him in a surprised tone.

"Naw nigga. I haven't. I wasn't geeked for slim like you were."

Devyn kissed her teeth while rolling her eyes. "Bow always been bae. You tripping. It was actually a decent movie," She said while grabbing her car keys off the coffee table. "Come give Mommy some love." She summoned over her baby girls.

The sound of their sneakers thumping against the hardwood sounded out in the silent apartment as they scurried her way, hugging her tight as she kneeled in front of them. My heart warmed at the sound of her placing kisses on their lips. Devyn is such a great mother and my heart backflips every time I witness her interact with them. She's so strong for holding it together after losing her husband.

"What time y'all got to be there?" Dallas asked as Devyn stood upright, running her hand through her straight hair.

"3:30. I still need to go get her. I'll let you know how everything goes."

Not too long after the twins' birthday, Dallas' mother condition had worsened leaving her to go for dialysis three times a week for about four hours. I knew how bad it was weighing on Dallas but of course, he wasn't speaking on it. Actually, he was doing very good at concealing his feelings about the whole ordeal. I knew otherwise, though. I know it was tearing him apart witnessing his mother deteriorate right before his eyes. It was bothering me as well seeing as though I've grown closer to Ms. Raye over these past few months.

Standing at a distance, I watched Dallas nod his head, obviously uncomfortable with their conversation pertaining to their mother. He ran his hands down his face, shaking his head while sighing deeply.

"Ight man. You coming back to get them or want me to keep them for the night?"

Devyn's brows rose, "You don't have to work tomorrow?"

"Naw."

"Of course you can keep them!" She replied in an excited manner, smiling from ear to ear. "Cole asked me to go out with her tonight too, so this is great."

I loved Cole. She was Devyn's best friend whom I met at the girls' birthday party. Surprisingly, we hit it off. It was as if she lived off a natural high which I truly enjoyed - she brought such positive energy.

Dallas chuckled as his sister turned to head towards the front door. "Tell little ugg I was said wassup."

I giggled, thinking back on how I flipped on how he and Cole interacted with each other. On the outside looking in, you would think they'd like each other by how much they chose to annoy the other. Once bringing it up to Dallas, he made sure to sit me down with Cole and clear the air. After hearing how they *really* felt about each other, I found it amusing that I thought such thing. Cole was like another sister to him and annoying each other came with the bond.

Devyn smiled, fanning her brother off. "Alright girls. Be on your best behavior for your uncle and auntie."

"We will!" They replied in unison while swinging their feet up and down as they sat on the couch watching TV.

"AYE!" Dallas hollered before Devyn got out the front door fully.

"What boy?!" She said with a hint of annoyance in her voice, looking back.

"Call me next time. Y'all popped up during a special moment."

I laughed, lightly pushing the back of his head before rounding the couch to fill the empty space on his left as the girls sat on his right.

"Special moment my ass…" She laughed, holding onto the doorknob while looking at us both. "I called you endless times Dallas, even Shia. I already knew what was up once I didn't get an answer from neither of you."

We both laughed as she waved before blowing us air kisses, "I'll see y'all. Don't make me an auntie yet, little rabbits." She said before closing the door leaving us in a fit of laughter.

"You look so pretty Uncle Dally." Yani cooed as her little hands cupped my cheeks.

It's been about an hour since Shia been gone to get our pizza and wings. Not really in the mood to drive, I tossed her my keys without hesitation. This wasn't the first time I let her take my car to go do whatever she pleased. I shot her a text about ten minutes ago but still didn't receive a response. Honestly, I was getting worried.

"Pucker your lips," Yuri demanded, definitely revealing her older sibling bossiness.

I locked eyes with her while doing what she requested as she began smiling while putting red lipstick on my lips. I don't know why in the hell my sister would buy two five-year-olds a make-up kit. After Shia left, they practically begged me to be their muse and I couldn't refuse.

They're my babies - I'd do anything for them.

"Hold up a minute babies," I said causing them to cease their movements.

Grabbing my phone off my lap, I went to my recent calls and instantly went to Shia's name placing it to my ear. About two rings in, the locks on the front door were coming undone before my beautiful lady came walking through. Ending the call, I rose to my feet as the twins rushed to her legs, jumping around excited for their favorite food.

My brows furrowed noticing the tear stains upon Shia's chocolate cheeks as she smiled weakly while placing the food on the table. Not a word was said nor did she look my way before hurrying to my room, closing the door behind her.

"Go wash your hands." I watched as they scurried to the bathroom, bickering with one another that could be heard over the running water.

"AYE! Chill with all that!" I rose my voice so they could hear me over the water. Within seconds, their bickering stopped.

Moving towards the kitchen, I washed my hands before placing a slice of pizza and two wings on each of their plates. Grabbing two plastic cups out the overhead cabinet, I poured a suitable amount of Hawaiian Punch in each. I watched as they hurried to the table while I placed their plates in front of them before going back to get their cups.

I smiled at the sight of them clasping their hands together, heads bowed as they began praying in unison. It was such a beautiful sight knowing my nieces knew the Lord and made sure to express their thanks. Giving them one last look, I moved towards my room slowly opening the door.

Shia was balled up under the covers, sniffing.

"Baby," I called, remaining my distance.

From time to time, Shia would still have her mood swings. Dr. Jones finally took her off the meds since she'd improved greatly and getting closer to her halfway mark of sobriety. But in all actuality, I believe the mood swings are apart of who Shia naturally is. The fact she's going without something she was used to, just intensifies it.

Sighing, I softly closed the door behind me before trekking the short distance to the bed. Sitting by her feet, I leaned over touching her body through the covers.

"Baby. What's wrong?"

No response.

I hated when she got like this. Shutting down on me and shit. She hated when I did it and I'm working on it for her so it'd be nice if it was reciprocated.

"Come on baby. We talked about this. You don't like me shutting down so why you doing it?"

"I don't wanna talk about it Dallas." She mumbled into the covers, aggravation and pain lacing her tone.

"But we bout to though." I wasn't about to allow her to push me away with her funky attitude.

Taking a hold of the covers, I roughly pulled them off her body. She quickly sat upright, arms flailing before lazily falling into the sheets, locking her fiery eyes with mine. I focused in on how her eyes held a red tint to them meanwhile the intensity demanded my attention. Not cowering under her gaze, I returned the same expression.

Shia loved to bitch people - that was her "thing."

My face twisted once her cupped hands flew to her mouth, giggling.

How one minute she's crying then soon as she look at me she's laughing?

"What?" I asked, head cocking to the side.

"Before we get into this talking thing, I suggest you go wash your *face* off. I can't take you serious bruh." She suggested, putting an emphasis on face as her open hand went in a circular motion in front of her own.

It had completely slipped my mind that Yani and Yuri had went color crazy on my face. I chuckled, finding it funny along with being happy that it removed some of the tension in the room. Rising to my sock clad feet, I headed towards my master bathroom, washing my face clean of their mural.

Shia was now sitting in Indian-Style in the middle of the bed, somewhat hugging herself.

"Come 'ere baby." I summoned her over with a head nod as I sat on the edge of the bed.

A small frown found its way to her full lips as she maneuvered her small frame off the bed, rounding it before finding herself standing between my legs. The whiff of her natural scent invaded my nostrils as she looked down on me, pain plastered across her pretty mien. My hands gravitated towards her wrist, giving them a slight tug as she sniffed.

"Talk to me, Shy." My left hand moved towards the back of her thick, right thigh rubbing gently.

"I saw her." She softly spoke with her head hung, doing everything to not keep eye contact.

I licked my lip, "Saw who?"

Her eyes shifted to me for a second before meeting the floor once again. Using my bent index finger, I rose her head forcing her eyes to meet mine.

"Saw who baby?" I asked again, hoping that this time she'll reveal the person behind making her upset.

"My mother."

July 15, 2016: Clinton, MD

Looking my face over one last time, I flipped the visor up as it created a soft thud meeting the car ceiling. Grabbing my phone and wallet out the passenger seat, I swung my short legs out the car standing to my full structure. The last sound heard was me putting on the car alarm as I trudged across the parking lot towards Pizza Hut.

I rolled my eyes once noticing the few bodies already lined up, glad that we called ours in about 30 minutes ago.

Mace
<u>Received</u>
Hold bra. The nieces walked in on y'all fucking?
That's traumatizing... for them, anyways lol.

I giggled after reading over Mace's text. After what happened earlier, Mace was the first person I texted. He always got a kick out of my wild stories so I knew this one would have him fully entertained. My fingers moved rapidly across the screen typing out my response, moving forward slightly as the line moved.

Mace
<u>Sent</u>
Lmao. No nigga. They ALMOST caught us.
They never walked in. It felt like they saw us though.

I smiled, stuffing my phone into the front pocket of my jeans as I approached the counter.

"Hello. How are you? You picking up or placing an order?" The young female on the other side of the counter greeted me.

"Picking up for Shia. It was pizza and wings." I called out as she began looking for our food.

After showing me the food and ringing me up, I comfortably sat the large box on my arm with the wings on top of it. Walking towards the door, I turned backwards using my backside to push it open.

"Thank you." I expressed my gratitude to the unknown person holding the door open for me.

My heart skipped a beat once meeting those identical brown hues I thought I'd never see again. She looked exactly the same, if not better. It'd been five years since I've seen her - since my 21st birthday. That was the day I left behind my "mother," childhood home, and all the fucked up memories to come with it. During that period of not being at home and sleeping wherever with my boyfriend, my drug abuse became worse.

That's when heroin became my best friend.

I took a step back once her hand gravitated towards me as if she wanted to caress me. I'm guessing she could sense my standoffish demeanor which had her taking steps back as well. I felt stuck. Now that I was sober and clear headed, she'd been crossing my mind countless times lately. What I would say to her. How much I hate her for not believing me and not protecting me. But now that she was standing in arms reach, everything I mentally practiced couldn't exit my lips.

"Shia." She broke the thick silence between us, making me cringe at my name falling from her lips. "We need to talk."

I scoffed, rolling my eyes. Oh. Now she wants to talk? For years, I wanted to "talk" to my mother and let her know how her new husband took advantage of me at night. But not once did she believe me. Matter of fact, she didn't even want to hear it. In her eyes, I was just a liar that didn't want to see her happy.

Scanning my hues over her slim thick frame, I mentally thanked her good genes for blessing me with such a well sculpted body. Even after all these years, she looked damn good. Her hips still poked out perfectly with her thighs holding a healthy weight to them. Her stomach was still flat with an ass that sat out more than mine. Her rich chocolate skin was blemish free, still making her very easy on the eyes.

"I gotta go." I completely shut down her request, heading towards the car.

My nerves went haywire once hearing her calling my name, feet shuffling across the pavement after me. The more I ignored her, the more it hurt. I spent so many years hating her when all I wanted was her. That's all. I wanted my mother to believe me, protect me, or better yet, just love me.

But she didn't, and because she didn't, it made it that much easier to hate her. Now here she was trying to wiggle her way back into my life, and the little girl in me wanted to welcome her with open arms. But I knew better. I'm not forgiving her that easily. Fuck that. She deserves to feel the pain I've felt for years.

I turned around quickly once feeling her hand touch my shoulder, shooting daggers with my eyes forcing her to step back with hands up in surrender.

"I just want to talk Shia, please." She begged, pleading with her eyes.

Gripping the sides of the pizza box, I tried to keep my temper at bay but it was building pretty quickly. How does one not communicate with their child for five years then just pop up wanting to talk? As if I owe her that.

"About WHAT?!" My voice escalated, voice cracking due to the pain my heart was enduring in this moment.

It's crazy how she still had this hold on me.

Her brown orbs looked around the parking lot as if she didn't want to catch any onlookers. Me on the other hand? I could careless.

"Everything."

I looked at her as if she had two heads, rising my brows. "Don't you think you're a little too many years late? I'll pass Selena. Goodbye."

The warm tears cascading down my cheeks rolled faster as I vividly replayed the interaction with my mother in my head while telling Dallas. His hands were holding mine the entire time, bringing me some sort of relief like he always does. Having Dallas in my life has made living *that* much easier. It might sound insane but I know for a fact that Dallas is my soul mate. God didn't just bring him my way for nothing, out of nowhere.

He sighed as his tall frame towered over mine once standing up. His long limbs wrapped tightly around my body, making my heart jump at the serenity engulfing me once being in his hold. I loved how protected he made me feel.

I dug my face into his shirt, bawling as his fingers raked through my hair. I relished in the feeling of his pouty lips connecting with the skin of my forehead, providing a gentle kiss.

"Damn baby. You're full of so much pain. You gotta let go and let God."

"I-I c-can't…" My voice trailed off, giving up on speaking due to me being so choked up.

"There's no can't when it comes to God. Trust and believe, He will work it all out. You just gotta put it in His hands. Trust Him. Let Him take that load off you. You carrying all this un-forgiveness isn't hurting nobody but yourself. You gotta let go baby. As much as it hurts, you have to." He spoke soothingly in my ear, sending trembles down my spine.

That's the thing… I couldn't just **let** go. I wanted to hate her so she could feel what I felt all these years. Letting go was too easy. She deserved to endure hell on earth like I did.

Book XVII.

August 27, 2016: Fort Washington, MD

❝Baby.❞ His early morning, husky voice quickly brought me out of my deep slumber causing me to roll on my side bringing the covers over my head.

"I don't want to get up." I pouted into the covers, annoyed with the fact I had to go into work today.

A deep scowl took over my visage once feeling his warm hand slowly running up the back of my thigh towards my ass. Looking over my shoulder, my body began quivering once locking into his salacious gaze. Tucking my bottom lip into my mouth, I took my time running my orbs slowly over his structure noticing that no clothes were covering him. The muscles in his shoulders twitched as he shook my leg making my ass jiggle.

"Stop babe." I giggled as he squeezed my one cheek forcing me to bite my lip.

It was like this man never got tired of sex. Last night we went at it for an hour straight, and if I didn't fake fall asleep on him, we'd probably been aiming for an extra one. I don't know how he did it. He had the stamina for himself and then some.

My heart fluttered once seeing his tongue sweep across his bottom, juicy lip with those unruly brows of his climbing his forehead. My eyes fell on his face moving down his perfectly sculpted abdomen before concentrating on the thick, long member that was at full attention. Squeezing my thighs together, I tried to keep my hormones at bay at the thought of how good he felt inside of me.

Dallas chuckled, looking down at himself before bringing his eyes to meet mine once again. The corners of his lips contorted into a crooked grin showcasing those deep dimples.

"You want us to slide in that?" He teasingly questioned, squeezing my ass again.

Swiftly, I turned on my back leaning back on my elbows as Dallas slowly climbed onto the bed hovering over me. My hands moved to his cheeks pulling his face towards mine, pecking his lips softly.

"Ugh, your morning breath girl." He teased, his minty breath fanning against my nose.

"So," I muttered, raising my head to kiss his lips again as he smiled.

My mouth fell agape once feeling his fingers swipe at my opening, making me wetter than I already was.

"Aww. We got you wet baby?" He seductively asked in my ear earning a moan from me as his fingers passed my wet folds, curving inside of me.

"Mmm."

"Hm? What you say?" His soft, teasing tone alone was driving me insane and his tongue running up the side of my neck wasn't making it any better.

I squirmed beneath him, hands gravitating towards his strong shoulders once feeling his head poke at my entrance.

"Mm…" I softly pushed against his chest, "Boo. I got to get ready for work." I whined, hoping he'd let me out of his hold.

He kissed my chin while slowly entering me. "Naw baby, you're halfway in now. I'm proud of you. This some celebrating. Happy 6 months Shy."

My eyes rolled back once Dallas filled me to the hilt after expressing his happiness for my sobriety.

Shit. He was in me now, so there was no stopping him.

I moaned before giving his chest a small jab forcing his intense eyes on me, stopping his strokes.

I smiled weakly pointing my small index finger at him, "*just* a quickie. And thank you, boo. Couldn't have done it without you." I couldn't begin to explain how good I felt being sober - it was a feeling that couldn't be put into words.

He shook his head, "Naw baby. You could've done it without me but God is the one you couldn't have done it without."

He was right. I couldn't have done it without God but little did Dallas know, I couldn't have done it without him either.

⌾≈⌾

Babe
<u>Received</u>
You still sore baby?

Rolling my eyes, I ignored Dallas' text returning my phone to my dresser before heading back into my closet. That early morning quickie turned into an hour making me 15 minutes late to work. At the moment, Dallas was on my bad side… kind of. There was no way I could stay mad at him long.

"OW NIGGA! QUIT IT!" Kris shrieked with a loud smack against Mace's chest following.

A smirk crept across my face after looking over my shoulder and noticing the grimace settling amongst his pink lips. I shook my head, chuckling before refocusing back on the task at hand. Not only were we celebrating my six months of sobriety, we were celebrating Mace's as well. While at work, Kris insisted that I called her on my break which she expressed how she was taking us out for dinner. I didn't think it was necessary but she wasn't taking no for an answer.

Mace laughed, "Where are you taking us?"

"It doesn't matter. Just know your ugly ass will leave satisfied." She snapped back.

I laughed to myself still shuffling through my clothes. These two together were a sight to see; they never stopped arguing.

He smacked his lips, "Ight little titties."

"You better stop talking shit before this threesome turns into a twosome real quick."

Turning around, I faced my best friends holding up a black, halter dress against my body for their approval. Looking between them two, I couldn't hold back the smile fighting its way to my lips at Mace's silly expression. His hand was holding his chest looking at Kris with wide eyes.

She chuckled, holding up her index finger to him. "Don't Mace. I already know where you're about to go with it."

He smiled, kissing his teeth before leaning back on his elbows as his legs dangled off the side of my bed. "You the one being all nasty n' shit. Mace didn't say nothing."

I giggled as their eyes fell on me. "What y'all think?"

"I'm not a pimp and y'all not my hoes. Find something else to wear, Shia." Mace joked, smacking his lips once Kris pushed the side of his head.

"Shut up." Kris spat before looking back to me, "It's fine Shy."

Mace's face twisted as he quickly rose to his feet, rubbing the back of his neck. "Keep touching me dawg…" He mumbled but was loud enough for us to hear.

"Huh? What you say Mace?" Kris taunted while cupping her hand around her ear, leaning his way.

I laughed at Mace rolling his eyes before those green, piercing hues locked on me running over my curvy figure.

My brows climbed my head, "You bout to say something smart?" I questioned, already knowing how annoying Mace loved to be.

A soft chuckle broke his lips. "Naw. *Actually*, before Ms. Heavy Hitter put her hands on me…" He nodded his head Kris' way, "I was gonna say that the dress is straight."

I smiled wide, "I'm glad you both like it!" I happily spoke, clenching the dress tight before heading towards my bathroom to get dressed.

August 27, 2016: Upper Marlboro, MD – *Kobe's*

"The fuck!" Mace's voice heightened, holding his arm up in front of his eyes while leaning back from the large fire rising from the teppanyaki grill in front of us.

There were a few giggles from the other people sitting at the c-shaped table with us at Mace's foul language. Every time we went out together, he was always embarrassing us especially with that vulgar mouth of his. Kris had brought us to a Japanese steakhouse and I was enjoying it so far; I've never had someone cook my food in front of me so this was an exciting moment.

"Stop touching me girl!" Mace spat towards Kris who'd just nudged his side hard, forcing his shoulder into mine.

I giggled, shaking my head while focusing my attention on my vibrating phone that was in my lap.

Babe
<u>Received</u>
Where tf you at slim?
Don't ignore me.

I laughed out loud gaining a few looks including my best friends. Mace's lips turned down slightly as he leaned in my direction, attempting to look at my phone as I pushed him away.

"Move nigga!"

He laughed, "Who that? Bro?" He questioned with raised brows as he focused on the cook flipping his wide Due Buoi spatulas before mixing up the cooking meats and vegetables. "Or you fuckin' around?"

I crossed my eyes, annoyed with the fact I've even introduced the two. The only friend I was aware of Dallas having was his best friend and unfortunately, he lost him. With me knowing how easy it was to get along with Mace, I felt Dallas needed his good energy and to my surprise, they hit it off well. Even though they annoyed me when together, the bond they were building was fulfilling.

"Bro?" I said, kissing my teeth, still annoyed with him assuming there was another man in the picture.

His green hues shifted to me, nodding slowly. "Yea nigga. Bro." He said, putting an emphasis on the term of endearment.

I giggled softly, "Whatever." My fingers moved swiftly across my phone screen, deciding to respond to Dallas since I've been ignoring him since earlier today.

Babe
<u>Sent</u>
Out... with my best friends.
What do you want?

Placing my phone in my lap, I turned my attention back to the cook with a frown spreading across my lips once seeing him signal me to open my mouth. While replying to Dallas, I noticed him throwing pieces of chicken and shrimp into people's mouths for them to catch. I wasn't really in the mood to do so but once receiving a nudge to my side from Mace, I found myself opening my mouth for the soaring food.

"Just like that." Mace whispered, forcing me to laugh before holding my palm up to the cook. "I'm sorry. I'm ready." I voiced once getting myself together as everyone focused on me with a smile.

Snickering, I could see Kris and Mace out of my peripheral staring hard as hell with anxious expressions making the moment that much funnier since I was two drinks in. I wasn't a drinker at all but since we were celebrating, I thought two drinks wouldn't hurt. Why not? Opening my mouth, I leaned to the right catching the piece of shrimp in my mouth as everyone at the table began clapping.

My hand gravitated towards my face trying to cover my mouth as I smiled, not being able to stop laughing. Those two drinks had a hold on me which felt good. Pushing my hair behind my ear, I grabbed my cup taking a sip while cutting my eyes towards the two to my left.

"Whaatt?" I dragged out, smiling with heavy lids.

Kris pulled her plate to her as I practically bounced in my seat once watching the food fall on my own.

"You turnt. That's what."

"Shut up," I mumbled, waving her off as Mace chuckled.

My phone vibrated in my lap once picking up my fork ready to dig in. Sighing, I returned my fork to my plate before picking up my phone. A small smirk contorted my plump lips once reading over Dallas' text.

Babe
<u>Received</u>
Oh yea?
I'll see that ass when you get home.

I knew my words would get to him - the main reason I said what I did. Getting a rise out of him was exactly what I was aiming for.

August 27, 2016: Camp Springs, MD

Huffing out of frustration, I rummaged through my purse for my set of keys to Dallas' apartment. The fact it was dark on top of the two drinks was making such a simple task a difficult one. I smiled weakly, happy once feeling the cold metal in my hand. After unlocking the door and closing it behind me, I quickly took off my heels - I despised wearing them. Sneakers were more my speed. Throwing my keys on the dining table before launching my purse on the couch, I moved towards the kitchen placing my bag of leftovers on the island.

"Baby," I cooed while stumbling down the hallway.

I grabbed my head trying to calm the headache that was beginning to grow. Never again was I drinking. This wasn't for me. Pushing his bedroom door open slowly, I peeked my head in seeing Dallas sprawled on his back, mouth slightly agape and sound asleep. The light from the TV bounced against his face, making his sharp features detectable even in the dark. I truly enjoyed watching him sleep. There were nights I'd lay next to him staring just because it was such a beautiful sight to me.

Twisting my face, I reached towards my back unzipping my dress allowing it to fall to the floor at my ankles. I was in a lazy mood tonight which explained me kicking it to the side and crawling onto the bed towards my handsome beau. Running my hand up his chiseled chest, I placed my cheek on his skin instantly hearing his heartbeat. Noticing that he didn't budge from my presence, I looked up to him locking my brown hues on his chin.

Pushing myself up, I kissed it softly earning a clear of his throat before his arm wrapped around my waist, hand rubbing the small of my back.

"You smell like alcohol." He mumbled, twitching his nose while slowly peeling his eyes open fixing those brown eyes on me.

Immediately, I regretted those drinks. Knowing he was far in on his sobriety and here I come, stumbling in off alcohol wasn't a good look. Especially since I was his partner, his support.

"I'm sorry," I mumbled, tearing my gaze from him unable to look him in the eyes any longer.

"What you sorry for? You don't owe me shit." He kissed his teeth.

The anger lacing his tone was making me uncomfortable and annoying me at the same time. I never did well with people snapping at me. Sighing, I pushed myself up from him, preparing to make my exit to the living room. It was obvious he had an attitude and this wasn't his first. Lately, he'd been on the edge and I've been doing everything in my power to not retaliate.

So if sleeping on the couch would prevent an argument, the couch would do for the night.

Leaning over, I reached for a pillow before his callous hand wrapped around my wrist. His eyes bucked open, running over my barely covered frame.

"Where you going?"

"The couch." I dryly retorted, hoping he'd catch a taste of his own medicine.

He fell silent for a moment, just staring me in the eyes. His hold on my wrist released before he started nodding slowly.

"Ight. Goodnight." He nonchalantly responded, leaving me feeling as if my plan backfired.

As badly as I wanted to spazz out, I chose against it. All I know is that when he woke up in the morning, I wouldn't be here.

September 5, 2016: Fort Washington, MD

"Where's Dallas? Why you not up his ass right now?" Blake teased, giggling while plopping into the couch next to me bouncing her shoulder off mine.

I rolled my eyes, annoyed with not only her but the fact it's been over a week, Labor Day to be exact, and a lot of things have changed between us. The change was happening on his end, not mine. We'd spend time here and there but it was nothing compared to how we normally would. Even though him becoming distant was making me upset, I was trying to respect his space. Kissing my teeth, I looked to my right at Blake before quickly folding my legs next to me.

"Shut up," I mumbled, shifting my gaze back to the TV that was playing *Love Jones*.

"Girl. Stop moping around. Let's go do something."

"I don't want to." I quickly responded, hoping she'd get the point and leave me alone.

Tink
<u>**Received**</u>
I'll be back home later on.
I missed y'all like shit

A smile spread across my face once reading over Tink's text as my fingers moved rapidly on the screen.

Tink
<u>Sent</u>
We missed you more boo!
Come over when you get here.

"Tink is coming back today!" I said happily earning a smack of the lips from Blake.

"That damn girl talks to you more than me." Blake pouted, folding her arms across her chest in exaggeration.

It was true. Tink and I grown very close over the past couple of months especially when Dallas and I became a couple. She became the little sister I always wanted.

Tink
<u>Received</u>
I'll be through there tomorrow boo.
Gotta be with the fam.
Dallas didn't tell you today is Aaron's anniversary?

September 5, 2016: Camp Springs, MD
Chewing on my lip, I eyed the bottle of Hennessey sitting in arm's reach. Two years into my sobriety and all I could think about was drinking today. Being an ex-alcoholic and losing my friend two years ago to a drunk driver was taking a toll on me. Once losing Aaron to drunk driving - something I used to do too often - it scared me towards sobriety. Knowing someone like me killed my best friend was the only thing that encouraged me to put the drink down.

Yet, I found it ludicrous that I was considering putting that intoxicating fluid back into my system. Shia coming in that night tipsy triggered something in me - that alcohol demon I wasn't trying to revisit. And it was as if she picked the perfect time to bring alcohol into the equation nearing Aaron's anniversary which brought me more to the edge.

It doesn't make sense to me right now that I'm actually considering drinking when I can just find strength in you, God. Father, give me that same strength you provided me with to get through this day like last year.

279

As if on cue, pulling me out of my thoughts, the vibration of my phone shifted my gaze towards it dancing across the coffee table. I leaned forward, huffing, nowhere in the mood to talk to anyone. I'd been ignoring everyone all day.

Did they not get the point?

"Hello." I dryly answered, clearing my throat while scooting further down into the couch.

"Dallas, baby. Where are you?"

Shooting my eyes towards the ceiling, I ran my left hand down my face. "Home. I'm good Ma." I quickly responded, already knowing where this conversation was headed.

She sighed softly, "Baby, I'm praying for you. I know it hurts sweetie but you sulking in that apartment will only make you feel worst. You get out for a breath of fresh air today?"

My leg began shaking out of annoyance. The Lord knows how much love I have for my mother but her attempt at trying to make me feel better was doing the complete opposite. Instead, it was irritating me.

She was doing a bunch of talking that I could care less about hearing right now.

"Ma," I cut her off.

Silence fell over us.

"I'll talk to you later. I'm not really in the mood. I love you though." I rushed out.

"I understand. I love you more. Come by and see me tom—" I frowned once hearing her cough uncontrollably.

"You good Ma?" I asked, concern lacing my tone.

Her coughing subsided, "Yes baby. I'm fine. Come by tomorrow."

I nodded as if she could see me, "I'll be through there. Get some rest, ight?"

She chuckled lightly, "I'll try. Stay out that head of yours."

A small smile worked to my pouty lips, but the pain still remained heavy in my heart. I missed my best friend. My brother. Once returning my phone to the table, my eyes shifted towards the

Hennessey bottle. I jumped once hearing the sudden knock on the front door.

"The fuck dawg!" I mumbled out of vexation.

"Baby. It's me." Her voice came out mumbled from being pressed against the door.

My heart unexpectedly picked up its pace once hearing her sweet, soft voice - I missed it so much. Even though I didn't want to be bothered, something had me rising to my feet ambling towards the door.

"I know you're in there. I can feel you." She spoke again, sending chills down my spine.

How does she do it? Make me want her so badly. Make me gravitate towards her with just her words alone.

Coming to the conclusion that alcohol wasn't the answer, I trekked across the room picking up the fifth of Hennessy before breaking the seal and pouring the fluid down the drain. If I kept the bottle around any longer, more than likely I'd drink it. A wave of relief took over my body watching the empty bottle fall into the trash bin.

The sound of the chain lock hitting against the door sounded before I twisted the lock, pulling the door open. Her eyes met mine, hands clasped together in front of her. Her long hair was in two French braids and she was dressed in a white V-neck and gray sweats. Despite the bagginess, she still looked beautiful, like always.

"I know you don't want to be bothered, but you need me right now. I want to be here for you."

In spite of my current mood and wanting to be alone, I pushed the door open wider while stepping to the side allowing her entry.

Yet again, I don't know how she does it.

Ever since Shia waltzed her way into my life, she turned it upside down. I never knew what it felt like to love a woman that I was intimate with, but I knew what I felt for her was real.

It was love.

After locking the door, I moved towards her enclosing the space between us quickly. I needed to hold her. My tall structure towered over her small one as I threw my arms around her, holding tight. Once having her in my arms, I felt some sort of release. I didn't shed one tear today, but in this moment, my eyes began brimming with tears.

Her small hands rubbed my back in a soft manner as I wiped at my tears, sniffing.

"Baby. It's okay. Let it out." She said softly as I squeezed her tighter.

God, what did I do to deserve someone as beautiful as her?

These past few weeks I've done nothing but draw back from her, and here she was, still loving on me in my weakest moment. Father, you knew what you were doing when you brought us to each other.

My shoulders rose and dropped rapidly as my tears seemed to fall in sync with the fast movement. My breathing became labored, digging my face into the crook of her neck, trying to bring myself to a state of calmness. This hurt so bad. Two years later, and I still feel empty.

"Th... this hur... hurts so bad." I managed to speak between sobs, wiping at my face after removing my face from her neck.

I can't believe I'm crying like a bitch right now.

The pads of her thumbs wiped beneath my eyes as she intensely stared into mine, sympathy swirling within her brown hues. Her warm hands cupped my cheeks, tilting my face down to get a better view of my visage.

"I know it hurts boo. But you have to hold onto all the good memories and find happiness in that. Just like you tell me, baby, God gives His toughest battles to His strongest soldiers. Aaron is doing far better where he is now than being here with us."

As she offered me words of encouragement, I felt a burst of energy flow through my chest. This couldn't be the same female I'd met months ago who wouldn't even utter God's name. Hence, here she is, nourishing me with words I'd use on her. It's amazing how God works. I knew it was just a matter of time before He began working on her heart again.

Book XVIII.

October 27, 2016: Fort Washington, MD

Turning up my nose, I threw a jab into Dallas' naked back as his contagious, cute laugh filled the air.

This nigga always thought it was funny farting out of nowhere.

"You fuckin' stink, Dallas!" I yelled, delivering another hit to his back while removing my naked body from his.

We'd walk through the door no more than 30 minutes ago and the first place we headed was the shower, like always. Since the first time we took a shower together, it's been the routine for us. With neither one of us in a rush to get dressed, I gave in to giving Dallas a massage since that was all he was talking about on the way here.

I jumped, nudging him with my elbow once feeling his hard-on poking my ass. "Stop," I giggled while dodging his hands, moving out his reach.

A jolt shot to my wet folds as he flashed me a sexy look, biting his lip. Lately, we'd been having so much sex and actually, I was tired. But with Dallas, it was the complete opposite. He loved sex more than me which resulted in him sliding in me about two to three times out of the day - **we** need a break.

"You want us to take care of you?" He teasingly asked while slowly ambling my way, dick sitting straight in the air.

I shook my head frantically, "No boo. I'm tired. I want to cuddle." I pouted, throwing my head back in exaggeration.

I laughed at the twisted expression settling on his face as he trapped me between the wall and his body. His warm hands slowly moved to my plump ass, squeezing hard, earning a hiss from me. I whined, stomping my foot into the ground while leaning my head against the wall.

"Babyy," I whined as he placed soft kisses on my exposed neck, sucking lightly.

"Hm?" He murmured into my neck, sending vibrations against my skin making the hairs on my skin began to rise.

"Stop baby," I said just above a whisper, trying to do everything in my power to remove his warm skin from mine.

Dallas sighed deeply, pulling his face from my neck locking his brown eyes with mine. "Forreal? You just want to cuddle?" He questioned with sadness lacing his tone and a defeated expression settling on his face.

I nodded, mutely giving my answer.

He smacked his lips, "Ight…. mean ass." He mumbled his last words, but I heard him clearly.

I bit my lip focusing on the flexing muscles in his back as he moved towards the bed, and that cute butt of his. I quickly followed behind him, excited that I'd got my way.

"That's still my name in your phone?" I asked with a tipped brow, hoping he'd changed it by now.

"Yea. Cause it's my damn ph—" His words were cut short as I hit him in the chest with the back of my hand.

"Change that shit." I spat out in a playful manner, even though I knew he would take it seriously.

His face deadpanned as he tightened his lips together. I tried my best to fight back the smile pulling at my lips, but the look on his face was priceless. I truly enjoyed annoying Dallas. He kissed his teeth while slowly nodding, getting his bottom half situated under the covers as I did the same. He continued looking at the TV, not paying me any mind at all. Resting my cheek on my hands, I studied his side profile focusing on how his jaw clenched as he swept his tongue across his juicy, pouty lips.

I frowned once he jerked his arm away from me. "You not going to cuddle me?" I asked in my baby voice, contorting my lips into a pout.

"Naw slim." He spoke in a dry tone, pausing shortly before looking my way. "I'm not." He finished, shifting his attention back to the TV.

I moved my body wildly in an exaggerated manner, throwing a fake temper tantrum. Out the corner of my eye, I caught the crooked grin sitting on his face. He chuckled once I pushed him softly forcing him to look my way. My lip flew between my teeth as a jolt shot to my love below before traveling up to the apex of my thighs, making me bite my lip harder. Even though we'd been overdosing on sex lately, that happened to be the only thing sitting on my mind, seeing as though we were in our birthday suits in each other's arms reach. The look he was giving me was making matters worst as well.

I turned my full lips downward at him, "Baby." I put on my sexy tone knowing it was hard for him to resist.

He smacked his lips, "Man, come here with yo mean ass." His deep voice rumbled as he outstretched his long arm in my direction.

I smiled wide, quickly moving to his side to bask in his body heat. My heart tingled once feeling his lips against my shoulder for a quick moment before pressed against mines. Every time we kissed, I felt like it was our first one all over again. I loved how he still made me feel when I first fell in love with his big head ass. Slowly peeling my eyes open to lock with his, I puckered up my lips once more satisfied when he placed another peck on them.

"Thank you." I smiled, getting situated in his side as he wrapped his arms around me while turning his frame towards me.

I threw my left leg over him as his large structure began getting comfortable entangled with mine. I sighed deeply once feeling his cheek rest against my naked chest, closing my eyes immediately. I felt a nap coming on.

"Hmm." I hummed once hearing Dallas mumble words against my skin.

With my eyes still shut, I used my fingers to play in the few rough curls resting on his head, using it as a distraction to keep me awake.

"What you say, boo?" I softly voiced, scratching his head knowing exactly how he loved it rubbed.

"I asked do you mind taking Ma to her session tomorrow?" He responded, bringing a wave of nerves to my body just off his question alone.

It wasn't like I'd never been alone with his mother before because we'd spent plenty of time together. But I'd never think he'd request something of so much importance of me - our relationship was truly blossoming in a good direction. The fact he was trusting me, with his mother, was mind boggling - but flattering, nonetheless.

"You can just drop me off in the morning and use my car. She gotta be there at 3:30, and just hit me when y'all done." He finished, already deciding for me due to his pre-plan.

I guess he took notice of my silence because I felt his face removing from my chest, bringing his heavy eyes towards mine. One of his thick, unruly brows climbed his forehead in question.

"Is that cool, baby? I'm not trying to press you. I just really need you to do this for m—" I cut his rant short by placing my palm against his chest, feeling his heartbeat off the connection.

"Boo, I got you. Don't worry." I assured him, smiling.

I'm just still in a state of shock that he's trusting me with his mother - this really meant a lot to me.

October 28, 2016: Uptown, Washington DC

Crossing one hand over the other taking the turn onto Dallas' mother's street, I sang along to H.E.R.'s "Wait for It" off *H.E.R. Vol. 1.* This album was absolutely everything - and I had Blake to thank for putting me on to it. Due to her love for listening to music while cooking, I managed to hear the entire album and fell in love instantly. It's been on a daily rotation ever since. Killing the ignition, I flipped the visor down before using my index finger to spread an even amount of Aquaphor on my plump lips. Smacking them together while pushing the visor back up, I pulled the keys out the ignition before hopping out the car.

My 'Flu Game' Jordan 12's ascended the concrete steps leading to the front door. Before hitting the top step, the door was swinging open revealing his smiling mother. The last time I saw her - about a week ago - she was looking pretty well. But today, it was the total opposite. Her entire appearance exuded exhaustion. More weight was stripped from her beautiful face and the bags sitting under her almond shaped eyes, along with the cane in her right hand displayed her fatigue state. I frowned, hurrying to her side as she closed the door behind her once stepping onto the porch.

"Hey, Ms. Lady." I greeted, happy to see her meanwhile taking ahold of her free arm, making sure to support her well.

One thing I admired most about her was regardless of how she was feeling, she'd always smile and be in the best mood. She'd always tell me how she wasn't fighting this battle alone and God always has the last say so.

Her faith in God was inspiring and she *always* spoke about Him with so much adoration. I loved it.

"I got it, baby." She reassured me, me still hesitant on letting go.

My eyes shifted towards her shaking knees forcing my hands to return to its prior position. "I'd rather help you down these steps first then it's all yours beautiful."

Out the corner of my eye, I caught her smile as we began our short journey down the porch steps. Just as I said, I released my hold once both of her feet were securely against the pavement.

Babe
<u>Received</u>
Ma not giving you a hard time, is she?

Within seconds, we were getting into Dallas' black, 2-door Dodge Challenger as I brought life to it. The light on my phone caught my attention just as I was about to put the car in drive. Retrieving my phone from the cup holder, a small giggle broke my lips at his text. My gaze fell on his mother once hearing her question. I nodded, shifting my gaze back to my phone replying before returning it to its previous spot.

"Yea. It's your son. Asking if you were giving me a hard time…" I chuckled under my breath once noticing the weak smile tugging at her thin lips. "You ready Ma?"

I frowned once hearing the deep sigh part her lips followed by a head nod as she got situated in the leather seat.

"I can't stand this loud ass car…" She mumbled before returning to her regular tone, "I'm ready baby."

That was the first *real* smile she has given me since entering her presence. I knew it was nothing personal but instead, I knew the sickness was taking a toll on her. She was now in kidney failure and on the kidney transplant waiting list. Even though we've been praying for her constantly, it was beginning to feel like God was preparing us for her departure.

October 28, 2016: Mitchellville, MD
Rubbing my hands together aiming to gather heat within them, I moved them up and down my arms. My full lips contorted into a small

frown as my orbs danced from the bottom of Dallas' mother's small frame towards the top of her head. Noticing her eyes closed, I took this moment to observe the two tubes taped to her arm, blood flowing freely through them. My heart tightened at the sight before me; I couldn't stand seeing her like this.

"There you go… staring again."

A smile worked its way to my face once seeing her eyes slowly peel open, locking with mine. I giggled from her words, knowing exactly what she was making reference to. We'd been here for about an hour now and unfortunately, she'd kept catching me staring from time to time. It wasn't like I was trying to be rude but this was something I'd never had to witness before. It was heart-wrenching but oddly, I couldn't keep my eyes off her.

"I'm sorry Ma. How are you feeling?" I questioned, immediately mentally cursing myself once the question left my lips.

I laughed once seeing the funny expression she was shooting my way, brows sitting high on her forehead.

"My bad. That was a dumb question." I swiftly tried to recover.

She shook her head, eyes fluttering. "No baby. It wasn't. I'm feeling alright. I hate these long hours of this but God shall see me through it all."

See. How was she so positive? Dallas was identical to her in regards to their faith in God.

Babe
<u>Received</u>
What y'all doing?
I miss my girls!

"Your son is a mess." I voiced, bringing a smile to her face.

"What he talking bout now?" She responded as if she was annoyed with me mentioning him; I knew otherwise.

I turned up my nose, typing away at my screen rapidly before Dallas got the chance to annoy me with a second text. He had a habit of being impatient resulting in him sending back to back texts.

"Asking what we were doing and how he miss us." I voiced, playfully rolling my eyes.

I laughed once catching his mother roll her eyes as well before waving me off with her free hand. "That boy is too much."

"I agree," I sided with her, giggling.

The exaggeration of someone clearing their throat forced my eyes to his mother's, only to see her face lit up with excitement. Her mouth was agape in shock as her hands flew to cup her mouth, tears welling at her lids.

"What are you doing here?" She questioned, somewhat choked up over her words as she fanned the person to come closer.

My brows furrowed as I turned around to catch the stranger's gaze. My eyes widened, mouth falling apart in surprise once focusing on the woman who looked identical to Dallas' mother.

What the hell.

He never told me his mother was a twin, and **identical** at that.

October 28, 2016: Capitol Heights, MD

Removing my Volkswagen uniform top, my thick, unruly brows deepened once receiving a jab to my arm from Shia while settling in the passenger seat of my car.

"What the fu—" My words were cut short once she spoke up.

"Why didn't you tell me that your mother was an identical twin?" She shrilled, hitting the steering wheel.

I looked at my steering wheel before looking back to her with a crazy look, "Chill on the car bae."

Her plump lips - that I wanted to kiss so badly - pursed together as her pretty face contorted into a mug, folding her arms across her chest. "Dallas." She spoke sternly causing me to chuckle.

I shrugged, resituating myself in the seat by scooting further down while lowering the backrest. Work had a nigga beat. After the first car maintenance, I lost count on the all the other ones we had lined up for the day including walk-ins.

I sniffed, rubbing my nose. "Cause… it wasn't something that crossed my mind with everything going on." I was hoping that answer would keep her quiet for awhile.

"But…" She began.

I guess I was wrong.

"But what baby?" I asked, resting my head into the headrest focusing my heavy eyes on her.

I studied her beautiful side profile as she focused on the road, falling into a daze as she spoke. I wasn't paying attention to one word she was saying. Instead, I was thinking about how I wanted to get between those thick thighs later on. Her head shot in my direction, frustration etched across her visage.

I chortled running my hands down my face, "My bad baby. What was you saying?"

"Fuck it Dallas." She seethed, waving me off dismissively. "I'm taking my ass home."

As much as I hated her funky attitude, I loved seeing her get worked up - she was the cutest when she was mad or annoyed.

A crooked grin crept to my lips, "Naw. You coming home with me."

"Hm. That's what *you* think." She responded smartly, kissing her teeth.

Reaching for her thick thigh, I gave it a nice squeeze earning a small hiss from her. This little sex "break" she had us on wasn't going to last. I'll be damned if she had me laying next to her damn near every night and not giving up the cheeks. The tip of my fingers trailed up and down her inner thigh, loving how she began squirming in the seat before swatting my hand away.

"Damn girl!" My voice escalated, laughing.

"Then quit it then!" She shot back, a smile tugging at her lips.

I know she loved these hands on her.

I sighed, "Ight then. Don't be begging for this dick later on." I teased, grabbing myself as she looked at me out the corner of her eye, biting her lip.

She kissed her teeth, rolling her eyes. "I'll never beg for that shit. Like I said, I'm going home and you and your little man can go the other way."

"Yea. We'll see." I responded, knowing she was going to be singing a different tune later on.

October 31, 2016: Uptown, Washington DC

I hissed, quickly standing to my full structure once feeling Dallas' large hand smack against my ass forcing my hand instantly to my backside. Looking over my shoulder, a heavy scowl distorted my countenance once catching the teasing smirk sitting on his beautiful, pouty lips.

"STOP nigga!" I whined, unusually becoming fed up with him touching me within 24 hours.

Every since we slipped into our matching costumes - Harley Quinn and Joker - he hasn't been able to keep his hands off me. With us both being a fan of *Suicide Squad* and having a wild connection mirroring the attached couple, we decided they would be the perfect pick for our first Halloween together. I was excited not only because this was my first time celebrating Halloween, but because I was spending it with the man I love and his family.

"Fuck you mean stop? I'm tearing that ass up tonight Miss." He put on his best Joker voice that sent a jolt to my core - seeing him in this get-up was such a turn-on.

Turning my body to face him, my lustful brown eyes locked onto his white painted face admiring his striking features even with it covered. I giggled at his green hair due to me spraying a temporary hair dye on it about an hour ago. My hues traveled down his long frame taking in the modern Joker attire. A long, purple faux leather trench was clothing his upper body revealing his chiseled abdomen that I put fake tattoos all over. Two thick gold chains were sitting around his neck, a pair of blue pants securely around his waist, and a pair of black shoes on his feet.

He looked damn good. Edible, if you asked me.

"I like the sound of that, Puddin." I responded, referring to the nickname given to Joker by Harley.

Just like Dallas' costume, mine mirrored the outfit Harley Quinn sported in the movie. Not wanting to be bothered with a wig, I practically begged Blake to straighten my kinky curls leaving it in a bone straight state - not a kink in sight. After splitting it into two high pigtails and leaving two strands of hair on each side out in the front. I had her spray the middle blonde, the left pigtail blue and the other pink.

A red and white t-shirt, with the words "Daddy's Lil Monster," squeezed my upper half leaving a bit of exposed tummy skin. A red and blue bomber jacket with gold lining with the words "Property of Joker" embedded on the back sat on top of that. Sitting on top of a pair of fishnet stockings, a matching pair of spandex shorts clung to my plump ass like a second skin with a chunky, gold and black belt around my waist. Wanting to be on the comfortable side, I decided on wearing black high-top chucks rather than the heel boots she'd wore.

I blushed at the sight of Dallas' brown hues ogling my well-endowed figured. My curves were always apparent but with what I was wearing tonight, they were demanding attention from any onlookers. Tucking his lip between his teeth, he grabbed himself with lust dancing within his eyes turning me on even more than I already was.

"I'm going to fu—" His words were cut short by Yani - dressed up as Betty from *The Flintstones* - rushed his legs, making him stumble a little.

I giggled once seeing the vexation spread across his face which I knew stemmed from the fact he didn't get to share his nasty words with me.

Dallas hoisted Yani into the air, swinging her little body earning a loud laugh from her before placing a big kiss on her cheek. He looked her over, smiling. I absolutely adored watching him interact with his nieces - it was such a beautiful thing to witness.

"You look good mama. Where's your sister?" He asked, looking towards the door waiting for Yuri to pop up any moment.

I laughed once seeing Yani nod her head towards the door. "Downstairs with Mommy. Mommy told me to come get you two."

"Oh yeah? She did, huh?"

She nodded swiftly, "Uh huh. She did."

"Ight. Let her know we'll be down there." He said, returning her back to the floor.

"Okay." Her squeaky voice sounded, running off just as quick as she came in.

I hissed, feeling my body heat go up a couple notches once having Dallas' arms wrap around my petite waist. His massive hands moved up and down my thighs as I stood in front of the mirror, putting in my stud earrings. I smiled once locking eyes with him through the mirror. His chin rested softly on my shoulder with that crooked grin sitting on his lips.

"You look beautiful, baby." He complimented, making my heart feel as if it was going to burst just off four words alone.

God, what did I do to deserve such a good man?

My cheeks heated as the corners of my full lips curved upward, "Thanks, baby. You look handsome, like always."

A chill traveled down my spine once feeling the connection of his lips against the skin of my neck. My shoulder twitched from his touch - the way this man made me feel never could be put into words; he's amazing beyond verbal description. Raising my hand, I cupped his cheek before turning my face to place a quick peck on his cheek.

"Come on. Dev gon' think we up here fucking in a few." His deep voice spoke against my skin.

He chuckled, squeezing my ass earning a yelp from me as I slapped against his chest. "You always playing." I giggled.

"Ima be playing with more than your ass tonight, Miss." He responded with a sneaky grin blessing his pouty lips.

October 31, 2016: Washington, D.C. – *Capitol Hill*

My chunky brows met in the middle of my forehead as I watched my nieces run ahead of us. Shia's arm was wrapped around mine while Devyn and Cole fell not too far behind us.

"Slow down girls!" Shia yelled, instantly making my heart heat up due to her love for them.

My biggest fear was them not liking her. Honestly, I felt they liked her more than me which had my jealousy surfacing occasionally but I was grateful that Shia fit in so well with my family. I glanced over my shoulder, making sure the two drunks behind us was still standing upright.

"Y'all good?" I questioned in a teasing manner.

Devyn smacked her lips, making me only imagine the face she was making.

"Of course we good… nigga." She responded smartly, speaking for the both of them.

I chuckled, "Yea. Ight."

I looked to my right, scanning my brown orbs over Shia's small frame appreciating every curve God blessed her with. I couldn't help but smile once seeing her do the same.

"What you looking at?" She asked.

"You." I quickly responded, sweeping my tongue over my bottom lip.

"What about me?" Her voice was laced with curiosity as her free hand rose to rub my arm.

"Everything, baby. God really brought you in my life at the right time." I expressed as we came to our tenth and last house of the night.

My eyes landed on Devyn's backside as she moved ahead of us in her skimpy pirate costume. Moving towards her daughters, she offered a smile to the elderly woman at the door placing candy in their bags. The nudge on my arm pulled my eyes back to Shia.

"Aww. I love when you get soft on me, baby."

Rearing my head back slightly, I gave her a funny expression at her confession. Her perfectly arched brows furrowed, confusion sitting amongst her visage. I guess she didn't realize what she said. I laughed once seeing her jaw drop as her small hand pushed against my chest.

"You play too much." She giggled, making my smile grow even wider.

Our heads turned towards my nieces once hearing the shuffling of their small feet across the pavement rushing in our direction.

"Auntie Shy!" They yelled in unison, hugging her legs tightly as she rubbed their backs.

I watched them lovingly as she stooped to their level, pulling them both into a tight embrace making my heart swell at the sight alone. Shia's face was full of excitement as she allowed them to show her all the candy they retrieved from the night. Out my peripheral, I saw Cole and Devyn laughing while moving our way.

"Dallas!"

My brows rose in question once hearing my sister's voice, pushing my full attention towards the two best friends.

I offered her a head nod, "Wassup?"

"You ready?" She questioned with heavy eyes, stupid grin contorting her lips. "We need to get back to Ma."

I nodded, already knowing we were out here long enough. The girls had enough candy to last them for days, maybe even weeks.

October 31, 2016: Uptown, Washington DC

Raising my balled fist to the wooden door, I placed two soft knocks against it before hearing my mother's soft voice welcoming me in. Pushing the door open slowly, I peeked my head in before revealing my full frame. She was sitting upright in the bed under the covers with heavy eyes and a weak smile on her face. Her eyes shifted towards me from the TV as I moved further into the room, a glass of water in hand. She was due for her night time medication so I knew she'd been requesting a glass sooner than later.

"Wassup Ma." I greeted, placing her glass on the nightstand before leaning over to place a kiss on her cheek.

"Hey, baby." Her weak voice sounded, bringing a small frown to my lips.

This was the most difficult thing to witness. I was watching my mother deteriorate right before my eyes. God, why you doing me like this man? You know my mother is my world. Without her, it wouldn't be no me. I wouldn't even know how to function.

"How you feeling?" I asked, scanning my eyes over her frail mien which was plucking at my heart strings by the seconds.

She smiled, "I'm still here, ain't I? I'm blessed baby. How was the trick-or-treating?"

The corners of my lips turned upward at the thought of my outing with my ladies. This was my first year dressing in a costume for Halloween - I had Shia to thank for that. She'd never celebrated Halloween before with her family and honestly, growing up, my mother never used to let us celebrate it either. Once Devyn had the twins, all that changed. Devyn made it known that despite our religion, she wanted the girls to enjoy a night of being able to dress in whatever character they chose. Devyn expressed that she'd wish our mother would've let us enjoy our childhood as well but to be honest, I wasn't tripping off that shit.

I rubbed the back of my neck, nodding slowly. "It was cool. We had fun. The girls did too."

"And Shia? How did she like her first year?" She asked, heavy eyes fluttering slowly as if she was tired. "Can you grab that bottle from over there for me, baby?" My eyes shifted across the room towards the dresser.

I sighed while rising to my feet, slowly trekking towards the array of drugs, reaching out grabbing the single bottle I'd knew she was due to take.

"Thank you, Dallas." She softly said while wrapping her slim digits tightly around the bottle before popping off the non-safety cap.

"No problem, Ma," I responded, taking my space back on the side of her bed. "But she loved it…" I chuckled as tonight's outing flashed through my head. "Prolly more than the girls."

A big smile spread across her face, "I'm glad she enjoyed herself. You know baby, I don't tell you this enough but I love the man you've grown into. It was difficult being a single mother raising you two, let alone trying to raise you to be a man. No mother is prepared to do it on her own. I was petrified of how I was going to teach you how to be a man, but I thank God He saw me through."

I smirked once she leaned forward, touching my cheek lovingly allowing it to sit there for a moment before speaking again with her hand dropping in the process.

"I brought some beautiful kids in this world and y'all turned out to be just fine. Seeing you treat Shia with so much respect is all I ever wanted for you. I see the look in your eyes when you look at her, baby. She's the one, and I want you to continue to keep her happy. Pray for her even when she doesn't pray for herself."

It felt like my body was reaching its maximal body heat as she expressed how much she idolized our relationship. Everything between Shia and I still felt surreal - I couldn't believe she barged her way into my life and created her special spot into my heart.

"Maannn Ma. You always want to turn all soft on me." I teased as she laughed, lightly pushing me with her leg.

"You know you love her boy."

I tucked my bottom lip between my teeth, nodding. "Yea… yea, Ma. I do. And you know what's funny?"

"What's that, baby?" She inquired, fully invested into me expressing my feelings which I normally don't do.

I looked straight ahead at nothing in particular, feeling her eyes boring into the side of my face. "I never knew I was capable of loving outside of y'all. I never knew I was capable of being…" My words trailed off as I locked eyes with her, becoming silent.

"Go head."

"In love," I said just above a whisper, incapable of believing that such feelings evolved for a woman that didn't have the same blood running through our veins.

She smiled causing me to do the same. "There's nothing wrong with being in love baby, especially when the person you're in love with loves you just as much. And Dallas, I'm quite sure you're not in it alone."

Rolling onto my side, I honed my attention in on Dallas as his large silhouette emerged into the room. For the past 20 minutes, I'd been laying here watching old re-runs of *Martin* waiting for him to return. Since he wasn't up for driving across town back to his place tonight, we decided to occupy his mother's guest room.

Raising my hand to cover my mouth as I coughed, we locked eyes as he looked over his shoulder once removing his shirt.

"You good?" His asked with raised brows.

I nodded swiftly, pulling the covers to meet just below my nose - I was *too* cold.

His response was a simple nod as he continued to remove his clothing, leaving his torso naked and basketball shorts hanging from his waist. I frowned once seeing him get settled on the bed, legs crossed at the ankles before digging his right hand in his shorts and throwing his left hand behind his head.

"What you looking at?" He questioned, keeping his gaze forward as I continued to admire his good looks from the side.

"You not cold?"

His eyes shifted to me for a second before breaking our gaze, smirking and looking down to his junk then looking back to me.

He swept his tongue across his pouty, bottom lip. "Naw meanie. I'm not cold. My man got me all warm."

I rolled my eyes, annoyed with the fact he kept calling me that dumb shit when I was far from mean. Well, I am mean but nothing like I used to be.

"You're disgusting."

A hearty chuckle erupted from him as he shrugged his shoulders carelessly. "You know I don't care especially since you love me and my disgusting ways." He teased before moving his tongue in a sensual manner making my body tingle.

I laughed, lightly slapping his arm before yawning. "I'm so tired."

"Then go to sleep then." He quickly conveyed.

My face deadpanned as I pursed my lips in annoyance. "Shut up."

"That's what I've been hoping for since I stepped in here." He dryly responded, not giving me any eye contact as he spoke.

"Dallas, stop playing with me."

His head shot my way with the most serious expression spread amongst his countenance, thick brows climbing his forehead slowly.

"Think I'm playing?"

"You better be."

He kissed his teeth, slowly nodding as his bottom lip slightly poked out as if he didn't take me seriously.

"You know I love you girl?" He stated more than asking me.

His words strummed away at my heart strings, making me realize how much the smallest things meant to me when it came to him. Dallas could never fathom how much I appreciated him taking the time to understand me and most importantly having patience. I know I'm not the easiest person to deal with, but I know you brought him my way God for a purpose. And all I can say is thank you especially since he brought me back your way.

I smiled, "I love you more baby. More than you'll ever know."

He sniffed, turning to me while leaning in leaving his lips hovering over mines.

"I doubt it." His soft breath bounced against my full lips before we were wrapped into a deep kiss.

I already knew this was going to be a long night ahead of us.

Book XIX.

November 26, 2016: Fort Washington, MD

Inhaling deeply, I released a heavy sigh as I sat on the bar stool watching Blake pace the kitchen floor frantically. Lifting my index fingers to my temples moving them in a circular motion, I shook my head while rolling my eyes. Blake was doing entirely too much. In two hours, we would be hosting our first Thanksgiving dinner and she was in complete panic mode. These past months of living with her, I've realized that when it came down to events, she was essentially a perfectionist - everything had to be immaculate.

Meanwhile, I was over here not making a big deal. I was excited because not only was Dallas and his family going to be in attendance but Kris and Mace were making an appearance as well. There was going to be nothing but love surrounding me and it had me on the edge of my seat, body surging with excitement. My eyes fixated on Blake once seeing the shot glass being shoved in my direction, filled to the rim with Henny. I frowned, second-guessing before throwing the intoxicating fluid down my throat. The last time I had a drink was the night Dallas was upset with me, but one shot or two would do especially with Blake running around like a chicken with her head cut off.

She was making me anxious. I was already nervous as is, and her frantic antics weren't helping soothe me in any way. Since I'm not much of a drinker, I wasn't aiming to get drunk. Meanwhile, I wanted to respect Dallas' sobriety as well. So going overboard was a big NO.

I frowned once seeing the shot glass being shoved my way once again. I smacked my lips, already seeing that Blake was trying to get me trashed. I grabbed the glass while tipping a brow her way simultaneously, eyeing her over the rim.

"I'm not getting drunk with you B."

She giggled while turning to the stove, pulling it open to check on the yams before closing it.

"I know. I know. I don't even want to see you drunk." She waved me off dismissively.

A smile contorted my full lips as I looked at my buzzing phone on the counter, running my index finger across the screen to answer the call then placing it on speaker.

"Sup Mace." I couldn't stop smiling as I placed him on speaker. "Got you on speaker."

I haven't talked to him in awhile. It felt so good to hear his voice, to feel his energy.

"Y'all need me to bring anything?" His raspy voice drawled.

"Ummm…" Blake dragged before she was cut off by Mace.

"Uh-uh, nigga. I'll stop you right there before you conjure up a shitload of things for me to get. I'm bringing soda!" He rushed, hanging up causing the loud beeping noise to sound throughout the kitchen.

We looked at each other and started dying of laughter. Mace was a damn character, I swear. There was not a moment talking to or being around him and he didn't make you laugh. He might as well become a comedian but he swore up and down that he'd freeze up on stage.

I think otherwise.

"I can't stand your best friend," Blake said, letting her laughter die off while shaking her head.

I smiled at the thought of Mace; I was so grateful for him. "You can't help but love him though."

"Yea. You right." Blake agreed, setting the finished deviled eggs on the counter along with the other trays.

"You need me to do anything?" I asked, standing to my feet while tugging at the white tank dress stopping just above my knees that was hugging me like a second skin.

"Nope. I'm about to shower so just keep an eye on the mac-n-cheese for me. CJ said he's on the way so listen out for him." She rambled, grabbing her phone before heading towards the stairs leading upstairs.

My white Moschino slides led me into the living room as I nodded, taking in all the information Blake quickly relayed to me. While plopping into the couch, my freshly done brows furrowed once reading the text from Dallas. Unfortunately, this holiday wasn't going too good thus far due to Ma's symptoms from her lupus surfacing at the wrong time. He said she'd been throwing up a few times since this morning, not being able to hold down a single thing. All of this was becoming too much. Not just because Dallas was hurting, but seeing her health decline speedily was one of the most painful things to witness.

She wasn't just Dallas' mother to me anymore - she was now **mine** as well. Especially since mine never did what she had to do as a mother.

Just as I was about to respond, my phone began vibrating in my hand alerting an incoming call from Dallas. Using my hand to push myself upright on the couch, I tucked a piece of my wavy hair behind my hair. For the past two weeks, I'd been sporting braids that Devyn did and once taking them out, I chose to keep them in their wavy state with a middle part. Accepting the call, I smiled once seeing my handsome love's face on the camera.

I giggled, "Back up boy!" I shouted, raising my tone over his loud background. "Where you at?" I asked with my face twisting in the process.

I watched as he continued to move around, air hitting against the speakers as he maneuvered his way through wherever he was. Silence finally came as I saw the familiar area he secluded himself in - his mother's bathroom. My lip turned up in disgust as I heard his belt unbuckling before he sat down on the toilet, propping his left elbow on his leg allowing his left cheek to lean against it. Using his right hand, he kept the phone in a good distance from his face.

I took this moment to admire his striking features as the soothing silence blanketed us.

"Baby, let's talk nasty." He suggested, raising his brows twice making me laugh at his freaky antics.

Lately, we've been back on our rabbit shit. It was damn near impossible to resist Dallas.

"Are you taking a shit?!" My voice rose, remembering that he was in the bathroom and he did, in fact, pull his pants down.

"What you think nigga?"

"Ugh. Bye. Call me back!"

He laughed, "Naw. You staying on with me."

I rolled my eyes, "I don't know what makes you comfortable enough to take a shit on FaceTime with me." I stated, leaning back allowing the back of my head to meet the armrest of the couch.

He smacked his lips, "The same way you think it's okay to take one on FaceTime with me."

He laughed once seeing my jaw drop, waving me off dismissively.

"I already know you're going to deny, but we both know that you been on FaceTime with a nigga AND even had me sit with you one night."

"YOU wanted to sit with me that night!" I countered, remembering that night vividly.

It was like we were attached at the hip. Everywhere I went, Dallas went, including the bathroom. I had no idea why we were being so attached that night, but we were. Neither one of us wanted the other out of their sight.

He smacked his lips, "Whatever girl."

I rolled my eyes, choosing not to respond. We stared at each other in silence. I began blushing once seeing him bite his lip, eyes moving across the little bit of body he could see.

"I can't wait to see you."

"You're seeing me now, Dallas." I joked, playfully rolling my eyes.

"You know what I mean. Show me a titty or something, baby."

The doorbell sounded, forcing my eyes in the direction of the corridor, giggling as I rose to my feet heading that way.

"No Dallas." I shook my head, reaching for the doorknob while keeping my face in view of the camera.

"Who that?"

"Your baby daddy!" CJ interjected in his most ratchet voice, making me burst out into laughter.

I lightly pushed him with my shoulder as he laughed, closing and locking the door behind him.

A smirk was sitting on Dallas' countenance while shaking his head, "He a trip man. I'll see y'all in a few, baby."

I frowned, making my brows meet in the middle of my head as I plopped back into my previous seat. "What? You hanging up on me cause of what CJ said?!" I teased, knowing it had nothing to do with my flaming friend.

"WHAT! I DON'T WANT YOU CHILD!" CJ yelled from the kitchen.

I laughed as Dallas smacked his lips, pursing those beautiful lips that I loved so much.

He blew me a kiss as I returned it, "I'll see you in a few, baby. I love you."

I smiled wide, "Okay. I love you more."

He smiled, creating those dimples in his cheeks that I absolutely loved. It felt so good to be genuinely loved by a man; I wasn't used to this. And as long as I've been living, I can't believe I've never experienced something so beautiful to share with someone.

This was what I've been waiting for.
This was what I needed.

November 26, 2016: Uptown, Washington DC

The sound of my mother regurgitating in the hallway bathroom had me cringing as I leaned against the door, hoping it was nearing the end. This has been lasting for at least five minutes now. To say this was breaking me down was an understatement. I was at my wit's end in regards to her health diminishing so rapidly before all of us. Not only was I an emotional wreck, but the past few days, I've been thinking about taking a drink.

It was taking everything in me to fight the urge I knew so well two years ago.

It was like I was itching for the liquor to be in my system.

This is when I know I have to take it to you.

Lord, I never like to question you, but why is she going through this? Why is someone so beautiful that you placed here suffering? Why does it have to be MY mother? The most painful part of this entire ordeal is that I'm helpless, and you know that. This is all in YOUR hands, and I just want you to come through for me. You know what she means to me. You know I can't lose her.

Raising my hand, I knocked softly on the wood, "Ma."

I was met with her loud coughing before she spoke, "I'll be out in a few Dallas, and then we can go. I'm fine."

She wasn't. I don't know why she felt the need to keep saying she was "okay," when it was evident she wasn't. I guess this all stemmed from her speaking nothing but positive things into the air. Honestly, her positive vibes were the only thing keeping my faith up. But at the same token, it was making me irritated as well because her being "okay" wasn't reality.

A heavy sigh brought my eyes to my sister, "She okay?"

I looked at the ground before meeting her eyes, clearing my throat while pushing myself off the wall to stand at my full structure.

"Ask her yourself. I'll be outside," I dryly responded before walking off.

I needed some air.

November 26, 2016: Fort Washington, MD

I threw my head back while laughing at Mace, "You're annoying."

He smirked, cutting his eyes at me.

"But you love me though."

That I did. I loved him crazy. It still amazed me to this day how close we got especially due to our rocky start. I never knew someone so annoying would become a person I held so close to my heart. It was hard to believe that I actually considered Mace one of my best friends.

"I do," I admitted, looking at his backside before he turned to face me while leaning on my dresser.

He'd just finished telling me about that same female that wouldn't give him play. Surprisingly, they were working on a "them." I was happy for him. Mace would make a great boyfriend especially since he was sober.

"Matter of fact, why she not here?" I questioned, wondering when I'd meet this woman he spoke so highly of. "When me and Kris meeting her?"

He smacked his lips, "Mannn. Y'all hoes not meeting her. Y'all gonna scare her away!" He laughed, dodging the hit I delivered his way.

"We not hoes!" I shrilled, giggling, knowing he was nowhere near serious.

He laughed while thumbing his chin, "I know. Y'all gonna meet; it just has to be the right time. But how you though? You doing good?"

Mace was aware of me seeing my mother after all these years and I knew he was concerned. Shit. I was concerned for myself. After interacting with her, all I could find myself thinking about was our awkward but tensed encounter. No matter how hard I tried to act like she didn't exist, she was the reason I was here today. And what made matters worse was that her popping up made me ponder on using.

"I'm good." I lied.

He narrowed his eyes at me, clearly not believing a single word I said.

"You're lying."

"I'm not." I quickly responded, hoping he'd drop the subject of how I was holding up.

If I elaborate any further, it'd do nothing but put me in a bad mood. Today was dedicated to good vibes. And good vibes were the only thing I was focused on.

I watched him nod, not saying another word.

"Whatever moe. Come on, let's go upstairs." He nodded his head towards my open bedroom door, me happy that he dropped the conversation as a whole.

Smiling, I sang and danced along to Maze & Frankie Beverly's "Before I Let Go" blasting through the speakers of the backyard. Before everyone arrived earlier, we set up a few chairs and tables since it was nice out. It wasn't too cold, but still, there was a nice breeze here and there. If it got too chilly, we were going to move everything indoors but for now, everything was going well.

I couldn't escape the delightful feeling as I held Kris' hands while we danced together, enjoying the moment. I've never been so content with my life.

My first Thanksgiving where I actually felt like I was surrounded by family. And the sad thing was that neither of my parents was in attendance.

The feeling of a hand on my back caused me to cease my movements, turning quickly and locking into Dallas' doting gaze.

This man loved me something serious, and you could see it in his eyes every time.

My baby.

Smiling wide, I pulled him into a tight hug before his lips were meeting mine.

"Ugh. Y'all can step off for all that shit." Kris scoffed while folding her arms dramatically, pouting.

Dallas smiled against my lips as I caught a glimpse of him flipping her off in my peripheral. I couldn't help but smile once receiving his final pecks, our foreheads becoming one in the end.

I loved his lips.

"MOVE nigga!" Kris said while pushing Mace away with her shoulder, mugging him heavily.

"You over here cock blocking, like usual?" He sneered, dodging her swat as he moved to greet Dallas with a brotherly embrace.

Even after they released from their slight hug, Dallas' arm snaked back around my waist like it was before. Every time we were in the presence of a man, he had to have some sort of physical contact with me. For example: holding my hand, standing behind me with his hands rested on my hips, or like now… arm around my waist.

I thought it was cute and very protective of him. I never had something so authentic, so it felt beautiful savoring in this feeling that I couldn't put into words.

It just felt so damn good.
I never wanted to let it go.

"When you get here fool?" Mace looked at Dallas, sweeping his tongue over his pink bottom lip out of habit.

"Not too long ago bra."

My giggling became faint as he placed a gentle kiss on my ear making me bite my lip. He was whispering all types of dirty shit in my ear that was putting me on the edge. I loved this feeling and hated it at the same time.

A chill traveled throughout my frame from the heat of Dallas' hand rubbing against my thigh, just near the cuff of my ass.

Mace scoffed, lip twisting at the sight of the both of us. He and Kris couldn't stand when we were all lovey-dovey in front of them. We could care less though.

"Uh-uh. Y'all not bout to annoy me with this overkill of PDA." Kris voiced, tugging on Mace's arm causing him to glare at her funny. "Come on Mace."

I laughed at the puzzled look contorting his features, brows meeting in the middle of his head.

"What the fuck is PDA?" Was the last thing I heard as she pulled him away, forcing me into a fit of laughter.

I figured he had no idea what it was, which explained why he was looking at her the way he did.

My laughing subsided as Dallas twirled me quickly to face him, wrapping me up in his stronghold. I could feel his heart beating against my chest which fell in sync with mine like it usually does. I giggled as he dramatically sniffed my hair before nuzzling his face into the crook of my neck - one of my spots.

He chuckled once I squeezed his face between my neck, hoping to stop his kisses. I moaned against my will, trying to wiggle out his grasp.

"Stop, baby," I whined, stomping my foot in a pouting manner while throwing my head back which gave him better access.

"Stop that whining shit. You making my dick hard." He grunted, raspy kissed tone turning me on even more.

I pushed him away once feeling the tip of his fingers playing at the bottom of my dress. A lustful smirk played at his lips, brown hues ogling my curvaceous frame. I blushed, breaking his gaze and looking to my cousin as she called my name.

"What?!" I yelled back, wondering what the hell she wanted.

Pursing my lips together, I cocked my head to the side once seeing the mini Polaroid camera in her hand. Dallas comfortably wrapped his arms around me from behind, chin resting on my shoulder.

"Smile, baby." He spoke softly in my ear as Blake rose the camera to her eyes.

I never got tired of this feeling: being in Dallas' arms. Smiling, I rested my hands on top of his as she took the picture. The mini Polaroid came out the side of the camera as she grabbed it, handing it to me.

"I can't stand how cute y'all are." She playfully said before walking off.

Turning to face Dallas, I placed a quick peck on his lips before he pulled me in for an even deeper one. This man always had me weak, knees trembling and all. Our lips parting sounded into the air as I smiled, in a daze, at the love of my life.

Looking down, I observed the photo of us that was now visible, smiling at how cute we looked. I couldn't believe I was in a healthy, loving relationship and sober. If you'd ask me two years ago did I see myself sober dating a God-fearing man, I'd laugh in your face.

This man standing before me was beyond amazing and at times, I didn't even feel like I deserved him.

"I'll be back." I shimmied due to the pressure building between my thighs.

His hand gripped my ass cheek, making me shoot him a dirty look. It's been a minute since our bodies have been entangled due to me wanting to slow down, but the thought of him being inside of me was becoming overwhelming.

"Where you going?" He asked, minty breath fanning against my visage.

"Bathroom. You can do a few seconds without me, babe." I patted his chest, pecking his lips again before turning to walk off.

From behind, I could feel his eyes on me the entire time.

Just how I liked it.

The center of his attention.

"Coming!" I yelled once hearing the knocking at the front door.

Everybody didn't get the memo to come around back?

Once opening the door, my heart skipped a beat… damn near stopped actually. Anger and pain rushed me all at once. The person standing on the other side of the threshold was the last person I wanted to see. But then again, there was that piece in me that's been waiting for this.

"What you doing here?" I dryly questioned, kissing my teeth with my hand firmly pressed against the door.

I watched as she nervously ran her hand up and down her arm, avoiding eye contact.

"Blake invited me. Can I come in?" She softly asked.

I didn't know I was tapping my foot against the hardwood until it was the only sound resting between us. It was taking everything in me to not slam the door in her face.

Why would Blake invite her? Especially on such an intimate event.

Pushing the door open wider, I stepped to the side allowing her full entry while using my free hand to welcome her in.

"Come in."

"Where's Shia?"

I looked back towards the house, hoping to see any sight of my girlfriend. For her to be going to the bathroom, it damn sure was taking a long time. I rubbed my hands along the front of my jeans while taking a seat next to my mother at one of the many tables.

"Bathroom," I responded, glancing at the house again before looking out into the yard at the many bodies moving around.

"She didn't even come see me."

I laughed once seeing the fake pout marring my mother's features. She and Shia had gotten so close over the past couple of months and I was grateful.

"She'll be back Ma."

She laughed, "I know baby…" Her voice trailed off, bringing her closed fist to her mouth as she coughed.

I watched as she looked around, her smile never wavering one bit. I commended her on how her lupus didn't affect that beautiful smile of hers. Regardless of how much pain she was enduring, that smile was there to stay.

"This is so beautiful. I'm glad you brought me Dallas. I needed this." She confessed, bringing a tingly sensation to my body.

She had no idea.

Every single second spent with her was a blessing in itself.

I couldn't believe she was here.

For what?

My plan was to have a smooth day, full of love. Yet, here she goes, already turning my good day to bad just off her presence alone.

The muffled sounds of Montell Jordan's "This Is How We Do It" could be heard from where we stood in the corridor, awkwardly keeping a good amount of space between us.

My brown eyes took their time traveling over her frame identical to mine. Back then, I never realized how much I looked like her because I was high on a daily basis, completely oblivious to everything going on around me. But now that I was clean, I've noticed that our bodies were curvaceously built the same if mines not more.

"What you doing here?" My tone laced with irritation, repeating myself from when I first laid eyes on her.

"To talk things over."

I scoffed, rolling my eyes.

I couldn't believe this shit.

"I'm trying to figure out what exactly is there to talk about Selena." I smartly responded, shifting my weight to one side while crossing my arms.

My fiery gaze never let up from her, intensely picking her apart with my eyes. There were many nights I dreamed of this moment. Hoping I'd get the chance to inform her on the piece of shit she was. How she chose her husband over her own daughter. So many things I practiced constantly in my head, and now that the moment was here, I could barely form sentences.

No matter how much anger I had towards her, I still missed her.

There were times we had a bunch of happy moments… before him.

And those memories were the only ones I missed.

Her brown eyes fluttered, looking around before meeting my gaze again.

Tapping my foot against the hardwood, I was becoming impatient. I didn't owe her shit. So, if she was going to stand here like a mute just staring, then we could end this visit now.

"You gonna talk or you want me to show you the door?" I spat, my body slowly but surely beginning to fill with rage.

A heavy sigh released from her - the same thing she used to do when she was over my attitude.

"Shia…" She began, raising her hands attempting to calm me down.

"Don't do that shit. I'm calm. I'm not about to be in a minute, though."

Her face deadpanned as if she was going to give up on this - on me. If so, it wouldn't surprise me. I watched her intently, hoping she'd say anything… something.

What did I have to do for my mother to love me like a mother should?

I didn't ask to be here.

I smacked my lips, flailing my arms in the air, completely fed up with her silence. I found it absurd that I felt like I didn't know my own mother; that's because I didn't. Through my heroin addiction, me being sexually taken advantage of and her absence, she became a figment of my imagination. I forgot how it felt to experience that motherly love.

So now that she was here after all the damage, it did nothing but add fuel to my already fired up resentful heart.

"Man, you can go." I placed my hand on her shoulder, pushing her towards the door as she shrugged me off stepping to the side.

"No. I want to talk Shia, please." She pleaded with begging eyes.

Shifting my weight to one side of my body, I folded my arms across my chest.

"Talk," I flatly responded.

Her brown orbs moved around the room awkwardly, "Can we go somewhere more private?" She began moving out of nervousness, fiddling her fingers.

Huffing, I became hesitant at the thought of her being in my personal space but instead of being an asshole, I decided to hear her out.

"Come on." I gestured towards the stairwell leading downstairs to the basement.

Baby
<u>Received</u>
I'm fine. I'm handling something real quick.
Brb.

My thick, unruly brows met in the middle of my head once reading over Shia's text. Handle what? From her text alone, I knew there were important details she was leaving out like what exactly she was "handling." Choosing to not make a big deal out of probably nothing that would lead to an argument, knowing us, I returned my phone back to the table.

At least I know she's good.

"Everything fine?"
My mother's voice brought my eyes to her as she finished up her prayer, grabbing her fork to begin eating.
I nodded, "Yea. Everything straight. How's the food?" I asked once seeing her dig into the fried turkey that I happened to prepare.
Smiling, I watched as her eyes closed clearly enjoying the meal. I laughed making her eyes land on me with a small smile now spreading across her visage.
"You already know how I feel about your turkey, Dallas." She stated the obvious, making me smile wide before giving myself a pat on the back.
"Don't get cocky now! Remember who taught you!" She teased, pointing her fork at me.
Raising my hands in surrender, I turned my lips down. "I don't want no trouble big mama."
She laughed as I got more comfortable in the seat, scooting further down while extending my legs underneath the table. Moving my

eyes around the yard, I relished in the feeling of having all my loved ones here. Even though I no longer had my best friend, it felt like Shia was sent to help heal that wound. I knew his death would be something I'd never get over, but having her by my side definitely helped me cope better.

It hurt less.

Once hearing a familiar voice, my brown hues shifted to the small and feisty woman that I considered a little sister. It felt like forever since I've seen Tink due to her constantly being out of town and I missed her crazy. Even though we don't get to see each other like we used to, I was proud of her and the fact she was living out her dreams. She deserved every great thing coming her way.

I smiled, watching my mother place a kiss on her cheek as Tink hugged her from behind making sure not to squeeze too tight.

"Hey, Ma!" She greeted, throwing her silky dreads over her shoulder while moving towards me.

"I was just asking Dallas about you the other day. You out there with the celebrities, and forgetting about little ole' us." She teased, earning a laugh from the both of us.

Ma was always on joke time.

I kissed my teeth once Tink mushed me, her squealing once I brought her into a bear hug before placing a kiss on her forehead once releasing. I laughed once she punched me in the chest.

"You always doing that shit." She muttered, making sure Ma didn't hear her.

Tink's silky dreads slightly whipped against my chest once she turned to face my mother, heading to take the empty seat next to her. She ran her hand over Ma's short hair, examining her face as I took my seat again.

"You know I could never forget y'all. Y'all family, and family is everything." She expressed wholeheartedly.

As much as we meant to her, she meant even more to us.
Her and Aaron.

Looking her over, I couldn't help but admire how beautiful she was. I was her twin. She was half of the reason behind my beauty. It looked as if she spit me out herself. My eyes slightly began filling with water at the thought of all our good times.

All the times before him.

"So…" I trailed off, hoping that lit a fire under her ass to begin spitting out every apology I rightfully deserved.

She sat for a moment before speaking, "I didn't know, Shia."

Rearing my head back in disbelief, my mien twisted into one of confusion. After four years of her being out of my life, and the first thing she says is: I didn't know. When in actuality, she knew every damn thing! She just didn't want to believe it.

Releasing a slight chuckle, my eyes gravitated towards the ceiling in an attempt to fight the tears that were begging to exit my eyes.

"The fuck you mean? You didn't know?!" My tone escalated, anger stirring from deep within.

There was no way her bullshit was flying with me today.

"Just like I said, I didn't know, Shia!" She snapped back, resulting in me making it that much easier to lash out at her.

I kissed my teeth, "That's a bunch of bullshit, and you know it. You knew it. You knew since the first time I told you because I completely fell into depression… losing weight and all. Walked around the house as if it wasn't my home. You saw how he looked at me, and you didn't do a damn thing!" I fulminated, her standing in silence chewing on the inside of her cheek.

Everything was right in her face.
How did she *not* know her daughter was getting raped?

I pointed a scolding finger her way, "You *let* that man rape me, Selena! You let h—"

"LOOK! I didn't let him do SHIT!" She attempted to defend herself, moving closer to me with a mug painting her full lips.

The tension between us was thick, and honestly, I have no idea how long I could keep my cool. I wanted to put my hands on her.

Producing any type of physical pain was all I could think about, hoping it'd bring her at least half the pain I had to endure over the years.

I put my hands up in front of me, "You can stay right there. I'd prefer if you not get in my personal space." I warned, taking a step back while sizing her up.

"Shia, I really didn't know he was raping you, baby. I was so depressed over you—" She stopped abruptly, getting choked up as a lonely tear escaped her eye rolling down her cheek. She released a heavy sigh, "Your father's death really did a number on me. I… I—"

"Don't use MY daddy as your reason for not being a mother! YOU WERE SUPPOSED TO PROTECT ME!" I screamed, pointing to myself, reaching my breaking point. "Instead, you were more worried about getting FUCKED that you ignored the fact YOUR husband was fucking me against my will."

Before I knew it, my face was being turned due to a hard slap colliding with my cheek. All I saw was red as I lunged her way. Before making any contact, a pair of strong arms wrapped around my stomach as I tried my best to escape. Normally, at his touch, my body would instantly relax. But with all the anger I've built up for years towards the piece of shit standing before me, not even Dallas could bring me to a state of peace.

This bitch **must** get her shit rocked.

"Dallas! GET OFF OF ME!" I yelled, attempting to pry his hands apart.

"I'm STILL your mother, Shia! You will NOT disrespect me like that!" She shouted, moving back with pain and fury etched across her chocolate visage.

My face twisted from her voice alone. She had the audacity to put her hands on me when she didn't do HER job as a mother. After all these years of being silent and away, she pops back up thinking that I should respect her as MY mother?

FUCK… no.

"Aye man! I think it's best that you leave," Dallas suggested, slightly loosening his grip which made it possible for me to push away from him.

Her eyes widened once I jumped over the couch, punching her in the face before she got the chance to get away.

"OH SHIT!" Dallas shouted, swiftly grabbing ahold of me before I got the chance to hit her again.

"What the hell is wrong with you Shia?!" Dallas said through clenched teeth, shaking me simultaneously.

Angry tears flowed down my face while my chest heaved up and down; I couldn't find it in me to calm down. The sound of Blake's voice infuriated me even more as I brought my intense gaze to her. She stepped off the last step, arms out with a confused expression on her face. She gasped once laying eyes on my enemy, rushing to her side once grabbing a dry towel from near the kitchen sink to place against her busted lip.

I pointed to Blake, "THIS is because of YOU, B! The fuck would you invite her for?"

Dallas' hold still remained tight around my stomach, keeping me close to his front.

Blake shook her head, "Because you two need to talk, Shia… that's why." She rolled her eyes, still catering to my mother's bleeding lip.

Seeing my favorite cousin that was basically a sister to me comfort my mother was a painful sight. Why was she siding with her? Instead, I thought she'd be at my side, making sure I was good.

I chuckled in disbelief while shaking my head, "I can't believe you, man." I intently watched her grab an ice pack out the freezer before handing to my mother.

Blake rolled her eyes, "WHAT?! You can't believe what Shia?!"

The anger lacing her tone brought my face to confusion, in disbelief that she was going off the way she was. I shook myself out of Dallas' hold before giving him a piercing glance, forcing him to put his hands up in surrender.

I snapped my attention back to Blake, "YOU. How the hell you come in here rushing to her side instead of MINE?! Matter of fact, WHY would you even invite her?!" I stepped closer to her as she did the same.

Blake chuckled, using her thumb to strum on her bottom lip.

"Because you need to hear her out Shy!" Her voice rose an octave, me looking past her shoulder to lock eyes with my mother who was looking right back at me.

"Give me one good reason as to why I should."

Blake enclosed the space between us, stepping close enough for me to feel her breath on my face. She touched my shoulder gently, face softening in the process.

"Cause you need healing, boo."

I bit my lip, tapping my foot against the hardwood as I looked at the ceiling before back to her.

"Look at all the progress you made. You need to forgive, Shy. You owe yourself that. Walking around with all this hate in your heart towards the one person who played a part in your existence isn't doing a thing for you. You deserve true happiness. And it starts with her…" She pointed behind her. "That woman right there. It starts with forgiveness, Shy."

December 13, 2016: Uptown, Washington DC

I flashed her a boyish grin once seeing her full lips transform into a pout. I pecked her lips softly with my hand resting on the doorknob of the front door. The smacking sound of our lips releasing was the only thing heard before she rose to the tip of her toes, planting another juicy kiss on my lips.

She was trying to start something up.

"Baby, you know I gotta go to work. Stop tryna be slick." I pecked her lips one more time, opening the door as we pulled apart. "Let me know if the girls give you any trouble."

I nodded, resting my hand on the door while watching him descend the front steps. Once reaching the pavement, he turned to face me blowing a bunch of air kisses causing me to giggle. He was so affectionate and it was the cutest thing. When first meeting Dallas, I never would've guessed a relationship developing between us. The term grateful wasn't even close to how I felt about having Dallas in my life.

"I love you, Dally."

I laughed at the stoic expression sitting on his face as he ceased all his movements, twisting his lips at me.

"Whatever girl. I love you more. I'll hit you on my break." He yelled, stepping off the sidewalk into the street, rounding the front of his car.

My gaze was trained on him since he got into the car and pulled off. Releasing a deep sigh, I closed and locked the door. This became our routine. When I was off work, I'd pout for him to stay and have to watch him leave for work. Get happy that he was back home after an 8-hour shift, just for it to happen all over again.

This has been going on for a good two weeks now, since I haven't been home, doing everything in my power to avoid Blake. No calls. No texts. I genuinely didn't want anything to do with her at the moment. Of course, everyone was trying to convince me to "get over it," but I couldn't.

I'm angry.
I'm hurt.
There was no talking to me like this.

We locked eyes as I began my journey back upstairs, me not getting far before her calling my name pulled me back down the steps.

I leaned out, keeping a tight hold of the banister so I wouldn't fall.

"Ma'am?"

Her face twisted, looking exactly like Dallas causing me to laugh. Dallas was her twin and beyond just the physical appearance. From me spending more time with his mother, I realized that a lot of their traits are identical to one another's. Some good and some bad.

"What I tell you about that?!" She convened me over with her head.

Letting go of the banister, I brushed my hands against my black leggings. I hated how any and everything collected on this material, but whatever, leggings were clutch and went with everything.

I smiled wide, moving in her direction, "I know. I know. You hate when I call you ma'am." I plopped on the couch, diagonal from her favorite seat that she occupied.

"You know I do. *Yet*, you continue to do it." She voiced, playfulness lacing her tone.

How come my mother couldn't be like this?

"How you though, baby?" She asked with a tipped brow before sipping from her glass of water, returning it back to the coffee table in arms reach.

My head reared back at her interest of knowing my well-being. If anything, I should be asking how she was feeling. As the months went by, her condition was doing nothing but getting worse but regardless, she kept high energy and a beautiful smile.

How did she do it?
I fell into depression and ran full speed, head first to drugs.

But she handled this life-threatening disease with so much class, so much happiness. How could someone that was potentially at risk of dying to be in such a beautiful mood? The smallest things happened to me and I felt like I wanted to jump off a cliff. She was strong. And not the type of strength you would run into on a daily basis. Her type of strength was rare and something I truly admired; the type of strength I wish I had a long time ago.

Then maybe... maybe I wouldn't be so fucked up right now.

"I'm good." I simply said, bringing a frown to her face.
"So if you're so good, why aren't you talking to your cousin?" She tipped a brow, me rolling my eyes knowing that Dallas shared my business with her.
"Dallas can't keep his mouth closed." I pouted, making a disgusted face.
She chuckled, "It's not that. He's... he's just really worried about you, Shia. And honestly, I am too. Don't forget that I'm a mother so my instincts are kicking in strong especially since you're a big part of my baby's life. I want you to be level-headed, as well as him."
She paused for a second, sighing.
Where was this conversation headed?
"Shia... I just don't want you to relapse, and you being the reason behind Dallas doing the same. This might sound like I'm attacking you but it's far from that. My son's well-being is my main focus but I've gotten the chance to know you, and I know you're

invested in what you have with Dallas. I appreciate you, and I want to see you do great as well as him."

She paused again, looking around the room before locking into my gaze once again.

"I say all this to say, how are you feeling? I know seeing your mother wasn't easy and there is a lot of built up emotions between you two. Talk to me, sweetie… please." She begged with her words and eyes.

I broke our eye contact, feeling the tears wanting to surface. One thing I loathed most was expressing my feelings; I never did well with that sort of thing.

I shrugged, still not in the mood to elaborate on how I was feeling at the moment. I was nowhere near good.

"I mean… I'm just hurt. But I'm good." I shrugged, attempting to play off the constant pain I was undergoing.

She flashed me a look as if she didn't believe me. Who would though? It was clear as day that I was having an internal battle. My appetite has been shot lately and at night, I could barely get any sleep.

There were a few times I ruminated on the thought of sticking that needle in my vein, feigning to feel the rush of euphoria be injected throughout my physique.

But… I knew I couldn't.

No matter how shitty I felt.

I've come too far to relapse, forcing me to start all over again.

"You really think I'm going to believe that?" She asked, tipping a brow.

I remained silent, receiving a sigh from her. Her shoulders dropped in defeat. She nodded slowly, allowing it to sit in that that's all she would be getting out of me.

Like I said, expressing myself never been easy.

"You know what. How about this… I would really love if you join us for church on Sunday. Dallas promised to attend since it's our 10 year anniversary, and I'd love for you to come with."

The thought of church had me skeptical. It hasn't been that long since I've found my way back to God so the thought of attending church was pretty far-fetched. Looking towards the ceiling, I fell into deep thought before I felt her hand rest on my knee, bringing my gaze to hers.

"Just think about it."

December 13, 2016: Fort Washington, MD

Rolling my eyes once hearing him smack his lips, I swiftly turned to be met by his annoyed expression.

"Get. Out." He sternly voiced, shoving my shoulder with his hand. "I gotta go to work Shy."

Resting my head against the headrest, my plump lips turned into a pout as I began to whine.

"Maceeeee."

"Girl. You over there sounding like my girl, begging for the dick and shit." He grunted, adjusting himself making me scoff at the sight.

"Ew. You're annoying." I forcefully pushed the passenger door open before grabbing my bag between my legs from the floor.

I heard him chuckling as I emerged from his car, "I knew that'd light a fire under your ass."

I couldn't help but smile as I shut the door, leaning over to meet his piercing green hues. He wore a boyish grin, "Don't go in there acting an ass." He reminded, bringing a nod out of me.

I sighed, unable to verbally go along with his wishes, but I'd try my best.

"Have a good day at work. I love you ugly." I expressed, throwing my bag over my shoulder.

He quickly put the car in drive as I stepped back, "I love you more slim. Remember what I said." Was the last thing he said before throwing up the deuce and heading down the street.

Sighing, I turned facing the two-story townhome making a deep scowl contort my face. This was the last place I wanted to be, sad to say. My gaze shifted slightly towards the left focusing on Blake's car in the driveway, rolling my eyes as I began my trek towards the front door.

I was met with pure silence once unlocking and closing the door behind me. Looking around, I noticed there weren't any changes since I last been here two weeks ago. Trying my best not to make my presence known, I silently moved through the foyer towards the basement.

I smiled once entering my personal space without Blake being aware. After throwing my bag across the room near my closet, I plopped onto the edge of my bed, scrolling through Instagram for a few. Not being entertained, I leaned back to place it on the charger next to my nightstand.

Rising to my 5'5" structure, I rose to the tip of my toes while stretching my arms above my head. Crossing my arms to grab the bottom of my shirt, I pulled it over my head before jumping back once seeing Blake leaning against my door frame.

There were so many choice words I had for her but chose against it, mentally attempting to calm my racing heart. If she knew what was best for her, she'd leave now.

Rolling my eyes hard, I turned my back towards her without uttering a word. Stepping out of my jeans, I gathered my clothes while sashaying towards my laundry basket.

"So what the fuck, Shy. I'm guessing I'm a ghost?!" She sarcastically questioned, causing me to cringe out of annoyance.

You might as well be, I thought.

Keeping my lips sealed, I moved in her direction only to be blocked once trying to maneuver around her.

See.
I didn't have time for this bullshit.

Having to encounter Blake was something I tried my best to avoid, even though it was inevitable since she lived here too.

She stepped in front of me again as I aimed to move around her, this time making me smack my lips at her actions.

Sizing her up intensely, I kissed my teeth.

"You gon' move or naw?"

Throwing an annoyed expression my way, she cocked her head to the side.

"How bout naw?!" Blake sardonically responded, placing her hand on her hip while still remaining her solid block between me and my living room area.

Throwing my hands in the air allowing them to slap against my bare thighs, I decided to entertain the situation at hand.

"So what… you wanna talk, right?"

"What you think?" She sharply countered, making me even more annoyed than I already was.

"I thought you would've got the point by now especially since I never responded to your texts or answered any of your calls."

"I'm fully aware of you trying to avoid me, but you had to come home at some point. So we going to talk or no?"

I flashed a fake smile, "How bout no?" I rolled my eyes while pushing my way past her, this time making contact causing her to stumble back.

Glancing over my shoulder, I gave her a malicious grin only to receive a hard grimace in return.

"Really, Shy?!" She asked, surprised by my aggressiveness.

Pushing my bathroom door open, I locked eyes with her.

"Should've moved out of my way."

December 18, 2016: Camp Springs, MD

"Baby, hurry up," I yelled through the bathroom door after taking a glance at my watch, straightening my tie as I stood in front of my full-length mirror.

Church service started at 11 and in order for us to get a good park instead of being forced to go to the overflow, it was necessary that we leave out within the next five minutes. This was typical Shia behavior; not being ready on time. Looking myself over in the mirror, I smirked lightly admiring how well I cleaned up.

Knowing my mama would have a fit if I wasn't dressed in a suit, I was draped in black from head to toe. The suit she'd bought me about two years ago was being put to good use on this beautiful Sunday. Sniffing, I scratched within my thick, untamed curls before running my hand over my freshly cut beard. Getting up early yesterday morning, I got my hair shaped up along with my facial hair.

There was no way I wanted to hear my mother's mouth, especially on our church's anniversary day.

The sound of the bathroom door opening brought my gaze to my beautiful woman, looking delectable as usual. Biting my lip, my brown hues took their time scrutinizing her curvy body, enjoying her choice of attire. I chuckled once seeing her do a complete 360 - one of the things I've grown so accustomed to before one of our many outings.

"Boo. Do I look okay?" She sweetly asked with a twisted face as if she wasn't satisfied with her outfit.

That was nothing new.

"You look beautiful, Shy. Let's go."

Sighing, she moved to stand in front of me meanwhile looking herself over. Looking at her expression in the mirror, I focused on the cute frown sitting on her plump lips. I already knew what she was about to say, and we didn't have time for it.

"Naw. Naw slim. You're not changing." I kissed her neck, causing her to put by stomping her tiny feet against the floor.

"No really Dallas. Do I look fine?" She asked again, turning to face me as my eyes couldn't help but wander.

"Baby. It's Sunday. I'm trying to keep things G rated. Plus you trippen' cause God said to come as you are."

She giggled, nudging me with her shoulder bringing a laugh out of me as well.

"But I'm not gon' lie though. Them pants pretty distracting." I teased, causing her to gasp.

A magenta colored, flared shirt was loosely adorning her torso and a pair of grey, high-waist shimmery pants hugged her thick thighs. It looks like she was headed to a damn disco, but nonetheless, I was letting her do her. At the end of the day, we weren't headed to a fashion show but instead to receive the word of God.

"Shut up." She spoke through clenched teeth, delivering a hit to my chest with the back of her hand.

Chortling, I grabbed her hand placing a soft kiss on the back of it before pecking her lips.

"You look fine little girl. Now, come on. I don't wanna hear my mama's mouth." I pressed, grabbing my keys off the dresser before leading the way out my bedroom do

December 18, 2016: Clinton, MD

Putting the car in park, I was relieved that we easily found a space in the church main parking lot instead of the overflow. The sound of my Charger cutting off surrounded us as I looked to Shia, realizing how nervous she was. Reaching over, I touched her thigh in a comforting manner but received no movement from her.

"You good?" I tilted my head down as my brows climbed my head.

Realizing that she was in a daze, I softly slapped her thigh forcing her to look my way with wide eyes.

"What?" She softly asked, oblivious to the question I proposed.

My hand caressed her cheek, staring deeply into her brown eyes.

"Get out your head baby. You're working yourself up over nothing. It'll be over before you know it."

I watched as she nodded slowly, mulling over my words before shaking her head frantically.

"Yea. Yea. You're right. I'm going to be okay." She spoke in a shaky voice, obviously trying her best to convince herself.

"Look." I sternly voiced to get her attention, her head whipping my way from me squeezing her thigh.

"I'm right here with you. You gon' be good." I conveyed in a reassuring tone.

Her once scared expression quickly disappeared as she laced our fingers together, shifting her gaze to focus on our connection before meeting my eyes again.

"Thank you boo," She softly said.

"Always," I smirked, pecking her lips softly. "Now, let's go." I playfully said through clenched teeth with my lips hovering over hers.

She giggled, stealing another kiss that made my body weak for a second.

Lord, I don't know what I did to deserve her but thank you. Just… thank you.

"They're over there," Dallas whispered in my ear, nodding his head in the direction of his family.

The corners of my lips formed into a big smile once seeing Yani and Yuri in matching dresses. On our way to them, I took my time to observe my surroundings.

This place was beautiful. Even when I did attend church in the past, it was nothing compared to this. Huge would be an understatement. And there were barely any seats left.

Looking to my left, I admired the man that I'm madly in love with. Unknowingly, his jaw clenched which I noted was a habit of his that he was unaware of. Before I knew it, we were at the row where his family saved two seats for us. With his mother occupying the aisle seat, he leaned over placing a kiss on her cheek bringing a bright smile out of her.

As if her smile couldn't grow any bigger, it did once her eyes landed on me. This unexplainable warm feeling traveled throughout my frame once leaning over to hug her, a kiss being placed on my cheek in the process.

"Thank you for coming, baby. You won't regret this. God got something special in store for you today." She spoke so confidently.

Standing up fully, I smiled, trying my best to ignore the funny feeling running through my body at her words.

"Thank you for inviting me."

The pastor approached the podium. He was so handsome and looked young too. The choir's melodic voices diminished to a soft tone while allowing him to get situated. Looking around, I noticed people softly swaying from side to side. Some were standing meanwhile others were seated and completely indulged.

The music died down as the pastor begin smiling before placing his hands on the podium.

"GOOD MORNING FAMILY!" He yelled into the microphone resting in the holder as the congregation reacted to his greeting, returning it.

"I saaidddd… GOOD MORNING FAMILY!"

This time the congregation's response was louder making my eyes widen as I looked around, trying my best to adjust to my atmosphere. Lastly, I shifted my gaze only to find Dallas silent, intensely watching the man of the hour.

"First, I would like to extend a welcome to all of our first-time visitors. I see a lot of new faces out here." The congregation began clapping as I suddenly felt nervous, feeling singled out even though no eyes were on me. "But… I'm going to get to the nitty gritty today. I won't hold you long." He exclaimed, moving his hands for emphasis.

I watched him grab the mic before beginning to walk to one side of the stage. He sighed with a grin, "We about to talk today, church." He voiced, emphasizing the situation with his free hand.

The church fell silent as he slowly ambled back to stand in front of the podium. I could've sworn he looked directly at me once looking out into the fellowship. A tingly sensation worked its way down my spine as he began to speak.

He cleared his throat, "Today's sermon is called: The Never-ending Cycle."

He paused shortly before moving to the middle of the stage.

"How many of you have a friend that's been hurt by someone so they intentionally hurt them back? Or, a friend that's been hurt and can't find it in their heart to forgive?"

That same sensation revisited not my spine, but my heart this time as he chuckled, raising a finger.

"How about this… how many of you ARE that friend?!" He proposed the question, causing chattering amongst the people surrounding me and some nodding heads.

My brown hues followed his frame as he moved back to the podium, putting his glasses on with the mic in his other hand. Licking his fingers briefly, he swiped through the pages of the Bible.

"Colossians 3:13 says: Bear with each other and forgive one another if any of you has a grievance against someone. Forgive as the Lord forgave you."

Looking at us over the top of his glasses, he repeated his last words.

"*Forgive* as the Lord forgave you."

Sheesh.

This message was for me.

Forgiveness was my biggest battle right now.

Everyone's hues followed him back to the center of the stage as he began using his free hand, speaking.

"I've come to realize that many people simply don't want to forgive. Or better yet, they seek revenge on those who have hurt them. Do you know that it is *impossible* to walk this earth and not get hurt? There is no way around pain, whether it's physically, verbally, or mentally."

During his short silence, I digested his words, allowing them to seep into my heart.

"It's truly unfeasible." He finished, rushing back to his trusty Bible.

"Ephesians 4:31-32 says: Get rid of all the bitterness, rage and anger, brawling and slander, along with every form of malice. Be kind and compassionate to one another, forgiving each other, just as in Christ God forgave you."

His laugh sent a chill down my spine, "You see how we revisited that? Forgiving each other, just as in Christ God forgave you."

Briefly, I looked around, specifically looking at Dallas' mother noticing how indulged she was in the message. A smirk blessed my face once seeing the girls silently asleep, both tucked on each side of Devyn.

His voice rose an octave, "No matter WHAT they've done to you... FORGIVE!"

Forgive.

That word alone was hitting me like a ton of bricks especially since it was the one thing I was finding difficult to do.

"I see the look on some of y'all faces, probably thinking, *what I need to forgive them for?*" He stated in an amusing face, earning a few laughs including me. "You need to forgive them to allow the healing to begin, to break down that barrier that's blocking YOUR blessings. Forgiveness is not granted because a person deserves to be forgiven.

Forgiveness is an act of love, mercy, and grace." He voiced his last words softly, using his hand for emphasis.

Within the last ten minutes, I've realized how much he utilized the stage, which I loved. His energy was at an all-time high and contagious. It had me so anxious for his next words.

"Do you think that person that hurt you is thinking about you? No. But you're thinking about them though, right?"

Yup. I sure was.

"Whether it's on your mind how they hurt you or what you want to do to hurt them. Having unforgiveness in your heart is doing nothing but putting your energy where it doesn't belong. You're still mad, for what? Because they've hurt you, right? The damage is done. That pain you feel shows that you're alive."

I frowned, finding truth in his words. I hated being wrong. But the more I sat here, the more I realized how damaged I truly was. It didn't make sense for me to keep walking around so angry… so unforgiving.

He shook his head, "You better find some comfort in that you're STILL breathing. We have our KIDS getting taken out because people don't want to forgive." That statement created claps along with some words of agreement. "You better be thankful for that air moving through your body, so you CAN feel that pain." He sternly said, pointing his finger at us.

"Forgiving someone doesn't mean you have to be buddy-buddy again. Or suddenly that you agree with what they've done to you. The act of forgiving means you have released them from the wrong they've done to you."

This was starting to *really* hit me now.

"You have released yourself from anger. You have released yourself from anxiety. You have released yourself from depression." He began, causing me to ponder on numerous situations in my life. "That bitterness is no longer in your heart. That stress that affects your blood pressure is now under control. You finally have that weight lifted off your shoulders…" He shook his shoulders, adding effect. "…and find yourself in a great mood."

His passionate tone had my body shivering as he spoke so powerfully, making sure to get his point across. Retrieving the cloth from his back pocket, he gave his sweaty face a wipe. I was wondering when he'd rid himself of the sweat that the beaming lights were causing.

"You're no longer thinking about them, and how they hurt you." He transferred his cloth to the hand holding the mic.

"THATS…" He waved his index finger, "…what forgiveness does. It allows you to free yourself spiritually and emotionally."

"Today might not be your day to forgive. That's between you and God. But I'm telling you once He gets a hold of you and you… let go, it'll be a beautiful day. Not only will you notice the change but those around you as well. You'll be so high off the euphoric feeling of letting go that you will be asking yourself: *why I didn't do this a long time ago?*"

His words got a slow nod out of me, allowing everything to sink in, wondering how could I be so unforgiving to my own blood.

My mother.
My cousin.

"That hurt no longer has control over your life. Instead, YOU now have gained full control just by submitting to God, allowing yourself to trust Him to bring that emotional healing. I'm not telling you that that hurt goes away overnight. Nor will it go away within weeks. It maybe can take years, but as long as you let go and let God, you're already healed."

He smiled, shaking his head.

"I hope y'all hearing me today." People began clapping as he wiped his face again.

"I'm not telling you what TO do. I'm just here to tell you what you SHOULD do. I'm here to help YOU no longer have sleepless nights, tears of sadness, unnecessary lash outs."

A roar of claps and words from different people began erupting into the air as he began stomping his foot while speaking.

"I'm here to help you remove that cringe, smack of the lips or roll of the eyes when you hear their name. I'm here to help you get rid of that idea of payback."

"You forgiving them IS THE PAYBACK. You being able to live stress-free IS THE PAYBACK. YOU REAPING YOUR BLESSINGS IS THE PAYBACK!!!" His voice rose with every word he spoke, yelling his last sentence which sent a jolt to my heart.

Here was that wonderful feeling hitting me yet again. The presence of God. It was so pure. So warm. So comforting. I smiled as tears rolled down my eyes, knowing God used Dallas' mother to get me here today. The feeling of Dallas' hand grabbing mine brought my gaze to my love, absorbing his comforting smile.

The pastor paused, looking around at the congregation with them clapping and hollering while some rose to their feet. Moving back to the podium, he took a sip of his water before starting up again with a now softer tone.

"May every head bow..." He closed his eyes, signaling everyone else to do the same.

"Father God, I come to you today for the people before me. I ask that every broken heart in this room be mended. Regardless of their circumstances, move in their hearts to forgive the person who has wronged them. Just as you forgive us every single day."

With a bowed head, I couldn't resist the tears that fell down my chocolate cheeks from the words of the anointed man before us.

"Give them the strength to allow themselves to be open and ready for your healing. Help them to no longer talk about or dwell on the situation, but instead, find comfort within your love Father God. Through your healing, may their hearts be released of that unforgiveness spirit. In Jesus' name. Let the church say... Amen."

"Amen," I ended the prayer along with the church.

"Remember, hurt people hurt people. So the next time someone hurts you, just keep in mind that they're hurting as well. It's time to put an end to this never-ending cycle, church. Though it's easier to act on feelings, we must learn how to feel our way into doing. Wipe that slate clean. Be free."

"Forgive and let God."

Book XX.

December 31, 2016: Fort Washington, MD

"How I look boo?" Crossing my eyes, I looked over my shoulder as I sat on the side of her bed. My eyes scanned her frame quickly while biting my lip, enjoying her wearing one of my favorite colors. She turned a red and black flannel into an off the shoulder shirt, hiked up to expose a small portion of her flat stomach. A pair of black skinnies ripped at the knees that she grabbed on one of our many outings to the mall, squeezed her thick thighs like a second skin. A medium-sized black choker and gold chain with her name engraved on it stopped at the top of her shirt, meeting her cleavage. Glancing at her feet, I frowned once seeing the black chunky open-toe wedges sitting on her pretty feet.

"Edible as always, but kill the shoe bae."

Shia smacked her lips, "But why though?"

"Cause we going right upstairs. Duh." I pointed to the ceiling, stating sarcastically earning a hard eye roll from her.

I chuckled, placing my hands on my knees before pushing myself to my feet. Smirking, I slowly ambled her way while ogling her body as if it was my first time laying eyes on her. She giggled as I wrapped my arms around her waist, hers finding its way around my neck like usual.

Smiling, I gently placed my lips against her forehead, holding it there to make my love known.

"I love you, baby," I told her as if I haven't told her a thousand times or even more.

Raising to the tip of her toes, she pecked my neck before smiling wide, staring deeply into my eyes.

"I love you more."

I stole a kiss.

"You're right though. Fuck these shoes." She said while snatching the wedges off her feet, bringing her height down a few inches.

I slapped her ass, "For once you're listening to a nigga!" I teased as she shot me a lustful glare over her shoulder.

"Bitch SHUT UP!" CJ yelled at Blake before bursting out into laughter, holding his chest. "Don't be in here lying about the fact you don't suck dick."

Blake gave him a look while flipping her purple hair over her shoulder, "That's because I don't… bitch."

Kris smacked her lips, "I even know you're lying B."

It was nearing 10 o'clock meaning it was getting damn near close to a new year. I couldn't believe how fast the year flew by especially since I was now ten months clean. There were no urges, I was completely off my meds, and I was no longer seeing Dr. Jones. I could honestly say that things have been going great so far. My best friends were clean and are flourishing at their new jobs. Blake and I had made up a few days after the church service; there was no way I could stay mad at her knowing we lived under the same roof. Then on top of it all, she welcomed me into her home and rooted me on throughout this process regardless of my lash outs.

Smiling, I peered at my loved ones around me, never picturing my life to be full of so much love and support. They've helped me in more ways than one, each and every one of them in their own way. From the laughs, the hard truth, and helping me find my way back to God; I felt like I owed them my life. Despite how hard things may get, I knew there was no turning back to my addiction not only for myself but for them as well.

I was not going to be a disappointment.
I was not going to be a failure.

Looking over my shoulder, I ogled the handsome man I had the pleasure of calling mine.

"What you looking at?" He mumbled, kissing my back that had me biting my lip.

It'd been a few days since I got some of his loving, and there was nothing more than I'd love with him being in me tonight for the new year.

He thrusted his pelvis against my ass, earning a hiss from me.

"Want some dick?" He teasingly asked with that cute grin I've grown to fall victim to.

I nodded, biting my lip harder.

"Mhmm." I hummed, getting turned on rapidly.

Dallas was my kryptonite.
My new addiction.

"Bet. Come on." He thumped the side of my thigh signaling me to stand as he kept his front glued to my backside. "We'll be back." He voiced, grabbing my hand to lead me downstairs before they had a chance to respond.

"You and these fuckin' skinnies!" I fussed through clenched teeth as she giggled while I tugged at the ankle of her jeans.

"You determined baby." She poked with lust swirling in her eyes, leaning back on her elbows as her chocolate breasts jiggled by my movement.

Sighing out of relief, my dick got even harder once I snatched off her panties, licking my lips at the delicious sight.

"Mm. She gets prettier every time." I voiced, dropping my jeans and boxers in one motion, my shit sprinting into the air.

The way she was eyeing me stroke myself had me ready to bust a fuckin' nut. I couldn't believe how worked up this woman could get me off just a look. Hovering over her, I kissed her lips softly as she grabbed my dick, stroking it slowly. We fell into a deep kiss, our tongues fighting to be the dominant one.

"Fuck." I faintly whispered against her lips as she began rubbing the head of my dick against her wetness.

I bit the top of her ear gently once sliding into her wet cave, her moaning in my ear which gave me motivation. Feeling her juices slide down my piece, I picked up my pace as her moans got louder. I crashed my lips with hers to conceal the moans; I swear this girl gets louder every time.

"Mmm." She moaned into my ear as I buried my face into her neck, grabbing her left leg to dangle on my back allowing me to go deeper.

A smirk graced my visage once hearing her gasp, mouth dropping simultaneously. I couldn't help but admire how beautiful she looked in the midst of our lovemaking. I never would've imagined having a woman wide open like this, nor vice versa.

There was absolutely no time frame on falling in love with someone because Shia snatched my heart before I even knew it.

I wouldn't have it no other way, though.

"Oh naw slim!" Mace yelled, fanning his hand in front of his face like something smelled. "Y'all niggas was just fucking?!"

I smacked my lips before twisting them out of annoyance. This nigga Mace definitely knows how to be irritating, for no reason at all.

"No." I sharply responded, moving further into the living room where everyone was gathered.

"Baby, I 'ont know what you're lying for. I'm pretty sure they heard your loud ass." Dallas put me on the spot, causing me to gasp and hit him in the chest as he took a seat next to me on the floor.

Coughing on his drink, Mace patted his chest rapidly attempting to gather himself.

"Naw bruh. Actually, we didn't. Y'all faces said enough." He said, sipping his drink again.

I wish he'd choke on it again.

Out my peripheral, I could see Dallas' shoulders raising and dropping as he laughed at Mace's annoying ass. I didn't find shit funny.

"Anyways, where is your girlfriend that you speak so highly of?" I questioned, anxious to meet the woman that had my freak ass friend tied down.

Funny how quickly things change within a few months.

I caught his eye roll, "She was supposed to be here but ended up going out of town with her family."

"You sure she not ducking you, instead of out of town?" Kris poked, grinning at him over the brim of her cup.

Once hearing him smack his lips and the expression settling on his face, I knew he was ready to get into Kris' ass. I swear they loved bickering just for the hell of it.

"You sure you're not sucking me a *little…*" He squinted, holding his index finger and thumb just a few inches apart for emphasis. "...bit too hard right now?!"

Kris flipped her hair over her shoulder, "Don't confuse my mouth with your girl's." She clapped back causing us to laugh even harder.

Mace's face deadpanned before smirking, clapping his hands.

"Touché. Touché." He nodded in approval, obviously pleased with her comeback.

Kris smiled while standing, giving a curtsy before raising her hand to do a queen wave.

"Thank you. Thank you." Kris exaggerated, plopping back onto the couch.

"Y'all stupid." Blake voiced between laughs. "Let's play a game."

"Game?!" CJ slurred, causing me to shake my head as he accidentally bumped Mace while attempting to sit on the floor.

Mace's visage turned into one of concern, placing his hand against CJ's back to keep him from hitting his head against the floor.

"Damn slim. Need to slow down on that shit." He suggested with a twisted expression.

For the past hour, Blake and CJ had been throwing shots back which I honestly lost count, and they probably had too.

CJ waved him off dismissively, "I'm good."

He was nowhere near good. He was fried like shit.

Blake looked around the room, "Y'all down?" She proposed her question again, making sure to make eye contact with all of us.

Everyone shrugged, giving off different words of agreement.

"Hmm. Never have I ever kissed a girl." Kris announced, causing Mace to smack his lips instantly.

"Now we know you lying like shit." He called her bluff, making us all laugh.

"Nigga. Fuck You." She spat, flipping him the bird.

"Naaww. You good." He chuckled, taking a sip from his cup.

Ever since Shia introduced Mace to me, I gathered that the nigga was a nut; he was definitely the life of the party. And we were all fully aware that he loved picking with Kris, especially about what he assumed was her sexual preference.

I watched as everyone took a drink, excluding Shia and myself. She chose to enjoy tonight in a sober mind, fully supporting me and my sobriety. I appreciated her. She gave me a reason to love her more every single day.

I took a sip of my soda, still participating minus the alcohol.

"CJ you kissed a girl before?" Shia said in bewilderment, asking the question we all wanted to.

"Bitch. It was so elementary, tired as hell and a damn dare. Hated it. Been loving dick my whole life." He openly shared, bouncing from side to side.

I glanced at my phone, noticing that it'd just hit 11:50. Ten more minutes and we'd officially be entering 2017.

"Never have I ever gave bad head." Shia beamed as if it was one of her biggest accomplishments.

"You damn sure haven't," I mumbled, causing her to giggle and knock her shoulder into mines.

"Shut up." She murmured back.

"All that freaky shit you're always talking and you can't eat a snatch right?!" Kris exclaimed once seeing Mace take a drink.

"Ya damn right. The bitch got the lazy tongue. I was tired as fuck but she pressed a nigga out." He shrugged carelessly. "Then had the audacity to complain."

I chortled, watching Blake drink to Shia's statement.

"Awww. But I thought you haven't sucked dick before B." I called her out forcing her eyes to widen and everyone to look her way.

If she was any lighter instead of having a chocolate complexion identical to Shia's, then you'd truly see how embarrassed she was. I hated putting people on the spot but I had to do it. Just because she was lying so hard an hour ago, and now being caught in it.

Mace erupted into a loud laughter, "Caught your little ass in a lie. You over there tight as shit." He teased causing us all to laugh as well.

He siced EVERYTHING.

Just as Blake opened her mouth to respond, Shia cut her off starting the countdown as we all joined in.

"FIVE! FOUR! THREE! TWO! ONE!"
"HAPPY NEW YEAR!"

Smiling, I took hold of Shia's chin, giving her a loving kiss as she reciprocated it, me savoring the sweetness of her fluffy lips. Who would've ever thought I'd be walking into the new year with an amazing woman by my side? The corner of my lips curved even wider, thankful that I could call her mine.

I pecked her lips once again, hovering over them.

"I love you, mean ass."

She smiled, "I love you more boo."

Migos "WOA" blasted through the surround sound speakers of our living room. We rapped along to the song as I bounced, dipping at the knees to the beat as Dallas' arms draped over my shoulders. Shivers traveled down my spine from the close proximity of us two. He rapped the words in my ear from behind as we stayed in sync with the music, this moment reminding me of Tink's party.

The first time we danced together.

Feeling my phone buzz in my back pocket, I removed myself from Dallas' front to retrieve it. Looking at the text, I smiled big at Tink's text. What a coincidence.

"Better not be no nigga got you cheesing like that." Dallas playfully voiced, causing me to roll my eyes.

"Now you knoww."

He nodded slowly, rubbing his chin.

"Yea. You know better." He grinned seductively.

I returned my phone back to my pocket after pressing send.

"It was Tink. Wishing us all a happy new year."

His head cocked before twisting his lips.

"Well ain't that boutta bitch. She didn't even send me—" His words were cut short by his phone ringing.

"My bad, baby. It's Devyn." He informed me once looking at the screen, sliding his thumb across it to answer the call.

Smiling, I watched my handsome love go from excitement only for his face to drop instantly. I touched his arm softly, wondering what was going on due to the unpleasant expression contorting his features.

His eyes filled with water as his chest rose and dropped heavily, looking as if he was going to faint.

"Baby."

I touched his chest, trying to bring his eyes to meet mine.

"Baby. What's wrong?" I questioned in a concerned tone, hoping he'd answer me soon.

He ended the call, tears rolling down his flawless, caramel cheeks. There was only one woman that could have Dallas so emotional. Once he locked eyes with me, I knew it was bad news. The pain etching his face was enough to validate my assumption of the news he was about to drop on me.

"Sh…" He choked on his words as I touched his face, tears pooling my eyes as well.

"She's gone, Shy."

I pulled him into a tight hug, allowing my body to absorb his pain, hoping I was bringing him some sort of comfort in this horrible moment. Holding the back of his head as he cried into my neck, he held onto my body for dear life. I cried with him. The aching pain in my chest had me weak at the knees, but our strong embrace was enough to keep me standing.

I had Dallas, and he had me.

His mother was a blessing, especially when she treated me like one of her own. She showed me that motherly love I've been missing and yearning to feel so bad again. She always gave me words of advice, even when she knew I didn't want to hear it.

You brought Dallas to her. And you brought Dallas to me. Without those two, I wouldn't be loving you the way that I do. Thank you for blessing me in more ways than one. Throughout every battle I endured in life, I managed to conquer them with the solid support system you provided me with. I know there is a lot of more healing to be done, starting with my mother. Tomorrow isn't promised, and this was more than a wake-up call. I needed to make amends with her because you only gave me one mother.

What a way to start the new year.

Epilogue.

Wiping the beads of sweat from my forehead, my brown hues scanned the doctor's office we were currently sitting in. Once feeling Shia's hand connect with my shaking leg, I looked to my left, smiling at my beautiful woman. Glancing at her left ring finger, my heart warmed once focusing on just a small indication of our love.

This all felt surreal.

Merely two years ago, my life was in shambles after losing my mother. If it wasn't for the support of my family, friends, and now fiancé, I would've spiraled down straight to relapsing. She giggled, smiling softly making me do the same.
"Boo. Calm down." She tried to soothe me.

I couldn't.

This was life changing for us. We'll finally get to see the first look at our baby, and to say I'm ecstatic would be an understatement. It still was soaking in that not only I was about to be a husband, but a father as well. This feeling couldn't be put in words. I've never felt so good in my life.
I cleared my throat, "I can't. I'm happy as shit." I conveyed in a low tone to her, making sure no ears heard our exchange of words.
She beamed, making my heart jump.
"Me too," I responded, grabbing her hand to place a kiss on the back of it.
Just as she was about to speak, the calling of her name had our attention shifting toward the voice's direction. Placing my palm on her lower back, we both stood up simultaneously to head to our assigned room.

This was it.

Once getting settled in the room, I felt more at ease seeing as though I've been waiting for this moment ever since we found out she was pregnant.

"I've never seen you like this." She laughed, looking at me as she sat on the exam table.

I chortled, "This my *first* kid with your beautiful ass. How you thought I was gonna act?!"

She shrugged, twisting her face.

"Not like this. You've been shaking like a stripper since we woke up." She said, laughing as I stood to my feet.

"Shut up girl." I slowly ambled her way, placing a kiss on her lips once reaching her.

"Gimme another one." She demanded, puckering her lips up again as I obeyed her wishes. "Come in." She welcomed the person that softly knocked on the door.

Our gaze fixed on the short woman coming in and closing the door behind her. My heartbeat kicked into overdrive, knowing that the moment was now here. I couldn't stop smiling.

"Good morning. You guys excited about your first sonogram?"

Shia sighed, raising her shirt as the ultrasound tech began to put a pair of purple latex gloves on her hands. Smiling, she took a seat on the rolling stool next to the exam table as Shia leaned back.

"Damn sure is." I voiced, rubbing my hands together with a big smile before interlacing my fingers with Shia's.

She laughed, preparing everything needed for us to see our baby.

"Well alright, let's get this going. I know y'all want to hear the heartbeat and see your baby."

"We really do!" Shia squealed, squeezing my hand lightly as I placed a kiss on her forehead.

I can't get enough of her.

It felt like everything went in slow motion once seeing her spread the gel on Shia's stomach which made this even more surreal since she wasn't showing yet. I couldn't wait to watch her body evolve, tummy poking and all.

"It's not cold?" I asked her with a tipped brow.

She shook her head, "Nope. It's actually warm."

"That's because we have a warmer for the gel to prevent the discomfort for our patients." The tech butted in, moving the transducer probe against her smooth skin while looking at the screen.